KNOTTING WITH A STRANGER

A WHISPERING GROVE NOVEL

A COZY OMEGAVERSE ROMANCE

HARLEY KNIGHT

CONTENTS

KNOTTING WITH A STRANGER
A WHISPERING GROVE NOVEL

It started with a message to the wrong number... now I'm craving a stranger.

Running the bakery with my sister is my life—early mornings, endless dough, and just enough sugar to keep me sane. I don't have time for distractions.

But when I accidentally text a stranger, everything changes.

He's not just mysterious—he's sharp-tongued, wickedly charming, and far too good at making me forget common sense. What starts as playful banter turns into something more... something that stirs my Omega instincts in ways I don't understand. His words make me burn, his voice wraps around me like a promise, and when he finally asks to meet...
I panic.

Because no one this intense, this consuming, can be real.

I tell myself to forget him, but fate has other plans. A

snowstorm, a wrong turn… and suddenly I'm face-to-face with the man who's haunted my thoughts. Only he's not alone. His world is sharp edges and whispered threats, tangled in power plays and ruthless Alphas.

I should walk away. But his touch ignites something primal inside me, and resisting him feels impossible.

He says I belong to him.

But in a world ruled by Alphas, giving in might mean losing myself… and I'm not sure I'll make it out whole.

CHAPTER ONE

LILY

Wedding cakes have a way of knowing when you fear them.

I'm standing in my kitchen at five in the morning, staring at what should have been a perfectly good vanilla sponge cake but has instead become some sort of concrete monster. The mixer whirs pathetically, the metal spoon bent at an angle speaks of defeat, and I swear the batter just growled at me.

"Listen here," I tell it, brandishing my spatula like a weapon. "I've dealt with worse than you. Remember the Great Fruit Cake Disaster of 2024? Yeah, that's what I thought."

The mixture remains stubbornly silent. Defiant.

Through the kitchen doorway, I glance into the darkened storefront of Flour & Fable Bakery. Christmas lights from Main Street cast multicolored shadows through our festively decorated front windows, making the display cases shimmer. The snow falls in thick, lazy flakes outside, turning Whispering Grove into the inside of a snow globe. Somewhere, faintly, I can hear "White Christmas" playing from the speakers outside. The whole town plays festive tunes nonstop. I would feel enchanted on any other morning, but right now, I have bigger problems.

Like the fact that my sister, Hannah, is out of town for two days, allegedly picking up supplies, but more likely meeting the mystery man she thinks I don't know about. And I have a wedding cake due at 2:00 p.m. that's currently declaring war on my kitchen.

I blow a strand of dark hair from my forehead, sending a puff of flour across my face, while the industrial kitchen gleams around me, all stainless steel and professional equipment. We've come far from the days when we baked in our family's tiny kitchen. We learned everything from our parents. And we both dreamed of owning our own bakery.

The morning light catches on the copper pots hanging overhead, the specialty cake pans lining the walls, and the row of proofing drawers where tomorrow's bread slowly rises. I breathe easily... the place always calms me.

This is my kingdom. My safe haven. The place Hannah and I made our own after we lost our mom. Dad did his best, working double shifts at the local diner to keep us fed and to keep Mom's small bakery business going. She had inherited it from her mother a long time ago, and she then left it with us. But watching him try to juggle everything—raising two girls, working himself to exhaustion, attempting to keep Mom's recipes alive—left its mark on all of us.

A sharp knock at the front glass door startles me from my memories. Through the darkness of the shop, I can make out a familiar silhouette bundled in a thick coat, rapping impatiently on the glass.

"You have got to be kidding me," I mutter, wiping my hands on my apron. Mrs. Meadow. At five in the morning. Because of course.

The knocking gets more insistent as I hurry toward the door. Is she in trouble? "Coming, coming!"

Mrs. Meadow practically pushes her way in the moment I unlock the door, bringing a swirl of snowflakes with her. "This weather is dreadful."

"Mrs. Meadow, we don't open for another three hours..."

"Oh, pish posh. Hannah said I could pick up my order at five." She stamps snow from her boots—on our clean floor—and peers around the dark shop. "Though, I do worry why your sister would leave you alone like this. What if you went into heat, dear?"

I bite back a sigh. "Then I'd close up shop and deal with it like any other modern Omega. But seeing as I haven't experienced any heat in twenty-four years, I think we're safe for now." Especially since I haven't had any inklings yet.

I stare at my countertop, counting backward from ten at her words. The irony of a Beta lecturing me about Omega biology is not lost on me. Society considers them the balanced ones, the peacekeepers between volatile Alphas and fragile Omegas. Ha. Mrs. Meadow has probably never had a single hormone-induced thought in her perfectly regulated life, yet here she is, treating me like I'm one whiff of Alpha musk away from throwing myself at the nearest knot. Because obviously, that's all we Omegas think about—finding mates, making babies, and being good little breeders. Never mind that I've kept this bakery thriving many times on my own when my sister traveled.

Mrs. Meadow makes that little *hmph* sound that suggests she has *opinions* about modern Omegas. I leave her standing there and head to the counter where, sure enough, I find a box marked *Mrs. M — 5 a.m. pickup* in Hannah's messy handwriting.

My sister, ever efficient, must have prepared it before leaving. She also apparently forgot to mention it to me. Though, given how distracted she's been lately, constantly checking her phone and smiling at nothing, I'm not entirely surprised.

"Here you are, Mrs. Meadow. One special-order coffee cake." I slide the box across the counter.

She peers inside suspiciously. "Thank you, dear."

She tucks the box under her arm. "Well. I suppose you'll be managing alone until she returns?"

"I've got it covered." I gesture to the kitchen, where my monster cake batter awaits. "Just working on a wedding cake."

"Alone? Without help?" Her eyebrows shoot up toward her hairline.

"I don't need anyone to bake a cake, Mrs. Meadow."

"That's what's wrong with young Omegas today. So independent. In my day..."

I tune out the familiar lecture, nodding at appropriate intervals while mentally calculating how much time I'm losing. The cake needs to be done before opening, and I still have all the morning baking to do.

"I may only be a Beta," Mrs. Meadow sniffs, adjusting her coat. "But I've taught more young Omegas proper etiquette than you can count. My niece, bless her, followed every word of my advice and landed herself a wonderful Alpha husband." She looks me up and down. "Never make direct eye contact with unmated Alphas, dear. And do tilt your head—just so —to show proper submission. Those scent-blocking patches aren't optional during professional interactions, you know." She purses her lips as I fail to suppress a laugh. "And please, dear, don't laugh so loudly. It's most unbecoming of an Omega."

Finally, after what feels like an eternity of unsolicited Omega etiquette lessons, I manage to usher her out into the snow. The moment the door locks behind her, I race back to the kitchen, where my cake batter has, if anything, become even more menacing.

"Right," I tell it, rolling up my sleeves. "Where were we?"

The mixer makes an ominous sound in response. I need help. Hannah would know exactly what to do, how to save this disaster. I collect my phone, remembering the new number she gave me yesterday before leaving. Something about her phone contract ending and her number changing. Her new number is stuck to the fridge—hastily scrawled on a sticky note that's already curling at the edges. I can't help wondering if the change has something to do with that mystery guy she's been seeing or her sudden plans to leave town. She's been tight-lipped about both, which isn't like her at all.

Squinting at her messy handwriting, I type the number in and start messaging.

Help! Need to hide this body. It's bigger than expected, and I can't lift it alone. Bringing in reinforcements didn't help. May need to dissolve it in acid.

I set the phone down and return to battling the mixer when a response comes quickly.

Acid leaves evidence. Rookie mistake. I know a guy who specializes in these situations.

I snort, typing back while adding more flour to the mix. *Very funny. But seriously, this thing is turning into cement. I've tried everything short of an exorcism.*

Have you considered that maybe it WANTS to be cement? Follow your dreams.

I laugh, shaking my head at Hannah's response. *Since when are you this philosophical about baking disasters? Usually, you're all about experimenting.*

Sometimes, chaos is the best ingredient. Speaking of

which, what's your preferred method of body disposal? Asking for a friend.

I pause in my mixing. Since when does Hannah make criminal jokes? She's usually the serious one.

What happened to "murder is bad for business"? You feeling okay?

Murder is excellent for business if you know how to market it. "To die for" takes on a whole new meaning.

Something feels... off. I grab my phone, really examining it for the first time, then check the number against the Post-it.

Oh. Oh, no. OH, NO.

This isn't Hannah. The last number should be six, not nine.

I've been casually discussing murder with a complete stranger. My heart pounds as I stare at the screen. Another message pops up.

Though, if you're really struggling with disposal, I have some creative suggestions. Professional experience.

Professional experience? *Oh God.* I've accidentally contacted a hitman. I'm going to end up on a true crime podcast. Hannah will never let me live this down —assuming I live.

Should I just ignore it? Call the police? But before I can decide, another message appears.

Your silence is concerning. Did the body win?

Despite my panic, I find myself smiling. Whoever this is, they have a sense of humor. Maybe they're not a hitman. Maybe they're just someone who watches too many crime shows. Like me.

Um... So, funny story. I think I have the wrong number. I was trying to text my sister about a cake disaster...

Three dots appear immediately.

A likely story. That's what all murderers say. "Oh, I was just baking!" Meanwhile, there's a body in the mixer.

I swear it's just cake! Though, at this point, it might be classified as a weapon of mass destruction.

Pics, or it didn't happen.

I laugh, then glance around guiltily, as if Mrs. Meadow might materialize to disapprove of me flirting with strangers. Not that I'm flirting. Am I flirting?

Are you sure you want evidence of my crime? I type back.

I'll risk it. Show me your worst.

Heart racing—from panic or excitement, I'm not sure—I snap a quick photo of the kitchen disaster. Flour everywhere, bent mixer attachment, and the concrete-like batter in all its glory. I even make sure to get my flour-covered hands with pink nail polish in the shot just to prove I'm really baking.

Behold, the scene of the crime, I send.

The response is immediate. *This is the most beautiful crime scene I've ever witnessed. Though, your murder weapon needs work. Too obvious. Cake is amateur hour.*

His next message comes with a photo—a firm hand wrapped around a coffee mug, sleeve rolled up to reveal a muscular forearm that makes my breath catch. In front of him, just a plain white wall gives nothing away.

Can't all be professional destroyers of kitchens, he sends.

I bite my lip, studying that arm—not too hairy, but enough to tell me he's a man. Definitely works out.

A man with muscles who can also banter? Now that's dangerous.

"Dangerous" is my middle name, he replies. *Right after "Secretly Plotting Something."*

Oh? And here I thought you were just another pretty forearm in a mystery office.

I'll never tell. Though, I will say my sourdough starter has seen things.

The mixer grunts as it churns, reminding me that I'm supposed to be fixing a crisis, not chatting with a stranger about murderous baking. But I can't seem to stop.

Your sourdough starter sounds deadly. Does it have a name?

Bertha. She's beautiful and terrifying. Now, a baker like you would have a starter too... I won't believe you if you say otherwise.

I giggle, surprising myself. It's been a while since anyone has made me laugh so early in the morning.

Name?

I roll my eyes but find myself typing. *Chonky. He's my dad's legacy—three years strong and still terrorizing health inspectors.*

You let your starter commit crimes against public officials? I'm shocked and impressed.

I find myself giggling. *Hey, those rashes were purely coincidental. Probably.*

Probably?

What Chonky does in his free time is his business. I just provide the flour and turn a blind eye.

A criminal mastermind AND her accomplice. I'm talking to a wicked woman here.

I catch myself grinning at my phone like an idiot. *Says the man having an existential crisis over cake batter at 5 a.m.*

Fair point. I maintain that the batter started it.

I should be worried that this conversation feels so natural. Instead, I perch on a kitchen stool, the cake temporarily forgotten.

Judge all you want, but that cake mixture started it.

Victim blaming. Tsk, tsk.

The sky outside is lightening, snow still falling in thick flakes. Time is running out. I have to open the bakery, save a wedding cake, and start on the morning baking. However, I'm sitting in my flour-dusted kitchen, having the strangest conversation of my life.

So, the mystery texter continues, *do you often assault innocent baked goods this early?*

Only on days ending in Y. Do you often give murder advice to wrong numbers?

The interesting ones. Most people just say, "Sorry, wrong number," and disappear. You're the first to confess to a crime.

Technical point... I was asking for help with disposal. The crime was already committed.

Ah, so you're saying you need an accomplice?

Heat creeps into my cheeks. Am I really doing this? Flirting with a complete stranger about a fictional murder?

Depends. Are you offering?

The three dots appear and disappear several times, making my heart race. Finally.

I might be. I have very specific standards for my criminal partnerships.

Oh? Do tell.

Well, first, they have to have a sense of humor about homicide. Check. Second, they need to be creative with disposal methods. Check. Third...

I wait, breath caught in my throat.

They have to be willing to share their baking disasters with complete strangers at ungodly hours.

My cheeks hurt from smiling. *Check, check, and check. Though, I should warn you that I have standards too.*

I'm all ears.

First, they have to appreciate the criminal potential of baked goods. Second, they need to name their sourdough starter something appropriately dramatic.

And third?

I bite my lip, typing before I can second-guess myself: *Third... they have to keep me entertained while I try to save this wedding cake from itself.*

Challenge accepted. Though, I have to ask... is this cake for an enemy? Because if so, you're doing great.

I chuckle loudly, the sound echoing through the quiet kitchen. The morning light is growing stronger, the snow creating a cozy bubble around the bakery. And for the first time in longer than I can remember, something feels like it's beginning.

I should probably actually try to fix this cake, I type reluctantly.

Probably. I have to say, this is the most fun I've had before dawn in a long time.

My heart does a little flip. *Same. Though, I'm still not convinced you're not a serial killer.*

Says the woman who texted a stranger about hiding a body.

Fair point. For all you know, I could be the serial killer.

A risk I'm willing to take. After all, you seem pretty busy with that cake. No time for murder on the side.

I glance at the clock and wince. He's right, I really need to focus, but something makes me hesitate before putting the phone down.

I should go. Places to be, cakes to salvage.

The life of a baker turned criminal is never easy. Good luck with your victim.

I start to set the phone down, then quickly type one more message.

Thanks for being an unexpectedly fun accomplice.

The response comes fast. *And hey... if you need help hiding any other bodies...*

My heart stutters as I read the implied invitation. Before I can respond, another message appears.

Or, you know, if you just want to talk about non-homicidal things sometime...

The mixer chooses that moment to make a sound

like a dying elephant, and reality crashes back in. I have a cake to save, a bakery to open, and a very real life to deal with. This was fun, but...

But what? The practical part of my brain says to end it here. The Omega part of me, the part that's been dormant for so long, whispers something else entirely. My fingers hover over the phone's keyboard, torn between sensible and spontaneous. The next message I send could change everything—or end it before it begins.

Through the kitchen doorway, I see the snow continuing to fall, and somewhere in the distance, church bells chime the hour. Time to decide.

I begin to type.

Shame. I only date people who can handle a little murder and mayhem with their morning coffee.

Setting my phone down, I turn back to my kitchen nemesis with renewed determination.

In moments, the phone dings again, and I glance over at the message.

True, non-homicidal is overrated. But I might be persuaded to lower my body count...

My laugh bounces off the kitchen walls, surprising me. Shaking my head, I return to the wedding cake, unable to wipe the smile from my face. Who knew disaster could lead to something so unexpectedly delightful?

CHAPTER TWO

JAMES

A week of these daily chats with my mystery girl, and still, my restless feet carry me back and forth across the room as I wait for her message. I glance at my closed door—old habits die hard—before staring down at my cell phone again. Pacing helps me think, always has, but lately these conversations are the only thing that gets me moving. The phone feels warm in my hands as I read her last message again. Something about her responses makes my Alpha instincts stir—her quick wit, the way she combines chaos with humor. It's been a long time since anyone made me feel this... alive.

My room is small, sparse, but the morning light streaming through the window makes it feel less confining than usual. A few more weeks until I'm out of here.

I glance at her last message again, and the urge to

protect, to pursue, rises strong and unexpectedly. I haven't responded to anyone like this in years.

I should get back to work, I type quickly, then glance up at my shut door, at the gap beneath it for any shadows. All clear. *But I enjoyed our chat, Lily.* Something shifts in my chest when I type her name—it has ever since she shared it during our second conversation. Sometimes, at night, I catch myself saying it under my breath like a secret worth keeping. *Lily.* A simple name that's become anything but simple to me.

Giving up so easily, James? And here I thought you were hardcore.

I grin despite myself. *Trust me, sweetheart, I'm plenty hardcore. Just temporarily occupied.*

Mysterious. Let me guess—international spy? Professional ninja? Underwater basket weaver?

The laugh escapes before I can stop it.

If I told you, I'd have to kill you. And you've already got one body to deal with.

Fair point. Though, now I'm definitely intrigued.

Footfalls sound out in the hallway. I type faster. *Keep being intriguing, then. Maybe you'll find out someday.*

Is that a promise or a threat?

Both, I think. Neither. Everything is complicated right now. *Let's call it a possibility,* I send instead.

I like possibilities.

Her reply makes something in my chest tighten.

So, mysterious stranger, we've been chatting for a week,

and you haven't asked for photos once. Either you're not a creep, or you're playing a very long game.

I can't help the giggle that slips out. *If that's your way of asking for photos...*

Still grinning, I drop into my chair and stick my foot out, twisting to get the right angle. The canvas shoes almost gleam under the lights as I snap the picture against the industrial floor. *Here's a toe pic. Try to contain your excitement.*

Oh, my. How scandalous. At least buy me dinner first.

I would if I could. Unfortunately, I'm a bit... tied up at the moment.

The truth hovers dangerously close to the surface. But something about her makes me want to be honest—or as honest as I can be.

Tied up with Bertha the sourdough? she asks.

Among other things. Life's complicated right now.

Three dots appear, disappear, and appear again.

Yeah. I get that.

Something in the tone of her response shifts, and I ask. *Bad day?*

Not bad, exactly. Just... one of those days where everything reminds you of what you've lost, you know?

The vulnerability in her words hits something deep in my chest.

Yeah. I know exactly what you mean.

Sorry, didn't mean to get heavy. Usually, I save the tragic backstory for at least the second week of accidental texting.

Lucky me, I'm ahead of schedule. Want to talk about it?

Another pause. *It's just... my mom. She loved Christmas. The bakery was always her favorite place at this time of year. Some days, it feels like yesterday; others, it feels like a lifetime ago.*

My chest squeezes at my past, my shitty situation. Outside the window, snow continues to fall, each flake another reminder of all that I've lost. The white blanket covers everything, just like the silence that's smothered my old life, buried who I used to be. I think of my own losses—freedom, reputation, time. Some days, the weight of it all feels like drowning in that endless white, but hers feels heavier somehow.

How long?

Twelve years. I was twelve. My sister was fourteen. Dad did his best, but... well. Complicated.

I fight the urge to promise things I can't deliver. To fix, to heal, to wrap her in safety, and to make the world soft again. Fuck, it's been one week of messages, and I'm already in too deep. But what else do I have in here except these moments, these words that make me feel real again? Getting obsessed is dangerous, and I know better. But empty Alpha promises won't help either of us. Instead, I type, *Thank you for telling me.*

Thanks for listening. Most people get weird about grief. Like it has an expiration date or something.

Grief is grief.

Anyway, you know what's weird? Talking to you is easier than talking to most people I actually know.

Maybe because there's no pressure. No expectations.

Maybe. Or maybe you're just good at listening.

If she only knew how much these conversations mean to me too. These moments of normalcy, of connection, in a place designed to limit both.

Then the past hits without warning, sharp as a knife...

Rain drumming against the windshield, streetlights smearing orange through the darkness. The leather of my jacket creaking as I grip the steering wheel. I should've known better. Rick, my cousin, has always walked the line between legal and not, has always pulled this shit for as long as I can remember. But family is family and you trust them, right? So, why the fuck does picking him up in the middle of the night from the drugstore leave me questioning my decision?

The passenger door suddenly rips open. Rick dives in, face flushed with adrenaline, rain dripping from his hair. The metallic click of something heavy hitting the floor makes my chest tight.

"Drive!" His voice cracks. "Fucking drive, James!"

"What the hell did you—" The words die in my throat as I spot the duffel bag, catching the glint of metal—a gun—beneath his jacket. My stomach drops. "Fuck, tell me you didn't."

"Shut the hell up and drive, man!" He's sweating despite the cold, slamming his palm against the dashboard. "You're my ride, remember? That's what you fucking promised!"

"A ride home, Rick! You said you were picking up—"

"Move!" he shouts.

I'm jittery, knees bouncing, my gaze swinging to the

store he just rushed out of. No sign of anyone running out after him! Did he use the gun?

I'm already shifting into gear because that's what I do —I protect, I help, I fix things. Even when every instinct screams that this time, this time, *I've walked into some-thing I can't fix.*

We tear down a residential street, houses looming dark against the rain-heavy sky.

"Pull over now. Fucking now!" Rick suddenly lunges forward, snatching the wheel with his gloved hand and jerking us over the damn curb, and I hit the brakes.

"What the—" I grip the wheel tighter, shoving him away. "I'm not moving until you tell me what the hell is going on."

Rick is already grabbing his duffel, the door half open. "Sorry, bro. Had to be you. You're the only one they'd believe." His grin is something dark, something that makes my blood run cold. "Needed someone to take the fall. You know how it is."

Ice freezes me.

He vanishes between the shadows of the houses before I can react. That's when I see it—the gun he left on the passenger floor, just as the red and blue lights explode across my rearview mirror, turning the rain into a chaos of color.

A thundering knock at my door drags me out of my thoughts. Footsteps sound outside my door, their shadows appearing underneath. "You got visitors."

I have to go, I type quickly. But... same time tomorrow?

It's a date. I mean, not a DATE date, just... you know what I mean.

Her flustered response makes me smirk. She's fucking adorable.

I know what you mean. And hey... for what it's worth? I like our not-date dates.

Me too. Even if you're probably a serial killer.

Says the woman who started this with a body disposal text.

Touché. Stay dangerous, mystery man.

Stay sweet, baker girl.

The familiar jingle of keys comes, and I lift my head to the door. Frantically, I move to the bed and slide the phone into the hidden compartment I carefully hollowed out in the wall down by the bed's feet—worth every pack of cigarettes I'd traded for someone to help me carve it three months ago. The burner has already proved invaluable, even if getting it in here had cost me more favors than I care to count.

I adjust my shirt collar. The lock clicks, and Mike appears in the doorway. I meet his gaze steadily as I step into the sterile hallway. Our footsteps echo against the white-washed walls as he leads me through the maze of identical corridors. The air here is stale, heavy with industrial cleaner and resignation.

He gestures to a door, and I enter to find a few other locals already with their visitors. My gaze lands on my buddies, Hunter and Archer, and I immediately grin. Bastards are smirking just as hard. Their presence fills the white room with something that doesn't belong here—hope, maybe. Or a reminder of the world beyond these walls. A world I'll be returning to soon.

My lawyer made sure Hunter and Archer got on my pre-approved visitors list early on, right alongside my attorney and counselor. The paperwork wasn't fun, but it means they can skip half the security circus when they come. And thank God this place lets approved non-family do contact visits in the common room— none of that glass-barrier bullshit. Makes it feel almost normal. Almost.

I settle into the hard plastic chair with the ease of a man who knows his sentence is just a temporary inconvenience. Just a few more weeks... then freedom.

Hunter towers over most of the guards, his broad shoulders and rugged build clearly marking him as an Alpha, even if his scent doesn't give it away. Today, his black hair is windswept from the storm raging outside, and there's a fresh scrape above his right eyebrow— probably from another mountain adventure. He scans the room automatically, a habit from years of search and rescue work, before he takes a seat across from me at the table. The leather jacket he wears still carries traces of snow across his shoulders.

Beside him, Archer looks like he just stepped out of a business meeting, which he probably did. His golden-brown hair is perfectly styled, and his casual clothes are anything but casual. The kind of simple sweater that looks fucking expensive. But the amber eyes that meet mine belong to my buddy from when we were kids, running wild on Hunter's grandfather's land.

"Looking cheerful this morning," Archer notes as

they both lounge in their plastic chairs. "Finally excited about freedom?"

"Something like that. Seriously, it can't come fucking quick enough." They are the only family that matters anymore, if I'm honest. Hunter's grandfather took us all in during our roughest years—me running from my family's expectations, Archer escaping his family's criminal empire, Hunter reeling from losing his parents. The old man treated us all like grandsons, though only Hunter shares his blood. Even now, years later, we all still refer to him as "Grandfather." "What did you find?" I ask.

Hunter and Archer lean in close across the table. Hunter's jaw is tight, that muscle ticking the way it does when he's holding back fury. A quick glance at the door shows the guard's back is turned.

"Finally got through probate," Hunter mutters, his fingers drumming against the table. "After a fucking year of delays and bullshit from Travis and his cronies."

"And?" I ask, reading the tension in their postures. Something's wrong.

"It's only half a fucking map," Hunter spits out, barely containing his volume.

"Half?" I lean back, processing. "What the hell?"

Archer runs a hand through his hair. "Apparently, when their grandfather passed, the old man had one last trick up his sleeve. Split the treasure map in half— one part to Hunter's side, one to Travis's. Some bullshit about wanting the family to come together."

"Fuck that," Hunter growls, and I watch him struggle to keep his composure.

Losing his grandfather is still raw for him... for all of us. Grandfather Thorne had been everything to Hunter after his parents died. The man had raised him in that sprawling farm mansion in the mountains, teaching him everything from tracking to astronomy on those endless nights.

A memory rises through me, as clear as if it were yesterday instead of fifteen years ago. The four of us around a campfire on the vast Thorne estate, the stars impossibly bright above the mountains. Grandfather's massive frame settled into his favorite hand-carved chair, his silver beard catching the firelight, those ice-blue eyes twinkling with the flame's reflection. Even at seventy, he'd had the bearing of a mountain man half his age—shoulders as broad as a doorframe and hands that could still crack walnuts between his fingers.

"Now, boys," he'd rumbled, his voice as deep as thunder. "Let me tell you about my grandpa's daddy." He'd leaned forward, those eyes dancing. "Old Jefferson Thorne—though Lord help anyone who called him anything but Jed—wasn't your ordinary prospector. Man was brilliant as a whip and twice as quick. But..." He'd paused, taking a long pull from his flask. "Well, that taught him banks weren't worth the paper they printed."

I remember how we'd leaned in, teenage boys hanging on every word. Even then, Hunter and I had been planning, dreaming of the day we'd search for it ourselves. The firelight had cast long shadows across Grandfather's face as he continued.

"See, what Grandpa's father found wasn't just gold that made his hands shake when he wrote in that leather journal of his. Found something up in those caves that wasn't meant to be found. Something that made him convert every last nugget and dust speck to gems and plates within a month."

He'd stood then, all six feet, four inches of him casting a giant's shadow as he paced around the fire.

"Spent the next year burying it across our land. Five thousand acres of the meanest terrain the country could conjure. But here's the thing that'll curl your toes, boys…" He'd stopped, fixing each of us with that penetrating stare. "That cave system? Three men went missing in there the year after Grandpa's dad made his find. Search parties couldn't get more than half a mile in before their compasses went haywire. Found one man's boot, just the boot, caught in a crevice near an underwater stream."

"What happened to them?" Hunter had whispered, completely ensnared.

"Some say they got lost in the maze of tunnels. Others think they found what they were looking for and were met with foul play while hiding it. All I know is Grandpa's dad started carrying a rifle everywhere after that, jumping at shadows. Wouldn't go near those caves again, not for all the gold in the world."

"Come on, Grandfather." Hunter had laughed, but there'd been an edge of uncertainty to it.

"I'm serious." Grandfather had shrugged, settling back in his chair. "But tell me this... why did seven men vanish in spring when they tried to follow Jefferson Thorne's trail? Why did his own brother, Lincoln, disappear without a trace that same year?" His eyes had glittered dangerously in the firelight. "And why, my curious boys, did they finally find him frozen solid in his bed on the hottest day of August, clutching that journal and smiling like he'd seen an angel?"

I shake my head now at the memory. Grandfather had always been a master storyteller, spinning wild tales about the dangers lurking in those caves. Looking back, I figure he'd do anything to keep us from hunting for that treasure—even if it meant serving up horror stories with our s'mores. Can't say it worked, though. If anything, those stories just made the mystery more irresistible.

Most of those caves are gone now—collapsed, buried, or blown apart by decades of development to flatten more of the land. Sure, you can still see where the hills fold like rumpled blankets across the property, but pinpointing where those underground passages used to snake through the bedrock? That's another story entirely. We'd spent years following dead ends and false starts, checking every depression and outcrop across five thousand acres of stubborn terrain. Without some kind of map, we might as well have been throwing darts at shadows. And just when we were ready to admit defeat, we learned about Grandfather having the map, something he denied until his dying breath.

I breathe heavily. Sitting back in this sterile room, Hunter's knuckles are white as he grips the edge of the table.

"We've been planning this since we were kids," he says. "Mapped every inch of that terrain. Studied all the old surveys. Learned every story about where the searches went wrong. He never hinted that he had a map while he was alive or that he'd give Travis Fuckhead half of it. And now this fucking family therapy bullshit?"

"Travis is a fucking ass, and he won't share his half with us," I blurt.

"Fucking snake," Archer cuts in. "He got the lodge and half the grazing land, but they've been trying to get their hands on the main farming house mansion too, which went to Hunter. Like the lodge isn't enough."

"Hell, Travis never even visited him those last five years, so I don't know why he got half the map," Hunter adds, voice thick with contempt.

I lean back in my chair, the familiar ache of my family's betrayals rising up. "Yeah, well, blood doesn't mean shit sometimes. Mine proved that well enough." I gesture vaguely at our surroundings. "That's how I ended up in this fine establishment, remember?"

"Not long now for your release," Archer reminds me quietly.

"Counting down the weeks," I agree, plans already

forming. "And then we deal with your cousin, Travis." An idea begins to take shape, one that makes me smile. "You know, I've made some interesting connections here. People who specialize in making others... cooperative."

Hunter's expression shifts, understanding dawning. "James..."

"Nothing violent," I assure him. "But I know people who can make Travis's life complicated enough that half a map might look like a fair trade for peace and quiet."

"He's got a family, and I fucking hate defending him, but for his kids..." Archer starts.

"We'll leave them completely out of it," I promise. "But Travis? He's got some skeletons. Everyone does. Especially boys playing cowboy at the lodge while others do the real work."

"We'll see. For now, just lie low and get the hell out of this joint," Hunter states.

I smile, remembering Grandfather Thorne's words from another fireside night. "What was it he always said about wolves?"

Hunter's lips curl into a predatory grin. "The pack that hunts together..."

"Survives the winter," Archer finishes softly.

The guard shifts at the door, facing us, nodding in my direction to indicate time is running short. But it doesn't matter. A few more weeks is nothing after waiting eighteen months. And when I walk out of here, we're going to remind Travis why we've always been more wolf than sheep.

Even if we have to do it with half a fucking map.

Three Days Later

I'm lying in bed, staring at the ceiling after messaging Hunter, when my phone lights up. Lily's name appears on the screen. I turn onto my side, away from the door, keeping the light hidden as I type...

Shouldn't all good bakers be asleep by now?

Says the chef messaging me at midnight.

I smile. *You messaged me first.*

Fair point. I'm knee-deep in true crime documentaries and can't sleep. You?

Let me guess—trying to solve another small-town murder?

Hey, someone has to figure out why the local librarian vanished with all the first-edition cookbooks.

I muffle a laugh. *Pretty sure that's called theft, not murder.*

But what if she was silenced because she knew too much about secret recipes?

I sink comfortably into my mattress, lost in my world called Lily, typing away.

And here I thought I was the one who should be worried about criminal tendencies.

Please, the worst crime I've committed is putting pineapple on pizza.

My chest tightens at her casual joke. If she only knew.

That IS pretty unforgivable.

Nerd. So why are you up? Bertha giving you sourdough troubles?

The question hits closer than she knows. Truth is, nights are the worst here. When the walls feel closer and memories get louder.

Actually... thinking about my grandfather. The anniversary of losing him was last week.

There's a pause before her reply comes.

I'm sorry. Those anniversaries are brutal.

Yeah. Sorry to bring it up. I know you mentioned losing your mom and... I'm doing a shit job of this late-night conversation thing.

Nah, you're balancing the heavy and the light like a pro. Besides, Grief Club members get to talk about this stuff. It's in the bylaws. Anyway, want to play a game? Her text lights up my screen.

Depends. Does it involve more true crime theories?

Better. 5 Questions. And you have to be honest.

My stomach tightens. Honesty isn't something I can afford right now, but...

Hit me with your best shot.

First kiss—when and where?

I laugh silently into my pillow. *Behind the bleachers,*

freshman year. Belinda... can't remember her last name. She tasted like cherry ChapStick and immediately told me I was terrible at it.

OMG! 😬 *Mine was Bobby Wilson at a school dance. He missed my mouth entirely and kissed my nose.*

Smooth operator, that Bobby. I curl into my pillow, unable to get enough of her conversations.

Question 2. What's the one thing you'd grab if your place were on fire?

Easy one. *My father's cast-iron skillet. Been in the family for three generations. You?*

Mom's recipe book. Even though half the pages are stuck together with ancient cookie dough.

Question 3. I stare at the phone intensely.

How many serious relationships?

My chest tightens. *Two. Girlfriend for three years when I was in high school, then another for almost two.* I hesitate, then add: *You?*

Just one. Todd. College sweetheart turned cheating asshole.

I clench my jaw, surprising myself with how angry that makes me. *His loss.*

Question 4. The dots appear and disappear several times. *If you could go anywhere in the world right now, where would you go?*

I stare at the ceiling, imagining freedom.

Polignano a Mare, this tiny town in Puglia, southern Italy. Grandfather used to talk about it, where he often traveled and found his wife. Tiny restaurant right on the water, fishing boats coming in at dawn. You?

Japan. But not Tokyo... I want to find those hidden mountain villages where they've been making the same pastries for centuries.

You'd love it. Watched this documentary about their mochi traditions, the way they respect every step of the process. My mouth waters at the memories.

Tell me more about your Italian town.

My chest aches with wanting.

Imagine waking up to the smell of fresh bread and coffee. Streets so narrow that you can touch both walls. Every restaurant has red-checkered tablecloths and wine served in ceramic jugs. And the old women sitting in doorways will feed you until you burst, just because you smiled at them.

Sounds perfect. Take me with you?

The words hit hard. *One day,* I type, wanting to make it real.

One last question... Long pause. What's your favorite position?

I nearly choke, then muffle my laugh in my pillow.

For... cooking?

Playing innocent doesn't suit you, Chef. 😈

Heat floods my body. I shouldn't encourage this, but...

Depends on the kitchen counter height.

Good answer. But that doesn't answer the question.

Fuck. I shift, already hard. I reach down to adjust my cock.

That's dangerous territory, baker girl.

Too scared to answer?

More like too aware of what thinking about you in any position would do to me right now.

Oh.

Yeah. Oh.

Tell me anyway.

I picture her. *On top, straddling me. I want to watch your face, see what makes you bite your lip, hear every sound…*

There's a long wait before her reply comes.

Now who's being dangerous?

You started it. Your turn to answer.

Feels like an eternity waiting for her.

Against the wall, you behind me, taking control.

Christ. I try to steady my breathing.

You're killing me here.

Good.

I close my eyes, picturing her next to me instead of these concrete walls. I deliberately haven't asked what she looks like because I wanted to know her mind first. But now… fuck. I want to see her smile, taste her skin, feel her curves against me.

The phone vibrates in my hand.

Earth to James? Did I break you?

Just thinking.

About?

About how fucking much I want to be honest with her. Instead, I type, *About how much I like talking to you.*

Smooth recovery, Chef. But same.

We talk until her responses get slower, sleepier.

Until she's sending typo-filled messages about needing to be up for the morning rush.

Go to sleep, baker girl.

Sweet dreams, Chef.

Her last message comes through as footsteps pass my cell.

I turn my phone facedown. I'm so far past the point of no return with her, but right now, I can't bring myself to care.

CHAPTER THREE

LILY

"If I throw myself out of this moving vehicle as a reason not to attend the gathering, would that be considered dramatic or resourceful?" I ask from the back seat, watching snowflakes dance in the headlights of Hannah's Honda. She catches my eye in the rearview mirror, her dark-chocolate hair perfectly coiled in its French twist, one manicured eyebrow arching as she unconsciously taps her fingers against the steering wheel in time to the classical music drifting from the speakers.

"Dramatic," she says from behind the wheel.

"Resourceful," Dad votes from the passenger front seat, his weathered hands brushing down the length of the knitted vest he wears over a cream button-up shirt. Silver hair glints from the passing streetlights, and laugh lines deepen around the edges of his mouth. "And if you do it, I'm right behind you. Though, I recommend we claim food poisoning first. More dignified."

"You haven't eaten anything yet," Hannah points out, rolling her eyes.

Dad holds up his full travel mug. "This gas station coffee begs to differ. I can feel the salmonella forming already."

Hannah laughs. "That's just your annual case of Family Gathering Fever. Symptoms include sudden onset of excuses, mysterious ailments, and an overwhelming urge to flee north. And I'd join you in faking sickness, but you said we should do this for Mom."

"You're right," Dad agrees. "They're family, and your mom used to love these gatherings." He adjusts his vest for the hundredth time. "Though, to be fair, Martha's meatloaf tried to kill me last year."

We all burst out laughing.

"They're Mom's family," I say as more snow dusts the evergreens while we climb higher into the mountains. "Who, might I add, only remember we exist once a year when Great-Aunt Martha needs to prove what a generous and caring matriarch she is."

The car falls quiet except for Hannah's festive classical music on the radio. I stare at the lights of Whispering Grove fading behind us as we climb toward the wealthy northern enclave where Mom's family lives. Where they've always lived, looking down both figuratively and literally on our little town.

"I get it. When we lost Mom, or when Grandma went into a nursing home," Hannah says softly, "did any of them offer to help? To watch us while Dad worked doubles?"

"Martha sent a casserole," Dad offers weakly.

"That wasn't a casserole. That was a weapon of mass destruction." I remember the gray, gelatinous mass. "Pretty sure it violated the Geneva Convention."

"I'm not saying they're perfect." Dad clears his throat. "But they're all we have left of Mom's side. And maybe if we made more of an effort..."

"We're not the ones who should be making the effort," I say, more sharply than intended. "Where were they when Mom was keeping the bakery going while looking after Grandma because she needed round-the-clock care?"

"Your mother..." Dad says carefully. "She loved these parties despite everything. She'd light up just walking through Martha's door, no matter what awaited inside. So, we need to attend."

Hannah grins at me through the rearview mirror. I huff.

I think back to Mom dancing in the kitchen while mixing cookie dough. Mom laughing as she taught us to braid bread dough. Mom squeezing Dad's hand when Martha made comments about his *simple* career choices.

Mom choosing joy, even when it was hard.

"Ten minutes," Hannah announces, checking her phone. "That's our limit. Then someone is faking a stroke."

"Twenty minutes," Dad counters. "At least stay through appetizers."

"Fifteen," I offer. "And we create a signal. If anyone mentions our sad, single Omega statuses, we implement emergency evacuation procedures."

Hannah winks at me through the rearview mirror.

Dad frowns as Great-Aunt Martha's Victorian monstrosity comes into view. "Sweet mercy, did she add more lights?"

The house resembles something from a Hallmark movie that took a wrong turn and ended up in Vegas. Every inch is covered in twinkling lights, giant candy canes, and what appears to be a small army of animatronic reindeer. The effect is less festive and more *Christmas having a nervous breakdown.*

"I count three new inflatable snowmen," I report. "And... is that a life-size Santa sleigh on the roof?"

"With real bells." Hannah parks behind a line of much fancier cars than our practical Honda.

"Fifteen minutes is too long," Hannah mutters. "I'm downgrading to seven."

"Hannah," Dad protests.

"Five. Final offer."

He shakes his head at us.

I check my phone one last time before we head inside. Still no response from James. It's been days of silence and pretending it doesn't matter while knowing it matters far too much. My stomach twists with that now-familiar mix of worry and hurt. We'd been talking every day, building something that felt real despite the distance, and then... nothing. The rational part of my brain says there could be a hundred innocent explanations, but the rest of me keeps circling back to darker possibilities. Or worse—that I'd imagined the connection between us, read too much into every late-night conversation and shared secret.

The walk to the front door feels like a march to execution. Dad leads the way while Hannah and I drag our feet.

"Remember," I whisper. "If Cousin Rebecca starts in about her Alpha husband's latest promotion—"

"Sudden migraine." Hannah nods. "If Patricia mentions her Omega support group—"

"Spontaneous combustion."

"If Martha asks about grandchildren—"

"We run like hell."

Dad throws us a look over his shoulder. "I can hear you both."

"We know," we say together, grinning.

The door opens before we reach it, spilling warm light and the smell of cinnamon onto the snow-dusted porch. Great-Aunt Martha fills the doorway like a Christmas-themed battleship, all red velvet and perfectly coiffed gray hair.

"Hannah, darling!" She air-kisses both of Hannah's cheeks. "Casual outfit for such an event. Theodore, you're actually wearing a vest. How... comfortable. And, Lily..." Her smile tightens slightly when she turns to me. "Still working at the little bakery?"

"Still co-owning the successful business Mom

built, yes." I paste on my best customer service smile. "How's your hip replacement? Still setting off metal detectors?"

Hannah snorts. Dad elbows me. Martha's smile turns decidedly frosty.

"Do come in." She steps aside. "Everyone's in the parlor. Rebecca was just telling us about Charles's new position on the hospital board..."

I catch Hannah's eye.

The house might as well be Santa's workshop. Every surface holds some festive tchotchke. Every doorway sports mistletoe. Every window frames an electric candle.

But Mom used to love this. The thought hits me sideways, making my chest tight. She'd walk through these rooms, touching everything, exclaiming over new additions, genuinely delighting in the excess of it all.

Dad's hand finds my shoulder, squeezing gently. He knows. He always knows.

The parlor buzzes with expensive perfume and even more expensive gossip. Cousin Rebecca holds court by the fireplace, her Alpha husband, Charles, looking appropriately adoring as she details his latest achievement. Despite myself, I feel a pang at seeing them together—the easy way he anticipates her needs.

"Lily!" Patricia swoops in before I can find a defensive position. "Darling, you look... healthy. Still haven't found your Alpha match? You know, there are organizations that help Omegas who struggle—"

"Actually," my mouth says before my brain can stop it, "I have someone. He's traveling for work right now. James. He's a chef."

Dad's coffee mug pauses halfway to his mouth, then he sets it down on the table. Hannah's eyes widen slightly.

"Oh?" Patricia's perfectly plucked eyebrows rise. "How... nice. And what restaurant does he work at?"

"It's... complicated. He's starting at a new place. Very exclusive stuff, and I can't spoil the name until it opens up."

Oh God, I'm making it worse, but there's a part of me that's delighted to see them stare at me with something other than pity for a change. Well, except for Hannah, who's frowning in my direction.

Rebecca joins us, wineglass dangling from manicured fingers. "How ambitious. Though, I suppose it's a big step up from the bakery's... scale."

The way she says it makes our thriving business sound like a lemonade stand. Before I can respond, a burst of laughter draws my attention to the window seat, where Cousin Michael sits with his new Omega mate. They're lost in their own world, his fingers trailing absently through her hair while she leans into his touch. The contentment in their closeness makes something in my chest ache. What I wouldn't give to have someone stare at me like that.

"Excuse me." Dad straightens suddenly. "Lily, would you help me find Martha's library? I need to check something about... books."

"Yes!" I practically bump into him. "Books. Very important. Sorry, ladies. Family emergency. Book emergency. Emergency books."

We escape down the hallway, dodging the worst of the mingling, when Cousin Roger thrusts a plate of gray meatloaf and a fork into my hands, shoving a steaming new cup of coffee at Dad with a harried "You both need something!" Dad clutches the coffee like a lifeline as he leads the way to the one room that's always been a sanctuary in this house.

The heavy oak door closes behind us, sealing us into the familiar comfort of leather-bound books and mahogany shelves that stretch to the coffered ceiling. A fire crackles in the massive stone hearth, casting dancing shadows across the worn rug where we spent countless rainy afternoons as kids. The room still smells of lemon polish and old paper, exactly as it did when Grandma would read to us here, though Martha hasn't touched a single volume in the decade since she inherited the house. But she must use it more often, seeing as the fireplace is now blazing.

"That went well," Dad says as we settle by the fireplace on a leather couch. "Four minutes in and you've invented a boyfriend."

"To be fair, he's real. Sort of. Was real? Anyway, I don't want to talk about it."

He grins and studies me. "Everything okay?"

I poke at the meatloaf. "Is this thing moving?"

"Don't change the subject. And don't look too

closely at the meatloaf. Looking only makes it stronger."

"I just…" I struggle to find the words. "Sometimes I wonder if they're right. If I'm broken somehow. Every other Omega I know has had at least one heat by now and found their mate. I think even Hannah has met someone, even if she won't tell me about him yet, and she already had her first heat when she was twenty-one. Me? I still haven't figured out what they want."

"Hey." He sets aside his cup on the nearby coffee table, turning to face me fully. "You're not broken. You're like your mom—you do things in your own time, your own way. She didn't have her first heat until she met me, you know."

That surprises me. "Really?"

"Really. Doctor said some Omegas need the right connection first. The right timing." He smiles softly. "She used to say her heart had to be ready before her body could follow."

"I miss her," I whisper.

"Me too, kiddo." He wraps an arm around my shoulders. "But she'd be so proud of you. Both of you. Running that bakery, growing it so much."

"Even if I'm a sad, single Omega?"

"Hey." His voice turns serious. "You don't need an Alpha to be complete. Your mom would be the first to tell you that. She chose me because she wanted to, not because she needed to. There's a difference."

"Is that why you never…" I trail off, not sure how to ask.

"Never remarried?" He smiles sadly. "Hard to settle for less than perfect once you've had it. Besides, I had my hands full with two stubborn daughters."

"We weren't that bad."

"You once tried to mail Hannah to Canada."

"She deserved it! She told Martin Miller I liked him!"

"You were thirteen at the time."

The library door opens, and Hannah slips in, carrying three plates of something that looks significantly more edible than the meatloaf.

"Thought I'd find you here." She settles on the couch near me. "Brought reinforcements. Dumplings made with Mom's recipe."

"Thank you to both of you for agreeing to attend tonight," Dad announces, grabbing his plate, already wolfing one down.

"Anything for you," I say, setting down my meatloaf and taking a plate of dumplings. Hannah nods as she enjoys her meal, and Dad just smiles at us.

Hannah leans against my side. "Remember how Mom used to sneak us in here during these parties?"

"She'd tell stories about the books coming alive at night," I say softly.

"And dance with Dad between the shelves," Hannah adds.

For a moment, I swear I can smell Mom's perfume —vanilla and cinnamon and home.

The library feels warmer with us three together.

Less like hiding and more like choosing our own joy, just like Mom used to.

"Five more minutes?" Hannah asks softly.

"Ten," Dad and I say together.

"So, Lily," Hannah says, settling into a worn armchair now. "Who's James?"

I concentrate very hard on my dumpling. "Ah, no one. Had to say something to get them off my back."

"Yeah, right." Hannah's eyes narrow. "Sounded pretty real to me. The way you gave details about him..."

I shrug, meeting her gaze. "How about you enlighten us on who your secret lover boy is? You think I haven't noticed you sneaking off at night for a couple of days here and there, your hushed phone calls..."

The color drains from Hannah's face. Her fingers twist in her lap. "I wish that were a boy," she says quietly. "Trust me, it's not."

Dad reaches over and squeezes her hand, no questions asked. That's the thing about Dad—he knows when to push and when to just be there.

"You know," Dad says softly, his voice carrying that same gentle tone he used when we were kids and the world seemed too big, too scary. "Your mother always said the hardest battles we face aren't the ones thrown at us but the ones we carry inside." He looks between us, his eyes full of empathy. "Whatever it is, whenever you're ready... we're here."

Hannah smiles, which, in turn, has me grinning.

We sit in comfortable silence, sharing dumplings

and the quiet understanding that sometimes family isn't about blood or tradition or fancy parties. Sometimes, it's about hiding in libraries, plotting escapes, and knowing exactly who will help you hide a body— metaphorical or otherwise.

The bells on the rooftop Santa sleigh start to chime, making us all jump. Outside the library window, more snow falls, turning the world soft and quiet. My phone stays silent in my pocket. No messages from James even though it's Christmas Eve, but somehow it matters a little less now.

Mom always said the best things take time. Maybe she was right about that too.

"Ready to face the wolves again?" Hannah asks.

"Yeah," I say, standing up, joined by Dad.

Together, we head back into the Christmas Eve chaos, a united front against whatever the evening might bring. And if I find myself staring at the easy affection of Michael and his new Omega or the way Charles anticipates Rebecca's needs... well, maybe wanting something doesn't mean you're broken for not having it yet.

Maybe it just means your heart knows what it's waiting for.

CHAPTER FOUR

LILY

For most of the morning, I've been playing catch-up in the kitchen while Hannah handles the steady stream of customers filtering through our storefront. Flour & Fable Bakery isn't huge—just the long glass counter showcasing our daily offerings, the register area where Hannah works her magic with the customers, and the main domain— the kitchen visible through the wide archway behind the counter when the door is open.

Even with Christmas packed away and already one week into the new year, I'm still humming "Jingle Bells" while the industrial mixer whirs, my hands working through another batch of cinnamon rolls. They're still selling out faster than fresh coffee. These are Mom's recipe—the one that took her three years to perfect, tweaking the cream cheese ratio until it was exactly right. Even now, years after losing her, I still catch myself turning to share a joke or ask her opinion, usually right when I'm dusting flour off my favorite plum-colored dress that she would've lovingly scolded me for wearing in the kitchen.

Then, a new scent finds me, and I'm breathing it in deeper, unable to get enough. It stops me in my tracks.

Between one heartbeat and the next, my world narrows to that scent—bergamot, old books, and autumn leaves, with an underlying sweetness that makes my insides flutter.

I drift toward the kitchen archway. Through the open doorway, I spot Hannah manning the counter, boxing up pastries. The bakery is in full swing, regulars clustered around, the bell above the door chiming every few minutes with new customers.

But the usual comfortable chaos of our little shop fades to background noise as I step into the main bakery. Everyone keeps glancing up from their conversation, trying to be subtle about their staring and failing miserably.

Because there he is.

He's examining our display case with the same careful attention I've seen art curators give to priceless paintings, one long finger tracing the glass above a row of éclairs. Tall enough that he has to duck slightly under our vintage crystal chandelier, with the kind of presence that makes our cozy shop feel somehow smaller and larger at the same time. His hair glints in the morning light, turning it to a burnished gold.

My heart stumbles over itself when his gaze finds mine. Amber eyes are as bright as honey in sunlight. His mouth curves into a smile that feels like a secret shared between just us two. He strolls toward me like someone completely at ease in their own skin, and I find myself rooted to the spot, pulse thundering in my ears.

The way my body responds to his presence tells me everything my rational mind is still catching up to. He looks at me, his smile widening just enough to show a hint of a dimple in his left cheek.

"I hope you're the one responsible for those cinnamon rolls in the window," he says finally, his deep voice sliding down my spine like warm honey. "Because they're the most enticing thing I've seen all day." His eyes say otherwise, and the heat in my cheeks tells me I'm not the only one affected by whatever this is between us.

For a moment, I forget how to breathe.

Then I manage to find my words. "Most enticing thing all day? It's barely nine in the morning. I'd hate to peak this early." The words slip out before my brain can fully engage its filter, and fire slides up my neck.

Up close, his presence is even more overwhelming —a charcoal Henley that hugs broad shoulders, sleeves pushed up to reveal forearms corded with lean muscle. My eyes trace the sharp line of his jaw, those impossible cheekbones, and I'm convinced the temperature in the shop rises another few hundred degrees. I catch one more whiff of that intoxicating scent. God, who is this man, and why does it feel like my whole world just tilted on its axis?

His laugh is rich and genuine, and something in my chest does a little flip at the sound. "Oh, I wouldn't worry about that," he says, and the way his gaze shifts over me tells me he caught my double entendre.

Hannah catches my attention, her eyebrows raised in a way that says we'll definitely be talking about this later. I should care about that. I should care about a lot of things right now. But all I can focus on is the way his amber eyes haven't left my face, like I'm some rare first edition he's just discovered.

My knees actually wobble.

A slight smile plays at the corners of his mouth like he knows exactly what effect he's having.

"What can I get you?" My response comes out embarrassingly breathy. I clear my throat and try again.

Hannah chooses that moment to practically skip past, bless her evil heart, and the look she shoots at me can only be described as delightedly wicked as she *accidentally* bumps my hip while delivering a tray of fresh scones. The gentle nudge sends me a half step closer to him from behind the counter. She disappears with a satisfied little smirk.

The Alpha—and good Lord, is he ever an Alpha—prowls closer. There's no other word for it. He moves like someone who knows exactly how much space he takes up and how to use it to maximum effect. All the ladies in the bakery notice him, staring, gawking, lost in their own fantasies.

"What would you recommend?" His gaze never leaves mine, even as he surveys the display case.

My hands dip into the pockets of my apron, and I'm grateful for the space between us because my body is doing things it has never done before. Heat pools low in my belly, igniting into flames. My skin feels too tight.

"That depends. Are you feeling adventurous, or do you prefer to play it safe?"

Something sparks in those eyes. "Do I look like someone who plays it safe?"

No. No, he really doesn't.

"In that case..." I move along the display case, trying to ignore how his presence seems to follow me like a physical touch. How other customers Hannah is serving keep watching us. "The almond croissants are fresh out of the oven. Or there's our signature cinnamon rolls—Mom's recipe, actually."

"Oh?" Something like recognition shifts in his expression as I glance at him. "You grew up in the business?"

"Sort of." My response comes easier now, on familiar ground. "She started in our home kitchen, making baked goods for the store, before taking over the business." I gesture around the shop, pride mixing with the old ache. I don't know why I'm saying all this, yet I can't seem to stop. "My sister and I took over after... after she passed. Added our own touches while keeping her recipes alive."

"That couldn't have been easy." A softness coats his tone, as if he knows about loss too.

"Worth it, though." I straighten slightly. "Every time someone says our cinnamon rolls taste like home, or a bride cries over her wedding cake... that's Mom's legacy. That's what matters."

He studies me for a long moment, something unreadable on his face. "A woman who knows what she wants and builds it herself. Impressive."

The compliment settles warmly in my chest, different from the heat his presence inspires. This feels... real. Earned.

"So." I manage a real smile. "About those recommendations?"

"I'll trust your judgment." He returns the smile, and oh, that's not fair at all. "Surprise me."

I gather an assortment of our best sellers, adding one of our special chocolate Sin in a Box cookies. My hands still shake slightly when I pass him the bag, and when our fingers brush, electricity shoots straight through me.

His nostrils flare. His pupils dilate slightly. The air between us thickens with something that has nothing to do with baked goods.

"We're open every day except Mondays." I try to be professional, miss by a mile, and land somewhere around breathlessly interested. "Though, mornings are best for the croissants."

"Actually, I'm only in town for the day on business." His smile turns rueful as he leans slightly closer, and I catch a few women at nearby tables shooting daggers in my direction. "Local antiques dealer wouldn't stop raving about this place. Said your cinnamon rolls were worth crossing state lines for."

"Just the cinnamon rolls?" I arch an eyebrow, channeling my inner femme fatale, but pretty sure I look more like a flour-dusted disaster. "Our scones have been known to start minor turf wars."

He laughs, a ridiculously sexy sound that has me daydreaming about what it would feel like to be kissed by a man like him. "Is that why there's a line out the door? And here I thought it was the charming company."

"Smooth," I snort before I can stop myself. "Do you practice those lines in front of a mirror, or do they just come naturally?"

"Only to a beautiful baker." His eyes are dancing up and down my body, and I'm suddenly very aware of how the morning light streaming through our front windows reflects the brightness in them.

"Let me guess—you say that to all the pâtissiers," I shoot back while my heart flutters when his grin widens. I can't stop staring at that adorable dimple of his.

The bell above our door chimes as another wave of customers floods in, and he glances over his shoulder at the growing crowd.

"I should probably stop monopolizing all this

prime bakery real estate," he says, adjusting his hold on the bag of pastries, stepping back with obvious reluctance. Then he winks—actually winks—and I swear my knees turn to butter on the spot. "Thanks for making my brief stay in town memorable."

Just then, my phone dings in my apron pocket with a message from James.

Hey, baker girl. Missed chatting with you.

I stare at it for too long. He's been radio silent for weeks. Of course he'd choose this exact moment to resurface. I stuff the phone away in my apron.

Hannah rings up his pastries, and once the gorgeous customer pays, he slips out the door. I become acutely aware that every female gaze in the shop is locked on to me with laser focus.

"Ladies, our chocolate croissants are just as dreamy and far more attainable," I quip, earning a few grudging laughs. But even as I head back to my mixing bowls, I can't quite shake the lingering scent of bergamot and old books or the way his smile made the whole world feel a little brighter.

My phone beeps again, but I ignore it and jump into serving customers, as the shop is chaotically busy. When we're finally quiet, shelves close to empty, I head back into the kitchen, Hannah quickly on my heels.

"Well, well, well." She's leaning against the kitchen doorway, arms crossed. "That Alpha was interested in you."

"That was nothing." I busy myself with the abandoned frosting. "Just a customer."

"Lily, your scent changed the moment he walked in. I could smell it from the register." She moves closer. "Has that ever happened before?"

"No," I admit quietly. "Never. I don't... I don't react to Alphas. You know that."

She reaches out and squeezes my hand. "Maybe you just hadn't met the right one."

There goes my phone again, insistent. Hannah's gaze tracks over my apron.

"Speaking of the right ones... you've been awfully attached to that phone lately. Something you want to tell your big sister?"

"Nope." I pop the *p* sound, aiming for casual. "Nothing to tell."

"Really? Because you've been checking it a lot. And now this Alpha walks in, and your Omega practically purrs, which has never happened before. Is he the one messaging you?"

I focus very hard on piping perfect swirls of frosting. "It's nothing. Just... just someone else I text with sometimes. It's not serious."

"Uh-huh." Her tone drips skepticism. "And this *not-serious* person is James, right?"

"It's not serious. I mean, we haven't even met. It's just texts. Fun conversations. Nothing worth mentioning."

"That's why you're keeping it a secret?"

Sometimes, I hate how well she knows me. How she can see right through my defenses to the truth I'm trying to hide from myself—that I'm terrified of how real this feels, how much I looked forward to his messages, and how defeated I felt when he stopped sending them.

"I just…" I struggle to find the words. "If I tell people, if I make it real… then it turns out to be nothing…"

"Oh, honey." Hannah pulls me into a hug, her familiar scent—sugar cookies, coffee, and marsh-mallow—wrapping around me. "You're allowed to hope, you know. You're allowed to want things."

My phone buzzes a third time. Hannah releases me with a knowing smile.

"Go on, check it. I'll collect the empty baskets from the shelves in the shop."

Hands shaking slightly, I pull out my phone and read James's message.

Just wondering if you've committed any felonies today. You know, for research purposes. Also, hypothetically, what are your thoughts on Valentine's Day? Asking for a friend. Who might be me. Who might want to try asking about meeting up. If you're still interested.

I stare at his words, my stomach doing that familiar flip even as anger bubbles up. Two weeks of silence and he just waltzes back in with his charming serial killer routine? I'm torn between the urge to tell him off and the traitorous flutter in my chest at seeing his name on my screen again.

Oh, look who's emerged from witness protection. Should I alert the authorities that you're alive?

Ouch. Deserved that.

You think? I was THIS close to posting missing-person flyers with your chat avatar on them.

Would you have described me as "armed with questionable timing"?

Despite myself, I snort. *More like "Approach with caution. Known to disappear without warning and reappear with suspicious Valentine's plans."*

There's actually a reason for that. One I'd rather explain in person.

Hmm. Sounds exactly like something a serial killer would say.

Says the woman who knows specific details about body disposal, thanks to her true crime obsession.

Hey! Those are purely theoretical knowledge points. And you're deflecting.

A pause, then: *You're right. I am. Look, I know I messed up by vanishing again, but I swear I had a good reason. One that involves an emergency out of my control, location, and a series of unfortunately timed events.*

And you couldn't send a single "Hey, not dead" text?

Would you believe my phone got eaten by a mountain goat?

Now I KNOW you're making shit up. 🙄

He pauses for a moment. *Yeah... I am. But the truth is... unusual. And not great. And I've been beating myself up about going dark on you.*

That's... surprisingly honest. 😐

I owed you that much. I really messed up, didn't I? he responds quickly.

The fact that you know that helps. A little. Maybe. Jury's still out.

Fair enough. I miss our talks. And your terrible puns.

Hey! My puns are works of art. Unlike your disappearing act.

Meet me for coffee, and I'll tell you the whole ridiculous story. I promise it's worth hearing. And if it's not, you can add "pathological liar with a vivid imagination" to that missing-person flyer.

I bite my lip, staring at the screen. Meeting in person would make this real. Would risk turning this perfect bubble of connection into something that could disappoint. Or hurt. Or end. But there's something about the way he owns up to his mistake, the thread of sincerity woven through his playful words... Unless he's lying about that too.

Fine. Valentine's it is. And you're buying or baking. And it'd better be a REALLY good story about that goat.

Deal. Though, I should warn you, I clean up surprisingly well for a suspected serial killer.

I giggle. *Now who's getting cocky? I'll have you know I just had a very charming customer who set a high bar for mysterious strangers.*

Sounds like I have some competition. I'd better bring my A-game and best murder alibi.

You're ridiculous. And that's not the compliment you think it is.

And yet you're smiling right now. Aren't you?

I am, damn him. *I plead the Fifth. Now, stop fishing for compliments.*

Outside the kitchen window, snow starts to fall again. My thoughts drift between bergamot and old books, the mysterious stranger's wink that turned my knees to butter, and James's words that still manage to make me laugh even when I want to be mad at him. I'm standing in the middle of my bakery, suddenly understanding why my mother always said relationships were the most complicated recipe of all.

CHAPTER FIVE

LILY

The January morning rush finally ebbs around eleven, leaving the bakery smelling of vanilla and fresh coffee, dusted in flour like the snow outside. Our little shop sits quiet now after the chaos of post-holiday customers desperate for comfort food in the bitter winter cold. The industrial mixer hums as I work on a batch of Italian buttercream, trying to lose myself in the familiar rhythm of sugar and egg whites coming together. But every few minutes, my attention drifts to my phone, dark and silent on the counter, for another message from James. He's been quiet for the past week. Again.

Hannah has been watching me all morning, wearing that expression I know too well—the one she's worn since Mom died, as though she has to be both sister and mother now. I see her reflection in the polished display case as she approaches, her steps measured.

"That's the fourth time you've checked your phone," she says, reaching past me to turn off the mixer. "And you nearly dropped Mrs. Lyn's birthday order form in the sink earlier when you got a message. This isn't like you, Lily."

"I'm just expecting an important message."

"From James?" She tries to sound casual, but I catch the way her eyes narrow slightly.

Heat creeps up my neck. "Maybe."

"You can talk to me, you know." Hannah abandons her cleaning, leaning against the counter.

"You know that wedding cake fiasco right before Christmas when you left me all alone to do it?" I focus on arranging cream puffs on a golden tray, buying time. "When I was elbow-deep in cake and desperately needed your new number to complain about it?" I shoot her a look. "By the way, thanks for changing your number right in the middle of the busy season. Really, this is your fault, sis."

She rolls her eyes at me.

"Anyway, there I was, trying to type your new number, and apparently, my desperate finger hit the wrong number." I fidget with another cream puff. "And instead of, you know, ignoring the crazy person having a wedding cake meltdown, he actually wrote back."

"And you kept talking to the wrong-number guy?" The big sister tone creeps into her voice.

"He was actually really funny and made me forget about my stress!" I chance a look at her. "And then we just... kept talking."

"Lily..." Hannah stares at me deeply. "Have you even met him?"

"Not exactly." The cream puffs can't be arranged any better, but I keep fiddling with them anyway. "We've talked about everything, and he has this sourdough starter named Bertha. And he mentioned catching up, maybe on Valentine's Day." I trail off, seeing her expression. "What?"

"So you're sharing personal things with someone you've never met?" Hannah's voice has that edge to it, the one that says she's trying not to sound judgmental but definitely is. "Do you even know what he looks like?"

"Does it matter? I know it's a guy."

Hannah scoffs. "Yeah, maybe he's a serial killer."

I let out a strangled laugh, remembering our playful messages about murder. If she only knew.

"Or," Hannah continues, "what if he has a family? You know how many men do this? Prey on women online, especially Omegas—"

"He doesn't know I'm an Omega," I cut in. "I never told him that."

"Is James even his real name?"

The question hits harder than it should. "I... assume it is." But now doubt creeps in, the way it always does when Hannah gets that tone.

She pulls out her phone. "What's his number?"

"What are you doing?"

"Remember how we set up Ruby on those blind dates?" A slight smile crosses her face. "Well, one of them, Dominic, is a security specialist—basically a legal hacker. And he owes us one for introducing him to Ruby. If anyone can track down this number, it's him."

I hesitate, my fingers tightening around my phone. "Hannah..."

"Come on, Lily. Let me at least try. For my peace of mind?"

I stare at her for a long moment, then slowly recite the number. My stomach knots as she types it into her phone and messages it to Dominic.

"Done," she finally says, hitting Send. "Now we wait."

The next few hours in the bakery crawl by like molasses. Every time the bell over the door chimes, I jump. Every ping from a phone makes my heart race. I mess up three orders and nearly burn a batch of snickerdoodles. Hannah keeps shooting me concerned glances between customers.

Late afternoon, just as I'm pulling a tray of sourdough from the oven, Hannah bursts through the swinging doors from the front of the shop, her phone in hand. I freeze, still holding the bread paddle.

"Is it Dominic?" I ask, barely breathing.

She nods, eyes scanning her screen. "He says that based on the area code, he was able to triangulate—whatever that means—and narrow it down to a rural area. There's some kind of facility there..."

"What kind?" Something in my chest constricts as I watch her face.

"It's the Alpine Ridge Correctional Facility," she says carefully.

The world tilts sideways. "What?"

"Are you sure he said he was a chef?"

My mind races through our conversations. He'd talked about cooking, about recipes, about kitchen disasters, but had he ever actually said where he worked?

"Maybe..." My voice sounds distant to my own ears. "Maybe he's a guard there. That would explain the phone, right? And the weird hours, and..."

"Or," Hannah says gently, "he could have an illegal phone, and he's an inmate."

"No." But even as I say it, pieces start clicking into place. The vague answers about his work. The specific times he'd message me. The way he'd deflect questions about sending me photos of where he was. And never wanting to do a video call.

"He sent me a photo of his shoe, but he hasn't asked for photos of me," I protest weakly, pulling out my phone.

Hannah studies the image. "That could be anything. Prison kitchen uniform, for all we know."

My hands shake as I type to James. *Hey... what exactly do you do for a living? Where are you right now?*

"Lily..." Hannah reaches for my hand.

"He'll explain," I insist. "There has to be—"

"When did you last hear from him?"

"Last week. But he already told me he'd explain everything when we met."

Hannah's eyes fill with sympathy. "Of course he did. Probably when he gets released or escapes."

"Stop it." My stomach drops.

"Lily, you need to think about this. A man who won't tell you basic things about his life, who sends cropped photos—"

"He listened when I talked about Mom," I cut in, hating the way my tone breaks. "When I told him about finding her recipes, about how much I missed her. He understood that kind of loss. That wasn't fake."

"Or he's really good at what he does." Hannah comes around to my side. "Con men don't succeed by being obvious, Lily. They succeed by finding what people need and becoming exactly that."

My phone sits silently in my trembling hands. No response. No typing dots. Nothing.

"I need air." I head for the back door, but Hannah catches my arm.

"You need to delete and block his number."

"I need to know the truth."

"The truth?" Her tone rises slightly. "The truth is that you've been texting a prisoner who lied to you for weeks. Who knows what else he's lying about? His name? His crime? Whether he's even getting out?"

Each question lands like a blow. Because she's right—of course she's right. Hannah is always right about things. She was right about Todd in college, about David last year, about every red flag I've ever tried to ignore.

But this feels different. The way he wrote about his

grandfather's death, about grief and healing. The way he made me laugh. The way talking to him felt more real than any conversation I've had with any guy, ever.

"Give me the laptop from the counter," I whisper.

"Lily…"

"Please."

She hesitates, then slides it over. I go to the government inmate locator site and type in his name and correctional location.

Eight Jameses pop up. I don't know his surname. My gut aches, and I'm going to be sick.

I close the laptop.

"Get rid of his number," Hannah says softly. "Whatever this was… it wasn't real."

But that's the thing about real connections—they don't feel any less real just because they're impossible. They don't hurt any less just because you should have known better.

I stare at our last exchange. I could demand answers. Could tell him I know the truth. Could…

Instead, I set the phone facedown on the counter and turn back to my cream puffs. They at least make sense.

"You were right," I tell Hannah, hating the sympathy in her eyes as I turn toward her. I pick up my phone, thumb hovering over his number.

Then I block him. Part of me feels wrong on the inside…

Hannah reaches for me, gives me a huge hug, and then pulls back. "You did amazing, and now we need to figure out what we're going to do about the Anderson-Pierce wedding."

I blink at the sudden change of subject. "What about it?"

"Mike called. His delivery guy went to a different town first, and his truck broke down, so we're not getting our specialty flour shipment tomorrow. Could be weeks." She wipes her hands on her apron. "We need that chocolate-cherry cake for the tasting on Thursday, and you know regular flour won't give us the same texture for our baked goods either."

"Seriously? Could this day get any better?" I drop my head onto the counter.

"Actually..." Hannah's voice takes on that carefully casual tone she uses when she's trying to help. "Pike Mill's supply store has them in stock. I called them, but they have no staff to send for delivery. And all couriers are booked."

I lift my head. "Pike Mill? That's, like, three hours away."

"Exactly." She starts gathering empty mixing bowls. "You could take my car tomorrow morning. Crank up those awful breakup songs you pretend not to love. Maybe stop at that little coffee shop by the lake." She bumps my shoulder. "Sometimes, a drive is the best way to clear your head. Get some perspective."

"You just want me out of the kitchen before I stress-bake three dozen chocolate chip cookies."

"The fact that we're drowning in comfort cookies is purely coincidental." Her smile fades to something softer. "Seriously, though. Go for a drive. Scream along to Taylor Swift. Get some air that doesn't smell like sugar and regret."

I look down at my phone, no longer with his number. Memories that were beautiful, impossible things that were never meant to last.

"Yeah," I say finally. "Maybe I will."

CHAPTER SIX
HUNTER

The wind howls like a wounded beast, whipping snow against my windshield faster than the wipers can clear it. Even with the chains on my F-350's tires and the weight of the supplies in the back, I can feel the truck fighting against the gusts. Fucking useless weather report. They said the storm wouldn't hit until tomorrow, giving everyone plenty of time to prepare. Instead, it slammed into the mountains like a freight train, catching everyone with their pants down.

"What do you think, Thor? Weather service screwed us again, didn't they?"

The massive malamute in the passenger seat huffs in agreement, his warm breath fogging the side window. I reach over to scratch behind his ears. Thor's been my constant companion for years now, ever since I found him as a half-frozen pup during a rescue operation. Now he's a mountain of fur and muscle and better company than most humans I know.

"At least we got the supplies before it hit."

The bed of my truck is loaded with containers of shelf-stable food, medical supplies, and enough firewood to keep my cabin warm through what was supposed to be tomorrow's storm. The back seat is crammed with fresh produce and meat. Living in the mountains means you either stock up or starve, and I've seen enough winter disasters to know which I prefer.

Thor's ears suddenly prick forward, and he lets out a low whine. My hands tighten on the steering wheel as another gust tries to push the truck sideways. The road ahead is barely visible, just a suggestion of pavement beneath the growing blanket of white. In the mountains, storms don't just block roads—they erase them completely.

"Easy, boy. We know these roads."

Years of mountain driving experience keep my movements steady and controlled. I know every turn and switchback like I know the scars on my hands. I have to in my line of work as a rescuer. Can't save others if you can't find your way home.

The memory of my last mission—a family of tourists who thought winter hiking would be *adventurous*—makes me grimace. Got them out just before hypothermia set in, but it was close. Too close. People don't respect these mountains, don't understand how quickly things can go wrong up here.

Like my parents learned. Like I learned, watching the search teams dig for them through that avalanche, my grandfather's hand tight on my shoulder.

Thor's sudden bark snaps me back to the present. Through the whiteout, I catch a flash of red—brake lights, dim and distorted by the snow, but definitely there. I ease off the gas, squinting through the storm. As I get closer, the scene materializes like a photograph developing... a sedan. Its side end crumpled against the guardrail, listing dangerously toward the drop-off beyond.

"Fuck." The word fogs in the cab's warmth. From the way the trees are bending, the storm is going to get worse before it gets better.

Thor whines again, more urgently this time. He knows what comes next—we've done enough rescues together.

"Stay," I command, though I know he'll ignore me if I leave the door open. Grabbing my heavy storm gear—insulated gloves, waterproof jacket, and hat pulled low—I brace myself before opening the door.

The cold slams into me, driving needles of ice through every gap in my clothing. The wind nearly yanks the door from my grip as I force it shut, then battle my way toward the stranded vehicle. Snow pelts my face, the few inches of exposed skin already going numb despite my beard's protection.

There's movement inside the car—thank God they're alive and haven't tried walking for help. As I reach the driver's window, I catch my first glimpse of the person inside, and my breath sticks in my throat.

She's stunning—dark brown hair shot through with highlights frames a heart-shaped face, golden-brown eyes wide with a mixture of fear and determination. Her features are delicate, with high cheekbones and full lips currently pressed into a worried line.

When she rolls down the window at my gesture, I ask, "You need help?"

"Kinda stuck." Those eyes are even more striking up close, flecked with gold, studying me with wariness and hope. A few wild curls escape her hat, fluttering in the wind that whips between us.

Push it down. Focus on the job.

"We need to get you out of here," I tell her, assessing the car's position.

I see the uncertainty flash across her face—smart girl, she should be cautious—but I also see the moment she processes her situation, the same way I'm already planning our next moves. She glances at her phone, sighs, and sets it down. "I can't get a signal out here."

"You won't, and the storm's going to get worse. You're in danger staying out here."

She glances at the steep drop beyond the guardrail and lets out a shaky laugh. "So this isn't exactly how I planned to spend my day."

I half chuckle at her attempt to cover her fear. "You're safe. But I need to get you to the truck now, and this guardrail won't hold if the wind picks up more."

"That's... not terrifying at all." She swallows hard, then manages a wobbly smile.

The door protests as she pushes it open, but it gives way. The moment it fully opens, I see her body jerk at the full force of the storm. Without thinking, I reach out to steady her, and even through our layers, the contact sends a jolt through me. She's small and delicate compared to my bulk, but there's strength in the way she immediately starts fighting against the wind.

"I've got you," I assure her, and something in her posture relaxes slightly at the words.

She glances up at me, her eyes catching mine with sincerity. "Thank you for stopping. Most people wouldn't have, in weather like this."

Just as I go to respond, a sharp crack splits the air above the storm's howl. We both look up to see a massive pine branch, heavy with snow and ice, breaking free above us. Acting on instinct, I yank her against my chest, spinning us away from the car. The branch crashes down where we'd been standing, missing us by inches. Snow explodes around us in a white cloud, and I feel her cry out against my chest.

Her hands fist in my jacket, her face buried against me. My arms tighten instinctively, and for a moment, I'm overwhelmed by how perfectly she fits against me, how right she feels there.

"And this is why we need to move fast," I say roughly, still holding her close. "Can you run?"

She nods against my chest, then pulls back slightly. Even terrified and snow-covered, she's breathtaking. A tiny snowflake lands on her eyelashes, and I have to physically stop myself from brushing it away.

"What about my handbag and phone?" she asks.

"I'll come back for it. Right now, we need to get you somewhere safe."

Another crack sounds above us, and this time, she's the one who moves, grabbing my hand and pulling me toward my truck. I keep my body between her and the worst of the wind, but she moves with surprising speed despite her size, determination in every step.

"So you do this normally?" she calls out, still shaken as we push against the wind.

"Yep," I reply. "Rescue those in need up in these mountains. Though, finding you in this monster of a storm..." I stare at the whiteout conditions surrounding us. "That was pure luck."

Thor's barking grows louder as we approach, and I sense the woman falter slightly.

"That's just Thor," I tell her quickly. "He's friendly. And probably wondering what's taking us so long."

As if on cue, Thor's massive head appears in the back window, his tail wagging as he spots us. A surprised laugh escapes her, the sound nearly lost in the wind.

"You have a monster wolf in your truck?"

"Malamute. Though, he'd probably take that as a compliment."

We reach the truck. The side of the truck has my business logo—Peak Guardian Response. Her gaze traces over the logo on my side door. I help her into the passenger seat, where Thor immediately starts fussing over her, attempting to climb back into the front, his huge nose pressing against her, sniffing her, checking her for injuries in his own way. Her laugh this time is stronger, more genuine, as she buries her fingers in his thick fur.

"Hi, big guy," she says softly, and Thor responds by resting his chin on my shoulder, looking at me as if to say, *Can we keep her?*

"Stay with her," I order, though it's unnecessary—Thor has already appointed himself her protector. "I'll get your bag."

Fighting my way back to her car, I can't shake the image of her in my arms, the way she felt against me, the trust in her eyes when she looked up at me. Can't forget the way my entire body screamed to protect her, to keep her safe, to never let go.

The wind howls louder, driving sheets of snow between me and my truck, where Thor guards my unexpected passenger.

I push against the storm toward her sedan, yanking open the driver's door against the wind's resistance. Her handbag sits abandoned on the center console, a sleek leather thing that looks too delicate for these mountains, just like its owner. Next to it, her phone glows with a lost-signal warning. I grab both, along with a purple knitted scarf from the back seat, then secure the car as best I can. The wind nearly knocks me off my feet as I return to the truck, but the sight of her through the snow-streaked windows, fingers buried in

Thor's fur while she watches for me, makes the struggle worth it.

Her scent hits me the moment I climb into my truck—peppermint and vanilla with wild morning dew on mountain flowers underneath. Pure Omega, but different from any I've encountered before. Protective instincts surge, especially seeing how she's shivering despite having half a malamute in her lap.

"Thor, back," I command as my giant dog tries to push forward from the back seat but fails. "Sorry about him. He's usually not this... friendly."

She laughs, the sound brightening the storm-darkened cab. "It's okay. I love dogs." Her fingers find the spot behind Thor's ears that turns him to putty, his huge head sticking out between our two seats. "Though, I'm more used to the tiny things that fit in purses."

Thor practically melts, resting his massive head on her shoulder with a contented sigh. Traitor.

"He's an excellent judge of character," I say, carefully pulling out around her sedan. The snow is getting worse, if that's possible. "Usually takes him weeks to warm up to strangers."

"Clearly, he recognizes quality when he sees it." There's a smile in her voice. "But seriously, I can't thank you enough for helping me out."

"No thanks needed," I say. "Some things you just don't ignore." Then I crank up the heater, trying not to be too obvious about watching her in my peripheral vision. The cold has brought color to her cheeks, and snowflakes melt in her dark curls. She's beautiful, in an authentic way. Not polished or perfect, but alive and vibrant even while obviously scared.

"So," she begins as Thor snuggles closer. "Where's the closest town to get some help for my car?"

"Not in this weather." I focus on keeping us steady as the truck slides slightly. "My cabin is about twenty minutes up—assuming we don't get blown off the mountain." She arches an eyebrow, and I can't help but chuckle. "I promise I'm not a serial killer."

"Exactly what a serial killer would say." But she's smiling too. "Though, I guess Thor's a pretty good character reference."

"He's never steered me wrong." I navigate around a fallen branch. "Once we're there, you can try the land-line. Cell service is usually spotty up here even without the storm."

"You live here full-time?"

"Nah, I'm in Cedar Hollow usually. Come up here in the mountains with friends to ski, climb, get away from civilization. To escape, basically." A particularly strong gust hits us broadside, and I tighten my grip on the wheel. "Though, this storm came out of nowhere."

"You're telling me. The forecast said light snow, maybe some wind, which is why I'm here traveling to Pike Mill to pick up supplies." She scratches Thor's head absently. "Shows what they know."

"Weather up here has its own ideas." I steal another glance at her. She's still shivering slightly, so I edge the heat up higher. "You're not from around the mountains?"

"Whispering Grove. Run a bakery with my sister." Her tone warms when talking about it. "Been there all my life, but apparently, that doesn't make me any smarter about mountain weather."

"Whispering Grove is about an hour south of our location now. We won't make it back there in this weather."

She nods, clearly understanding.

"Right now, it feels like another planet." She peers through the windshield at the worsening conditions. "I don't suppose you have a secret helicopter stashed somewhere?"

"Fresh out of helicopters. Though, I do have hot chocolate at the cabin."

"Bribing me with chocolate?" Her laugh carries a nervous edge this time.

I catch her eye briefly. "I know this isn't ideal, but I'll get you somewhere safe. Promise."

She gives me a soft smile.

"So what did you need from Pike Mill?" I ask, genuinely curious about what would drive someone to brave these conditions.

"Specialty flour." She says it so seriously that I almost laugh. "My sister needs it for a wedding cake. I volunteered to pick it up because, apparently, I'm an idiot who doesn't check weather reports properly."

"Brave," I correct.

She smiles, and something in my chest tightens.

"Though, usually, my terrible decisions don't involve potentially freezing to death."

"Sounds troublesome." I work the steering wheel, fighting the blizzard that tries to pull us in every direction but straight.

She shrugs but is busy staring out the window, her hand clutching the door handle.

The truck slides again on a particularly bad curve, my stomach lurching, and her grip tightens.

"So, why a malamute?" she asks suddenly, still fussing over Thor, who seems determined to become one with her lap despite his size.

I guide the truck around another treacherous bend, trying not to focus on how her Omega scent seems to be seeping into my upholstery. I'll be smelling peppermint and mountain flowers for days. "I found him at a rescue site two years ago. Lost, starving, freezing. Refused to leave, and I couldn't let him go."

"Love at first sight?"

"More like stubborn determination. Reminded me of someone else who wouldn't take no for an answer."

"Ex?"

She's more perceptive than I gave her credit for.

"That obvious?"

"You got this little crease between your eyes. Like you bit into something that should've been sweet but wasn't."

Her description is so accurate that it makes me laugh despite the old ache. "Yeah, well. Some lessons you have to learn the hard way."

"Let me guess..." She hesitates, then gives me a tentative smile. "The job? Rescue work isn't exactly nine-to-five. Or maybe you spend too much time in the remote cabin with your buddies? Oh! Or it could be the classic 'my mother thinks you should have a more prestigious career' situation?"

I can't help but huff out a laugh at how far off she is. "None of the above, actually."

"Damn." She wrinkles her nose. "And here I thought I was channeling my inner detective. Those are usually the top three complaints I hear."

"From experience?"

"My cousin dated a forest ranger once. Her mother nearly had an aneurysm." She pauses, then adds more quietly, "But I'm sensing I'm way off base here."

I stare out at the storm for a moment. "She wanted the lifestyle until she realized it wasn't just a romantic fantasy. Thought she could... upgrade me, I guess. Turn the cabin into some kind of luxury retreat and kick my grandfather out."

"Ah. What a bitch!" The sympathy in her words isn't the condescending kind I'm used to. "Her loss, if you ask me." She shakes her head.

My chest unclenches. Unlike Vanessa, who looked at my cabin and saw a renovation project, this woman seems to understand that the mountains aren't something to be conquered or changed. Well, at first impression, at least.

"Hunter," I say suddenly, wanting her to know my name. Wanting to hear her say it.

"Hmm?"

"My name. It's Hunter."

She smiles, and damn if it doesn't light up the whole cab. "Fitting. Though, I hope you're better at hunting than you are at weather forecasts."

"Says the woman who drove into a blizzard for flour."

"Specialty flour," she corrects primly, making me grin. "Very different from regular flour. Life-and-death stuff."

"Clearly." The truck slides slightly, and she tenses, but I correct before she panics.

"I'm Lily."

I grin, rolling her name over in my mind. "Nice."

Thor huffs, rearranging himself so his head rests more firmly against her. I've never seen him take to anyone like this. Even with Vanessa, he maintained a polite distance. But with this woman...

"What got you into the bakery business?" I ask, wanting to keep her talking. Wanting to know more.

"It's a family business I run with my sister." Pride colors her response. "The bakery was in the family, and we still use our mom's and grandma's recipes."

"That's rare these days."

"Yeah, well, some things are worth preserving." She scratches Thor's ears thoughtfully. "Even if certain relatives think we should've sold it to the first Alpha with deep pockets who came along."

The bitterness in her tone surprises me. "Sounds like there's a story there."

"More like a novel. Or a Greek tragedy." She sighs. "Let's just say some people think Omegas need Alphas to be successful. That we're somehow incomplete without one."

"And you don't agree?"

"I think…" She chooses her words carefully. "I think finding your mate should be about connection, not convenience. About wanting someone, not needing them."

Her words hit something deep inside me. How many times had Vanessa talked about needing an Alpha who could provide properly? About status and security and all the things that had nothing to do with actual connection?

The woman beside me seems different. No artifice, no agenda. Just someone who knows who she is and what she wants.

It's more attractive than any designer perfume or practiced smile.

"You're different," I say before I can stop myself.

"Than what?"

"Than anyone I've met up here," I correct automatically, my focus split between her and the treacherous road. "Most people see the mountains as something to conquer. You talk about them like they're home."

"Maybe because they are." She looks out at the swirling snow. "I mean, not these exact mountains. But this life. The small town, the family business, the quiet beauty of it all. Some people might see it as settling for less. I see it as choosing what matters."

Thor whines softly, pressing closer to her, and I swear he's as caught by her quiet conviction as I am.

"Though, right now," she adds with a grin, "I'm seriously reconsidering my life choices. Including the one about driving in this weather."

"Nah, that was a great choice. Led you to us, didn't it?"

My response sounds flirtatious, but her laugh makes it worth it. "Smooth. Very smooth. Do all mountain men have such good lines, or are you special?"

"Definitely special. Just ask Thor."

"Ah yes, my new best friend." She rubs his ears again. "Though, I'm not easily impressed by flattery. Even if it comes with fur and puppy dog eyes."

"What about hot chocolate and a warm fire?"

"Now that... that might work."

I cut her another look, at the way she stares ahead, confused, the small crease on her brow as she focuses on the blurred road ahead of us. *She's beautiful.*

I shut down that thought quickly. She's stranded, possibly in shock, and definitely vulnerable. The last thing she needs is some Alpha getting territorial just because she smells like everything good in the world and laughs at his jokes.

But damn if it isn't tempting.

The wind howls louder as we climb higher, the truck's powerful engine straining against the conditions. Most vehicles would have given up miles ago, but I've modified this one specifically for mountain rescue. Though, usually, I'm not rescuing anyone quite so intriguing.

"Almost there," I tell her as we round the last bend. "Fair warning... my friends might be there and can be a bit..."

"Axe murder-y?"

"I was going to say *intense*, but sure, let's go with that."

She giggles, and I adore that sound. "Well, as long as they're equal-opportunity psychos. I'd hate to think I drove all this way just to end up in some gender-specific crime scene."

The laugh bursts out of me unexpectedly. "You really aren't afraid of much, are you?"

"Oh, I'm afraid of plenty." She absently strokes Thor's fur. "Heights. Spiders. My sister when someone messes up her kitchen organization system. But I figure if you're going to possibly die in a snowstorm, you might as well go out with good jokes."

"You're not going to die." The words come out more growled than intended.

She blinks at me, then smiles slowly. "No, I'm not. Because you found me."

The simple trust in those words does something to my chest I'm not ready to examine. Vanessa never trusted me like that—always questioned, always doubted, always looked for something better.

But this unexpected woman who talks to my dog and makes jokes about axe murderers... she trusts me after knowing me for less than an hour.

It's fucking terrifying when no other Omega has made me feel anything until now. And it's possibly the most attractive thing I've ever encountered.

The cabin comes into view through the snowstorm, and something primal shifts in my chest. My territory should be my sanctuary, but bringing her inside feels like inviting a storm more dangerous than the one howling outside. Because every trusting look she gives me has me wanting to prove her right—wanting to claim, protect, possess—and there's no shelter from that kind of hunger.

CHAPTER SEVEN

LILY

The wind nearly knocks me off my feet as Hunter guides me from his truck toward what has to be the most gorgeous cabin I've ever seen. Through the curtain of whirling snow, it rises like something out of a dream—three stories of rich wooden beams and windows, somehow both rustic and elegant. Stone chimneys pierce the white sky, smoke curling from their tops only to be whipped away by the storm.

I'm clutching my bag close when my foot slips out from under me on the snow-covered path, my stomach lurching up to my throat.

"Careful." Hunter snatches my elbow, steadying my balance. His touch sends warmth shooting through me. "Steps are icy."

Thor bounds ahead of us, his dark fur collecting snowflakes as he leads the way to the wraparound porch. The property around us is cleared for maybe fifty yards before the forest closes in, but at the moment, everything blends into a world of white. In better weather, this place would most likely be breathtaking. Right now, I'm just grateful it exists.

"This is yours?" I manage through chattering teeth. Though, the word *cabin* doesn't do it justice. This is the kind of place that should be featured in luxury magazines, with its all-natural materials and perfect proportions. "Are you secretly a movie star in hiding?"

His laugh is rich and deep, barely audible over the howling wind. "Inherited it from my grandfather." Something flares across his face—pain, maybe, or a memory. "Come on, let's get you inside before you freeze."

The door opens to a great room that steals what little breath I have left. Soaring ceilings with exposed beams draw my eye up, up, up to a chandelier that looks like it's made from naturally shed antlers. A huge stone fireplace dominates the center of the room, flames already crackling merrily behind its iron screen. Two deep leather sofas flank a coffee table that looks like it was carved from a single tree trunk, while oversized armchairs and what appear to be the world's most inviting bean bags are scattered around the hearth.

"Oh my God," I gasp, dropping my bag by my feet as Hunter shrugs off his jacket and tosses it on a hook. I fumble with my snow-covered boots to get them off. My fingers are so numb I can barely manage the laces.

"Here." Hunter kneels in front of me, and my

breath catches at the sheer... maleness of him, crouched at my feet like some dark fairy-tale prince. Those capable hands work the frozen knots of my boots quickly, and I have to remind myself that staring is rude. But honestly, how am I supposed to look away when he's right here, brow furrowed in concentration, strong fingers moving with such care? My hands physically ache to run through that thick, dark hair, then trace the trim beard along his sharp jaw.

When he stands, towering over me, I nearly whimper. His shirt stretches across a chest that belongs on a model, and those shoulders... God, those shoulders. I'm pretty sure I could spend hours counting the ways his muscles move under the fabric. Then his scent hits me—pine and woodsmoke mingled with crisp mountain mint—and my Omega instincts surge so violently that I have to grip the wall in the living room to stay upright. It's not just a scent; it's a primal call that makes every nerve ending spark to life, my body recognizing something my mind can barely process. The urge to lean in, to submit, is so overwhelming that I have to bite my lip to hold back a whine.

"Let me take your coat," he says in a low and rich tone that makes my toes curl like he has no idea what impact he has on me. I still can't believe an Alpha can affect me like this.

Control yourself. You have no idea who this stranger really is!

I force myself to look away first, but not before I catch the slight tremble in his hands—like he's fighting just as hard to maintain control. An Alpha struggling to keep his composure... because of me. The thought sends another wave of heat through my body, and I silently curse my Omega biology for making everything so impossibly intense.

I manage to slip my boots off without falling over —a miracle, given how my knees have apparently turned to jelly—and he helps me out of my coat. His fingers brush my shoulders, and I swear the temperature in the cabin spikes ten degrees.

I'm not usually the type to swoon, but if there was ever a moment to start, watching this mountain of a man handle me like I'm made of glass while looking like he could bench-press a truck... yeah, this would be it.

"Thanks," I whisper.

His ice-blue eyes meet mine for a moment that stretches like honey. Heat floods my cheeks, and I quickly look away.

He hangs my coat on a hook on the wall near the door, and with my bag in hand, I gravitate toward the fire, where Thor has already sprawled out. The malamute's tail thumps against the rug-covered floorboards as I approach, and he shifts to make room for me.

I twist around to find Hunter's gaze lingering on me. Everything about him radiates "Alpha," from his broad chest to the jagged mark along his jaw—like lightning caught in skin, disappearing beneath his collar and making me wonder just how far that scar traces down. But what catches me most is how he doesn't try to hide it, doesn't angle his face to shadow it. He wears it like he wears everything else—with a quiet, unshakable confidence that makes my heart stumble.

"Thank you again," I say, flexing my frozen fingers toward the flames. "For finding me, rescuing me. I don't know what I would have done out there."

"You're safe now. That's what matters." His deep tone holds a note of finality that sends a shiver down my spine. "Let me check the landline. Cell service is spotty up here, even in good weather."

He disappears down a hallway with Thor on his heels, leaving me. The great room feels simultaneously cozy and vast, with windows that reveal the storm that has turned the world white, and something about the isolation makes my skin prickle. I grab my phone from my bag—still no service. Just great... Hannah is going to freak out with worry when I don't return home in this storm. I send her a message just in case reception returns, and it can be delivered, telling her what happened and whereabouts I am... should anything happen.

I exhale loudly, reminding myself to calm down. The guy rescues people for a living. Surely he won't hurt me, right?

I distract myself by studying the room more closely. Everything speaks of money, but not the showy kind. This is old wealth, lived-in luxury. Family photos line one wall—mostly of Hunter with an older man who must be his father or grandfather, often in climbing gear or rescue situations. In one, they're rappelling down a sheer cliff face together. In another, they're teaching what looks like a much younger Thor to walk in deep snow.

"Line's dead," Hunter announces, returning. "Storm must have taken down some poles. Cell service is out too."

"Great." I try to smile, attempting not to freak out about being alone with a stranger in his cabin. Then again, he has done nothing but help me so far. "Hope I'm not being a burden..."

"Not at all." Something flares in his eyes. There and gone so fast I almost miss it. "Gives us something to do, being stuck indoors."

Heat floods my body at his tone, at the way his presence seems to fill every corner of the room. Before I can respond, a door I hadn't noticed swings open, revealing a gleaming kitchen beyond—and a face that makes my heart stop.

He freezes in the doorway, amber eyes widening in recognition. It's him—the gorgeous stranger from my bakery the other day, the one whose ridiculous flirting and devastating smile had me fumbling about. Even in casual clothes, he radiates the same magnetic aura that drew me in before.

What is he doing here?

His golden-brown hair is slightly tousled now, a few strands falling across his forehead in a way that makes him look impossibly more handsome than the polished version I first met. He's in dark-wash jeans that fit him perfectly and a crisp white button-down with the sleeves rolled to his elbows, revealing strong forearms and an intriguing compass rose tattoo on his right wrist. The shirt is untucked, top buttons undone just enough to seem effortlessly sexy rather than deliberate.

For a moment, we just stare at each other. I'm acutely aware of how I must look—half drowned, hair a mess, probably mascara everywhere. Yet the way he's looking at me makes my knees weak. His tall frame, easily over six feet, towers over me with an athletic build that tells me he works out regularly. There's something almost predatory in his graceful move-ments as he shifts his weight, like a big cat deciding whether to pounce.

His gaze roams over me, and that smirk blooms into a full, heart-stopping smile that deepens at the corners of his eyes. "Well," he drawls. "If I'd known a little blizzard was all it took to get you to show up at my door, I'd have done a rain dance weeks ago."

"You two know each other?" Hunter's ice-blue eyes lock on to me, then shift to the newcomer.

"Not formally." The stranger's voice is exactly how I remember it—smooth with an edge of amusement. "But she bakes the best cinnamon rolls I've ever tasted."

"You remembered." The words slip out before I can stop them.

"Hard to forget." His gaze dances over me, and heat

soars through me. "Though, I'm pleasantly surprised to see you so soon again, especially at my friend's place." He glances at Hunter. "Met her at a bakery in Whispering Grove last week." The way his amber gaze lingers on me speaks volumes. His casual stance masks something dangerous and compelling I remembered from our first meeting—an obsessive attraction to him that felt anything but healthy.

"Small world," Hunter adds. "I found Lily here about five miles back, her car half off the guardrail." His tone turns grim, that deep timbre sending involuntary shivers down my spine. "Another hour out there in this freezing storm..." He doesn't finish the sentence, but the weight of what he's not saying hits me like a physical blow.

I wrap my arms around myself, the reality of how close I'd come to freezing to death finally sinking in.

"I brought her here until the snow passes, since we were close to the cabin."

"Archer Sterling." The flirt from the cafe steps toward me, his expression shifting to a playful one that doesn't quite mask the predatory intensity beneath.

"Archer." I try to steady my voice, testing his name on my tongue.

My body betrays me, instinctively drawn to their Alpha presence. The tingle between my thighs deepens. This is a dangerous situation for an Omega like me. Alone with two Alphas in a cabin.

"Well, you know what they say—when the GPS says take a scenic route during a storm, always listen to it." My throat dries as I try to hide my reaction to them, though my attempt at humor falls flat.

The heat in Archer's gaze makes it clear he's not thinking about GPS or pastries.

"Storm's settling in for a few days from the look of it. Seems you're stuck with us," Hunter adds.

"Right," Archer corrects with a wolfish grin. "Though, the moment someone sends up a flare in this weather, you'll be suited up faster than Lily can frost a dozen cupcakes. Remember that ice storm last winter? You were halfway up the mountain before dispatch even called."

My gaze darts between them, not quite following. Archer must catch my confusion, and nods toward the wall where I'd seen the photos of Hunter hanging in simple wooden frames.

"Our resident hero here can't help playing superman on the mountain. Search and rescue is less of a job and more of an obsession."

The pictures click into place—Hunter in tactical gear and harnesses, rappelling down cliffs, his team around him.

"Someone has to save the tourists who think hiking in flip-flops is a good idea," Hunter deadpans.

"Says the man who once jumped out of a helicopter because the radio was spotty," Archer counters.

"That was one time!"

"Three times. I've got photos."

I find myself standing in front of the fireplace, unable to get close enough to the heat. Thor is back, taking a spot next to me while the guys are behind the couches.

"So, what you're saying is I managed to get myself rescued by the guy who makes other rescue teams look lazy?" I ask Hunter.

"You got it!" He winks, and my heart somersaults. Does he even realize what he's doing to me? "Better than a man who turned an entire room in his home into a rare-book sanctuary."

"That's an original Hemingway you're mocking," Archer defends. "Some of us appreciate things that don't involve climbing gear and protein bars."

"You installed a climate control system just for your books."

"A signed first edition of *The Old Man and the Sea* requires certain standards, you mountain savage." The warmth in Archer's tone takes any sting from the words. "Not all of us want to live like we're still sleeping in caves."

"Says the man who spent more on a single book than my truck cost."

"That Fitzgerald was an investment!"

I glance back and forth, unable to stop grinning at their banter.

Their laughter makes me forget for a moment that I'm stranded in a storm with two men who radiate enough Alpha energy to power a small city. *Almost* forget, anyway—my body hasn't quite gotten the memo about playing it cool.

Even my breathing has gone shallow, and I find

myself swaying subtly toward them like they're generating their own gravitational pull. The warmth pooling in my belly has nothing to do with embarrassment and everything to do with the way Archer's eyes keep finding mine or how Hunter's deep voice seems to resonate through my entire body.

I catch myself wondering what that rare-book collection looks like, then mentally shake myself. *Focus, Lily. This is not the time to geek out over first editions, no matter how many episodes of* Antiques Roadshow *you've binged.* Though, I have to admit, a man who gets this passionate about books is dangerously appealing to my inner literature nerd.

I swallow hard. I'm alone with two strange men during a huge storm. True, one of them made me weak-kneed in my bakery last week, and the other apparently saves lives for a living, but still. The true crime buff in me is cataloging all the ways this could go wrong.

Isolated cabin in a storm? Check.

No cell service? Check.

Two impossibly gorgeous men who are probably serial killers because isn't that always how it goes in true crime shows? The handsome ones are always hiding something sinister. For all I know, that rare-book collection could be bound in human skin, and Hunter's rescue photos could be his way of picking out victims. I've watched enough *Dateline* to know that "mountain rescue specialist" could easily be code for "knows all the best places to hide bodies."

I almost laugh at my own ridiculous thoughts. Most murderers don't bicker about books and climbing gear like an old married couple.

But the way they're both looking at me makes my skin flush despite the chill.

Grandma's warnings about Alphas echo in my head. *They'll make your body betray you, little flower. The trick is not letting them see how much.*

Too late for that, Grandma. Way too late.

"I need to check the backup generators. Storm like this, we could lose power." Hunter's grin does little to mask the commanding presence that seems to roll off him in waves. "Thor, with me."

The massive malamute that had been eyeing me from his spot by the fireplace rises, padding after his master. At least one of them seems to know what personal space means.

"Good, I'll handle the tour, then." Archer's smile spreads, and my stomach does that annoying flip thing again. "Unless you'd rather wait for our host, seeing as it's his place?"

"Go ahead," Hunter calls over his shoulder. "I won't be long."

The moment Hunter disappears down what I assume is the basement door, thunder crashes outside. The storm sounds closer now, angrier, like it's trying to remind me why I'm stuck here. Archer steps closer, and immediately, I'm enveloped in his intoxicating scent—bergamot and old books and male, leaving my head spinning. Why does he smell so good?

"Shall we?" He gestures into the hallway. "I promise there are no secret passages, and you're perfectly safe here."

I arch an eyebrow at him, thinking of the small Mace I carry in my bag, just in case. I tuck the bag under my arm. "That's quite the specific reassurance there."

"I can see the worry in your eyes." His amber gaze softens with understanding. "And I don't blame you. But this place… it's home while you're here."

"Well, as long as there's a decent kitchen," I quip, trying to mask how his earnestness makes my heart flutter. "Though, I have to warn you, my mom's recipes have been known to cause addiction. Strictly the legal kind, of course."

His laugh is warm and rich. "Ah yes, the famous family secrets. I look forward to trying more of your baked goods."

"I once had the mayor's wife camp outside my shop at five a.m. for the last slice of my apple pie."

"Now that's a story I need to hear." He takes a step up the staircase, then turns back to me with a grin. "Perhaps over coffee? I make a mean espresso."

"Careful there—a baker never reveals her secrets." I climb the first step, deliberately ignoring how the shadows seem to shift and stretch along the walls. "But I might be persuaded if this espresso of yours lives up to the hype."

"Actually, before we head upstairs, let me show you around on this floor," Archer mentions, his hand ghosting near the small of my back as he guides me down the step and into a hallway of rich mahogany panels. Even that almost touch sends shivers racing along my spine.

The first door he opens makes me gasp. "This is a bathroom? It looks like a spa retreat." My words echo slightly in the vast space. Cream marble stretches from floor to ceiling, centered around a sunken whirlpool tub that could easily fit four people. The whole room glows with soft ambient lighting. "Is that... a waterfall shower?"

"And a sauna through there," he adds, pointing to a door, clearly enjoying my reaction. He watches me take it all in, grinning. "Nothing better after a day in the snow. The heat seeps right into your bones."

I'm about to respond when he leads me to the next room, and all words die in my throat. The kitchen is... magnificent. Copper pots hang from a rack overhead, gleaming in the natural light that pours through floor-to-ceiling windows. A massive island of blue-veined marble dominates the center, surrounded by professional-grade stainless steel appliances. The walk-in pantry could fit my entire apartment's kitchen inside it.

"I think I'm in love," I breathe, running my fingers along the cool marble. "Two ovens... an eight-burner gas range... and is that a proper proofing drawer?" I spin to face him, not even trying to hide my excitement. "This is like every baker's dream kitchen come to life. Why does Hunter have such a fancy kitchen?"

"According to Hunter, when their grandfather renovated the place a couple years back, some hotshot interior designer talked him into it," Archer details. His lips quirk into a half smile. "Though, I doubt all this fancy equipment gets used half as much as it deserves. Especially not since Hunter's idea of cooking is takeout."

Hunter leans against the doorframe, that devastating smirk playing across his lips. "It's yours to use whenever you want. Something tells me you'd put it to better use than we do."

"Careful with those kinds of offers," I warn, even as my mind races with possibilities. "I might never leave. You'll come down one morning to find the whole place smelling like cinnamon and vanilla."

"Sounds terrible," he deadpans, but his attention on me never leaves. "How ever will I cope with fresh-baked goods appearing in my kitchen?"

I laugh, the sound surprisingly free and easy, despite my body's constant awareness of him. "Oh, so that's your evil plan. Lure the baker in with a dream kitchen."

"Is it working?" His voice drops lower, and my pulse leaps through my veins.

I meet his gaze, allowing myself a small smirk. "Maybe. But I still need to see the upstairs before I make any decisions about moving in," I joke, though I also want to see what I'm dealing with in the house, given that I'm stuck here until the storm passes.

His smile calls me to follow him up the stairs.

They creak under our feet as we ascend. The walls are lined with more black-and-white photographs—mostly mountain landscapes, though I catch glimpses of what must be Hunter's rescue missions.

"Hunter has... expensive taste," I manage, trying to focus on anything but how Archer consumes my attention.

"He inherited the place as is," Archer says with a slight smile. "Most of us grew up visiting here for as long as I can remember. Since losing his grandfather, he spends more time here than back in town now—it just feels like home."

We reach the landing, and Archer pauses. Lightning flashes through the windows, illuminating his features in sharp relief. "He lets us stay here whenever we want or when we need to get away."

The hallway stretches before us, all dark wood and plush carpeting that muffles our steps. More art, more photographs.

Archer leads me past doors that probably hide rooms bigger than my bedroom. We pass a library that makes me stop dead in my tracks. Floor-to-ceiling shelves stuffed with leather-bound volumes, reading nooks tucked into window alcoves. But something else catches my eye—a silk bra draped carelessly over a leather armchair, its deep red a stark contrast to the room's masculine energy.

Archer follows my gaze. "Hunter entertains sometimes."

"I can see that." I glance around the ornate foyer,

trying to act nonchalant, but I feel my cheeks flushing. "Though, I admit, in a house this grand, I half expect to hear the beating of a hideous heart beneath these floorboards."

Archer stops so abruptly that I nearly bump into him. When he turns, his gaze is alight with something I haven't seen before—a raw enthusiasm that transforms his whole face into something full of excitement.

"Did you just quote Edgar Allan Poe?"

I can't help the grin that spreads across my face. "Maybe."

"More than maybe," he says, his lips stretching into a wide grin. "I haven't met many people who can casually drop *The Tell-Tale Heart* into conversation."

"My grandmother's fault, actually." I pause, oddly pleased at the way he's looking at me—as if I'm a book he can't wait to open. "She used to read Gothic poetry to me when I was young. She loved it, and I guess it rubbed off on me."

"And Poe was your favorite?" There's something almost hungry in the way he leans against the wall, waiting for my answer.

"He understood darkness," I say. "Not just fear, but that strange place where terror meets beauty. I must have read *The Tell-Tale Heart* a hundred times."

"The guilty man who can't escape his own conscience," Archer murmurs, and something flares in those eyes. "Or perhaps the sane man trying to convince himself he isn't mad."

"Both, maybe." I return his stare. "That's what

makes it brilliant, isn't it? I heard you talking with Hunter about first editions," I add, curiosity finally getting the better of me. "You collect them?"

Something soft and vulnerable flickers across his face. "I have a few back at my place in town." He pauses. "My biggest obsession is my 1845 copy of "The Raven" from the *New York Evening Mirror*. Found it in an antique shop when I was twelve. My mom used to read Poe to me during thunderstorms."

The raw honesty in his words makes my heart squeeze. "That's incredibly rare."

"'Deep into that darkness peering, long I stood there, wondering, fearing,'" he says, eyes distant with memory. "Those lines... they meant everything the year I lost my mom. Still do. Sometimes the darkness you're staring into isn't just darkness—it's everything you're afraid to face, everything you've lost."

"I love that you know it by heart," I say, surprising myself with how gentle my response sounds.

His gaze finds mine again, and something electric passes between us. We're standing closer now, though I don't remember moving.

"What about you?" he asks. "Any other lines that stayed with you?"

"'We loved with a love that was more than love,'" I quote softly, my heart thundering in my chest. The words feel dangerous here, alone with him in this cabin, but I can't seem to stop myself.

His breath catches. For a moment, he's perfectly

still, looking at me like I've just handed him a key to something precious.

"You really are full of surprises."

I should step back. Should break this moment before it overwhelms us both. Instead, I find myself asking, "What other secrets are you hiding besides your love of Gothic poetry?"

"Many," he freely admits, his smile turning enigmatic. "But somehow, I think you might be the most dangerous one that's walked through these doors."

His eyes lock with mine, and the intensity in them makes my breath deepen. For a moment, we're both perfectly still. Him towering over me. Pulse on fire in my veins. I've never met anyone else who enjoys Gothic literature such as I do.

"Come on," he says finally. "There's more to see upstairs."

I follow him, trying to ignore how every step feels like I'm moving closer to something I might not be ready for... but can't seem to resist.

We pass a bathroom where an open door reveals marble and chrome and a bottle of what I'm sure is obscenely expensive men's cologne.

The next room Archer shows me is clearly a gym. He leads me to the end of the hall, opening a door to a room that somehow manages to be both luxurious and cozy. A window seat overlooks the mountains—or it would if the storm weren't turning everything into shifting shadows. The en-suite bathroom is bigger than my kitchen.

"This is you. Your haven until the storm passes," he says.

I try not to think about the implications of being in the same home as him and Hunter. Or how the storm seems to be pressing us closer together in this space that suddenly feels very small.

"I should let you get settled," he says, but doesn't move.

Thunder rolls outside, and I swear I can feel it in my bones. Or maybe that's just the effect of having him so close, his scent surrounding me, his height making me feel deliciously small.

"Right," I manage. "Settled."

His chuckle grows loud, and he gives me a wink as he backs away, making me to wonder what exactly I've gotten myself into. And why the prospect of seeing him again thrills me more than it should.

He leaves me alone, and I stick my head out into the hallway to notice that he's gone. Hearing the muffle of voices downstairs, I assume it's Archer and Hunter chatting.

That's when I find myself staring at a photo that stops me in my tracks.

The black-and-white image shows two people outside what looks like an old-fashioned bakery. One is clearly Hunter's grandfather, based on the other photos, decades younger but with the same strong features. And the woman beside him, laughing at something out of frame...

"Wait." My voice sounds strange to my own ears. "That's... that's my grandmother. In her first bakery."

CHAPTER EIGHT
ARCHER

I'm chopping carrots in Hunter's kitchen, the thud of the knife against the cutting board almost drowning out the howling wind outside. Fuck, the blizzard has gotten worse in the last hour, turning the windows into solid sheets of white. Something about the storm feels wrong—too intense, too purposeful, as if it's trying to keep us all trapped here. As if it's hiding something out there.

"You know," Hunter states from behind me, and I glance back to see him rustling through his walk-in pantry. "You don't have to cook." He emerges with a jar of honey-roasted peanuts, but there's tension in his shoulders I've never seen before. "We could just..."

"What? Order pizza?" I keep chopping, harder than necessary, trying to focus on anything but her peppermint candy scent lingering in the air. Even here, even now, it's driving me crazy. Making my hands shake. Making my instincts surge with every breath of Omega

I take. "In case you haven't noticed, we're kind of trapped here."

"We've got supplies. Protein bars, trail mix…"

"Your idea of food is exactly why I'm cooking. Some of us actually like to taste what we eat."

Hunter watches me, his expression knowing. "She's getting to you."

"Shut up."

"The mighty Archer, losing his cool over an Omega." He's trying to keep his tone light, but there's an undercurrent of worry. "Never thought I'd see the day. You're usually so…"

"So what?"

"Controlled. Distant." He studies me. "This one's different."

I point the knife at him. "You want to cook your own damn dinner?"

He raises his hands in surrender, but his eyes are serious. "Just… the way she looks at us like…"

"How?"

"As though she's just as affected as we are. And that's dangerous, considering we had no plans to take an Omega. Well, not yet, anyway."

Soft footsteps on the stairs draw our attention. Thor appears first, followed by Lily. She's wrapped in one of the bedroom's thick blankets, but it does nothing to mask her scent. My knife slips, nearly taking off my finger.

The blanket has slid slightly off one shoulder, and I trace the exposed skin where her shirt has been pulled down. Those soft curls of hers are even more untamed, dark brown waves with golden highlights shining from the hallway light. They cascade past her shoulders, framing a face that makes my breath catch every time I see it.

"Thor kept pawing at my door. Apparently, he's not familiar with the concept of being left alone." She scratches his head, and I study her delicate fingers moving through his fur. "But he's too adorable to ignore."

My gaze drifts to the gentle curve of her neck where it meets her shoulder, to that tiny cupcake tattoo peeking out behind her ear. She's got spirit. It has me wanting to see just how far that spirit goes.

"He's appointed himself your guardian," Hunter explains, sliding the jar of peanuts across the counter. "Hungry?"

She approaches cautiously, taking a few nuts. Her fingers tremble slightly, but she doesn't back away. She pops a peanut into her mouth, and I find myself tracking the movement of her throat as she swallows.

"So," she says, leaning against the counter with forced casualness, taking us both in. "Is this what you Alphas do for fun? Rescue stranded Omegas and force-feed them peanuts? Because I have to say, as far as kidnapping scenarios go, this is pretty tame."

I chuckle. "Only the special ones."

Her eyes meet mine, a flash of heat there, blood rushing. "Lucky me." She picks up another peanut, rolling it between her fingers, Hunter watching her with barely a blink of an eye. "Though, I have to admit, I had no idea Alphas cooked. That's not in any of the fairy tales I remember."

"Maybe you've been reading the wrong stories," I add.

She tilts her head, considering me. "Maybe I have." Her tongue darts out to catch a bit of salt from her lip, and my grip on the knife tightens.

Hunter clears his throat loudly. "Hey, I just remembered—I've got some clothes that might fit you. My cousin leaves stuff here for when she visits in the summers, as she visits us from Australia."

"That would be amazing," Lily murmurs, but her eyes linger on me. "Though, I'm starting to think the blanket look works for me. What do you think, Archer?"

My name on her lips does things to me, dangerous things. "I think—" I start, but Hunter cuts me off.

"Clothes," he says firmly. "Before you catch pneumonia. Or drive our resident chef to injury." He pointedly eyes the way I'm gripping the knife.

Lily's laugh is like honey, sweet and scandalous. She knows exactly what she's doing... purposely teasing me. She straightens, adjusting her blanket with deliberate slowness.

"Lead the way."

I stare at them heading upstairs, my hands clenched on the counter. Every one of my instincts screams to follow, to not let her out of my sight. The Omega who challenges me, who meets my gaze without flinching, who looks like everything I've ever wanted... I return to finishing the stew, throwing it all in a big pot on the stove with the rest of the ingredients.

Hunter comes back alone, his expression casual but distracted. "She's all set up there. I'm heading out to check our firewood supply. With this storm continuing, I want to make sure we have enough logs to keep the place warm."

"Hunter..."

"Everything's fine," he says, but there's something in his tone I can't quite read. He grabs his coat and heads out.

My mind keeps drifting back to her. The way she smiled at me in the bakery, how she teased and flirted. I reach down to adjust my cock, trying to get comfortable. I should leave her alone.

But somehow, I'm already moving toward the stairs, drawn up like a puppet on a string. From the moment I first saw her, she has occupied my thoughts and filled my dreams. Each step brings her scent closer —sweet, intoxicating, dangerous. It wraps around me, pulling me forward until I'm standing outside the spare room.

The door is open, and she's there in jeans and a loose hoodie among the shelves of clothes, looking lost in thought. When she turns to find me in the doorway, she startles slightly, taking an instinctive step back. Fuck, she's gorgeous.

"Sorry," I say, staying in the doorway to give her space. "Just checking if you're settling in okay?"

"Thanks," she says, trying for a light tone, but I notice the slight tension in her shoulders. "I have to warn you... my track record with men trying to help me isn't great."

"No?"

"Let's just say that, last week, one offered to help and ended up wearing his coffee instead of drinking it." She busies herself with examining the shelves, but I don't miss her quick glance my way. "Though, I suppose you've already proved yourself somewhat less awful than most."

"High praise."

"The highest." She reaches for another sweater on the top shelf but can't quite grab it. I stay where I am, making sure to keep my distance.

"I can get that for you," I offer. Then, with a small grin, I add, "Promise not to be awful about it."

She laughs, and fuck, she sounds beautiful. Some of the tension eases from her posture. She steps aside, letting me grab the sweater for her.

As I hand it to her, our fingers brush briefly, and the contact sends electricity through me. I take a deliberate step back.

"The bakery prepared me well for careful handoffs."

"Ah yes, the great pastry-to-customer transfer. Very delicate business." She hugs the sweater to her chest, but her eyes are sparkling with humor. "What brought you in on that day, anyway? Was it really a recommendation by someone else?"

"Fate, I like to think, seeing as I was in town to deliver a purchased antique piece," I say without thinking, then wince at how cheesy it sounds. "Or maybe just really good timing."

She arches an eyebrow. "That's what you're going with? Not 'I was desperately craving a croissant'?"

"Would you believe both?" I lean against the door-frame of her bedroom door again, keeping the casual distance between us. "Finding out the baker was as interesting as her pastries was a bonus."

She's smiling. "How long have you known Hunter?" she asks, settling back on the edge of the bed. The question seems safer than addressing the electricity still crackling between us.

I absently run my thumb over the compass rose tattoo on my wrist—a habit I picked up years ago. "Since we were kids. His grandfather took us both under his wing when I moved to town. Taught us everything about surviving out here in the woods."

"You weren't always local, then?"

Something in her genuine curiosity makes me want to open up.

"No. Mom and I moved around a lot when I was young. Running from..." I hesitate, choosing my words carefully. "Family complications. We finally settled here." I don't mention that it was our last move together, that within months, she was gone, leaving me with only her books and the sound of her voice reading Poe in my head.

Her eyes drift to my wrist, to the tattoo there. "That must have been hard, moving so much."

"It was. Never knew which direction we'd end up next." I look down at the compass rose. "Got this after she passed. The rose was for her—Rose was her name. The compass..." I pause, memories washing over me. "For all those years we spent searching for somewhere safe."

"So sorry for your loss." She freezes, the corners of her sweet lips drawn down.

"I was fourteen when I thought I was invincible. Decided to explore the woods alone even though the weather was turning."

Interest sparks in her eyes. "Let me guess—it didn't end well?"

"Got completely turned around in the snow. Couldn't see three feet in front of me. And I swear..." I shake my head, remembering how terrified I'd felt. "I swear there was a wolf following me. Could hear it padding through the snow, getting closer."

"Was there really a wolf?"

"Never found out. But I climbed a tree so fast I ripped my favorite jacket. Sat up there freezing my ass off, convinced I was going to die, when I heard this booming voice say, '*Boy, what the hell are you doing up there?*'" I grin. "Hunter's grandfather. And behind him, this gangly kid who was already taller than him. That was Hunter and the first time I met him."

She laughs. "At least you have a good excuse for being stranded," she says, shaking her head. "Last spring, my car died right outside of town during this massive thunderstorm. River was flooding, roads were washing out... and there I was, stuck on this little rise of land that was getting smaller by the minute."

"How'd you get out of that one?"

Her cheeks flush slightly. "Promise not to laugh?"

"Absolutely not."

She rolls her eyes but continues. "The flood rescue team showed up in this big truck. Very heroic. Very dramatic. And I..." She covers her face. "I was so startled by their sirens that I slipped right off the hood of my car into the mud. Had to be fished out looking like some kind of swamp creature."

The laugh bursts out of me before I can stop it. "I thought you said it was a heroic rescue."

"Oh, it was. Nothing more heroic than fishing a mud-covered girl out of a ditch while she's cursing about her ruined shoes." She laughs too.

"See, this is why I stick to tree climbing. Much more dignified."

"Yes, very dignified. The proper way to flee from imaginary wolves."

Something in my chest loosens. When she smiles so freely and unguardedly, it's more captivating than any deliberate flirtation could be.

I lean closer, drawn by her warmth and her smile when I near.

That's when her attention lifts to something

behind me. Moving past me—the brush of her body against mine sending electricity through my veins—she stops in front of a photograph in the hall.

"That's..." She reaches out, touching the glass. "I wanted to ask you or Hunter about this photo."

I follow her gaze to the black-and-white image—two people outside an old-fashioned bakery. One is clearly Hunter's grandfather, decades younger but with the same strong features. And the woman beside him...

"That's my grandmother," Lily whispers. "In front of the bakery. But why... how...?" She turns to me. "Hunter's grandfather... did he know her?"

My heart stops for a moment, and I shrug at the implication. "I... maybe. Could be." My mind races through possibilities because what if... they're related? "Fuck, it would be interesting to find out, wouldn't it?"

"Interesting?" She studies my face. "That's one word for it."

The notion hangs heavy in the air between us. I want to tell her it doesn't matter, that whatever connection might exist between their families won't affect what *I'm* feeling for her, but the words stick in my throat.

"You should probably check on that stew before it burns," she finally says and retreats to her room.

As soon as her door closes, I head downstairs, taking the steps two at a time, my mind spinning. I need to talk to Hunter. I need to see if he knows anything.

The front door bursts open before I reach the bottom step. James stumbles in from the storm outside, clearly having just arrived at the cabin, covered in snow, his bulky shoulders made more imposing by the heavy winter gear. His face is pale with cold and frustration. He was due here an hour ago.

"The roads," he gasps, collapsing against the wall. "They're all blocked behind me. Ain't anyone leaving the woods anytime soon. Barely made it here."

"Good, you got here, then."

He removes his boots, then shrugs off his coat.

I lift my head, calling out, "Hunter! Got a minute?"

Hunter emerges from a back room. "What's up?"

"That photo upstairs, the one of your grandfather outside the old bakery? Who's that woman with him? The one with all the curls?"

"What?" Hunter's brow furrows. "Hell if I know. Someone he worked with, I assume. Never really asked about it. Why?"

I can't help the grin spreading across my face. "Well, our guest says that woman is her grandmother."

"What the fuck!" Hunter's eyes go wide, his gaze shooting to the ceiling. "Are you sure?"

"Pretty sure. Which could mean..." I wiggle my eyebrows at him. "You might be related to the prettiest baker in town."

"Shut the fuck up," Hunter growls, but there's shock written all over his face. "Grandfather never mentioned..."

"Well, guess you've got some family history to uncover." I clap him on the shoulder. "Though, this definitely puts her out of your league now, bruh."

"What are you two yapping about?" James interrupts. Prison didn't soften his edges—if anything, it made them sharper. He's all muscle and threat, even casually leaning against the wall.

Hunter straightens. "We've got a guest staying until the storm passes. Young woman from Whispering Grove who got into an accident nearby because of the snowstorm."

"A woman from a bakery?" James's eyebrows shoot up, something predatory crossing his face. "Here?"

"Back off," I say, lowering my tone. "She's not looking for company."

"Wait." James's face changes, recognition flickering in his eyes. "You said she's from Whispering Grove?"

Hunter steps forward, tension radiating off him. "Yeah, and she's staying here for now. So don't fucking start with your shit, understood?"

"Me?" James raises his hands, but there's something calculating in his smile that I don't like. "When have I ever caused trouble?"

"You want the list chronologically or alphabetically?" I ask, keeping my tone light even as I position myself between him and the stairs.

"Look at you two," James sneers, but there's a glimmer of amusement in his eyes. "All protective of some female you just met."

"Says the man who once punched a guy for looking at Hunter's ex wrong," I remind him with a grin.

"That was different," James grumbles. "Guy was a creep. I'm a gentleman. So, Hunter... Should we start calling you her brother?"

"Don't start," Hunter warns, but there's no heat in it. He heads toward the kitchen. "Since you're both so concerned about my possible family tree, you can help bring in more firewood before this storm gets worse."

"Always with the manual labor," James sighs dramatically, but he's already shrugging his coat back on.

"You could always go back to prison labor instead," I suggest helpfully, ducking the glove he throws at my head.

And just like that, we're back to being teenagers hauling wood for his grandfather, complaining the whole way but doing it. Some traditions you don't mess with.

CHAPTER NINE

LILY

The hot shower is exactly what I needed. Staring at myself in the mirror, where my skin is flushed pink from the heat, I take my time combing through my damp hair. The bathroom is impressive for a cabin—spacious, with high-end fixtures and the kind of water pressure my bakery building can only dream about. Hunter's cousin must be organized, leaving everything from hair products to lotions neatly arranged on glass shelves. I've helped myself to some leave-in conditioner that smells like vanilla and almonds.

I debate putting my hair up before deciding against it. Something about being in a house full of Alphas makes me want to keep it down, like a curtain I can hide behind if needed. The borrowed clothes fit better than they should—soft gray leggings that hug my curves without being too tight and an oversized cream sweater that feels like being wrapped in a cloud. It falls off one shoulder slightly, exposing more skin than I'd usually show around Alphas.

The thick socks I found are ridiculous—covered in little foxes that make me smile despite everything. Definitely not what I'd expect to find in a cabin full of Alpha males. I wiggle my toes in them, wondering about the cousin who left them behind. What kind of woman spends enough time here to have her own wardrobe? More importantly, what kind of Alphas keep a fully stocked woman's bathroom, complete with fancy hair products and lotions?

"Get it together, Lily," I mutter, leaning closer to the mirror. My eyes are bright in a way that has nothing to do with temperature. I look... different. Softer without my practical clothes and flour-dusted apron. More vulnerable. "You've handled worse than being stuck in a cabin with two ridiculously attractive Alphas." A pause. "Okay, maybe not worse. But different. Definitely different."

I smooth some frizz from my hair, wishing I had my normal products. Hannah would know exactly what to do—my sister has always been the put-together one, while I'm usually more concerned with what's in the oven than what's in my closet.

The thought of her makes my chest ache. She must be worried sick. I check my phone again—still no signal, my message stuck in digital limbo. "Sorry, sis," I whisper to my reflection. "Guess you'll have to handle the morning rush alone tomorrow.

"At least they're not the Big Bad Wolf type," I

mutter, then laugh at myself. Though, Archer in the kitchen earlier... the way he moved, the intensity in his eyes when he looked at me... *Stop it, Lily. These are real, potentially dangerous men who just happen to have rescued you from a storm.* A storm that's still raging outside the window, turning the world white.

I dig the Mace out of my wet clothes and slip it into the pocket of my borrowed leggings. Not that I really think I'll need it—something about these men, about this place, feels safe. Maybe too safe. That's what scares me most—not that they might hurt me, but that I might not want to leave.

Thor is sitting exactly where I left him when I peek out the door, his tail thumping against the hardwood. "Still on guard duty?" I rub under his chin, and he leans into my touch with a contented grumble. "At least one male in this house is straightforward about his intentions."

My stomach growls at the smell of something delicious and savory wafting up the stairs. Whatever Archer is cooking, it smells divine. Thor's ears perk up, and I laugh.

"Yeah, I'm hungry too. Might as well face the music, right?" I take one last look in the mirror, adjusting the sweater. "What's the worst that could happen?" As soon as the words leave my mouth, I regret them. *Never tempt fate, Lily.* Especially not when you're already living in what feels like the setup to either a horror movie or an adult film. My skin crawls, but I shake it off. I'm not going to scare myself.

I hear the guys speaking as I approach the kitchen —deeper than before, a new voice in the mix. It sends something dangerous sliding down my spine. My heart stutters, but I force myself to call out, "Hello?" Better than lurking in doorways like some sort of creeper.

The conversation stops. I step into the kitchen and freeze, my breath catching in my throat.

Wait!

There's a third Alpha now? And God, he's... magnificent. That's the only word for it. He's perched casually on the counter, one leg dangling, the other bent at the knee. His dark copper hair is slightly messy, probably from the blizzard, and his storm-gray eyes fix on me with an intensity that sends my heart into a pounding race. He's dressed simply—dark jeans and a charcoal Henley that does nothing to hide his broad shoulders. But there isn't anything simple about the way he carries himself, the quiet confidence that screams "predator."

A burn scar traces up his left forearm, visible where he's pushed up his sleeves.

Everything about him radiates controlled power, like a knife wrapped in silk. The kind of man my father always warned me about. The kind that makes all those warnings seem worth ignoring.

"Lily, this is James." Hunter catches my hesitation. "He's always here, like Archer. We practically grew up in this cabin." He's leaning against the fridge, beer in hand, completely at ease. The three of them look like a pack, I realize. A dangerous, beautiful pack that I've somehow stumbled into.

James?

My mind stutters on the name. Not my James—not the guy I've been messaging since way before Christmas, the one whose texts make me smile at my phone like an idiot. Then he vanished, and I discovered he might be in prison. Nope, that can't be him. What are the chances? This has to be a coincidence. Yet something about him calls to me.

I never actually spoke to James—we only messaged each other—so I can't even say I'd recognize his voice. But this James... God, his tone alone could make me come apart at the seams if he whispered in my ear. Deep and rich, with just enough gravel to make my stomach flip.

I mentally shake myself. *Control yourself.* But it's hard when I'm surrounded by three gorgeous men who radiate Alpha energy as though it's their personal brand. And this isn't that James anyway, so I need to chill.

"Welcome to the madhouse," James says, and his voice is pure sin, leaving my skin tingling. He runs a hand through his hair, dislodging snow crystals. "Barely made it through the storm to get here. It's the apocalypse out there."

"Dramatic as always," Hunter snorts, but there's obvious affection in his tone. He moves to clap James on the shoulder. "She doesn't need you scaring her with your apocalypse theories."

"Hey, I calls it like I sees it." James hops down from the counter with a grace that shouldn't be possible for someone his size. He's taller than the other two, practically built like a football player. "And what I see out there ain't natural."

"Nothing about this weather is natural," Archer adds from the stove, where he's stirring something that smells like heaven. "But that's a problem for tomorrow. Right now..." He tastes whatever is in the pot and nods. "Dinner's ready."

The three of them together are fascinating to watch. Hunter grabs bowls while James snags the silverware, setting them on the counter all in one place. Archer swats at both of them when they try to steal tastes of the food. It's clear this is their space, their sanctuary. And I'm the intruder.

I lean against the counter, suddenly hyperaware of my position—alone in a remote cabin with three strange men. My rational mind whispers warnings, but my body betrays me with a current of electricity that zips through my veins whenever their gazes find mine.

"So, what brings you out in weather like this?" James asks. His attention locks on to me, and the intensity in it—a mixture of curiosity and something deeper—sends a ripple of sensation across my skin, like fingers trailing down my spine.

"Flour run," I admit, aiming for casual while my pulse hammers wildly at the base of my throat. "For the bakery I run with my sister."

"A baker, huh?" James's mouth curves into a half

smile that awakens butterflies in my stomach. "In Whispering Grove?"

I tilt my head, surprise momentarily overriding the warmth spreading through my chest. "You know the town?"

"I get around," he says vaguely, something guarded flickering behind his eyes. "Small towns have the best… stories."

"And the best gossip," Archer adds, sliding a steaming pan onto the table. "James is our resident mystery man. Gets twitchy if you ask too many personal questions."

"Fuck that," James protests, an undercurrent of tension in his words.

"You absolutely do," Hunter jumps in, a playful gleam in his eye. "Remember when that hiker asked where you were from, and you just stared at her until she backed away?"

"I was thinking!"

"Yeah, thinking about how to disappear into the woods." Archer laughs.

My fingers fidget with the hem of my top as I watch them, my skin flushed and sensitive. I should be scared. I should be planning my exit strategy. Instead, I'm wondering what James's stubbled jaw would feel like against my palm.

"So, Flour Girl," Archer says, interrupting my thoughts. "What's your poison? Wine? Beer? Something stronger to take the edge off being stranded with three strange men in the woods?"

"Archer!" Hunter smacks him with a dish towel. "Way to make it sound like we're creeps."

"Hey, for all she knows, we could be." Archer winks at me. "But then we'd be terrible at it, feeding you first."

A laugh bubbles up unexpectedly from my throat. The sound seems to please James, whose eyes soften as they hold mine.

"Earth to Lily." Hunter's remark breaks through the charged atmosphere. "You planning to eat standing up?"

I blink, realizing I've been lost. Archer is ladling out what looks like heaven—chicken and vegetable stew, perfectly mashed potatoes, and garlic bread that makes my mouth water just looking at it. The guys are already moving toward the living room, bowls in hand.

"Coming," I say, grabbing my own bowl. Thor follows at my heels as we settle on the couches around the crackling fire. The malamute plants himself at my feet, a furry guardian angel. Hunter is in an armchair, and James and Archer are on opposite ends of the large couch, leaving me the love seat. Giving me space.

The first bite of stew makes me moan embarrassingly. "Oh my God."

"Good?" Archer is studying me with that intense gaze of his.

"I take back every doubtful thing I ever thought about your cooking skills." As I keep eating, I say, "This is amazing. Where did you learn to cook like this?"

"Self-preservation," Hunter answers for him. "We were tired of protein shakes and granola bars."

"Hey, some of us evolved past the *hunt and grunt* stage," Archer shoots back.

"Barely," James adds, and they all laugh.

The sound does something warm and dangerous to my insides. I'm fascinated by their dynamic. My gaze keeps drifting to all three of them as I continue eating.

"You okay?" Hunter asks softly. "You went somewhere else for a minute."

"Just thinking about my sister," I lie. "She'll be worried."

"The phones should work once the storm is gone," he assures me. "In the meantime..." He reaches for something, and suddenly, a screen is descending from the ceiling, a projector humming to life. "Movie?"

"Seriously?" I look around the rustic cabin with new eyes. "You have a hidden theater system?"

"Among other things," Hunter says cryptically, staring at me, and my cheeks heat up instantly. "This place is full of surprises."

"Show-off," James mutters, but he's smiling.

"Just because you prefer your entertainment more... physical," Hunter starts.

James throws a pillow at him with deadly accuracy.

"Children," Archer sighs, but his eyes are amused. "More stew?"

I nod gratefully, and he takes my bowl. When he returns, his fingers brush mine as he hands it back, sending sparks up my arm. I catch James observing the interaction, something dark and hungry in his eyes.

We settle in to watch some action movie I barely register. The storm rages outside, but in here, it's warm and comfortable. Almost too comfortable. James stretches out on his end of the couch, all graceful danger, and I keep staring at him. He reminds me so much of the James I used to text—the dry humor, the quiet intensity—but that James is gone, locked away somewhere for who knows what. I blocked his number the moment I found out, even though part of me wanted to hear his side. Wanted to believe there was more to the story.

"I should head up," I say when the movie ends, standing perhaps too quickly. My head spins slightly, though whether from the fire's heat or the company, I'm not certain.

"Sure you don't want to stay for another?" Hunter asks. "I've got the entire Marvel collection."

"Tempting, but..." I gesture vaguely upstairs. "Should probably get some rest. Thank you for dinner, Archer. And for..." I wave my hand around, encompassing everything. "All of this."

"Our pleasure," James says softly, and something in his tone leaves me shivering.

I practically run up the stairs to my room, Thor following close behind. My back hits the locked door, and I slide down it, breathing hard. "Okay, calm down. Just until the storm passes. You can do this."

But can I? With Hunter, who's somehow turned

this cabin into a haven, and maybe we're related? I should have asked him, but in their presence, I forget my thoughts. Then there's Archer, whose cooking and kindness defy everything I thought I knew about Alphas. And James... who can't possibly be my James, but who makes my whole body hum with recognition.

Thor whines outside my door, a comforting sound. At least I have one ally in this madness.

"Stop it," I tell myself firmly. "Stop staring. Stop flirting. Stop thinking about any of them as anything but Alphas who are helping you out. Stop wondering if James is..." I press my hands to my heated cheeks. "Just stop."

The storm howls louder, as if laughing at my predicament. And somewhere below, I hear their deep chuckles, and my heart does a traitorous flip in my chest.

I am in so much trouble.

CHAPTER TEN

JAMES

Sleep is impossible. I stare at the cabin's dark ceiling, my mind racing with thoughts of her. Of all the places, of all the storms... Lily. My Lily. It has to be her—how many Omega bakers named Lily could there be in Whispering Grove who run a shop with their sister? The coincidence is too perfect, too precise.

Her scent still lingers in my nose from earlier—vanilla and peppermint. Exactly how I'd imagined she'd smell during those long nights exchanging messages, when I'd lie in my cell, dreaming about the woman behind the words. But the reality of her is so much more than I could have pictured.

Those curves hidden beneath her clothes—soft, inviting, the kind a man could lose himself in. She's petite compared to me, barely reaching my shoulder, but there's a fullness to her that makes my hands itch to explore. And that wild hair of dark curls—I wanted to bury my face in them, feel her, smell her.

Her eyes, though—golden-brown, almond-shaped—lingered on me when she thought I didn't notice. They haunt me most of all. The way they widened when she first saw me before her guard went back up. I'd memorized every word she'd ever written to me, built an image of her in my mind, but nothing prepared me for the living, breathing woman.

She's more beautiful than the fantasies that kept me sane in the darkest hours in that hellhole, more tempting than the freedom I fought for. And make no mistake, Lily is mine. She just doesn't know it yet. The storm that brought her to me wasn't chance—it was fate. And I intend to claim what fate has delivered.

The mattress creaks as I shift, frustrated. I'd message her if I could, but our conversations ended abruptly over a week ago when they caught me with the burner phone in prison. That almost cost me another year inside—as if eighteen months weren't enough for a crime I didn't even commit.

Thank God for expensive lawyers. My family name might be mud now, but at least it saved me from doing more time after they busted me with the burner phone. The lawyers had gotten me out on technicalities and procedural errors.

I'd planned to find her the moment I got out, but two days of dealing with lawyers and catching up with Archer and Hunter in our hometown had stolen my time. Today was supposed to be the day—the day I crossed the mountains to Whispering Grove to finally pay her bakery a visit. I told Hunter and Archer I'd stop by the cabin since they were there to do some hunting, seeing as it sat right between both towns.

But then, right in the middle of my drive through the mountains, this fucking storm hit out of nowhere.

Now, it's worked in my favor. The universe has a twisted sense of humor that way.

I see her face when I close my eyes—the delicate curve of her jaw, the way her hair falls in waves past her shoulders, how her face glows when she laughs. All those nights in the cell when I'd lie there constructing her from bits and pieces of our conversations. Her wit, her intelligence, the way she could make me laugh even on my darkest days—I'd known she'd be beautiful inside, but this...

The sheets tangle around my legs as I get up. Standing still is impossible. I need to move, need to think, need to figure out how to handle this. The hallway is dark and quiet as I step out, but my feet carry me to her door before I can stop them.

She's in there. Lily. The woman who made me laugh when I wanted to put my fist through a wall, who understood loss and pain and healing in ways no one else did. The woman who sent me pictures of failed desserts at midnight with captions like *Pretty sure this is what murder victims' last meals look like.*

My hand hovers near the handle, not touching. The memory of her in the kitchen earlier makes my chest tight. Everything about her calls to something primal in me, something that wants to claim and protect and possess.

"Fuck," I whisper, stepping back. I can't push this. Can't rush it. She's already nervous about being trapped here with three Alphas—but finding out one of them is a convicted criminal she used to text with? That might freak her out, send her into a panic. Except she has no idea about my past... not yet, anyway. I have to take this slowly so I don't spook her. This needs to be handled carefully.

The storm rattles the windows, and cold flares in my bones despite the cabin's warmth. The sauna downstairs calls to me—it'd always been my go-to when I'd needed to clear my head before I landed in prison. The stairs creak softly as I descend, my mind still full of her.

The spa room is one of Hunter's grandfather's better ideas—a full facility with a steam room, a sauna, and a small pool. The old man believed in luxury, even in a hunting cabin. I strip down, grab a towel, and step into the cedar-lined sauna. The heat hits immediately, and I pour water over the hot stones, watching steam hiss up into the darkness.

The heat seeps into my muscles, but it does nothing for the tension building inside me. I keep picturing her curled up on that love seat, her lips parted when she tasted Archer's stew, the softness of her laugh. My cock hardens, and I don't fight my reaction.

I envision telling her the truth, seeing recognition

dawn in those eyes. Visualize her understanding, wanting me despite everything.

My hand slides lower, gripping my thick cock as I imagine her straddling my lap, her drenched pussy sliding over my dick. Fuck! She'd be pressed against me and the sounds she'd make... Her skin under my hands, her back arching, her voice gasping my name, her full breasts against my chest as I lean down to take one into my mouth.

I palm my cock harder, faster. In my mind, she's everything I dreamed of during those lonely nights—soft and warm and perfect.

Release hits quickly, a growl escaping me. I use my towel to catch the ribbons of cum spewing free.

For a moment, everything is perfect.

Then I hear a small gasp from the doorway.

My eyes snap open. On the other side of the glass door, illuminated by the dim spa lights, stands Lily. She's wearing sleep shorts and a tank top, her hair loose around her shoulders, her gaze wide as they meet mine. She's flushed, whether from embarrassment or heat or something else, I can't tell, but she's the most beautiful thing I've ever seen—all tender curves and sleep-mussed hair.

For one endless moment, we stare at each other—then she flees. Her footsteps echo on the stairs.

"Fuck." I clean up quickly, grinning despite myself. The look on her face—shock, yes, because she watched me, but for how long? Interesting.

With a towel wrapped around my waist, I find

myself outside her door again. I hear her pacing inside, the floorboards creaking with each step. My instincts scream to go to her, to explain, to claim, but that would only frighten her.

Every muscle in my body tenses as I struggle against the urge to break down this door between us.

"Fuck," I hiss through clenched teeth, resting my forehead against the cool surface of her door. My palm presses against the wall beside it, fingers splaying as I try to ground myself. The beast inside me claws at my restraint, demanding I take what's mine.

I can smell her through the door—that intoxicating blend of vanilla and peppermint, now laced with fear and something else. Something that makes my blood run hot. My breathing turns ragged, each inhale feeding the fire burning in my veins.

I listen to her movements, tracking her like prey. One turn of the knob is all it would take.

Pushing away with a strangled sound, I run trembling fingers through my hair as I force myself to back up. Not like this. Not when she doesn't know who I am. Not when I'm this close to losing control.

Instead, I retreat to my room to grab a notepad and pen. Old-school communication, since phones are useless in this storm. Then I return to her door. Settling with my back against the wall near the door, I start to write.

"Shouldn't all good bakers be asleep by now?" Then I slide the note under her door. There's a pause in the pacing, then the sound of paper being picked up.

A moment later, a note slides back. "Says the man who clearly can't sleep either. You had other activities to keep you occupied." 😐 The little drawn emoji makes me smile.

"Fair point. Though, I'm not the one wandering into saunas at 3 a.m." 😏 I add my own emoji, just like old times.

Her reply comes quickly, written on the back of my note. "That was an accident! I was exploring. I didn't expect... that. I should have knocked first."

"Exploring strange houses in the middle of the night? Someone's been watching too many true crime shows." I start a fresh page, remembering how we used to debate the merits of different murder weapons.

Her next message has a poorly drawn knife sketched in the corner. "Hey, in my defense, most murders happen in homes the victim is familiar with. I'm just being cautious."

"By wandering around alone? Pretty sure that's how horror movies start."

"Please. I'm clearly the final girl in this scenario. I've got all the qualifications—tragic backstory, practical shoes, and excellent situational awareness."

"Is that what you call walking in on private moments?"

There's a longer pause before her response. "I prefer to think of it as gathering evidence. Never know when you might need blackmail material."

My laugh is probably too loud for the late hour. God, I've missed this—her quick wit, the way she can turn any situation into a joke. "Blackmail? That's cold, baker girl. All those true crime shows are affecting you."

The next note takes longer to arrive because she most likely recognized the nickname I used to call her. Baker girl. When the message does return, her handwriting is slightly shakier. "How did you know I watch true crime?"

This is it. The moment to be honest, to tell her everything. My pen hovers over the paper for a long while before I write. "I've missed our chats."

The silence from her room is deafening. Then, very softly, I hear her gasp. The sound is followed by complete stillness—no more pacing, no more notes.

I wait for what feels like hours, hoping for another note to slide under the door, but nothing comes. Finally, when the first gray light of dawn starts to creep through the windows, I stand and make my way back to my room.

Sleep still won't come, but now for entirely different reasons. She knows. The ball is in her court. All I can do is wait, hoping she'll give me a chance.

The storm howls outside, but for once, I don't mind being trapped. After all, she's here. And maybe, just maybe, this is exactly where we both need to be.

CHAPTER ELEVEN
LILY

The morning sun filters through the cabin windows. I've barely slept, the confession from James playing on repeat in my mind like a suspense movie I can't stop watching. Every time I think about it, I want to be both sick and giddy at once. Butterflies perform an entire circus routine in my stomach, while my brain screams "Danger!"

How can I be terrified, furious, and excited simultaneously? Something is seriously wrong with me. Of course he would be drop-dead gorgeous. Of course I would fawn all over him like a lovesick teenager. Why couldn't it just be a simple attraction? But no... he had to be him.

The clock on the microwave reads 6:42 a.m. My mind won't shut off. Questions circle like vultures. What did he do? How long was he in prison? Is he dangerous? And most disturbing of all—why am I still attracted to him, knowing what I know?

Hot liquid suddenly burns my fingers, snapping me back to reality.

"Shit!" I hiss, yanking my hand away as coffee continues pouring from the pot, overflowing the mug's rim. I lunge for the dish towel hanging from the oven door, nearly knocking over the sugar canister in my haste. Dark brown liquid spreads across the counter like a miniature flood. The rich aroma of French roast fills the air, a pleasant scent at odds with my frantic scrambling.

While I mop up the mess, my mind races ahead to Hannah finding out. My sister's words echo in my head. *The truth is that you've been texting a prisoner who lied to you for weeks. Who knows what else he's lying about?* If he was a guard working there, he wouldn't be hiding it, right? The man I've been sharing my thoughts with, flirting with, dreaming about, *is* a criminal.

Just perfect. Another stellar pick from my impeccable taste in men. Dad would be so proud.

The coffee soaks through the thin towel, staining my fingertips brown. I throw it in the sink and grab another, crouching to wipe up the puddle on the floor. My hair falls in my face, and I blow it away in frustration.

"Three strikes and you're out, Lily," I mutter to myself. "First, the wannabe rock star who stole your credit card. Then, the charming accountant with the secret wife. And now..." I trail off, scrubbing harder at a stubborn drop. "Now a convict. You really know how to pick 'em."

Heart racing, I finally get the kitchen cleaned up and grab my coffee-filled mug. That's when I hear it—a soft exhale behind me that wasn't there a second ago.

"Morning."

The single, deep, male's word sends an electric current racing up my spine. I turn, and there he is, leaning against the doorframe of the kitchen. My throat goes dry.

James is not just handsome—he's sinful. That copper hair tousled from sleep, falling across his forehead in a way that calls to me. His jaw, shadowed with stubble, clenches slightly as our eyes meet. He's wearing a simple black T-shirt that stretches across shoulders broad enough to make the doorframe seem small, the fabric clinging to muscles that ripple with the tiniest movement. A vein runs down his forearm, prominent and masculine. Storm-gray eyes watch me closely and leave me covered in goose bumps, as if he's cataloging every detail, searching for weaknesses.

There's something feral about him in the morning—less polished, more dangerous. A small scar cuts traces along his jawline. Marks of violence that only enhance his appeal, which says something deeply concerning about my psyche.

I try to catch my breath without being obvious. In that split second, I make a decision: I'll act like I know nothing. Because how exactly do you casually bring up "So, prison, huh? What were you in for? Nothing murder-y, I hope?" And God, all those serial killer jokes I made in our messages...

"Sleep well?" I ask, aiming for nonchalance but landing somewhere closer to breathless. My fingers tighten around my mug, seeking something solid to ground me.

One corner of his mouth quirks up. It's not quite a smile—more like he's laughing at a private joke. "Not particularly." His eyes never leave mine, unblinking, unwavering. The intensity in them has me feeling like prey being assessed by a predator who isn't really hungry but might hunt for sport.

I take a sip of coffee to hide whatever expression might be betraying me. It burns my tongue, but I welcome the pain as a distraction from the heat building elsewhere in my body.

"So, looks like the storm is even worse this morning." Outside, the snow continues to fall in thick, heavy flakes, obscuring everything beyond a few feet of the glass.

His grin widens, predatory and knowing. "It sure is." Simple words that somehow carry the weight of a threat—or a promise.

I'm dying on the inside, melting like sugar in hot water. My legs feel unsteady, my skin too tight, too sensitive. Every nerve ending stands at attention, hyperaware of his presence, the distance between us, and the air molecules that separate our bodies.

He pushes off from the doorframe with the lazy grace of a panther and crosses to the coffee maker. The kitchen suddenly feels like the size of a postage stamp. He doesn't touch me as he moves past, but the heat radiating from his body might as well be a physical caress. I can feel it dancing along my bare arms, making the fine hairs rise.

My breath locks in my throat. I step sideways, trying to maintain some distance, but my hip bumps against the counter. There's nowhere to go. He reaches for a cabinet above my head, his arm creating a momentary cage. I catch a whiff of his scent—cedar and something darker, richer, with an undercurrent of raw masculinity that makes my toes curl inside my socks. My knees actually wobble.

He pulls down a mug, deliberately slow, his bicep flexing inches from my face. When he lowers his arm, his knuckles brush against my shoulder. The touch is so brief I might have imagined it, but the trail of fire it leaves on my skin is unmistakable.

"Excuse me," he murmurs in a low rumble that I feel more than hear. He's close enough that his breath stirs the curls by my ear.

I nod jerkily and slide farther along the counter, putting precious inches between us. My heart pounds like I've just sprinted uphill.

He pours his coffee. The quiet domesticity of the action feels somehow obscene, given the electricity crackling in the air between us. He doesn't add cream or sugar, just lifts the mug to his lips and takes a sip, eyes closing briefly in apparent satisfaction.

"How do you like it?" I blurt out, then immediately

want to sink through the floor when his eyes snap open, darkening with something that looks suspiciously like desire.

"Like what?" he asks neutrally, but there's a twitch at the corner of his mouth that suggests he knows exactly what effect he's having on me.

"The coffee," I clarify, feeling heat rush to my cheeks. "Sweet? Bitter?"

"Black," he says. "I prefer things... unaltered." His gaze rakes over me slowly, from my curls to my borrowed sweatpants, lingering on the places in between. "Pure."

I nearly choke on my own sip of coffee. Is he flirting with me? Or am I reading into things because my hormones have apparently overridden my common sense?

"I, um..." My words tangle. I never stammer. Ever. My quick wit is my superpower—the thing Hannah always says will either make me famous or get me killed someday. Right now, my brain has apparently decided to take a vacation, leaving me with nothing but basic motor functions and an embarrassing awareness of how my nipples are tightening beneath my thin sleep shirt. "It's hot."

His eyebrow rises fractionally. "The coffee?"

"Yes. The coffee. What else would I—" I stop myself, feeling like I'm digging my own grave with every word. "Just... hot coffee. Good. Morning. Necessary."

"Articulate," he says dryly, but there's that twitch at his mouth again.

"I'm not awake yet," I manage, trying to gather the scattered pieces of my dignity. "Half a cup minimum before I form complete sentences."

"Noted." He leans back against the counter opposite me, creating a blessed space between us, though his gaze maintains its hold. "You always this jumpy in the morning?"

"Only when I'm trapped in unfamiliar cabins during blizzards." I glance down momentarily at my mug. "Not exactly a normal Tuesday for me."

"Is it Tuesday?" A shadow crosses his face. "I've lost track."

I wonder if that's a side effect of prison—losing track of days. The thought sobers me.

The toaster dings behind me, making me jump. My coffee sloshes dangerously close to the rim of my mug. I spin around, grateful for the distraction, and grab my toast with trembling fingers. My hands are shaking so badly that I nearly drop the plate.

I feel his eyes on my back, a physical weight between my shoulder blades. The kitchen feels too warm, too small, too charged with unspoken things. I move to the refrigerator, desperate for something to do with my hands, with my body that seems determined to betray me at every turn.

Opening the refrigerator door, I welcome the cold air on my flushed face. *Get it together. You are in control. Don't let his presence affect you. He's just a man. An incred-*

ibly attractive, possibly dangerous man who makes your insides liquefy, but still just a man.

I'm so focused on my internal pep talk that, suddenly, he's behind me, his massive frame blocking the light from the window, heat emanating from him like a furnace. I freeze, one hand on the refrigerator door, the other clutching my plate so hard my knuckles turn white.

He doesn't touch me. He doesn't need to. I can feel the solid wall of his chest inches from my back, sense the controlled power in his body. His arm reaches past me into the refrigerator, his sleeve brushing against mine so lightly it might be accidental—but nothing about his movements feels accidental.

"Excuse me," he says again, voice pitched low, intimate.

My breathing turns shallow, my pulse a staccato rhythm in my throat. I can't move. I'm pinned in place by nothing but his presence and my own traitorous body.

He takes his time selecting what he wants—butter, I realize, watching his long fingers close around the dish. The moment stretches, elastic with tension. Then he withdraws, taking a step back, and I can breathe again.

I snatch the jam. My hands shake as I arrange my meager breakfast on the counter.

"Maybe if the storm lets up, it'll be a good time to head out," I say too brightly, spreading jam on my toast with unsteady hands. "I mean, there's not much food in the fridge anyway, right?"

I laugh nervously, the sound high and unnatural to my ears.

"Oh, there's plenty of food," he says, tone casual but eyes intent. He gestures with his butter knife when I glance at him, the movement somehow graceful despite its mundanity. "Have you not seen the fridge downstairs? It's filled with game—all kinds of meat. We could live out here for six months without leaving."

His hands are large but strangely elegant, with prominent veins and a dusting of copper hair across the knuckles. They're strong hands, capable of violence—or tenderness.

The thought makes my stomach flip.

"Six months?" I gasp before I can stop myself. "Perfect place to kidnap and keep someone trapped."

The moment the words leave my mouth, I want to crawl under the floorboards. My cheeks burn as I stare fixedly at my half-buttered toast. *Way to go, Lily. Bring up kidnapping to the ex-con. Brilliant conversation starter.*

James pauses mid-bite, regarding me with an unreadable expression. Then he laughs, the sound rich and dark like melted chocolate but with an edge that raises the hair on the back of my neck.

"You've got quite an imagination," he says, amusement laced with something sharper.

I shrug, trying to seem casual despite the warmth still flooding my cheeks. "Occupational hazard of watching too many true crime shows."

He takes another bite, chewing thoughtfully. "Got a new favorite? Let me guess... Something with a charismatic detective who always gets her man?"

The question feels loaded somehow, as if there's a subtext I'm missing. "Actually, I prefer the cold cases," I find myself admitting. "The ones that go unsolved for years until some tiny detail breaks everything open."

His eyes glint.

I take a too-large bite of my toast.

Silence stretches between us, vibrating with tension. Sweat gathers at the small of my back, dampening my shirt. The simple act of eating breakfast has never felt so fraught with meaning, so dangerous.

"Wanna see the fridge with the excess game?" he asks suddenly.

I stare at him, curiosity warring with self-preservation. His expression is neutral.

Say no. Do NOT go to a basement with a criminal, Lily. Have you learned nothing from every true crime show ever? This is literally how women end up as cautionary tales.

"Sure," I hear myself say, nodding like a puppet.

Stellar idea. They'll find your body in spring when the snow melts. Especially as I've seen no sign of Archer or Hunter yet.

Even as my rational mind screams warnings, something deeper, more primal, pushes me forward. A need to know, to understand the man behind those storm-gray eyes. To see if the James from our messages still exists somewhere inside this dangerous stranger.

He grins and says, "This way." He doesn't wait to

see if I follow, just turns and walks toward a door I hadn't noticed yesterday. His confidence borders on arrogance—he knows I'll follow.

Grabbing one of my jam-slathered toast slices while he carries his coffee, I trail after him like he's the Pied Piper and I'm a particularly susceptible rat.

The staircase creaks under our weight, the sound ominous in the silence. James descends, not bothering to turn on the lights until we're halfway down. When the bulb flickers to life, I blink in the sudden brightness.

The basement is surprisingly well finished—pine paneling on the walls, decent lighting. The image of Hunter or Archer hitting it, muscles tensed, sweat glistening, flashes unbidden through my mind.

I take another bite of my toast.

My attention swings to the two massive chest freezers against the far wall. Pristine white, industrial-sized.

The kind Dexter might have used to store body parts.

"Those are… big," I manage. My imagination runs wild with gruesome possibilities. What if the meat inside isn't deer or boar? What if—

"Thinking about bodies again?" James interrupts my morbid thoughts. He stands closer than I expected, observing me with that same unreadable expression. "I can practically see the wheels turning."

I force a laugh that sounds hollow even to my ears.

"Hazard of the true crime obsession. You start seeing serial killers everywhere."

"Even in me?" His tone drops, becoming something darker.

I meet his gaze and see something there that makes my breath lodge in my lungs—a knowledge, an understanding that goes beyond our brief acquaintance. It's the look of someone who knows exactly what you're capable of.

"Perfect for hiding the bodies, right?" he continues when I don't answer, moving toward the nearer freezer. The casual way he says it, combined with the gleam in his eye, sends a shiver down my spine.

I giggle, the sound slightly hysterical. "Only a killer would know."

He pauses, hand on the freezer lid, and turns to look at me. Mirth flashes in his eyes. The muscle in his jaw works as he stares at me, and for one terrifying, exhilarating moment, I wonder if I've pushed too far.

Nice going, Lily. Antagonize the criminal. Smart move.

But then his expression softens into something almost like amusement. "You've got guts. I'll give you that."

Before I can respond, he heaves open the lid of the nearest freezer. Cold mist billows out, momentarily obscuring its contents. "See? All deer and boar, according to Hunter. He's been busy the last few weeks."

I step closer, against my better judgment, and peer inside. And sure enough, there are neatly wrapped packages labeled in black marker: VENISON STEAK, BOAR ROAST, BACKSTRAP. The organization is meticulous, almost obsessive—packages arranged by cut, by date, by animal.

"Hunter is an organized guy," I comment, trying to sound casual despite the way my heart hammers against my ribs from being in James's presence.

"Everything has its place with him."

I nod and bite into my toast nervously, finishing it in three quick bites. A dab of jam catches at the corner of my mouth, and I flick it away with my tongue.

When I look up, James is staring at my mouth with such fire that I feel it like a physical touch. His pupils have dilated, darkening his eyes to nearly black. The air between us thickens, becomes charged.

"You've got—" he starts.

"What?" My own response is barely a whisper.

He reaches out slowly, deliberately, and brushes his thumb across the edge of my lips. "Jam."

The touch is brief, clinical almost, but it sears through me like a brand. He pulls back his thumb, a smear of red on the pad, and—my heart stutters—brings it to his own mouth. His eyes never leave mine as he sucks the jam from his skin.

I can't breathe. I can't think. My entire existence narrows to this moment, this man—the way his lips close around his thumb and the knowing look in his eyes as he watches my reaction.

"Sweet," he murmurs, and the word hangs in the air, loaded with meaning.

"Well, better head back up," I say. I turn toward the stairs, desperate to escape before I do something incredibly stupid—like throw myself at an ex-con.

But he's there, right in front of me, moving with that unnatural speed and grace that seem at odds with his size. My back hits the wall beside the staircase before I realize what's happening. He places his coffee cup on a step behind me, caging me in with his body without actually touching me.

I should be terrified. A rational, self-preserving woman would be reaching for her phone, for a weapon, for anything. Instead, I'm fighting the urge to close the inches between us, to press my body against his and discover if he's as hard, as hot, as he looks.

What's wrong with me?

"Are we going to keep playing this game, or can we talk about the elephant in the room?" There's an edge to his tone. His breath smells of coffee.

"I-I don't know what to say," I stammer, my heart threatening to pound right out of my chest. With my palms flat against the wall behind me to keep them from quivering, I fail miserably.

"That I know it's you, Lily." He leans in more, close enough I can see the different shades of gray in his irises and the individual bristles of stubble along his jaw. "My Lily. The one I used to chat with for hours, who drove me crazy, who had me smiling to myself when I should have been sleeping. The one I even dreamed about."

The confession hangs between us, raw and honest.

Part of me thrills to hear it—to know I affected him as deeply as he affected me—but the other part, the part that knows about his secret, recoils.

"You didn't," I scoff, trying to regain some equilibrium. "Dreaming? That's a bit much." My defenses rise automatically.

He shrugs, one shoulder rising and falling in a graceful motion that draws my attention to the strong column of his neck and the way his T-shirt stretches across his chest. "That's the impact you had on me."

"What was it?" The question slips out before I can stop it, a dangerous curiosity I can't seem to suppress. "The dream."

He's so close now that I feel the swish of his breath on my face. I'm struggling to breathe, my body burning up from the inside out. I clench my thighs together as he leans in farther.

"You want to know?" His tone drops to a rough whisper that seems to bypass my ears and go straight to my core. "You were tied to my bed."

My breath catches. "What?"

"Wrists bound to the headboard with my belt. Nothing else—just the belt and my marks all over your bare skin." His eyes darken further, becoming almost predatory. "You'd been fighting me, spitting fire like you always do in your messages, challenging me, pushing me. So I showed you what happens when you push an Alpha too far."

I swallow hard, my mouth suddenly dry. This isn't

the safe, sanitized dream I'd expected. This is hungry, burning hot, dangerous. It should frighten me. It doesn't.

"You were begging," he continues. "Not for me to stop—but for me to go harder, faster, to mark you up so you'd feel me for days afterward. Your nails dug into your own palms every time I bit down on your throat, your breasts, and the inside of your thighs. And when you came..." He stops, a muscle working in his jaw as if the memory is too intense. "When you came, you screamed my name so loud I thought the windows would shatter."

Heat floods my body, pooling low in my belly. I'm acutely aware of every inch of space between us, of how easy it would be to close that gap. My lips part involuntarily.

"That's... a very specific kind of dream, and hot," I gasp. Then I mentally shake myself, reality crashing back in. "I mean, no. Not hot. Not at all."

Liar, a voice whispers in my head. I'm soaked through just from his words.

His mouth curves into a knowing smile. "You're a terrible liar, Lily," he murmurs. "Your pulse is racing." His gaze drops to my throat, where my heartbeat must be visible, then back up to my eyes with naked hunger. "Your cheeks are flushed." His free hand hovers near my face, not quite touching. "And your pupils are blown wide."

I turn my face away, unable to maintain eye

contact without revealing too much. "You're imagining things."

"Am I?" His fingertips finally, *finally* make contact with my skin, turning my chin gently but firmly back toward him. The touch is an inferno, sending sparks down my spine, my body shuddering beneath him. "Tell me you don't feel this, and I'll back off."

I open my mouth to deny it, to lie, to protect myself from whatever this is, but the words won't come. I can't lie—not about this, not with his gaze seeing straight through me.

"I have to go," I blurt suddenly, ducking under his arm and pulling away. His hand shoots out, catching my wrist in a grip that's firm but not painful.

"Lily."

"No, I don't think we should continue... anything." My words shake despite my best efforts. "I need to be able to trust you, and I don't." The words come out in a rush, more honest than I planned.

His expression shifts from desire to confusion, his brows drawing together. "What are you talking about?"

I pull free from his grip and take a steadying breath. My hand trembles as I push a curl behind my ear, buying time. *Just say it. Rip off the Band-Aid.*

"Look, I know you were in prison, and you never once were truthful with me about that."

He flinches, just slightly, but it's enough to confirm what I already suspected. My sister had been right all along.

Damn!

His face goes through a rapid succession of emotions—shock, anger, and something that might be shame—before settling into a carefully blank mask. "How did you...?"

"Does it matter?" I back toward the stairs, suddenly very aware that I'm alone in a basement with a man I know nothing about—except that he's been incarcerated. "You lied to me."

"I didn't lie," he says. "I just didn't tell you everything."

"A lie of omission is still a lie," I counter, finding my footing on the first step. "And it's a pretty significant thing to omit, don't you think? 'Hey, by the way, I'm messaging you from prison.'"

His jaw clenches. "It wasn't like that."

"Then what was it like?" I demand, anger rising to combat the fear and disappointment churning in my gut. "Please, explain to me how you accidentally forgot to mention you were behind bars while we were sharing our deepest secrets."

"Lily—" he starts, taking a step toward me.

I hold up a hand. "No. I need... I need to process this." I turn and climb the stairs, heart pounding in my ears, tears threatening despite my determination to hold them back.

Now I'm not only stuck in a house with three Alphas, but one of them is a criminal who lied to me. A criminal I'm still, despite everything, painfully attracted to.

For all I know, they all are. Criminals, that is.

And the worst part? That doesn't terrify me nearly as much as it should.

CHAPTER TWELVE
ARCHER

The ancient mahogany desk beneath my fingertips carries the scars of generations, much like the half map spread beneath the heavy sheet of glass atop it. Hunter's grandfather had a flair for the dramatic—splitting a treasure map in half between cousins who can barely stand to breathe the same mountain air.

Flames crackle in the stone fireplace across the study. The room wraps around Hunter and me like a leather-bound embrace—our sanctuary in the cabin fortress. Floor-to-ceiling shelves groan under the weight of books and weathered journals. The scent of aged paper and woodsmoke feels more like home than any place I've ever owned.

Outside, the snowstorm batters the windows with increasing fury. White noise to accompany our treasure hunt.

"This symbol here"—I tap the glass, my reflection

ghosting over the faded parchment—"could be Devil's Peak or Widow's Crag. Both have that distinctive split."

Hunter sprawls in the leather chair opposite me, boots propped on the edge of the desk. His massive frame dwarfs the furniture.

"Grandfather always said the treasure was hidden where the mountain holds its breath," Hunter mumbles around the toothpick in his mouth.

I snort. "Poetic bullshit. The old man never gave a straight answer in his life."

"Why start now, right?" Hunter grins. "Though, I still think he left these riddles because he knew we'd lose our fucking minds trying to solve them."

"You know what this reminds me of?" Hunter asks, leaning forward to tap the corner of the map.

"If you say that time in Aspen with the twins, I will end you."

He barks out a laugh. "Jesus, Arch. I was going to say Grandfather's scavenger hunts when we were kids."

"The ones where the prize was always some obscure philosophy book?" I grin at the memory. "You bitched for weeks about the Nietzsche."

"Because I was eighteen and wanted cash for beer, not existential dread." Hunter rolls his eyes. "Still read it, though."

"Because Grandfather would quiz you." He grins softly.

The fire pops loudly, sending a cascade of sparks up the chimney. Thor barely twitches from his position on the hearth rug, his silver-gray coat glowing copper in the firelight.

"Twelve fucking months," Hunter states. He traces a finger over what might be a river, might be a boundary line. "Just over a year ago, the stubborn bastard left us."

I nod, knowing words aren't needed. Hunter's grandfather took me and James in—lost boys with nowhere to call home. Me, after my mother passed when I was fourteen, and James a few years later. The old man gave us more than shelter; he gave us purpose, stories, brotherhood. Now, at thirty, I should feel like a man, but back at this cabin, with James at thirty-two and Hunter at thirty-four, we may as well still be those reckless kids who were sneaking out past curfew, daring each other to jump from the highest branches, and laughing like we had nothing to lose.

"Remember when he used to tell us about his father burying Spanish gold?" I ask, grinning at the memory. "Said he traded moonshine for a chest of doubloons from a pirate who'd sailed up the Mississippi."

"Then it was Confederate treasury the next time." Hunter chuckles.

"And Blackbeard's personal stash after that." I shake my head, pouring two fingers of whiskey from the crystal decanter on the side table. The amber liquid blinks in the firelight as I slide a glass toward Hunter. "Crafty old son of a bitch couldn't keep his own lies straight."

Hunter raises his glass. "To Grandfather. May his treasure be worth all this bullshit."

"To Grandfather."

We drink in unison.

"This could be a creek bed." I point to a thin, wavy line after setting my glass down. "Or a trail. Either way, it seems to lead to this structure here." The crude drawing could be anything—a cabin, an outcropping, a tree.

"If this snow would let up, we could do another search on the grounds to try to find these landmarks," Hunter mutters, glancing toward the window, where white fury continues its assault outside. We only received the map from Grandfather's will last month in December, and with it snowing every other day up in the mountains, we've had no luck trying to mark the map.

"What if we're looking at it wrong?" I walk around the map to look at it upside down. "There's no compass rose on the map. No indication of which way is north. So it could be this way."

Hunter's gaze narrows. "Sneaky motherfucker."

"He always said we needed to change our perspective." I drain my glass.

We spend the next hour making notations on a transparent overlay, marking possibilities and probabilities. Two grown men built like bears hunched over a treasure map like boys on an adventure. The irony isn't lost on me.

Hunter stretches, his spine popping like gunshots

in the quiet room. "I'm getting a caffeine IV before I go cross-eyed." He rubs his face. "Fuck, we've been at this most of the early morning."

"Time flies when you're losing your shit over chicken scratch," I mutter, not looking up from a particularly puzzling cluster of markings.

"I'm gonna check on James," Hunter adds, collecting our empty glasses. "See if he's managed to climb out of bed yet."

"How's that going? Him and the baker girl?" I ask, rolling my shoulders to ease the tension.

Hunter's mouth quirks. "Wouldn't tell me shit when I asked yesterday, but they were eye-fucking each other last night by the fire. There's something there."

"She could be your relative," I suggest with deliberate nonchalance.

Hunter's face sours instantly. "That fucking photo doesn't mean a goddamn thing. Her grandmother standing next to Grandfather in some ancient snap proves exactly jack shit."

I chuckle at his vehemence. "I get it. I'd be pissed too if I lost my shot with a girl who looks like that."

"You're a real asshole, you know that?" Hunter flips me off, but there's no heat in it. "Besides, she's way too sweet for any of us."

"Not your type?"

"She's a dream, and I'd even share her with you two ugly bastards to be with someone like that." As he heads for the door, his words circle in my mind... We'd once shared a girlfriend when we were younger until she moved out of town. "Want anything from the kitchen? Besides your dignity?"

"Black coffee. And fuck you very much."

"Love you too, princess," he calls over his shoulder, the door clicking shut behind him.

Alone again, I lean closer to the glass, squinting at a peculiar marking. A boulder? A building? A goddamn Rorschach test? This map is deliberately obtuse.

The door creaks open to the room.

"Either Grandfather was secretly a modern pirate, or this is where he buried all those terrible Christmas sweaters," I mutter, assuming Hunter has returned.

"I'd vote for the sweaters. No one disappears that many reindeer cardigans without a plan."

I jerk my head up at the unexpected female voice. Lily stands in the doorway, one hip cocked against the frame, arms crossed over her chest. I study the challenging tilt of her chin, the wild curls framing her face like a dark halo.

Thor is on his feet before I can respond, his massive form bounding across the room with a speed that belies his size. The same animal who once held an intruder at bay for three hours without so much as blinking now whines like a puppy, his tail sweeping the floor as he reaches Lily.

"Well, hello to you too, handsome," she croons, dropping to her knees. Her tone shifts to that ridiculous baby talk females reserve for animals and infants.

"Who's the goodest, fluffiest mountain wolf? Is it you? I think it is!"

Thor, the traitorous bastard, flops onto his back, exposing his belly—a vulnerability he shows to precisely no one. His tongue lolls from the side of his mouth, and I swear to God he's grinning.

"Christ," I mutter. "Eighty pounds of muscle and tooth reduced to jelly by a head scratch."

Lily glances up at me, still running her fingers through Thor's thick fur. "Jealous?"

The question hangs between us, loaded with possibilities. I lean back against the desk, crossing my arms to mirror her earlier stance.

"Should I be?"

She rises to her feet in a fluid motion that draws my eye from her white sneakers, up the denim clinging to shapely legs, and past the narrow waist to the casual long-sleeved shirt with a neckline that teases rather than reveals. Her hair falls in chaotic spirals past her shoulders, several shades of brown mingling together like the inside of an expensive chocolate.

She strides into the room, Thor padding beside her like an oversized shadow.

"What's with the glass table?" she asks, sidestepping my question as she approaches. "Secret plans to take over the world?"

"Half a treasure map for this property," I reply, watching her reaction.

Her step falters. "You're shitting me. A real one?"

"I shit you not."

She approaches with newfound caution, as if the map might rear up and bite. "Like, a real *X*-marks-the-spot treasure map? Pieces of eight? Buried chests? The whole *Pirates of the Caribbean* deal?"

"Well, no *X* yet," I admit, shifting to make room for her beside me. "That's probably on the other half."

She peers down at the yellowed parchment, her shoulder not quite touching mine. The scent of vanilla and something sugary washes over me, mingling with an undercurrent of warmth that reminds me of freshly baked bread. It stirs something primal and hungry that has nothing to do with food.

"One of your antique purchases?" she asks, glancing up at me through thick lashes.

"Not quite. It's an inheritance. Hunter's, technically. His grandfather left it to him and his cousin... separately... so they'd finally make up."

"That's diabolical," she says, but there's admiration behind her words.

"That was the old man's style," I agree, shifting slightly so our arms brush. The contact is brief but electric, yet it lingers on my skin, the hunger to pull her back against me savage. "Always playing the long game."

"So, there's actual treasure here? On this property?" Her eyes dart around the room with fresh interest, lingering on the rows of books. "What is it? Gold? Jewels? First edition Hemingways?"

"That's what we're trying to figure out." Her enthusiastic smile leaves me grinning. It's refreshing, this unguarded curiosity. "The map's not exactly *National Geographic* quality."

Our shoulders touch now, and neither of us moves away.

"Well, at least you know that's a water well," she mutters, pointing to the very symbol I'd been puzzling over seconds before.

I blink, looking closer. "A water well? You sure?"

"Pretty sure. See the little handle drawn on the side? Classic well shape. My dad restored an old one in our backyard—don't ask me why, but he has a thing for *functional artifacts*, as he calls them." She traces the shape with her fingertip, leaving a smudge on the glass. "Definitely a well."

I stare at it, then at her. "Fuck, you're right. There are three wells on the property, so that narrows it down."

Her smile is quick and satisfied. "You're welcome."

The storm outside howls like a wounded wolf, rattling the windows in their frames. Lily flinches, her earlier confidence cracking just enough to reveal the fear beneath.

"Not a fan of storms?" I ask quietly.

She shrugs one shoulder. "Not a fan of being stranded in them. My sister has probably filed a missing-person report by now."

"I might be able to help with that," I say, remembering what I'd set up earlier. "Come here."

It's not a request, but not quite a command either.

Something in between that has her raising an eyebrow, but following nonetheless.

I lead her to the other end of the study, where a round oak table sits surrounded by leather chairs. On the table is an antique radio set, a 1940s two-way radio I restored last summer.

"Is that what I think it is?" she asks, touching the polished wooden case with careful fingers.

"If you think it's a shortwave radio that can reach Whispering Grove from here, then yes," I explain, pulling out a chair for her. "The antique store in your town—Yesteryear's Treasures—has a matching one. Martin and I use them when the lines go down."

"You're fucking kidding me." The curse sounds charming from her mouth. For a moment, I think she might cry. Then she does something that genuinely surprises me—she leans in against me, brushing up close, and I get a lungful of that delicious Omega scent that promises to destroy me.

The feeling of her pressing against me sends heat pooling low in my belly.

"Thank you," she murmurs against my chest. "My sister must be worried sick."

We sit side by side at the table, our knees bumping beneath it. I adjust the dials with practiced precision, hyperaware of her watching my every move.

"So, you collect stuff like this, not just books?" she asks, scooting her chair closer to see better. Our legs press together from knee to thigh.

I nod, focusing on the radio to distract from the

heat of her touch. "I also have a weakness for communication devices."

"Are all collectors this hands-on with their hobbies, or is it just you?"

I glance at her. "Meaning?"

"Most collectors I know keep their precious finds behind glass. You're actually using yours." She gestures to the radio.

"I find beauty in function," I say simply. "What's the point of a perfectly restored engine if you never hear it run?"

Something soft shifts in her expression as her mouth lifts into a beautiful smile. I have the distinct feeling of being reevaluated, recategorized from whatever initial box she'd placed me in.

The radio crackles and spits static as I adjust the frequency. "Martin should be in the shop today, assuming he hasn't been snowed in himself."

"And if he has?"

"Then we try again tomorrow. Storm's not going anywhere."

Her knuckles whiten where they grip the edge of the table. "Let's do this."

I dial out the store's call sign, feeling Lily's eyes on my profile. We wait several minutes with no response. She sighs, shoulders slumping.

"Maybe try once more?" she suggests, leaning closer until I can feel her warmth radiating against my side.

I oblige, repeating the call. Just as I'm about to give

up, the speaker comes to life with a burst of static, followed by a gruff voice.

"Yesteryear receiving. That you, Archer? Over."

Lily jolts forward, her hand landing on my thigh in her excitement. The sudden weight of it sends a jolt of fire straight to my cock, my balls drawing in. If she notices my tension, she doesn't show it.

"Martin, it's Archer. I have someone here who needs to send a message to her sister in town. Over."

More static, then: "Go ahead. Over."

I hand Lily the microphone, our fingers grazing in the exchange. The contact lingers, neither of us pulling away until the radio crackles again impatiently.

"Hello?" Lily finally says. "This is Lily from Flour & Fable Bakery in Whispering Grove."

"Well, I'll be damned! Lily Parker!" Martin's words boom through the speaker. "Your sister's been raising hell all over town looking for you. Over."

She laughs, the sound rich and warm against the backdrop of the howling storm. Her entire face transforms, worry lines smoothing away, eyes crinkling at the corners. It's like watching the sun break through storm clouds.

"That's why I'm calling," she says. "Could you please tell Hannah that I'm safe? I got into a minor accident in her car in the storm, and I'm staying at a cabin until it passes."

She glances at me, and I recite Hunter's address, which she relays to Martin.

"I'm with"—she hesitates, glancing at me again—

"Archer and his friends. They helped me when my car got stuck. Please tell her not to worry. I'm fine."

"Will do, Miss Lily. Your sister will be relieved. That storm's a nasty piece of work. You're lucky you were found. Over."

"Very lucky," she agrees, her eyes meeting mine with an intensity that makes my blood simmer. "Thank you so much."

She hands the microphone back, our fingers tangling together longer than necessary. I turn off the radio but make no move. We sit there, facing each other, my legs parted, so she's almost nestled between them.

"Thank you," she says again, softer. "At least now Hannah will just think I've been abducted by mysterious mountain men."

I laugh, the sound rusty even to my own ears. "Is that what we are?"

"You tell me, rare-book dealer with a private radio network and half a treasure map." She twists a curl around her finger, the gesture unconsciously seductive. "You're not exactly what I was expecting."

"And what were you expecting?"

"I don't know. More... backwoods? Less"—her free hand waves vaguely in my direction—"elaborate cabin mansion."

"Disappointed?"

"Intrigued," she corrects. "It's not every day a girl gets rescued by three Alphas who look like they could bench-press a moose but discuss literature over dinner."

I move in my seat toward her, closing some of the distance between us. "And what kind of guy does a baker from Whispering Grove usually encounter?"

She mimics my sitting posture, bringing our faces closer together. "The kind who think *The Great Gatsby* is a cocktail and poetry is what happens when song lyrics rhyme."

That startles another laugh from me. "The dating pool is that shallow, huh?"

"Calling it a pool is generous. It's more of a puddle." Her gaze drops to my mouth for a fraction of a second. "A very small, very disappointing puddle."

"And yet here you are, stranded in a cabin with three strange men in the middle of nowhere. Most would consider that a horror movie setup."

"Maybe I've read too many Gothic novels. The isolated manor, the mysterious host, the forbidden secrets..." Her lips curve in a half smile. "Though, I'm still waiting on the ghost."

"No ghosts," I assure her. "Just legends of buried treasure and a dog who has apparently fallen in love with you."

On cue, Thor whines from where he settles at her feet, his massive head resting on her sneakers.

"My father would love this place," she says, looking around the book-lined walls. "He's always fiddling with things in our backyard. Solar-powered gadgets, irrigation systems for his garden. Last year, he built this rainwater collection system that's actually pretty clever."

The abrupt change of subject feels deliberate, as if she's steering us toward safer waters. I allow it, curious about where she's taking this.

"Sounds like a handy guy to have around," I say. "Self-sufficient."

"He had to be after Mom died." Her tone lowers, turning to face me completely in her seat. "Single dad with two girls. He learned to braid hair from YouTube tutorials."

The vulnerability in her admission tugs at something inside me.

"I built a solar-powered reading lamp when I was young," I offer, surprising myself.

Her eyes widen. "Really?"

"My mom was sick before we lost her. Too weak to get up from bed. I wanted her to be able to read at night without straining herself."

Lily's hand finds my forearm, her touch warm through the fabric of my shirt. "I'm sorry," she says simply. "Mine's in Whispering Grove Memorial Gardens. Plot 33B. I leave daisies every Sunday."

No platitudes, no awkward sympathy. Just understanding, clean and sharp as a knife's edge.

"Hunter's grandfather stepped in after my mother passed," I continue, the words coming easier than they should. "Became the father figure I needed. The old man had a way of collecting strays."

"I get it," she says quietly. "No matter how much time passes, they're always there, aren't they?"

The understanding in her eyes embraces me. I lean forward, reaching up to brush a strand of hair from her face. My fingertips graze her cheek, and she doesn't pull away.

"Exactly," I murmur.

Her hand slides from my arm to my chest, palm flat against my heart. Her fingers splay over the muscle there, and I wonder if she can feel how it thunders beneath her touch. We're close now, too close for strangers, but we don't feel like strangers. Her eyes drop to my mouth, and I lean closer, drawn by something I can't—and don't want to—resist.

I lower my attention to those pretty lips, and everything in me tightens with savage hunger. With a desperation to lean in and claim her. My hand slides to cup her jaw, thumb brushing her lower lip. The skin there is soft, pliant. I'm salivating to taste her.

The door bangs open with the subtlety of a gunshot.

She jerks apart from me as Hunter strides in, carrying a tray with steaming mugs. His eyes flick between us, taking in our flushed faces and close proximity. A knowing smirk spreads across his face.

"Brought hot chocolate," he announces, setting the tray down on the desk. "Saw you enter the study and figured you'd want some warming up."

"Thanks," Lily says. She stands and pulls back, but

her eyes keep darting to me with a heat that promises
this isn't over.

What surprises me is how they also flick to Hunter,
lingering on the breadth of his shoulders, the strong
line of his jaw. There's interest there—subtle but
unmistakable. My body tenses, not with jealousy but
with a sudden, predatory awareness.

Hunter catches it too. Our eyes meet over Lily's
head. His eyebrow rises a fraction—a question. I give a
barely perceptible nod—permission.

"I called my sister," Lily tells him, accepting a mug
of chocolate. "Well, sent a message through the
antique store. She knows I'm safe now."

"That's good," Hunter adds. "Family shouldn't
have to worry."

Lily smiles up at him, and I watch the effect it has
on my oldest friend—like a man seeing the sun after
months of darkness. It's the same effect she had on me
moments earlier.

"Don't let him fool you with the intellectual
routine," Hunter warns, eyes twinkling, glancing over
at me, Lily's stare following. "Man's got a storage unit
full of switchblades and another with vintage motor-
cycle parts. Regular Jekyll and Hyde."

"Really?" She turns to me with renewed interest.
"Switchblades?"

I shrug. "I appreciate craftsmanship in all its
forms."

"He's being modest," Hunter continues. "Show her
the one you're carrying."

Lily's eyes widen. "You're armed?"

I reach into my pocket and withdraw a folding knife, pressing the release to expose the blade. It's Italian, hand-forged in the 1950s, with a mother-of-pearl handle inlaid with silver filigree. Beautiful and lethal in equal measure.

She doesn't recoil as many would. Instead, she leans closer, studying the blade with open admiration. "It's gorgeous," she murmurs. "Functional art."

"Exactly," I say, oddly pleased by her assessment.

Hunter watches our exchange with knowing eyes. "Arch here has expensive taste in *everything*."

Lily's cheeks flush, but she doesn't look away from either of us. If anything, her posture becomes more confident, chin lifting in silent challenge.

"And what about you?" she asks Hunter directly. "What do you collect?"

"Trouble, mostly," he answers with a wolfish grin.

I close the knife and pocket it, never taking my eyes off Lily as she banters with Hunter. The storm howls outside, but inside this room, something else entirely is brewing—something wild and hungry that sparks between all of us like electricity before a lightning strike.

And for the first time since Hunter found her stranded on that snowy road, I find myself hoping the storm lasts a very long time.

CHAPTER THIRTEEN

LILY

The warmth of the hot chocolate seeps through the ceramic mug into my palms as I stand close, trying not to stare at Archer's hands as they trace the aged parchment on the table. The treasure map—well, half of one, anyway—sprawls across the polished mahogany underneath the glass top that I assume is for keeping it protected.

"These coordinates here." Archer points to the edge of the map. "They might lead to the entrance of the old mining system, but we've never been able to pinpoint it."

Hunter leans forward, his broad shoulders blocking the warm glow of the fireplace. "The topography has changed significantly since this was drawn. Landslides, forest growth... Nature has a way of reclaiming what's hers."

I take a sip of my hot chocolate, enjoying the rich sweetness as I inspect the faded lines. "Have you tried using modern satellite imaging and overlaying the old map?" I suggest, reaching out to trace a mountain range with my fingertip over the glass top.

Hunter's eyes light up. "That's—"

The study door creaks open, interrupting whatever he was about to say. James stands there, taking in the scene—me, Archer, and Hunter huddled over the treasure map—with a slow, measured stare that lingers on my face just long enough to make my cheeks burn.

His mouth curves into that knowing smile that sets my pulse racing, despite my determination to remain unaffected. He saunters into the room with his casual confidence, closing the door behind him with a soft click that somehow feels final, like the turning of a lock.

"So, have we officially got a fourth treasure hunter with us?" He directs the question to Archer and Hunter but keeps his attention fixed on me. "She knows our secret now..."

He winks, and suddenly, I can't breathe. My lungs forget their fundamental function as James slides into the armchair nearby, stretching his long legs toward the fire as shadows dance across his face, highlighting those sharp cheekbones.

"Are you into treasure hunting, Lily?" Hunter asks. He reaches for my now-empty mug, and our fingers brush as I hand it to him. The simple contact sends a rush of heat through my body that has nothing to do with the fire or the hot chocolate.

Hunter's laugh is low and smooth as he notices my

reaction. "Your face is flushed. Is the fire too warm for you?"

I shake my head, not trusting my voice.

"She's a natural," Archer says, striding closer. "Sharp eye for detail. She'd make a perfect member." The way he looks at me leaves me feeling like I'm the treasure they're seeking.

"So, what exactly are you boys looking for?" I ask. "Gold? Jewels? The lost ark?"

"That's the million-dollar question." Archer leans against the desk, arms crossed. "The legends vary. I'm hoping for knowledge. Ancient texts, maybe. Something that explains the history of this region better than our current records."

James scoffs. "Always the scholar." He tilts his head, studying me with those penetrating eyes. "I'm in it for the thrill of the hunt. The prize is secondary."

Somehow, I don't believe him, but maybe I'm just being paranoid, seeing as he lied to me all those weeks that we chatted and grew closer, with me grasping onto every message he sent me. Do Hunter and Archer even know about our conversations? That we've spoken more than they realize? From their relaxed postures, I'd guess not.

"What about you, Lily?" Archer asks. "If you could find any treasure, what would you hope it to be?"

I consider this for a long pause. "Truth of why they needed to bury a treasure," I say finally, looking directly at James. "I've always valued truth above all else."

Something flickers across his face before his mask of casual arrogance returns.

"Truth can be the most dangerous treasure of all," he says quietly.

Hunter's eyebrows draw together. "Getting philosophical on us, James?"

"Just stating facts," James replies.

The room feels smaller, the air thicker. My skin prickles with awareness as the three of them seem to form a loose circle around me—Hunter to my left, Archer directly across, James lounging by the fire yet somehow dominating the space.

"Are you okay?" Hunter asks, brow furrowed. "You look... hot."

"I'm fine," I insist, though I'm anything but. Every nerve ending in my body feels like a live wire. "When will this storm let up, right?"

Archer glances toward the window, though all we can see is the white snow pelting the glass. "Forecast says most of the week."

A week. A week trapped in this house with these three men whose mere presence seems to be triggering something primal in me. My mother's words echo in my mind —her careful explanations about Omega biology, about how some Alphas could trigger stronger reactions than others, especially during times of stress or isolation.

"Cabin fever setting in already, Lily?" James asks with a rumble. "It's only day two."

I force myself to meet his gaze steadily. "I'm simply

concerned about work. Some of us have responsibilities."

"We *all* have responsibilities," Hunter says seriously. "Mine are just on hold until this storm passes. Or if I get called in for an emergency search and rescue task," he explains, and I notice how his posture straightens slightly with pride.

"That's impressive," I say, remembering the well-stocked meat freezer I'd glimpsed earlier. "I saw the game in your basement freezer. You hunt well too."

"I do." He nods. "Tracking comes naturally to me—animals or people." There's something in the way he says it, a predatory edge beneath the matter-of-fact statement, that sends a shiver down my spine. "My grandfather taught me to track and hunt before I could even read. Said it was more important to know how to find your way and feed yourself than to know your ABCs."

"Priorities," I murmur, smiling despite myself.

"He was right, though," Hunter continues, his attention holding mine with an intensity that makes my breath catch. "I've used those skills more often than anything I learned in school. When you're tracking, you have to notice everything—disturbed soil, broken twigs, the way animals go quiet when a stranger passes. It's all about paying attention to what most people miss."

The way he says it makes me wonder if he's tracking me now, noticing every quickened breath, every flush of my skin, every involuntary reaction to his presence.

"So, what's your theory?" I ask, gesturing to the map and trying to redirect. "You have half a map to a treasure you can't identify. What's the plan once the weather clears?"

The three exchange glances, a silent communication passing between them that speaks of years of friendship.

"The other half of the map was given to my cousin, Travis, in my grandfather's will, so I'll first try to get him to give me his half," Hunter explains, his jaw tightening slightly. He glances at me momentarily. "After our parents died, Grandfather took me in, but Travis got shipped off to his mother's family. Nasty people who didn't treat him right, from what I heard. Travis has held a grudge against me ever since, convinced I somehow stole his place." He shakes his head, his brow pinching with frustration. "The bastard even resented it when Grandfather took in James and Archer years later—as if that was another personal slight against him. Didn't bother to visit Grandfather in his final five years, even knowing how sick he was getting."

"And why that fucker won't part with his half of the map," Archer barks. "We've been trying for weeks."

"That's why we're going to use our map to track it down ourselves," James chimes in, tracing a line on the parchment with his finger. "We have enough to work with."

Hunter nods, determination etched into his

features. I can see they're men who don't give up easily, who are set on finding this so-called treasure. There's something exciting about their resolve and single-minded pursuit.

The guys return their attention to the map, pointing out landmarks and theories, completely in their element. They lean in, arguing over interpretations and sharing ideas. But James keeps glancing my way when he thinks I'm not looking.

"I need some fresh air," I announce, suddenly feeling the need to escape his stare, to put some distance between us.

"In a blizzard?" Hunter asks, concerned.

"Just... air. Different air." Not one filled with Alpha scents that seem to be deepening. I'm not making sense, and I know it.

"You okay?" James asks, that sly grin returning. He knows exactly what effect he's having on me.

"Perfectly fine," I manage, forcing a casual smile.

I head out of the study, maintaining my composure until I'm safely in the hallway. Then I lean against the wall, breathing heavily, trying to sort through the riot of sensations coursing through my body.

What's wrong with me? James lied to me about being in prison, yet I still react to him like a compass needle to magnetic north. And it's not just him—Hunter's strength and Archer's intensity affect me just as strongly. It's like my libido has kicked into overdrive.

And what did I almost do earlier? Nearly kissed

Archer. As if I'd completely lost my mind—or my self-preservation instinct.

My fingers drum against the wood-paneled wall as I try to steady myself. When I'm anxious or overwhelmed, I need to do something with my hands. Baking. Yes, baking will help.

I make my way to the kitchen and locate the pantry —a walk-in space stocked surprisingly well for a remote cabin. I grab flour, sugar, and baking soda, then scan the shelves for chocolate chips. Finding them, I pile the ingredients into my arms, already planning the cookie recipe in my head.

"Going to feed an army?"

I whirl around, nearly dropping everything. Hunter fills the doorway of the pantry, his massive frame blocking the exit. In the confined space, his presence is overwhelming—all broad shoulders and woodsy scent that reminds me of pine trees after rain.

"I, uh—" I laugh, shifting my precarious tower of baking supplies. "When I get nervous, I like to bake."

One corner of his mouth lifts. "Do we make you nervous?"

I bite my lip, considering how honest to be. His eyes track my movement, darkening slightly. "A bit. I don't really know you all, and I've never been this close to an Alpha for so long, let alone three. I'm starting to understand what my mother once told me about the impact they have on Omegas." I swallow hard. "It's... a lot."

His smirk deepens. "And the same could be said

about the impact you're having on us." He steps closer, taking the bag of flour from my arms. "Let me help you with that." His fingers brush mine deliberately, lingering longer than necessary.

The contact leaves me buzzing, and when I glance up, I can tell he felt it too, by his sly grin.

We're standing so close in the narrow pantry that the heat radiating from his body envelopes me.

"Thanks," I murmur, grabbing vanilla extract and salt while he relieves me of the heavier items. I reach past him for the cinnamon on an upper shelf, and my arm brushes against his chest. Even through layers of clothing, the contact feels electric.

"Sorry," I whisper, though I'm not sorry at all.

"Don't be," he replies. He doesn't step back to give me space, forcing me to navigate around him, our bodies in constant near contact in the confined area.

"Why do you have so much baking stuff, anyway?" I ask, scanning the impressive collection of cake pans and cookie sheets on the metal shelves. "Do you bake?"

"Sometimes I have friends pop over, and they like to bake."

"Like girlfriends?" The question slips out before I can stop it, accompanied by a telltale blush.

Hunter smiles as he studies me. "They are girls and friends, yeah. And sometimes more."

I remember the bra I spotted yesterday. "Well, I don't expect Alphas like you three to be without girls hanging off you and Omegas ready to go." I force a laugh and try to squeeze past him, but he shifts, effectively caging me against the metal shelving.

"If that's your way of asking if we have Omega mates, the answer is no." His voice drops lower, rumbling in his chest. I can feel the vibration in the scant space between us. "We're not with anyone right now. Well, I know about me and can only assume for the other two, based on conversations we've had."

My attention is drawn to the strong muscles of his throat. "Not even James? He never spoke of anyone?"

Hunter raises an eyebrow in my direction. "Should he have?"

I shrug, trying for nonchalance. "Just curious about the dynamic between you three. You seem close."

"We are." He doesn't elaborate. "James has a darker past, but he means well. Even he doesn't tell us everything, especially about his love life."

"And what about your private life?" I ask, surprising myself with my boldness.

His lips quirk up at one corner. "What do you want to know?"

Everything, I think, but instead say, "For starters, are you going to let me out of this pantry so I can actually bake something?"

He chuckles, low and deep, but doesn't move immediately. "I kind of like you right where you are."

His attention drops to my lips for a heartbeat before he finally steps aside, allowing me to slip past him. As I do, I'm aware of every point where our bodies nearly touch, the sensation of contact making my skin tingle.

I hurry into the kitchen, where I set everything down on the counter. My heart pounds as I arrange ingredients in the order I'll need them—a small attempt to create order in the chaos of my emotions.

"What are you making?" Hunter asks, setting down his armload and taking a seat at the island counter across from me.

"Chocolate chip cookies," I reply, finding comfort in the familiar routine. "I need to keep my hands busy, and when I'm nervous or anxious, they're what I drown in." I offer him a tight smile.

He sets his massive forearms on the granite countertop. In the bright kitchen light, I can fully appreciate his rugged beauty with hair that falls just past his ears, a strong jaw dusted with a short beard, and eyes the color of the bluest summer day. He wears a simple Henley, sleeves pushed up to the elbows, revealing muscular forearms crossed with old scars. Unlike James's sleek, dangerous vibe or Archer's intense energy, Hunter radiates a steady, earthy strength.

Those hands—large, capable, with thick fingers that could probably do some amazing things... I imagine those hands on my skin and quickly look away, focusing intently on measuring flour.

"Can I help?" he offers.

"Keep me company?" I counter, reaching for a mixing bowl. "Tell me more about yourself. When did you start doing search and rescue?"

I begin mixing some butter.

"After my parents passed," he says, a shadow crossing his features as I glance up. "Avalanche took them when I was young. Grandfather raised me after that."

I pause in my mixing, recognizing the familiar pain of early loss. "God, I'm sorry."

He shrugs, but I can see in his eyes that the old wound still aches.

"It shaped me. Made me want to save others from similar fates." His stare meets mine, deep and sincere. "What about you? What shaped Lily into who she is today?"

The way he says my name—soft, almost reverent—sends a shiver through me.

"My mother died when I was young too." I add sugar into the bowl, focusing on the task to keep my response steady. "My dad did his best, but raising two girls alone wasn't easy for him. Mom loved flowers, so every weekend, I get a fresh bunch for my home, which always makes me feel like she's still with us. We normally take a bunch of flowers to my grandmother too, who is in a nursing home just out of town. She loves flowers." I pause for a long moment, lost in trying to bat away the tears that always come when thinking of my family. "I barely remember my mom some days. Just fragments—the smell of her perfume, the sound of her laugh. And I don't want to forget her."

"You never will. She is always with you." He

watches me add eggs next and then beat in the vanilla extract. "What's your favorite scent?"

The question catches me off guard. "Hmmm."

"Everyone has one. A smell that makes them feel instantly at home or happy."

I think about it as I add flour, baking powder, and salt to the bowl. "The smell of cookies. It's sweet, comforting, and inviting," I decide aloud. "You?"

"Pine forest in early morning," he answers without hesitation. "When dew is still clinging to everything and the sun hasn't quite burned through the mist."

I can picture it perfectly—Hunter in his element, moving silently through misty trees at dawn, tracking, hunting.

"Favorite food?" I ask, stirring the mixture.

"I'm boring—Bolognese with extra garlic and Parmesan."

"Sounds divine," I say. "Mine is my grandmother's apple pie with homemade cinnamon ice cream. It's heaven in a bowl."

"I would have guessed something with chocolate," he teases.

"That's for comfort, not a favorite," I correct him with a smirk. "Important distinction."

"So, what other distinctions do you make?" he asks, leaning forward slightly. "What else comforts you besides chocolate?"

There's something easy about talking with Hunter. The conversation flows naturally as I finish mixing the dough.

"Want to help roll these into balls?" I ask, pushing the bowl toward him along with a parchment paper–covered baking tray.

He nods, washing his hands at the sink before joining me. When he returns to my side, standing close enough that our elbows brush, I have to remind myself to breathe.

His large hands are surprisingly deft as he rolls perfect spheres of cookie dough.

"You're decent at this," I observe. "Are you sure you don't have a girlfriend somewhere? You seem skilled in the kitchen."

A shadow passes over his face. "Just the one from years ago that I told you about in the truck. Vanessa." He focuses intently on the cookie dough, rolling it between his palms with perhaps more force than necessary. "Let's just say she never had faith in me, and that ended up being our downfall. Got to have trust in any relationship." His eyes flick to mine, searching for something. "What about you? Anyone waiting for you back home?"

"No," I admit, shaking my head. "My last relationship ended about a year ago. He was a Beta, but it wasn't serious, in all honesty. More like overcoming boredom." I laugh at how lame I sound.

The kitchen door swings open, and James and Archer enter, both sniffing the air.

"What smells so divine?" Archer asks, scanning the kitchen.

"Chocolate chip cookies," I explain, nodding toward Hunter.

James watches us, something unreadable in his expression as Archer dives in to wash his hands and help with the rolling. I made a triple batch, so there's plenty to do.

"I have a great idea for tonight," James announces suddenly. "To keep us entertained."

"Sounds crazy already." Archer laughs. "Your ideas normally are. But they're fun."

Hunter chuckles in agreement, and I find myself curious despite my wariness of James.

I refuse to ask what he has planned. I won't give him the satisfaction of thinking I care that much. Instead, I turn to put the first two trays of cookies in the oven, Hunter's words echoing in my mind.

Got to have trust in any relationship.

And trust is exactly what's missing between James and me. So why can't I stop my heart from racing whenever he looks my way?

James never stops staring at me. Hunter moves beside me, reaching over my head to grab a plate from a high cabinet, his chest brushing against my back momentarily. The contact, brief as it is, sends another wave of heat through me. From across the kitchen, Archer looks at the freshly baked cookies with undisguised hunger that seems directed more at me than at the treats.

"So, what's this great idea of yours, James?" Hunter finally asks, breaking the charged silence.

James's slow, predatory smile worries me. "A fun game," he says. "Best way to pass the time in a storm."

I feel a dangerous thrill race through my veins.

"Unless you're afraid of a little fun, baker girl?" James adds with challenge behind his words.

"I'm not afraid of anything," I lie, despite the heat rising to my cheeks.

Hunter's hand brushes against my lower back. "Good," he murmurs. "This should be fun, then."

Three pairs of eyes watch me like predators sizing up prey. I know this will only lead to trouble. But as the storm rages outside, I find myself nodding.

"Fine," I say. "But don't blame me when this goes sideways."

James's smile turns wolfish. "Oh, I'm counting on it."

CHAPTER FOURTEEN
LILY

"You want to play truth or dare?" I gasp at the three men lounging around the coffee table. An empty whiskey bottle lies on its side at the center, waiting to be used.

"Why not?" James grins, leaning forward from his spot directly across from me on the semicircular couch that faces the huge fireplace. "Perfect game for a storm-locked night."

I reach for my bourbon and Coke, taking a sip. I don't normally drink much, but tonight calls for something to take the edge off. The fire crackles in the background, casting dancing shadows across the room and providing most of the light, along with a few strategically placed lamps. Thor is snoring away in front of the fire, not bothered by our chatter.

"Seriously?" I laugh, though I can't deny I'm excited. "Are we fifteen?"

"What's the matter, Lily?" Archer asks from his

position on the couch between James and Hunter. "Scared?"

"Of you three?" I quirk an eyebrow. "Terrified." My tone makes it clear I'm anything but.

Hunter chuckles beside me, his body radiating warmth even with the few inches of space between us. "Come on, it'll be fun."

"Fine." I grab another chocolate chip cookie from the bowl before the guys devour them all. "But I reserve the right to walk away when this inevitably gets out of control."

"We all know how this goes, right?" James asks, his dark gaze gleaming with mischief. "We've all played before?"

All three men turn to look at me expectantly.

I roll my eyes. "Yes, I've played truth or dare before. I'm twenty-four, and I did go to school, you know."

"Just checking," James smirks. "But this game is my own variation, as it includes the spin of the bottle. Whoever it points to gets asked 'Truth or dare?' by the spinner. No passes, no chickening out."

In all honesty, I no longer care about the rules with how my body buzzes under their attention.

"And what happens in the cabin stays in the cabin," Archer adds with a wink.

"Original," I deadpan, but I can't help the flutter in my stomach. This is probably a terrible idea, but after two days trapped inside with mounting tension, I need some kind of release, even if it's just the thrill of a party game.

"Ladies first," James says.

I take another fortifying sip of my drink, then lean forward and spin the bottle. It rotates several times before slowing to point at Archer with the base facing me.

"Truth or dare?" I ask, meeting his gaze.

"Truth," Archer answers, leaning back confidently. Messy hair frames his face. I hadn't noticed before how his sharp cheekbones bring out how damn gorgeous he is.

I consider what to ask. Something not too tame but not immediately crossing lines either.

"What's the greatest number of orgasms you've given a girl in one night?" The question comes out bolder than I intended, and I blame the bourbon.

Hunter coughs beside me, clearly surprised at my choice.

Archer's grin widens slowly. "Seven. Would've been eight, but she passed out."

"Bullshit." James laughs, throwing a balled-up napkin at him.

"Swear to God," Archer holds up his hand. "Ask Vanessa."

Hunter goes rigid beside me. "Vanessa?" he repeats. "Who dumped me?"

The temperature in the room seems to drop ten degrees. Ouch!

Archer's eyes widen fractionally. "Shit, man, I forgot—"

"You fucked my ex?" Hunter's tone remains eerily calm.

"It was after you broke up," Archer adds quickly. "Way after."

"How long after?" Hunter demands.

Archer lifts his chin. "Like… two damn years later."

"You're lucky she means nothing to me, and you can do better than that," Hunter says, but there's no real heat behind it anymore. He shakes his head and takes a long drink.

Does this mean Vanessa still holds on to his heart? I sure as hell don't care, yet there's fire climbing up my neck to see the passion in his attack.

"Wow, you guys have quite the crowd of girl-friends," I tease, trying to lighten the mood. It doesn't surprise me that they have a caravan of girlfriends in their pasts. I've had five boyfriends in my time, and not one worked out.

All three men look at me as if suddenly remembering I'm there, witnessing their dirty laundry.

"It's the damn past," Hunter says with a shrug. "We were younger and stupider."

"Speak for yourself." Archer grins, reaching for the bottle. "I'm still as stupid as ever."

The raised voices must have woken Thor from his spot by the fire. He stretches, then hops up on the couch near me and flops his head down, lying on his side, already sleeping in seconds. Someone has a good life.

The men are still chuckling as Archer spins, and it lands on James.

"Truth or dare?" Archer asks.

"Truth," James answers, taking a sip of his whiskey. The amber liquid glints as he raises the glass, highlighting his sharp jawline and the slight stubble darkening it.

"Worst thing you've ever done during sex that you don't regret?" Archer asks with a gleam in his stare.

James considers this, his expression darkening in a way that sends shivers down my spine.

"Tied a girl up in an abandoned factory," he says finally. "Left her there for hours while I went out, came back, and finished what we started."

"Jesus, James," Hunter mutters.

"She asked me to," James adds with a half smile. "Begged, actually. Said the fear of not knowing if I'd return made everything more intense."

I shift in my seat, both disturbed and intrigued. These aren't the kind of men I usually spend time with; that's for damn sure.

"Your turn," Archer tells James, who spins the bottle. It lands on Hunter, with Archer at the base. I'm kind of relieved the bottle seems to be ignoring me for now.

"Truth or dare?" Archer asks.

"Truth," Hunter says. Heat from his body radiates toward me, his smell a faint woodsy scent. It's addictive.

"Have you ever thought about fucking someone

while you were fucking someone else?" James asks bluntly.

I chuckle. "I'm seeing a pattern here. Too scared for dares, hey?"

James winks at me as if he knows something I don't... like he's saving the dares for me. I take a long sip of my drink.

"Yes," Hunter answers.

"Details, man," Archer presses. "Who was the fantasy? Who was the reality?"

Hunter runs a hand through his dark hair, making it stick up slightly. "No details needed." He grins evilly.

I try to picture Hunter—solid, steady Hunter—fantasizing about one woman while fucking another, and I see him doing it. He has a dark edge to him.

He takes the bottle and spins. It points at me.

My heart skips a beat. "Truth," I say quickly, not trusting what dare he might come up with.

Hunter looks at me, his blue eyes reflecting the fire-light. "What's your darkest fantasy?"

"Pass," I say automatically.

"No passes," James reminds me, looking entirely too interested in my answer.

I glare at him, then look back at Hunter. All three men are staring at me expectantly. The bourbon in my system gives me just enough courage to think I can answer.

"Being completely at someone else's mercy," I admit quietly. "Blindfolded, tied up, not knowing what's coming next or who's touching me." I feel my cheeks flush but force myself to maintain eye contact with Hunter. "Complete surrender of control."

The room falls silent except for the crackling of the fire. I can practically feel the shift in energy, the sudden tension thick enough to cut with a knife.

Hunter's pupils dilate slightly. "Interesting" is all he says, but the way he says it makes my stomach flip.

I quickly reach for the bottle, desperate to shift attention away from myself. I spin it hard, watching it whirl several times before stopping on Archer.

"Truth or dare?" I ask, praying that he chooses truth.

"Dare," he counters with a challenging smile. "I'm not hiding behind truths all night."

Damn it. I rack my brain for something that won't escalate things too far.

"I dare you to do your best impression of the person to your right," I say, nodding toward James.

Archer grins and immediately straightens his posture, adopting a brooding expression. He fixes me with an intense stare.

"I'm James," he says in a deep, exaggerated voice. "I like to pretend I'm mysterious and dangerous because it gets me laid. I own seventeen identical black sweaters because I read once that Steve Jobs did the same thing, and I secretly wish I could pull off a turtleneck."

Hunter bursts out laughing while James scowls.

"Fuck, I don't sound like that," James protests, but his lips twitch with suppressed amusement. "And for the record," he adds, "I own twelve black sweaters, not seventeen."

I laugh, genuinely amused by their banter.

Archer spins the bottle, and it lands on me with the base on Archer this time.

"This thing is rigged," I state, but no one else is protesting.

"Truth or dare?" he asks, smirking.

I hesitate. Truth has already gotten me into trouble once. "Dare," I say, bracing myself.

Archer's smile widens. "I dare you to take off your top."

My gaze widens, and I hear Hunter inhale sharply beside me. James leans forward, studying my reaction carefully.

For a moment, I consider refusing, but there's a challenge in Archer's facial expression that awakens something defiant in me. I hold his gaze as I set down my drink, then grasp the hem of my sweater. With deliberate slowness, I pull it over my head, revealing the black tank top I'm wearing underneath.

Archer's expression shifts from triumph to disappointment to appreciation in rapid succession. The tank reveals more of my shoulders and collarbone and my bra straps but is otherwise perfectly modest. All three men stare at me, and I can't help the small thrill of satisfaction that runs through me at having subverted Archer's expectations.

"Clever girl," James murmurs, raising his glass in a mock toast.

I grasp the bottle and spin it hard. It whirls several times before landing on Archer.

"Truth or dare?" I ask sweetly.

"Dare," he says immediately. "I'm not backing down."

"I dare you to take off your pants," I reply, feeling a rush of boldness. I assume he'll have boxers underneath—a taste of his own medicine.

Without a moment's hesitation, Archer stands and unbuttons his jeans, shoving them down in one fluid motion. My eyes widen as I realize he's not wearing anything underneath.

A huge, half-erect cock stands there, almost at eye level with me from across the table, and I find myself instantly looking away.

"God!" Yet I can't stop thinking of how big he is, how he manscaped, and the boldness that has me blushing.

He's completely commando. He grins at my shocked expression as I glance up.

"Jesus Christ, Arch!" Hunter exclaims while James bursts into laughter. "Put that away before you poke someone's eye out!"

I quickly avert my gaze again because I can't stop staring at it. "Okay, bad dare," I stammer, feeling my face flush crimson. "Put them back on."

"What's the matter, Lily?" Archer teases, taking his time pulling his jeans back up. "Surprised?"

"Traumatized is more like it," I retort, but I can't help laughing despite my embarrassment. James just reclines there, grinning. Bastard is enjoying seeing me squirm.

"Your turn to spin, Archer," he reminds him.

"I think I need another drink first," I mutter, downing the rest of my bourbon and Coke.

James gets up to refresh our drinks, returning with mine. I take a sip and nearly choke at the burn of the significantly stronger drink.

"Trying to get me drunk?" I ask.

"Just enhancing the experience," he replies with a wink.

James keeps his attention on me while Archer spins the bottle. It lands between Hunter and me, pointing slightly more toward me.

"Truth or dare?" Hunter asks.

Something in his tone makes me hesitate. "Truth," I say, deciding it's safer.

He leans closer, his knee brushing against mine. "Have you ever fantasized about more than one man at once?"

I nearly choke on my drink. His question hits too close to home, especially considering my attraction to all three of them.

I take a deep breath, steadying myself. "Fine. Yes."

"We need details," Archer presses, leaning forward.

"That wasn't part of the question," I counter, grabbing the bottle and spinning it before they can argue.

It lands on James with the base on me.

"Truth or dare?" I ask, meeting his gaze steadily.

"Truth," he says.

The alcohol emboldens me. This is my chance to get some answers. "Have you ever been to prison?"

The room goes suddenly still. Hunter and Archer exchange glances, clearly surprised by my question.

"Yes," James answers simply, his expression unreadable.

"How long were you in there for?" I press, ignoring the confusion from the others.

"Eighteen months."

"Did you kill someone?" I tense all over.

James's jaw tightens. "No. I was framed and wrongly blamed for a theft I didn't commit."

"You often lie to people?" I continue, the words coming rapid-fire now.

"Uh, seems like a lot of questions without any bottle spinning," Archer interjects, looking between us. "Have the rules of the game changed?"

I ignore him, my focus entirely on James, who hasn't broken eye contact.

"Only when I don't want to scare someone away," he answers quietly. "When I want a chance to properly tell them the truth later."

"So you're okay with leading someone on, making them believe you're something you're not?" I challenge.

"What the hell is going on?" Hunter asks, looking between us. "Did you two know each other before this weekend?"

"No," James says firmly, at the exact moment I say, "Yes."

Archer's eyebrows shoot up. "Well, this just got interesting."

"We'd been texting for weeks," I clarify, still glaring at James. "He never mentioned he was in prison."

"You two were texting?" Hunter asks, something unidentifiable flashing across his face. "Oh, so that was the burner phone you got busted with in prison? The one they threw you into isolation for, for an extra week, before the lawyers got you out?"

James shoots Hunter a warning look, but the damage is already done.

"It started with a wrong number," I explain, the words tumbling out now that the secret is out in the open. "I texted him, thinking it was going to my sister. We got to talking, and then... we just kept going."

James appears uncharacteristically flustered. "Lily—"

"Don't," I interrupt. "You flirted with me for weeks. I told you things I've never told anyone else. And all that time, you were lying about who you were."

"I wasn't lying about who I was," James argues, leaning forward. "Just... certain details."

"Like the fact that you were in prison?" I counter, my knee bouncing—nerves, anticipation, and dread all twisting inside me. A voice in my head warns me not to do this now, but I can't stop. Not when the anger has been building for so long. Not when he disappeared without a word. Not when he never told me the truth.

The room goes quiet. Hunter and Archer exchange surprised glances.

"That's not something you drop into casual conversation," James murmurs. "'Hey, by the way, I'm getting out of prison soon. Want to keep texting?'"

The words hit hard, knocking the air from my lungs. I stare at him, my throat tight, my pulse pounding in my ears. The messages—the late-night conversations that felt so real, so safe—had all been built on a lie. I let myself fall, let my guard slip, believing I knew him. And now, I don't know if anything between us was ever real.

Shame burns through me, hot and unforgiving. How could I have been so naive? How could I have let him in without ever questioning who he really was? My heart clenches painfully, the weight of betrayal settling deep in my chest.

Has he been laughing at me all this time? Amused by how easily I trusted him?

I swallow hard, but the lump in my throat refuses to go away. I want to scream at him, to demand why— why he thought I didn't deserve the truth—but I can't find the words. Because underneath the betrayal, underneath the anger, there's something far worse.

This hurts.

More than it should. More than I want to admit.

"I was going to tell you," James insists. "I wanted to explain in person. I had plans to visit your bakery yesterday, then this storm hit. And here we are."

"So, this has nothing to do with the treasure map?" Archer interrupts, looking confused.

"No," James and I say in unison.

"This is about him leading me on for weeks," I continue. "Making me believe he was someone he's not."

"I never lied about who I am," James repeats. "Everything I told you about me—my likes, my thoughts, my feelings—all of that was real."

"Except the part where you were in prison," I point out.

The damage was already done. The words are out, cracking the fragile thread of control I've been clinging to. My chest tightens, the weight of it pressing down, suffocating.

How am I supposed to believe him now? How am I supposed to trust that he's innocent—if he even is—when he's already proved he can keep something this huge from me? I had built an image of him in my mind, a version I felt safe with, someone who had been honest in ways that mattered. But was it ever real? Or had I fallen for a stranger who only gave me pieces of himself?

James exhales, rubbing the back of his neck, his expression unreadable.

"Yes," he concedes. "Except that."

The room falls silent as the truth settles between us, thick and heavy. Can I forgive this? Can I even begin to believe that the man in front of me is someone I can still trust?

Because right now, I don't know if I can.

"Well," Hunter says finally, clapping his hands together. "This is all very dramatic, but can we get back to the game? Or should we just start throwing punches now?"

His attempt at humor breaks some of the tension. I take a deep breath, trying to calm my racing heart.

"Game," I say firmly, my heart hammering in my chest, my face feeling like it's on fire. I really wish I hadn't asked him those questions in front of the other two, but better to be transparent, right?

"Your spin, James," Hunter reminds him.

James stays silent at first.

Then he reaches for the bottle, giving it a forceful twist. It spins for what feels like forever before pointing at Archer with the base toward me.

"Truth or dare?" I ask, still feeling the aftershocks of adrenaline from confronting James.

"Dare," Archer says without hesitation. "Let's lighten things up."

I consider for a moment. "I dare you to do your best pickup line on Hunter."

Archer grins and immediately turns to Hunter, batting his eyelashes dramatically. He slides closer, placing a hand on Hunter's massive forearm.

"Are you a campfire?" he asks in a husky voice. "Because you're hot, and I want s'more."

Hunter shoves him away as we all burst out laughing. Thor beside me grumbles, which is most likely more to do with us probably being too loud for him.

"That was terrible," Hunter groans.

"But effective." Archer winks. "You're blushing, big boy."

"Fuck off," Hunter mutters, but he's smiling.

Archer spins the bottle, which lands on me and him again.

"You're popular tonight," James comments.

"Truth or dare, Lily?" Archer asks.

"Dare," I say, deciding that truth is much more dangerous tonight.

Archer's smile turns wicked. "I dare you to kiss Hunter. Not a peck—full-on, with tongue."

I laugh nervously. "Is this high school?"

"Do it!" Archer insists.

I look around at their faces—Archer grinning expectantly, James frowning slightly, Hunter stretching his neck with a mixture of anticipation and uncertainty.

Then I'm staring at James, the bridge of his nose pinched, jawline tight. Part of me wants to make him hurt for lying to me.

"Sure," I say with forced casualness, setting down my drink and turning to Hunter.

He's sitting next to me on the couch, his large frame suddenly very close. I face him fully, hesitating as a thought strikes me.

"The photo upstairs of your grandfather and my grandmother..." I gnaw on my lower lip nervously. "Do you think... are we related?" I cringe as soon as the words leave my mouth.

Hunter reaches over and gently pushes a strand of hair behind my ear, his fingers lingering against my skin. "I bet my life on it that we're not. My grandfather shared a lot with me, and he had one love in his life—my grandma—and a lot of business friends. He was more likely an investor in her bakery."

I glance at the other two, who study our exchange with curious expressions.

"Nothing wrong with kissing cousins... relatives," Archer teases with a smirk.

"Fuck you," Hunter barks, but his hand is already on my arm, drawing me closer, tugging me onto his lap.

I use the momentum to straddle him, finding a surprising bravery for something I want despite the trembling in my limbs.

"Of course..." I laugh nervously. "I mean, if we were cousins, we'd know, and hell no to kissing..."

He chuckles, rubbing the back of his knuckles down my cheek in a gesture that's both reassuring and possessive. There's still darkness in his words, in his eyes, and part of me isn't entirely certain. If this comes back to bite me, I'll be devastated to discover I'm attracted to my cousin or whatever.

"Don't overthink it," he murmurs. "Deep breaths, okay?"

My confidence falters. What am I doing? This isn't me—I don't straddle near strangers on dares. But before I can retreat, Hunter's large hands come up to cup my face, his touch surprisingly gentle for someone so strong.

He leans in, giving me every opportunity to back away. When I don't, his lips meet mine with the gentlest pressure. The kiss starts slow, exploratory, as if we're finding our way to each other through darkness. His lips are warmer and softer than I expected, moving against mine with restrained passion.

Then something shifts. Hunter makes a low, growly sound in the back of his throat, and suddenly, the kiss deepens. His hands slide from my face to my waist, then to my back. My body responds instinctively, curving into his, a small sound—embarrassingly close to a purr—escaping my throat.

No one has ever kissed me like this before. It's consuming, elemental, like being caught in a riptide. His tongue traces the seam of my lips, and I open to him without hesitation. The taste of whiskey and chocolate mingles between us as his tongue strokes against mine, confident but not demanding.

His hands span my back, pressing me closer until I can feel the solid wall of his chest against mine. Beneath me, I can feel his hardening cock, his hips shifting subtly upward. He's massive everywhere, and the realization sends a jolt of electricity down my spine.

One of his hands tangles in my hair, angling my head to deepen the kiss further. The gentle tug against my scalp draws another sound from me, half gasp, half moan. I'm floating, drowning, burning—all at once. My fingers grip his shoulders, feeling the coiled strength beneath his Henley, then slide up to the nape of his neck, where his hair curls against my fingertips.

His mouth moves against mine, his hand lowering

to my ass, holding on tight. The heat of him beneath me, the woodsy scent of him filling my lungs with each ragged breath. It feels both endless and too brief. I don't want it to end.

Someone clears his throat loudly, followed by a nudge against Hunter's shoulder, shaking us. Hunter and I part reluctantly, both breathing heavily. I lick my lips instinctively, tasting him still, while his gaze tracks the movement with a craving that makes me shiver.

"Fuck, you're addictive," Hunter murmurs. "Like the kind of candy that ruins a man—sweet, sinful, and impossible to quit."

Slowly, I become aware of the room around us again. Archer stares at me, his earlier playfulness replaced by something darker, more primal. James's eyes burn with what looks distinctly like jealousy, his jaw tight and his shoulders tense. The energy in the room has shifted dramatically, a palpable current of desire that makes the air feel thick and charged.

I remain on Hunter's lap for a moment longer, acutely aware of his arousal pressed against me, twitching, and his hands tight on my waist. His gaze has darkened to the color of the ocean. He looks like he wants to devour me whole.

"Well," I finally manage. "That was... something."

"*Something* is one word for it," Archer murmurs, shifting in his seat.

I slowly extricate myself from Hunter's lap, my legs embarrassingly unsteady as I settle back onto the couch beside him. His hand lingers on my thigh for a moment before reluctantly withdrawing.

James studies the exchange with hooded eyes, swirling the remains of his whiskey before draining the glass in one swallow. The tension in the room has become almost unbearable—unspoken lust hanging in the air between us.

"I think I've had enough excitement for one night," I say, trying for casual but hearing the slight tremor in my words. "Thanks for the game."

"Running away, Lily?" James asks softly, and there's something in his tone that makes me want to prove him wrong.

"Not running," I counter, meeting his gaze steadily. "Just tired."

"It is getting late," Hunter agrees, though his expression tells a different story—one where sleep is the furthest thing from his mind.

I stand, gathering my sweater from where I'd tossed it earlier. "Good night, boys. Try not to get into too much trouble without me."

Thor is instantly on my heels.

Forcing myself to walk—not run—to the stairs, I sense all three sets of eyes tracking my every move-ment. Only when I'm out of sight do I allow my composure to crack, hurrying down the hallway to my bedroom. Thor gets to my room before I reach it, nudging the door open and scurrying inside. I find him already at the end of my bed, stretched out, ready to sleep.

I close the door behind me and lean against it, my heart thundering against my rib cage. What just happened down there? What was I thinking, kissing Hunter like that in front of the others? And why did it feel so incredibly addictive?

I press my fingers to my bruised lips, still tingling from his kiss. I can still taste him, still feel the pressure of his hands on my body. And worse, I can't stop picturing James and Archer looking at me afterward— like they were imagining themselves in Hunter's place. But James... fuck, he was fuming.

Good.

He should suffer.

Low voices drift up from downstairs, too muffled to make out words. Are they talking about me? Laughing at how easily I melted for Hunter? Or making plans for who gets to try next?

The most terrifying part is that some small, reckless part of me wouldn't mind if they were.

I slide down against the door until I'm sitting on the floor, hugging my knees to my chest. A soft whine draws my attention to Thor, who pads across the room toward me. His blue eyes watch me with an intelligence that seems almost human as he nudges his head against my arm.

"At least someone's checking on me," I whisper, making room for him.

Thor doesn't hesitate, pushing his large head into my lap with a soft huff. His fur is thick and soft beneath my fingers as I absently scratch behind his ears. He settles against me, a warm, solid presence that grounds me when everything else feels like it's spinning out of control.

"You're amazing for caring so much," I tell him, burying my fingers in his ruff. "Is this your job? Comforting distressed Omegas after your master is done with them?"

Thor just blinks up at me, his weight a reassuring pressure against my legs.

This storm needs to break soon. A few more days trapped with these three Alpha men, and I might do something truly stupid.

The thought sends a delicious shiver through me that has nothing to do with fear and everything to do with a desire I didn't know I possessed until tonight. Thor seems to sense the change in me, nudging my hand when I stop petting him.

"Sorry, buddy. Just having an existential crisis over here." I resume stroking his fur, finding comfort in the rhythmic motion. "Your owner has really complicated my life, you know that?"

I need to get a grip. They're virtual strangers, and at least one of them has already lied to me. This isn't a romance novel or a fantasy—it's a precarious situation that could go very wrong, very quickly.

Thor rests his chin on my knee, his steady gaze somehow reassuring. He doesn't judge me for my conflicted feelings, doesn't expect me to be anything other than what I am in this moment.

"What would you do?" I ask him quietly. "If you were me?"

He gives a soft *woof* that makes me smile despite everything.

"Yeah, that's what I thought you'd say."

I push myself up from the floor and move to the bed, Thor padding faithfully beside me.

He jumps up onto the end of the bed, turning in a circle before settling down with a contented sigh, his watchful eyes never leaving me. Whatever comes next, at least I'm not facing it completely alone.

CHAPTER FIFTEEN

I'm too wired to even consider sleep. My lips still tingle from Hunter's kiss, and my mind keeps replaying the confrontation with James. What a damn mess. I've somehow managed to get entangled with not one but three impossibly attractive men in the span of two days. And the storm outside keeps howling like it's enjoying my predicament.

A soft knock at my door freezes me mid-step from my pacing. My heart performs an Olympic-level gymnastics routine in my chest. Hunter? After our kiss. Or James? Has he come to explain himself further? To apologize for the deception? I'm not ready for round two of that emotional roller coaster—not when I'm still sorting through the complicated feelings his revelation stirred up.

Thor's head pops up, sniffs the air, then plops back down, confirming it's not a danger.

I don't answer the knock, hoping whoever it is will

assume I'm asleep and go away. I've hit my quota of drama for one night, thank you very much.

"Lily? You still breathing in there, or did Hunter's kiss actually kill you?" Archer's voice, playful yet somehow concerned, filters through the door.

I smirk to myself, warmth curling in my chest. Archer always makes things feel lighter, as though I'm not drowning in the mess of my own emotions. With him, it's easy to breathe—even when my world is anything but.

I don't hesitate and move quickly toward the door, cracking it open just enough to peek through.

"If I say I'm dead, will you go away?" I tease.

My breath locks in my lungs at the sight of him. Archer stands with one hand propped against the doorjamb, his tall frame backlit by the dim hallway lights. The shadows dance across the sharp angles of his face, highlighting those ridiculous cheekbones. His brown hair, which looks like it would be silk between my fingers, falls even more messily around his face.

I've dated attractive men before, but Archer belongs in another category entirely—the kind of beauty that's almost painful to look at directly, like staring at the sun after being in a cave. His black V-neck stretches across broad shoulders, and even in the dim light, I can see the definition of muscle under the fabric. A silver chain glints at his throat, disappearing beneath his collar.

"Hi," I manage.

"Just making sure you didn't spontaneously

combust from all that... tension downstairs," he says, the corners of his mouth lifting. "You bolted out of there like your ass was on fire."

"Yeah, well, finding out your texting buddy was in prison while you were spilling your guts to him, followed by straddling and making out with his friend... let's just say my night has been more eventful than my entire last year," I reply, leaning against the frame. "I should start charging admission to the disaster that is my life."

Archer's eyebrow quirks up. "I'd pay to watch. Seriously, though, you okay? James can be a real piece of work sometimes."

"Define *okay*." I laugh, the sound slightly unhinged even to my own ears. "I'm trapped in a snowstorm with three men who look like they walked out of some romance novel cover shoot. I mean, do you guys moisturize with unicorn tears or something? One of whom I've been secretly crushing on for weeks despite never having met him, another whose kiss nearly made me forget my own name, and then there's you—" I cut myself off, realizing I'm rambling like a lunatic.

"There's me," he repeats, taking a small step closer. "What about me, Lily?"

The bourbon is still humming in my veins, making me bolder than I should be. "You're the one who insisted Hunter and I kiss. Was that your twisted plan all along? Or do you just enjoy watching?"

"My plan?" He raises an eyebrow. "I assure you, I don't usually play matchmaker for Hunter. Man gets plenty of action without my help." He leans in slightly, close enough that I can smell his cologne—something woodsy with a hint of spice. "And for the record, I much prefer participating to watching."

"Could have fooled me," I retort, but I'm smiling now too, despite myself. There's something about Archer that lures me to him, even as he sets my nerves on fire. "And what was with the impromptu strip show? A warning would have been nice. I wasn't prepared to see... all of that."

He laughs, the sound rich and warm, spreading through me like honey. "You dared me to take off my pants. I took off my pants. I'm a man of simple logic." His gaze glitters with unrepentant devilry. "And I never pass up an opportunity to make a memorable impression. Judging by how red you turned, mission accomplished."

"Mission traumatized," I mutter, fighting a grin. "I'll need therapy for years. Possibly decades."

"Liar," he states softly, leaning in just slightly. "You liked what you saw. Your eyes did this thing"—he widens his own eyes in an exaggerated expression of shock that morphs into appreciation—"before you pretended to be horrified."

Heat floods my cheeks, but I refuse to back down. "You seem very confident for someone who might have caused me psychological damage."

"Oh, I'm always confident," he says with a grin that should come with a warning label. "It's part of my charm. That, and my big—"

"Don't you dare finish that sentence," I interrupt, holding up a finger.

"Heart," he finishes innocently. "What did you think I was going to say?"

"Nothing gentlemanly, that's for sure."

My pulse stumbles, betraying me. The teasing should be easy to brush off—I've handled his shameless flirting before—but there's something different this time. Fire lingers in his gaze, a challenge, a promise. My breath catches for half a second before I force myself to roll my eyes, pretending I'm not affected. But my body knows the truth. And so does he.

"Guilty as charged." His gaze drops to my lips momentarily. "It was hard, you know."

"What was?" I ask, embarrassingly breathy.

"Watching you kiss Hunter," he admits, his playful tone giving way to something more serious. "When it's all I've been thinking about since our almost moment in the study earlier." He shifts his weight, moving imperceptibly closer. "You know, when you were practically undressing me with your eyes while we used the radio."

"I was not," I sputter, then see the gleam in his expression. "You're insufferable."

"So I've been told. Usually right before I'm told how irresistible I am."

"Don't hold your breath for that second part," I say.

"Well," I add lightly. "Maybe it wasn't meant to be. Me and Hunter, I mean."

"I doubt that," Archer murmurs, and suddenly, he

seems much closer, though I don't recall him moving. "I don't believe in coincidences, Lily. You showing up here, during this storm... it feels like fate with us four. Like the universe was tired of watching us stumble around separately and decided to lock us all in together until we figured it out."

"Fate?" I gnaw on my lower lip, trying to maintain my composure despite the heat building low in my belly. "That's quite the line. Do you practice these in front of a mirror, or do they just come to you in the moment?"

"Not a line," he says, reaching out to tuck a strand of hair behind my ear. His fingers brush my cheek, leaving a trail of fire in their wake. "Just a feeling I've had since you walked through the door. Like you were meant to be here." His voice drops to a near whisper. "With us."

I should step back. I should close the door and get my head on straight. Instead, I ask, "And what else do you feel?"

His eyes darken, pupils expanding to nearly swallow the amber. "That if I don't kiss you soon, I might go a little insane." He traces the curve of my jaw with his thumb. "Or a lot insane. I'm already halfway there just looking at you."

My body betrays me, a rush of warmth flooding through me at his words. It's complete madness—I've known this man for all of two days, just kissed his friend less than an hour ago, and am nursing a broken heart over another man's deception. Yet I'm drawn to him like a moth to the flame, unable to resist the gravitational pull of his presence.

"That would be a terrible idea," I whisper, even as I shift my weight slightly forward.

"The worst," he agrees, his gaze locked on my lips. "Completely irresponsible."

"Reckless," I add.

"Absolutely." His hand comes up to cup my cheek, thumb brushing across my lower lip. "May I come in, Lily? Or would you prefer to give the hallway a show?"

The simple question, asked with such restraint when everything about his body language screams desire, breaks something loose in me. I step back, grabbing a fistful of his shirt, and pull him into my room.

"I'll take that as a yes," he says as he kicks the door closed behind him.

In an instant, I'm pressed against the wall beside the door, Archer's body a solid mass of heat against mine. His hands frame my face as he studies me for one breathless moment.

"You're stunning," he murmurs, his thumbs tracing my cheekbones. "Like, unreasonably beautiful, with a scent that fogs my brain and a wit that challenges me. It's actually annoying. Do you have any idea what you do to me?"

Before I can respond with something appropriately snarky, his lips are on mine, and whatever witty retort I might have made dissolves into a soft gasp. If Hunter's kiss was a tide pulling me under, Archer's is like being struck by lightning—sudden, electric, and consuming.

His lips are firm and insistent, claiming rather than asking. One hand slides into my hair, tugging just enough to tilt my head back farther, deepening the kiss with a groan that vibrates through both our bodies. My hands clutch at his shoulders, feeling the coiled strength under the fabric of his shirt.

When his tongue sweeps across my lower lip, I open to him without hesitation. He tastes of whiskey and something darker, something uniquely him that makes me crave more.

His hands move from my face to my waist, then lower, gripping my hips and pulling me tighter against him. He holds me harshly, possessively, and the realization of him longing for me draws a soft moan from my throat.

In one fluid motion, Archer lifts me, hands gripping the backs of my thighs as he presses me more firmly against the wall. My legs wrap around his waist instinctively. I roll my hips against him, drawing a sharp inhale from him.

"Fuck, Lily," he breathes against my lips. "You're going to be the death of me."

"At least you'll die happy," I quip, breathless and dizzy with desire.

He chuckles, the sound dark and promising, before capturing my lips again in a kiss that's somehow even more intense than before. His hands knead my thighs, fingers digging in just enough to make me gasp, and I grind shamelessly against him, chasing the delicious friction.

His lips leave mine to trail along my jaw, then down my neck, finding a spot just below my ear that makes me whimper. He lingers there, alternating between gentle bites and soothing swipes of his tongue that have me arching against him, my fingers tangled in his hair.

"I need to taste more of you. Need to know if you're this delicious everywhere."

The words send a fresh wave of heat through me, pooling low in my belly and making me throb with want. When our mouths meet again, the kiss is hungry, almost desperate. His tongue strokes against mine in a way that replicates what he wants to do to me, and I tighten my legs around him involuntarily.

Archer carries me from the wall to the bed, never breaking the kiss. He lowers me gently onto the mattress, following me down until he's hovering above me, his weight supported on his forearms. His hair falls around my face like a curtain.

Thor hops off the bed and trots right next to the door, where he flops down and falls back asleep.

Archer's body fits perfectly against mine, his hips nestled between my thighs. He rocks against me, slow and deliberate, creating a friction that has me gasping into his mouth. One of his hands slides beneath the hem of my tank top, fingers splaying across my ribs, his thumb brushing the underside of my breast.

I arch into his touch, moaning, eager for more, but some last shred of sanity manages to break through the fog of desire. This is too much, too fast, too complicated. I place a hand on his chest, gently pushing.

"Wait," I say softly, my breathing still uneven.

He freezes instantly, then pulls back enough to look into my face. "Everything okay?" There's genuine concern in his gaze, no hint of frustration or disappointment.

"I just... I can't do this. Not tonight. Not with everything..." I gesture vaguely, unable to articulate the chaotic tangle of emotions I'm feeling.

For a moment, I think he might try to persuade me, but instead he presses a last, gentle kiss to my lips before sitting back on his heels.

"Rejection," he sighs dramatically, hand to his chest as if mortally wounded. "My one weakness."

Despite everything, I laugh. "You'll survive, I'm sure."

"Will I, though?" he asks, giving me an exaggerated pout. "I may need medical attention. CPR at the very least." He leans closer. "I've heard mouth-to-mouth is most effective."

I laugh again, pointing to the door, but I'm smiling too hard for my action to have any bite.

He stands, smoothing his rumpled shirt, and gives me a bow. "Whatever my lady desires." As he straightens, his expression softens into something more genuine. "Lily, I haven't felt like this for anyone else in... well, ever."

The simple honesty in his voice catches me off guard, making my heart flutter.

"That's just the whiskey talking," I deflect, suddenly uncomfortable with the vulnerability between us.

"Nope," he says, popping the *p* sound. "It's all you. The whiskey just gave me the balls to admit it." He moves backward toward the door, grinning. "Well, the drink and the knowledge that you've now kissed two-thirds of the household. I'm just evening the playing field."

Is he actually keeping score? The thought should be ridiculous, but with Archer, I can never be too sure. His smirk is lazy, all effortless confidence, but there's something sharp in his gaze, like he's testing the waters, waiting to see how I'll react.

I narrow my eyes, refusing to give him the satisfaction. Dangerous territory.

"Good night, Archer," I say, throwing a pillow at him, which he snatches from the air with infuriating grace.

"Sweet dreams." He grabs the doorknob. "I know mine will be starring you in various states of undress." With a last wink, he slips out, closing the door quietly behind him.

I flop back onto the bed, staring at the ceiling, my lips tender from his kisses, my body still humming with unfulfilled desire. What the actual hell am I doing?

It's like I've stepped into some alternate reality where I'm suddenly the kind of woman who does these things. The kind who straddles a near stranger during a drinking game, who pulls another into her bedroom at the first hint of attraction. The kind who attracts godlike Alphas. I barely recognize myself.

And yet... I can't bring myself to regret it. Not Hunter's kiss that ruined me. Not confronting James about his deception. And certainly not how perfectly Archer's body felt against mine.

I press my fingers to my lips, remembering the different ways they kissed me—Hunter's kiss starting gentle and building to something overwhelming, Archer's kiss immediately desperate and consuming—and I wonder, against my better judgment, what James's kiss would be like. Would it be calculated and controlled, like the man himself? Or would there be an unexpected wildness under that composed exterior?

The fact that I'm even thinking about this has me groaning and yanking a pillow over my face. This storm needs to break soon—before I do something truly reckless. As if falling for all three of them at once isn't already dangerous enough.

My best friend, Ruby, ended up with three men, and I won't lie—I was jealous when I found out. But what happens when the storm passes, the heat of the moment fades... and these mountain men I'm stuck with decide I was never meant to be theirs?

With the taste of Archer still on my lips and the memory of Hunter's hands on my body, I know sleep is a lost cause tonight. I might as well start planning how

I'm going to face them all at breakfast without spontaneously combusting from embarrassment.

Or worse, desire.

CHAPTER SIXTEEN

I can't sleep.

My skin feels too tight, as if it's containing something ready to burst. The sheets tangle around my legs as I toss and turn, my body refusing to cool down despite the cold air seeping through the cabin windows. It's 2:00 a.m., according to the glowing clock on the nightstand, and I've been staring at the ceiling for hours.

Every time I close my eyes, I see Hunter's and Archer's faces inches from mine, feel the ghost of their lips against mine, hands on my waist. Then the image shifts, and it's James's dark, possessive stare as he watches me kiss another man.

"God damn it," I mutter, kicking off the covers. "What is wrong with me?"

I pad across to the window and wrestle it open, immediately regretting the decision as icy wind and snow blast into my face. The storm hasn't let up at all;

if anything, it's intensified. The trees beyond the glass bend and sway like dancers caught in some frenzied ritual, snow swirling in hypnotic patterns.

I battle against the wind to close the window again, finally managing to slam it shut. I lean my forehead against the frigid glass, hoping it will cool my burning skin.

"Why am I so hot?" I whisper to the empty room. It's like my internal thermostat is broken. This has to be more than just the lingering effects of Hunter's kiss or the alcohol from earlier. It's like something inside me is awakening, something primal and hungry I'm not sure I can control.

Not heat. I refuse to consider that possibility.

My stomach growls, giving me a perfect excuse to leave the confinement of my room. Food. That's what I need—something cold from the fridge to cool me down and satisfy the gnawing emptiness inside.

Pulling on an oversized sweater over my sleep shorts and tank top, I quietly open my door. The hallway is dark and silent, everyone presumably asleep after our eventful evening. I tiptoe down the stairs, wincing at every creak of the wooden steps.

The living room is cast in deep shadows, the dying embers in the fireplace providing just enough light to make out shapes but not details. The howling wind outside masks my movements as I feel my way along the wall toward the kitchen.

When I reach it, I head straight for the fridge, squinting against the sudden brightness as I pull it open. The cool air is a blessing against my heated skin, and I take a moment just to stand there, letting it wash over me, before scanning the contents.

Strawberry yogurt. Perfect. I grab a container and turn around to see I'm not alone—and I freeze in place, nearly dropping the container.

A figure sits at the kitchen table in the dark, perfectly still, watching me. I blink, my sight slowly adjusting to see James slouched in a chair with a half-empty whiskey glass in front of him. The faint glow from the fridge highlights the sharp planes of his face, his eyes like deep pools reflecting tiny pinpricks of light.

"Fuck!" I gasp, clutching the yogurt to my chest. "You scared me. Creepy much? Do you often sit in the dark watching people?"

His lips curl into that infuriating half smile. "Only the interesting ones."

I roll my eyes, trying to mask how his voice—low and rough with late-night whiskey—affects me. "And what makes me so interesting? The fact that I like midnight snacks?"

"Among other things." He takes a slow sip of his drink.

I go to grab a spoon from a drawer. "Couldn't sleep either?" I ask, aiming for casual.

"How could I?" There's something dangerous in his tone that makes me glance his way.

He stands in one smooth motion, setting down his glass with a soft clink against the wooden table. His movements are deliberate as he approaches, like a predator who knows his prey has nowhere to run.

"It's been killing me," he says. "Watching you kiss him."

Before I can respond, his hand slams against the refrigerator door, closing it and plunging us into deeper darkness. I'm caught between his body and the counter near the fridge, his arms caging me in. I set the yogurt and spoon on the counter behind me.

"You did that to punish me, didn't you?" he asks, his face now inches from mine.

I can smell the whiskey on his breath, mingling with something darker, more primal—cedar and smoke and male. My heart hammers against my ribs, but I refuse to show fear.

"Maybe I did," I challenge. "You lied to me."

"I'm not the one who couldn't wait," he growls. "I was supposed to be your first kiss."

The crazy in his voice should alarm me, but instead, it has me intrigued. Which is insane. I barely know this man—except I do know him, don't I? All those late-night text conversations, those whispered confessions. The man who made me laugh when I couldn't sleep, who listened when I talked about my mother, who shared bits of his soul in the safety of digital distance.

"You've been mine since that wrong-number text," he whispers. "You know it."

I push against his chest, creating just enough space

to breathe. "You're insane, you know that? We texted for a few weeks. That doesn't make me yours."

"Doesn't it?" He doesn't move back, staying in my personal space. "Tell me you haven't thought about me every day since we started talking. Tell me you weren't disappointed when you realized I wasn't some random wrong number."

"I was pissed," I correct him. "Because you lied to me about who you were."

"I never lied about who I am," he insists, running a hand through his dark hair in frustration. "Just... didn't reveal certain details."

"Like prison? That seems like a pretty big detail to omit while we were playing the *Questions* game."

His jaw tightens. "What was I supposed to say? *By the way, Lily, I'm texting you from a prison cell. Hope that's cool?*"

"You could have told me. And that you were about to get out!"

"I was going to tell you," he says, eyes locked on mine in the dim light. "In person. I was planning how to meet you, how to explain everything. And then suddenly you're here, in the cabin, looking at me like I'm a stranger." He sighs, dropping his forehead to rest against mine in a gesture so intimate that it steals my breath. "I fucked up. Is that what you want to hear? I was a coward."

"Better," I murmur, aware of his proximity, the heat of him bleeding into me, making my already over-heated skin burn hotter.

"You're still punishing me," he accuses softly. "With Hunter. I saw the way you kissed him, Lily. That wasn't just a dare."

I should deny it, but I can't quite bring myself to lie. "Maybe I wanted to see if what we had was real or just some digital fantasy."

"And?" His breath fans across my lips. "What's the verdict?"

"The jury's still out," I say, trying and failing to sound unaffected. "Hunter is quite the kisser. I like him and Archer."

A low growl rumbles from his chest, and his hand comes up to cup my face, his thumb brushing roughly across my lower lip. "You want to drive me crazy, don't you? Is this payback?"

"Not everything is about you, James," I say, but I don't pull away from his touch.

"This is," he says with absolute certainty. "This— us—it's been building since that first text."

"There is no *us*," I protest weakly. "There's just a bunch of text messages and a lot of lies."

"Tell me you didn't feel something when we were talking every night," he challenges. "Tell me you didn't wait for my messages, think about what I might be doing, wonder what I looked like."

I swallow hard, remembering the nights I'd fallen asleep with my phone in my hand, screen glowing with his words. The way I'd smile like an idiot at his jokes. The way my heart had raced when conversations turned deeper, more intimate.

"That doesn't change anything," I insist. "You still lied."

"Then let me make it up to you," he says. "Let me show you who I really am. I'll tell you everything about how I got set up and sent to prison wrongly."

"So enlighten me," I challenge. "Who is the real James?"

"The same man you've been talking to for weeks," he grunts. "The one who knows you love true crime documentaries but have to sleep with the lights on afterward. The one who listened to you talk about your mother's lemon pound cake recipe that you can't quite get right. The one who told you things I've never told another soul."

My chest tightens at the reminder of those conversations, the intimacy we built message by message. I told him about nightmares that still plague me. He shared stories of his family, of feeling like an outsider his whole life, of dreams to start his own bakery shop one day and follow his passion. Things he'd never admitted to anyone.

"I didn't make that up, Lily," he continues. "That was real. All of it." His eyes search mine, as if gauging whether I can handle it. "I was stupid, trusting, and naive. I believed my cousin Rick needed me to pick him up one night, but I unknowingly became his getaway driver. Then he pissed off, the bastard, leaving me to face the cops. But I got him back, as I reported him to the police for having drugs at his place, and he's serving time across the country in another prison."

"That's something, I guess." I study his face in the dim light, trying to reconcile the man I thought I knew with this new information.

His hand slides to the nape of my neck, fingers threading through my hair. "How much longer, Lily? How much more do I have to pay?"

The heat of his touch sends sparks down my spine, and I have to fight to maintain clarity. "I don't know what you want from me."

"Yes, you do." His eyes drop to my lips. "The same thing you want from me."

I should push him away. Tell him to go to hell. Storm back upstairs and forget this conversation ever happened. Instead, I find myself swaying closer.

"This is a terrible idea," I whisper.

"The best ones always are." His other hand skates to my waist, pulling me closer. "I'm done with games, Lily. You're mine."

His dominance ignites something savage inside me. I grab his shirt, yanking him down to my level.

"Prove it," I challenge.

His mouth crashes down on mine, tension exploding into a kiss that's nothing like Hunter's gentle exploration. This is raw, demanding, obsessive. His lips claim mine with a brutality that matches the inferno burning through my veins.

I respond with equal fervor, fingers tangling in his hair, lifting myself up on tiptoes. We stumble about, our kiss never breaking. I knock the yogurt container off the counter. It clatters to the floor, but neither of us cares enough to stop.

"Been thinking about this," he growls against my neck, teeth scraping the sensitive skin. "Every night since we started talking."

"Shut up," I gasp, not wanting reminders of his deception now, not when his hands are doing wicked things to my body.

We move through the kitchen, knocking into chairs as we go. His mouth never leaves mine for long, returning again and again like he can't bear to be separated from me.

We crash into the living room, bumping against the coffee table hard enough to send magazines scattering across the floor. The sound seems impossibly loud in the quiet house, but I'm beyond caring if we wake the others.

James maneuvers us toward the couch, and we collapse onto it in a tangle of limbs. The impact knocks us off-balance, and we roll to the floor, landing in front of the fireplace. The movement stirs the embers, causing them to flare briefly, illuminating us on the rug.

He pins me beneath him, looking down with a savagery that steals my breath. His weight should feel oppressive, but instead, it grounds me against the storm of desire threatening to sweep me away.

"This is what I've imagined," he says. "What I've needed. Craved." His hand brushes hair from my face with surprising tenderness, a stark contrast to the desperation of moments before. "And I can't let you go now."

The words should terrify me. They should send me running. Instead, I pull him back down to me, surrendering and claiming all at once.

"Then don't," I whisper against his lips.

His mouth captures mine again, gentler this time, but no less controlling. His hands slide under my tank top, calloused fingers tracing patterns on my overheated skin. Every touch burns, feeding the inferno inside me rather than soothing it.

"Your body's fucking burning up," he murmurs. "You want me, don't you?"

"Yes," I gasp, the word ripped from somewhere primal inside me as his hand slides higher on my thigh. "God, yes."

"Say it again," he demands, teeth grazing my earlobe. "Tell me how much you want me."

"I need you," I whisper, fingers digging into his shoulders. "I've wanted you since before I knew your face."

He groans, the sound vibrating through his chest against mine. "That's right, baby. You're fucking mine. You've always been mine."

His hand slides between my legs, spreading them, and I gasp at the first touch against my pussy, hot even through the thin fabric of my sleep shorts.

"So wet for me already," he growls approvingly. "Been thinking about this for so long, Lily. Thinking about how you'd feel, how you'd taste."

Before I can process his words, he kneels between my legs, looking up at me with dark hunger.

"James, maybe we…" I start, but the words die in my throat as he hooks his fingers into the waistband of my shorts and underwear, dragging them down my legs in one swift motion.

Then he spreads my legs wider, his gaze lowering, his tongue sliding over his bottom lip with pure, unadulterated hunger.

"Fuck, look at you," he breathes. "So deliciously perfect."

The cool air hits my exposed skin. Then his mouth is on me, and I cry out, my back arching off the floor.

His hand immediately comes up to cover my mouth. "Gotta be quiet, baby," he warns, his breath hot against my sensitive flesh. "Unless you want company."

The thought of the others hearing, of being discovered like this, should mortify me. But it actually thrills me.

James returns, his tongue taking long strokes, sucking and flicking my clit. I bite down on his palm to keep from screaming as his tender nibbles send me convulsing with arousal.

My hips rock against his mouth. His free hand grips my thigh tight enough to bruise, holding me in place as he devours me—tongue plunging into me, lapping at me. I've never had a man go down on me. Sure, I've been fingered and played with, even had sex, but fuck me, nothing compares to a mouth devouring me.

It's soft, but starved, and I moan louder against his palm. My fingers tangle in his hair, needing more of him inside me as I struggle to stay quiet.

When he replaces his tongue with two fingers, pushing into me roughly, curling them to hit just the right spot while his tongue continues its relentless assault, fingering me hard, fast, I shatter. The orgasm crashes through me like the storm outside, my body trembling as he keeps pumping into me, keeps sucking on my clit.

"That's it," he murmurs against my thigh, pressing hot kisses to the sensitive skin. "Come harder for me."

I'm still shaking, floating, when the sound of a door opening upstairs cuts through my haze.

Heavy footsteps cross the hallway, and I try to pull away, suddenly aware of how exposed I am. James doesn't let me. Instead, he moves up my body.

"I have no issues sharing you with my friends," he whispers against my ear. "They're my everything. But you're mine first."

The words send a shiver down my spine—equal parts fear and arousal. What kind of man says something like that? And why does it turn me on so much?

After a moment, the bathroom door closes, and we hear the sound of running water.

"Hunter," James whispers, but there's no guilt in his expression—only a predatory intensity that makes my knees weak.

"So, you want to share me with them?" I whisper.

He grins. "You said it was your fantasy during truth or dare, right? Leaving us to have our way with you."

I'm still spread wide, legs now wrapped around his waist, thinking how much I might love having all three men. Except, am I just dreaming that this is anything more than us stuck in a cabin and losing control of our inhibitions?

"I... I'm not sure we should do more," I stammer, still trembling from the orgasm buzzing through my body. "Even this... God, this was incredible, but moving fast."

James chuckles, a dark sound that vibrates through his chest. "Too late for second thoughts, baby. But I can be patient." He pulls back onto his knees, his attention dipping between my thighs.

I blush, seeing the way he stares at me.

"You have such a pretty pussy." He reaches down and pushes the tips of his fingers into me. "I'm fucking dying to put my cock inside you." Then he sticks them into his mouth, licking them, eyes rolling back like he's in ecstasy.

A buzz tingles deep in my stomach at the sight of his enjoyment, but then in moments, he helps me to my feet before grabbing and handing me my shorts.

My legs threaten to give out, but I quickly get dressed.

Before I can respond, he scoops me into his arms, one arm under my knees, the other supporting my back. I yelp in surprise, clutching at his shoulders.

"What are you doing?" I hiss.

"Taking you to bed," he says simply, carrying me toward the stairs as if I weigh nothing.

He moves silently through the house, avoiding the creaky steps I stumbled over earlier. When we reach my room, he pushes the door open with his foot and carries me to the bed, laying me down with surprising gentleness.

"I'll be dreaming about the taste of you," he murmurs, pressing a kiss to my forehead that's almost tender. "About all the ways I'm going to fuck you."

The crude words spoken so softly have me shivering. I should be appalled. I should tell him to leave. Instead, I find myself reaching for him, pulling him down for one more kiss.

He allows it, and I taste myself in his mouth. It's almost sweet, the scent strong. He pulls back before the kiss can deepen.

"Dream of me," he commands, his thumb brushing across my swollen lips.

"Good night, James," I whisper, already feeling the loss of his burning warmth.

He backs toward the door, his gaze never leaving mine. "Good night, Lily."

As the door closes behind him, I curl onto my side, my body still humming with satisfaction and a rising hunger. Whatever this is between us—dark and twisted and needy—it's only just beginning.

CHAPTER SEVENTEEN
HUNTER

Something rips me from sleep at 6:07 a.m. with the subtlety of a chainsaw.

Not a sound. Not a dream. Just that gut-level instinct I've learned never to ignore—the same one that's kept me alive on mountain rescues when avalanches were imminent. Something in the cabin is wrong.

I lie still, listening to the storm rage. Fucking blizzard hasn't let up—if anything, it's angrier than last night, like nature is having a tantrum. The wind screams against the windows, the glass frosted over with ice crystals that distort the predawn darkness. No one's getting out today. We're sealed in, trapped together.

That thought drags my mind to Lily. Images from last night pulse through my consciousness—her thighs straddling my lap, her lips soft against mine, that little whimper she made when I deepened our kiss. The memory alone stiffens my cock uncomfortably against the mattress.

"Shit," I mutter, shoving myself upright and pulling on sweatpants. Thor raises his massive head from his bed in the corner, those ice-blue eyes too damn intelligent for comfort.

"Just checking the place," I tell him, as if I owe the animal an explanation. "Go back to sleep."

He yawns, unimpressed, but rises to follow me anyway. Loyal bastard.

The hallway stretches dark and quiet as I pad down it, but that nagging wrongness deepens with each step. I pause outside Lily's door, listening. Nothing.

I should keep walking. It's none of my fucking business if she's still sleeping.

"Lily?" I call softly, rapping my knuckles against the wood. No response.

I push the door open, peering inside. The bed is made. The bathroom door stands open, dark inside. Her phone sits on the nightstand, still charging. Her slippers remain neatly placed beside the bed as if awaiting feet that never arrived.

Thor glides past me, nose to the floor, circling the room once before looking up with a soft whine.

"Yeah, I don't like it either," I mutter.

That twist of concern in my gut tightens like a corkscrew. The rational part of my brain says she's fine —just somewhere else in this oversized cabin. But fifteen years of search and rescue work have taught me that unusual patterns mean trouble. People don't vanish from their rooms without cause. She must be with one of the guys.

I stride down the hall to James's room, finding him asleep and on his own. Next, I move to Archer's room to check if she's with him and knock on his door.

After what feels like an eternity, the door swings open. Archer stands there looking like hell warmed over—hair sticking up like he's been electrocuted, eyes narrowed to slits, wearing only boxer briefs. But he's alone.

"Someone had fucking better be dead, Hunt," he growls, voice sandpaper-rough with sleep.

"Lily's gone," I say without preamble.

His eyebrows climb toward his hairline. "Gone, as in..."

"Room's empty."

Something shifts in his expression—surprise giving way to a sharper focus. "Since when do you keep tabs on when houseguests go to take a piss?"

I ignore the jab. "We need to wake James."

"Jesus Christ," Archer mutters, but he grabs a shirt from the floor, sniffing it before dragging it over his head. "Fine. But if she's just raiding the pantry, I'm going to kick your paranoid ass."

James hasn't moved from where he's sprawled across his king-size bed, one arm flung over his head, the other disappearing beneath the sheets. The room reeks of whiskey and socks.

"Rise and shine, asshole," Archer calls out, flicking on the lights with unnecessary enthusiasm.

James doesn't move. Typical. He could sleep through the apocalypse.

I cross the room and give his shoulder a hard shove. "James. Up. Now."

He groans, rolling onto his back. "It's too damn fucking early. Someone had better be bleeding out."

"Lily's missing," I say, the word catching slightly in my throat.

That gets his attention. He sits up immediately, eyes suddenly clear and alert in a way that makes me wonder if he was really sleeping at all.

"What do you mean, *missing*?"

"Her room's empty. Bed is made up."

An expression I can't quite read flickers across his face. "That's... interesting," he says carefully.

"Interesting? That's your response?" I snap, suspicion blooming. "What do you know, James?"

He raises his hands defensively. "Nothing. Just thinking maybe she couldn't sleep after last night's... activities."

My jaw clenches. Does he know something about what happened after we all went to bed?

"Get dressed," I order. "We're finding her."

"Yes, sir," James mocks, reaching for jeans draped over a nearby chair. "Always the fucking Boy Scout, aren't you, Hunt?"

I don't wait for him to finish, already heading for the door with Thor trotting at my heels. I take the stairs two at a time, scanning the living room as I descend. The fire that was roaring when we all turned in has burned to embers. The couch pillows are slightly askew, and there's an empty whiskey glass on the coffee table that wasn't there before.

The kitchen is empty except for Thor, who immediately abandons the search to slurp noisily from his water bowl. Traitor.

"Check the rest of the downstairs," I tell James as he appears behind me, still buttoning his flannel shirt. "Archer, front door."

"Since when are you giving orders?" James mutters but moves to comply, checking the living room more thoroughly.

Archer examines the entrance, opening the door and bending to inspect the outside. "Snow's undisturbed. She didn't leave this way." He straightens, frowning. "Though, I'm not sure why she would step into a fucking blizzard, anyway."

"People do stupid shit when they're scared or confused," I say, thinking of the dozens of search and rescue missions that started with exactly that scenario. "Let's split up. Check everywhere. She's got to be here somewhere." My gut tightens, panic spinning out of control.

James gives me a sideways look, something calculating flaring over his features. "You're awfully worked up over a woman who can obviously take care of herself. She's been here, what, three days? And suddenly you're her keeper?"

"Fuck off," I growl, not in the mood for his mind

games. "She's in my home, which makes her my responsibility."

"Ooh, territorial," Archer chimes in with a smirk. "Someone's Alpha instincts are showing."

"Both of you... shut it and search," I snap, stalking toward the back of the house.

We move through the house, having known every inch of this place since we were teenagers. Archer takes the basement. James searches the office, library, and west-wing guest rooms. I recheck upstairs more thoroughly, looking in closets and storage spaces that a curious guest might explore.

Nothing.

"Find anything?" James's question comes through my phone, the forced casualness not quite masking his tension.

"Nothing upstairs," I reply, frustration bleeding into my tone. "This is fucking bizarre."

"Basement's clear," Archer reports. "No sign of our little Omega. Though, I did find that tequila bottle we lost at New Year's. Score."

Something about the way he says *Omega* sends a jolt through me—a possibility I hadn't fully considered. The timing would be... catastrophic.

"Meet me by the mudroom," I say abruptly, clicking off before they can respond.

Acting purely on instinct now, I head toward my laundry room adjacent to the mudroom. It's not a place anyone would normally wander, especially a guest.

The door is slightly ajar. I freeze, suddenly aware of

a warm, honeyed scent emanating from inside—subtle but unmistakable. My body responds instantly and violently, blood rushing south, muscles tensing, a primal recognition that bypasses conscious thought entirely.

"Oh, fuck," I breathe.

I push the door open slowly, confirming my suspicion with a single glance.

The laundry pile I'd dumped on the folding table the other day has been transformed into an elaborate nest. Clothes are artfully arranged in a circular pattern, with my clean sheets—the ones I keep on the shelf above the dryer—draped in a way that creates walls and a soft center. And in the middle of this carefully constructed refuge lies Lily.

She's curled on her side, deeply asleep, her chest rising and falling with steady breaths. Her oversized sweater has ridden up past her hips, exposing the pale skin of her thighs and the edge of black lace panties. One white ankle sock is half off her foot, the other missing entirely. Her dark brown hair spills across the sheets like ink, framing her flushed face.

Most telling of all, she's clutching my Henley shirt —the moss-green one I wore yesterday—pressed tightly under her face. Another of my shirts, the black thermal I wear for night rescues, is bunched between her thighs.

My cock hardens painfully at the sight, a response so intimate and powerful that it's almost embarrassing. The flush on her cheeks, the slight sheen of sweat on her brow despite the cool air in the room—all confirm what her choice of location and my clothing already tell me.

"Fuck me sideways," I whisper, backing out and pulling the door nearly closed.

I emerge from the laundry room, and Archer and James arrive within moments. The second they round the corner, their reactions shift—nostrils flaring, pupils dilating as they catch the scent I'm now acutely aware is permeating the hallway.

"She's going into heat," I say bluntly. There's no point in dancing around it.

The three of us exchange loaded glances, the air suddenly thick with testosterone, with grunts.

Archer sniffs again, more deliberately. "Early stages," he murmurs, running a hand through his sleep-mussed hair. "Probably started during the night. Explains the truth or dare enthusiastic kiss."

"And why she was so warm," James adds, a strange note in his tone that has me glaring at him. What does he know that we don't?

"The storm's not letting up for at least five more days," Archer says, glancing toward the nearest window, where nothing is visible beyond a wall of white. "We're completely snowed in."

I growl, pacing a few steps away and back. "A heat-triggered Omega and three unmated Alphas trapped in a remote cabin during a blizzard. This scene is going to escalate, and fast."

"Or it's the setup to a very specific kind of porn," Archer quips, earning a murderous glare from me.

"It's up to her," James says, surprisingly serious. "Her body, her choice."

"She won't be happy," Archer adds.

"Nobody touches her unless she explicitly asks," I say, the words coming out more growl than speech. "I fucking mean it. We're not animals."

"Speak for yourself," Archer mumbles, but there's no real challenge in it.

James steps closer, meeting my gaze directly. "We'll help her through this," he says quietly. "However she needs us. But you need to check that possessive bullshit at the door, Hunt. You don't have any claim on her over us."

I want to argue, but he's right, damn him. I have no claim beyond a kiss that was part of a drinking game. The fact that my clothes are the ones she chose to nest with means nothing—I own this cabin, so my scent would naturally be most dominant.

"This isn't fucking about us," I state. "Let's focus on what she wants."

We back away from the door, huddling in the hallway so as not to wake her up.

"She needs to stay comfortable. Warm," I murmur, mentally cataloging the cabin's supplies.

"Food, water, pain meds," Archer adds. "Some Omegas get killer cramps in the early stages."

James nods. "And options. Real options, not just us throwing ourselves at her."

"What do you mean?" I ask, though I already know.

"Suppressants," James says. "If she wants them. Toys if she'd rather handle it alone. Safe spaces she can lock us out of."

"Jesus, James, she's not a prisoner needing escape routes," Archer says.

"She's an Omega in heat with three Alphas she barely knows," James counters sharply. "Trust me, she'll want options."

I take charge, as I always do in crisis situations. "I'll get food and drinks ready. Protein, sugar, hydration."

"I'll gather blankets, extra pillows, more nesting materials," Archer volunteers. "Maybe grab some of her own clothes from her room too. Familiar scents help. I'll set up a new nest for her that isn't in the laundry room."

"I'll check the backup generator and bring in more firewood," James says. "If the power goes out during this, we're well and truly fucked."

We disperse to our tasks like a well-oiled machine. In the kitchen, I begin preparing an elaborate spread—cheeses, cured meats, fruits, chocolate, nuts. Instinct drives me to provide, to care for, to demonstrate my value as an Alpha. I boil water for tea, prep the coffee maker, and then arrange juice and water bottles on a tray.

Archer enters as I'm slicing aged cheddar, his arms laden with blankets and pillows. He dumps them on a kitchen chair and eyes my preparations critically.

"You know what she actually needs isn't a five-star brunch, right?" he says, leaning against the counter. "She needs an Alpha knot. Cocks. Preferably three."

"She will work that out on her own terms."

"All I'm saying is, be prepared for her not to want your little picnic here," he states.

James comes in from outside just then, bringing a sharp blast of cold air and the scent of snow with him. His hair is dusted with white, his cheeks ruddy from the biting wind.

"Generator's good," he reports, setting down an armload of firewood. "Filled it up. Should last three days even with continuous use." He brushes snow from his coat. "You know not every Omega rushes straight into the desperate stage, right? Some take time to transition. Maybe we just take turns, giving her all the pleasure she desires. Put our tongues and cocks to good use."

"That's what I've been trying to tell him," Archer mutters.

"So we pamper her. Take care of her basic needs. And make it clear that we're here if she wants us, but we're not expecting anything unless she wants to," James adds.

"When did you become an expert on Omega care?" Hunter asks, arching an eyebrow.

Something dark passes across Archer's features. "I've been around," he says vaguely. "Learned a few things."

I watch him out of the corner of my eye as I arrange

food on a wooden platter. "Well, we offer her all of it, and she can pick and choose."

Archer turns to James. "Speaking of last night… we all good after what happened? Things got pretty heated."

James shrugs with exaggerated casualness. "That kiss? Please. It was a dare, not a marriage proposal."

My knuckles whiten around the knife handle. We all know he's not talking about Lily kissing me. There was history in the way they interacted, tension that went beyond physical attraction.

Archer notices my reaction. "That's not what I meant, and you know it."

James's expression sobers. "We talked afterward. It's complicated."

"What's complicated?" I ask, unable to stop myself despite knowing I'm walking into his trap.

"I never meant to hurt her," James says quietly, something like genuine regret in his words.

"No one ever does," I reply, the words bitter on my tongue.

"I fucked up," he says finally. "I know I did. And I'm going to make it up to her."

Something in his tone has me studying him more carefully. This isn't the usual James—smooth, savvy, always in control. There's a rawness to him I rarely see.

"I like her," he continues, still facing away from us. "Like, a fucking lot." He turns around, meeting first my stare, then Archer's. "And I know you two do as well. It's growing on you both, but I'm already too far gone."

He shakes his head, a humorless laugh escaping him. "Addicted to her, and it's not just the Omega thing. It's her."

Archer leans against the refrigerator, arms crossed. "Well, shit."

"Yeah," James agrees. "Shit."

"How long were you texting?" I ask, curiosity overriding my earlier anger.

"Six weeks," James admits. "Started as a wrong number, then we kept talking." A ghost of a smile crosses his face. "She made me laugh when nothing else could."

I've never seen James like this about a woman. Hookups, sure. Casual flings, plenty. But this vulnerability? Never.

"We've known each other our whole lives," James says, looking between Archer and me. "You two are the only real family I've got. So I'm telling you both straight—she matters. This isn't just about getting her through her heat."

Archer nods slowly. "Noted."

I study James for a long moment. We've been through hell together, the three of us. Shared everything—pain, loss, triumph, women. This is different, though. This feels like a line being drawn. A look into the future, instead of just today.

"I hear you," I say finally. "But remember—it's her choice. All of this. Who she wants, how she wants it."

"Of course," James states immediately. "Always her choice."

An understanding passes between us, unspoken but clear. We will all care for her during this heat, but what comes after—that's for Lily to decide.

"All right, enough with the feelings," Archer mutters, breaking the tension. "Let's finish getting this shit together for our girl."

Our girl. The phrase settles between us, and I like the sound of it.

We gather our supplies—the food tray, drinks, extra blankets, hot-water bottles, pain medication—and head back toward the laundry room. Archer carries a stack of pillows, trailing behind me.

"Think this is enough for her nest until we move her upstairs?" he asks.

"She'll rearrange everything anyway," I reply, leading us down the hall. "Omegas always do."

James follows with water bottles and a bottle of whiskey I hadn't seen him grab. "How did none of us notice she was approaching heat? We're not exactly inexperienced."

I pause, considering. "The storm. Barometric pressure changes can mask pheromones. Plus, she might be on suppressants that only just failed."

"Or the alcohol last night accelerated things," Archer suggests. "Wouldn't be the first time alcohol triggered an unexpected heat."

As we approach the laundry room door, a sound from within stops us in our tracks. A low, pained moan filters through the door, followed by another that sounds more distressed.

All three of us freeze, exchanging alarmed looks.

The moans intensify, sounding like genuine discomfort or pain.

"Fuck, she's hurting," I say, setting down the tray so fast that items slide off it. I reach for the door handle, protective instincts overriding everything else.

"Wait—" James starts, grabbing for my arm, but I'm already shoving the door open.

The sight that greets us isn't what I expected.

Lily isn't writhing in pain. She's awake, pressing my shirt to her face and inhaling deeply. Her body moves against another bunched piece of my clothing between her thighs, seeking friction. The sounds we heard weren't ones of pain at all—they were moans of pleasure mixed with frustration.

She pauses at our entrance. For one suspended moment, we all stare at each other, the air electric with wanton desires and embarrassment.

Her face blushes, but she doesn't move to cover herself or bolt from the nest she's created. Instead, her eyes lock with mine, pupils wide, lips parting and glistening.

"Hunter," she whispers, my name on her lips like a prayer—or a demand.

Behind me, I hear James exhale sharply. Archer mutters, "Holy fucking shit," under his breath.

I know, in that moment, that whatever happens next will irrevocably change everything between all of us. And I can't wait.

CHAPTER EIGHTEEN

LILY

My vision swims, the edges blurry and distorted like I'm underwater. The door to the room opens, flooding the space with light that hurts my eyes. Three tall silhouettes appear. For a moment, I wonder if I'm hallucinating—if the fever burning through my veins has finally pushed me over the edge into delirium.

I blink slowly, struggling to focus. My mind feels wrapped in cotton, thoughts sticky and disconnected. I clutch Hunter's discarded Henley tighter to my chest, burying my nose in the fabric. The scent grounds me and provides comfort that eases the burning under my skin. I've been huddled in this laundry nest for hours to lower the ache, fully aware of what I'm doing, but it's as though something in my mind clicked and I just needed to be surrounded by the Alphas' scents. I couldn't stop if I tried.

I remember the compulsion that drove me here—

the overwhelming need to surround myself with the three Alphas' scents and to create a safe space.

The air changes as they enter the room, becoming thick and heavy with their combined scents. Something deep within me stirs in response, and pain intensifies between my thighs. I press Hunter's shirt more firmly against my face, inhaling deeply to steady myself.

James approaches first, slowly. He kneels beside my nest, close enough that I can feel the heat emanating from his body.

"How are you feeling, Lily?" he asks gently.

Hunter hovers behind him, his expression unreadable, but tension radiates from his rigid jaw. Archer circles to my other side, studying me, head tilted slightly.

I struggle to form words, my throat bone-dry. "I feel... hot. Strange." My voice sounds foreign to my own ears.

Their scents make my head spin.

"Why do you all smell so... yummy?" I whisper, unable to stop myself.

James exchanges a significant look with the others before turning back to me. "Hey, baker girl, we think you might be going into heat."

I stare at him, the words not making sense at first. Then I laugh.

"Don't be crazy. I don't react to Alphas. Everyone knows that. This isn't—"

"I'm going to dispute that theory," Archer interrupts, gesturing to the elaborate nest I've constructed. "People who don't react to Alphas don't typically barricade themselves in laundry rooms with stolen clothes."

Something hungry and primal envelops me, and I shiver despite the fever raging through me. I glance down, knowing I've wrapped their clothes around me like armor and pressing another shirt between my thighs for relief. It's the only way to stop the ache.

But is that heat?

"So, you think it's really happening because—" I gasp, hugging Hunter's shirt tighter. "I'm stuck here with you three during a blizzard, and if I'm going into heat..." I can't finish the thought, the implications too overwhelming.

Hunter steps forward, crouching low in front of me, near James. "We'll look after you."

His words carry a weight beyond simple caretaking. My body responds with a rush of heat between my legs.

"I brought the couch cushions in here," I blurt out, gesturing to the far corner of the laundry room. "And the ottoman from the living room. I don't know why. I just... needed them."

James nods, a knowing look in his eyes. "You were building a proper nest. It's instinct."

"I'm not nesting," I insist, even as I smooth the edge of a sheet I've carefully arranged. "I just needed... something."

I watch through half-lidded eyes as they arrange their offerings around me—plates of food, bottles of water, more blankets and pillows. My focus keeps slipping, drawn repeatedly to the movement of their hands, the flex of muscles under clothing, and the fullness of their lips as they speak.

Archer gestures to my arrangement. "You've done well, but I can build you a better one. Something more comfortable, more secure."

I shake my head adamantly, a surge of possessiveness washing over me. "No, this is fine. I'm just fine here." I run my hand over the carefully constructed layers. "I'm not nesting. You're nesting."

As soon as the childish retort leaves my lips, I catch myself. What am I saying? I lift Hunter's shirt to my nose again, inhaling deeply. The masculine scent sends a wave of calm through me, momentarily dampening the fire under my skin.

"God, I'm losing my mind," I mutter. "It's like I'm hallucinating. And I have this pain in my stomach." My hands press against my abdomen, where a hollow ache has been building for hours. "It's not like cramps; it's like… emptiness." I look up at them, vulnerability washing over me as I admit, "These scents are what keep me calm." I gesture to the clothes surrounding me.

"Alpha smells." James nods knowingly. "Your Omega side is responding."

Sure, biologically, I'm an Omega, but I've never experienced the stereotypical reactions, the overwhelming responses to Alpha pheromones that are supposed to define the dynamic.

Until now.

The change is instant, like a storm breaking over me—wild and all-consuming. My skin prickles, heat blooming beneath my collar. My breath falters, heart racing too fast for my chest to contain. It's not just instinct; it's them. Their scent of strength, of something untamed, coils around me like smoke, weakening me.

Panic stirs in my chest. I can't let this control me. I can't—

"You okay?" Hunter's voice breaks through the haze, low and steady. Concern sharpens his tone. "You're breathing kinda fast."

"I'm fine," I lie.

"You sure?" His gaze sharpens, his brows knitting. "I can leave if you—"

"No!" The word escapes too fast, too desperately. My face burns. "I mean... I'm good. Really."

Hunter watches me a beat longer, then exhales through his nose like he's debating whether to push. Instead, he leans closer, his fingers reaching for me— slowly enough to give me time to pull away.

His hand brushes my brow, gentle and careful. His fingers are rough, calloused—strong enough to break me, yet somehow impossibly tender. His touch is electric, both cooling and burning simultaneously.

Without thinking, I capture his hand before he can withdraw, bringing it to my nose and inhaling deeply. My eyes flutter closed at the concentrated scent of him —earth, pine, and something uniquely male.

It's grounding and intoxicating all at once. My pulse skips, and for the first time since I woke up this morning, I don't feel like I'm drowning.

A sound escapes me, half sigh, half moan. My tongue darts out, tasting the salt of his skin before I can stop myself. The flavor explodes across my taste buds, and I moan again, louder this time.

"Oh God, I'm in so much trouble, aren't I?" I whisper, not really asking.

I curve toward Hunter instinctively, making soft sounds I've never heard from my own throat before. The ache grows, a throbbing emptiness that demands to be filled.

"Join me, please?" The words spill out unbidden, needy and raw.

"You can't say no, Hunter." Archer's words cut through my haze, an edge to his tone.

Hunter's eyes darken. "Have no intention to."

James stares at me with a darkness in his gaze, and part of me toys with the notion of dragging all three with me in here.

Hunter slides into the nest behind me, careful not to disturb my arrangement, distracting my thoughts. His chest presses against my back, arms encircling me, and the relief is immediate and overwhelming. I melt against him, sighing as some of the tension leaves my body.

"That feels right," I murmur. "The ache is... less."

My body fits against his perfectly, as if designed to complement him. The hard planes of his chest and stomach mold against my back, his thighs supporting mine. His heartbeat thumps strong and steady, slightly faster than normal.

Then there's his arousal near my rear, and instead of being alarmed, I find myself shifting subtly, seeking more contact. A low growl rumbles from his throat, vibrating through me.

"Sorry," I whisper, not sorry at all. "I can't seem to... control myself."

James and Archer just stare at us.

"We'll leave you for now," Archer says. "Let you settle in."

James doesn't move at first, then nods. "We'll prepare more comfortable nest arrangements. For all of us."

A flare of arousal washes over me at the thought of all three of them surrounding me, their scents mingling with mine.

Hunter's chest rumbles against my back. "Don't take too long."

James smirks. "Wouldn't dream of it."

"Try not to start without us," Archer adds, gathering blankets.

I study them through my haze, understanding dawning about what's coming. What we're all hurtling toward, inevitable as gravity.

As they turn to leave, a spike of panic shoots through me. "James," I call out.

He turns back, eyebrow raised in question.

"Soon, I'll need your tongue again," I blurt out, the

filter between my brain and my mouth completely vanishing.

The room goes still. Hunter stiffens behind me, and Archer's head whips around so fast I'm surprised he doesn't hurt himself.

"Again?" Archer repeats, his gaze darting between James and me.

James merely grins, a slow, satisfied expression spreading across his face. "Soon, baker girl. When you're ready for all of us."

"What the fuck happened last night?" Hunter demands, his arm tightening around my waist.

James shrugs, not bothering to hide his smugness. "A gentleman doesn't kiss and tell."

The memory of us by the fireplace, of his mouth working between my thighs, flashes vividly through my mind. My body responds instantly, and a rush of wetness makes me squirm against Hunter.

"You bastard," Hunter mutters, but there's something besides anger in his voice—a dark heat that matches the one building inside me.

"Later," Archer says firmly, pushing James toward the door. "We've got work to do."

They leave, closing the door behind them, and suddenly, it's just Hunter and me in the nest I've built. His lips press against my neck, warm and surprisingly gentle.

"You are so beautiful like this," he murmurs. "Wild and unguarded."

I laugh weakly. "I feel like a mess. I can't think

straight unless I'm near you or your scent." My fingers trace aimless patterns on his arm. "I barely slept last night, but once I woke, I was... overwhelmed. This need to be surrounded by things from all three of you. Your smells." Panic rises. "Please don't leave me."

His arms tighten. "I won't."

Something about the safety of his embrace, the security of being held so firmly, breaks open a vulnerability I usually keep tightly contained.

"Growing up, I had this fear of being left... after my mother died," I confess quietly. "My dad did his best, but he was devastated. Sometimes, I felt invisible." I turn slightly to see his face. "Then no Alpha would react to me. Like I was truly invisible. They might've dated me, but I had no effect on them. None." The memory of rejection burns almost as hot as the fever in my veins. "One guy told me I *might as well be a Beta* for all the reaction I got from him. Another suggested I see a doctor because, clearly, something was wrong with my pheromones."

I curl tighter into myself, the old hurt still raw despite the years. "I eventually stopped trying. Decided maybe they were right—something in me was broken."

Hunter's hand strokes my arm soothingly. "Maybe it wasn't the right time," he suggests. "Or maybe they weren't the right men. Because the moment you walked in, you blew us all away. Your scent, your presence." A confession rumbles from his chest. "Now, we're obsessed."

I feel the truth of it in the tension of his body, the careful way he holds me—restraining himself even as he provides comfort.

"But no rush," he adds, his tone shifting to reassuring. "We'll take it easy. Ready when you are."

I stiffen slightly at the implication. "Ready for rutting, right? Knotting me?"

The crude words hang between us.

Hunter's breath hitches. "Does it scare you?"

I consider lying, then decide against it. What's the point of pretense now when I'm literally nesting in his clothing?

"Fuck yeah," I admit. "What if I can't get enough during the heat?"

His chuckle vibrates through me. "That's not a problem, trust me."

His hand spans my waist, large and warm. "Not between the three of us... if that's what you want. All of us."

"Yes," I say, almost too quickly. Then I amend, "Yes, please."

The words taste foreign on my tongue, but once they're out, there's no taking them back. Heat rushes to my face, my skin burning as if I've just stripped myself bare.

Three.

I've gone from believing something was wrong with me—from wondering why my Omega side never reacted the way it was supposed to, why no Alpha ever stirred more than fleeting interest—to suddenly feeling everything all at once. And not for one Alpha... but for three. The thought leaves me breathless, a wild mix of nerves.

What if I can't handle it? What if this is too much, too fast?

But underneath the anxiety, there's a flicker of relief. Because I've wanted this. The hunger that's been gnawing at me since I walked into this cabin, the tension simmering just beneath my skin. I can't deny it anymore.

"I've been with a man before but felt almost nothing," I confess. "When we were together... it was fine but never intense. Never overwhelming. I thought maybe I just had a low sex drive."

"It wasn't your path." His fingers trace my collarbone, leaving fire in their wake.

His voice dips lower, rough with promise.

"Don't worry, cute angel. We will do things to you that you'll never forget."

My breath stutters. Those words should terrify me, and maybe once, they would have. But now? Now I'm burning for exactly that.

Heat pools between my legs at his promise.

"God, it's getting worse," I gasp, feeling a cramp roll through my abdomen. "I need... I don't know what I need."

That's a lie. I know exactly what I need. I need to be fucked, claimed, taken. A thought that I would normally bauk at, but instead, it sends another wave of heat through my core.

I shift against him restlessly, my hips moving of their own accord, seeking friction against the hardness pressing into my lower back. His arm tightens around my waist, stilling my movements.

"Easy," he murmurs, but I can hear the strain in his words. "Let's not rush."

"I can't help it," I whimper, my body betraying me with every passing moment. "It's like there's this... beast inside me. And it's getting stronger."

Behind us, the storm continues to rage, snow piling against the small window high on the laundry room wall. We're trapped here, all of us, for who knows how long.

Hunter's breathing changes, growing deeper and more controlled. His scent sharpens too, becoming more potent, and I realize he's fighting his own battle against ravaging me this very moment.

I turn to face him, needing to see his expression.

His eyes have changed, pupils wide. The warm blue has darkened to something more primal, more dangerous.

I reach up to touch his face, drawn to the intensity I see there.

He captures my wrist and brings it to his mouth, his teeth grazing my pulse point. The sensation shoots straight to my pussy, covered in tingles, making me gasp.

"I can easily forget myself around you," he confesses. "It comes with a kind of obsession that makes me want to kill any strangers for looking at you."

The darkness in his eyes promises both pleasure and pain, and I should be scared by the possession I see there. Instead, I find myself leaning into it, longing for it.

"Maybe I want you to forget yourself," I challenge, my own tone barely recognizable—husky, demanding.

His grip tightens on my wrist, his stare darkening.

"I'm so tired of being careful," I whisper. "Of controlling myself. Of feeling nothing." I press closer to him, my free hand sliding up his chest to curl around the back of his neck. "Make me feel something, Hunter. Make me forget everything but this."

His control snaps with an almost audible sound. His mouth crashes down on mine, hard and demanding, nothing like the gentle kiss we shared during the game. This is possession, claiming, devouring. His tongue sweeps into my mouth, and I open to him willingly, eagerly.

The taste of him is intoxicating, amplifying the fever in my blood. My body responds with a rush of heat and wetness between my thighs. I moan into his mouth, pressing closer, needing more contact, more friction, more of everything.

His hands are everywhere—tangling in my hair, sliding down my back, gripping my hips. He rolls us so I'm beneath him, his weight a delicious pressure pinning me to the nest I've created. The feeling of being surrounded by him—his scent, his heat, his strength—feeds something raw inside me.

He breaks the kiss to trail his lips down my neck, teeth biting the sensitive skin where my pulse pounds. I arch against him, offering more access, tilting my head in a gesture of submission that comes naturally, instinctively.

"Mine," he growls against my throat, the word buzzing through my skin.

"Yes," I gasp, the admission torn from somewhere deep and honest.

His hand slides under my sweater, calloused palm rough against the sensitive skin of my stomach. I suck in a breath as his fingers trace higher, brushing the underside of my breast.

I moan, desperate for him.

He groans, capturing my mouth again as his hand cups my breast fully, his thumb gliding across my nipple. Pleasure spirals through me, sharper and more intense than anything I've ever felt. Every nerve ending seems to have moved closer to the surface, every touch magnified beyond reason.

My hands fist in his shirt, tugging impatiently. "Off," I demand. "Need to feel you."

He pulls back just enough to yank his shirt over his head, revealing the muscles of his chest. I reach up immediately, fingers tracing the defined lines, exploring the dusting of hair that narrows across his chest. He's beautiful—all strength and burning hot, skin golden in the dim light. When my fingers reach the waistband of his sweatpants, he captures my wrist again.

"Slow down," he says. "We have time."

"It feels like we don't," I confess. "Like I'll burn alive if you don't touch me. All of me."

The need is overwhelming, a physical ache that grows with each passing minute. My hips shift restlessly, seeking friction, release.

Hunter's eyes darken further. "It might be more comfortable for you if I carry you to my bedroom."

I can't articulate it, not really. It's the rawness of this moment, the unbridled need that has stripped away all pretense. I don't want to lose that. I don't want to dilute it with the change of scenery in his bedroom.

"Here," I whisper. "I... I want it to be here."

He studies my face, his eyes searching for understanding. Then, slowly, a smile spreads across his face, a smile that's equal parts tenderness and primal hunger.

"Here," he repeats. "You want me right here, surrounded by laundry and the scent of detergent?"

I nod, my cheeks burning. "Yes," I whisper. "Please."

"As you wish," he murmurs with a grin. "But I'm warning you, pretty angel. Once we start, there's no going back."

I swallow hard, the adrenaline coursing through me.

"I know," I say. "I don't want to go back."

Heat radiates from his body against mine as his hands reach for the hem of my sweater, his fingers skimming my skin. He pulls it up slowly, deliberately, his gaze never leaving mine. The cool air on my skin is a delicious contrast to the burning heat within me.

His knuckles brush against my breasts, over my tight nipples.

My body pushes toward him like I have zero control.

Then he pulls the sweater over my head, tossing it carelessly onto the pile of clothes beneath us. His eyes roam over my exposed breasts, lingering on my hard, aching nipples.

"Beautiful," he breathes. "Absolutely beautiful."

He reaches out, one hand cupping a breast, his mouth wrapping around the other one, sucking my nipple, his tongue flicking it. The sensation is exquisite. My hips are already rocking, my body buzzing from the arousal cascading through me.

"Tell me what you want," he whispers against my skin.

"To be tied up," I gasp, the word barely audible. "I want... you touching me. Everywhere. Fucking me."

He chuckles, a growly sound, as he shifts above me. The heat of his body presses into mine, a delicious weight that has me arching instinctively. His hands skim over my skin before reaching down, rummaging through the scattered clothes beneath us. Then, fabric —soft, worn cotton—slides against my wrists.

I barely have time to process before he gathers my

hands, bringing my wrists above my head and binding them together with the shirt.

"I won't tie you to anything," he murmurs. "Not your first time with me, okay, angel?"

The endearment leaves me purring for him, batting my eyes at him. I test the hold, my fingers flexing against the makeshift restraint, and a soft, needy sound slips from my lips.

The unbearable, all-consuming need is addictive. I purr again, pressing my thighs together, desperate for friction, for relief.

"Then make me yours," I whisper, my body already his to ruin.

He leans back just enough to admire his work—my wrists bound, my body flushed and trembling beneath him. A grin pulls at his lips, his gaze dragging over me like he's savoring every inch. Not just looking—devouring.

His fingers hook into the waistband of my shorts and underwear, dragging them down slowly, as if he's unwrapping something rare, something meant only for him.

"You are everything I need." His voice is rough, but there's something almost reverent beneath it, something that makes my breath hitch.

He doesn't rush. Instead, he runs his palms over my bare thighs, spreading warmth and anticipation like a brand. His touch is slow, deliberate, mapping me with a kind of aching appreciation that has me trembling before he's even fully touched me.

"Every inch of you, angel." His lips brush my hip, his breath a wicked promise. "Every fucking inch is mine to taste, to worship, to claim."

My back arches, my hands above my head flexing in their restraints as he takes his time, his mouth exploring—pressing kisses, dragging his tongue in teasing strokes, nipping just enough to cover me in goose bumps.

He settles between my thighs, his hands firm yet tender as they spread me wider. The anticipation is unbearable, my entire body strung tight, aching for more. Then his gaze meets mine, dark and filled with something deeper than hunger. Something savage.

"You want me to take you?" he murmurs. "I want to feel you fall apart first."

I whimper, my body thrumming, heat pooling so fiercely I think I might shatter before he even pushes inside.

"Then stop teasing," I gasp, my head tipping back. I'm panting, my hips rocking, and I let my knees drop wider. "I need you."

His smile is slow, knowing. "Oh, angel," he breathes, bringing his hand to the apex of my inferno and spreading me with two fingers.

I groan. The touch, the desperation, is destroying me.

"I love how pink you are, how much you glisten." Then he drives two fingers into me, thick, long fingers that stretch me, and I cry out. Fuck me, but that's what I need.

My bound hands flex, fingers twitching as if they're desperate for something—anything—to hold on to. I arch, instinctively reaching, and my fingertips brush against the cold metal edge of the washing machine behind me. I grip it, the hard surface grounding me.

Hunter isn't gentle. I knew it the moment his hands claimed my thighs, the way he nudged me wider, his fingers pumping into me, causing that unrelenting stretch. He watches, completely focused, his grin dark and devastating as his fingers keep vanishing into me.

"So fucking beautiful," he murmurs, staring at me like he's looking at something priceless, something that belongs to him.

Pleasure coils tighter, spiraling higher, my breath coming in short, desperate gasps. I'm teetering right there—so close, so damn close.

Then he stops.

"No... don't stop!" I cry out, my hips rocking instinctively toward him, chasing the sensation, the release I was seconds from shattering into.

But he's already on his feet, leaving me aching, exposed, completely at his mercy.

Every line and ridge of muscle cuts like he was sculpted just for sin. My mouth goes dry. The way his abs flex, the deep V leading lower—he's beautiful in a way that steals breath, the kind that makes you forget your own name.

His hands move to his belt, the soft clink of metal snapping me out of my haze. My pulse thunders as he pushes his jeans down, leaving nothing between us. Nothing to hide how much he wants this—wants me.

Then he's kneeling, spreading my thighs farther apart, his hands gripping my hips as though I'm something to be savored. His gaze lifts, locking on to mine, full of promise, possession, and the wicked intent of a man about to make me his.

"Now," he breathes. "Let's see how long you can hold on."

My breath stutters, my body thrumming with the unbearable need he's just denied me. There's no mercy behind his eyes. Just heat, possession, the kind of brutality that promises I won't be the same once he's done with me.

His hands grip my hips, thumbs pressing into my skin as he drags me forward, pulling me closer until I'm right where he wants me. I'm trembling, my bound hands still clutching the back edge of the washing machine, trying to ground myself, to steady my thoughts, but it's impossible.

Not when he's looking at me like that.

"You have no idea what you do to me, do you?" he murmurs, and the rasp of it sends shivers through me. "All spread out for me, desperate, already shaking."

I purr. My thighs flexing, but his grip tightens, keeping me still. He's savoring this, taking his time, watching me lose myself beneath him.

And I am.

Every nerve in my body is alive, burning, my mind a haze of pleasure and frustration. The ache between my legs is unbearable, my body so primed, so ready, that I could shatter the moment he touches me again.

"Hunter…" I breathe his name, barely a sound, more a plea.

"That's it, angel." A slow smirk curves his lips, but there's something dangerous in it—something that tells me he isn't done playing with me yet. "Let me hear you."

Then, without warning, his mouth is on me.

My back arches, fingers clenching around the washing machine's edge as sensation slams into me. His tongue moves slowly, teasing, tasting, driving me higher and higher until I'm shaking apart.

I can't think, can't breathe, can't do anything but feel.

My thighs tremble as the coil inside me winds so tight I know I'm seconds from falling over the edge. I let out a gasping moan, my body tensing, ready to explode—

Then he pulls away.

I nearly sob at the loss, my hips jerking toward him, desperate for more, for anything to push me past the breaking point.

Hunter just watches me, his lips glistening, his smirk all dark satisfaction. "Not yet," he commands. "I want you completely undone when I finally take you."

I'm a trembling mess beneath him. "Please," I whisper, pride be damned.

His gaze darkens, and something shifts in him, something dangerous and unrelenting.

"Say it again," he growls.

I swallow hard, my pulse a frantic, stuttering beat. I've never felt this raw, this stripped bare, this completely at someone's mercy.

"Please, Hunter," I whisper again, my body burning. "I need you."

His breath shudders out, as if he's barely holding himself back. Then, in one fluid motion, he rises above me, positioning himself between my thighs, the heat of his cock pressing against my aching entrance.

He reaches up, unties my hands with a careful tug, and then brings my wrists down, pinning them beside my head. His fingers lace with mine, his grip firm, possessive.

His mouth brushes against my ear.

"Then hold on tight, angel, because I'm about to give you everything you've been begging for."

And then, he's inside me.

Fast, harsh, and... oh God, he's enormous. I cry out.

I can't do anything but arch beneath him. Hunter doesn't just take—he stakes his claim. And I feel it in every slow, deliberate inch as he buries himself inside me.

A groan rumbles through his chest, his forehead pressing to mine.

"Finally," he growls. "I've been waiting to feel you like this... wrapped around me, my cock buried inside this little pussy."

A shudder rolls through me, and I whimper, my body pulsing around him.

"Shh, angel," he soothes, rocking into me with slow, devastating thrusts. "You think I'm letting you go now?" He chuckles, dark and low, his lips brushing the edge of my ear. "Not a fucking chance."

His grip shifts, releasing my hands. His fingers trace along my arms, over my ribs, down to my hips, where he then holds me steady as he thrusts deeper, dragging pleasure through my body like fire licking at my skin.

"I'm going to fuck you every which way," he mutters. "Bent over the counter, legs wrapped around my waist. Facedown in my bed, where I'll keep you for hours. On your hands and knees, letting me watch as you come all over my cock."

A wrecked moan leaves me, my body trembling beneath him, every filthy promise making the heat coil tighter inside me.

"I'll have you in the shower, slick and dripping, my hands in your hair as I fuck you against the glass." His lips drag over my jaw, sending a full-body shiver through me. "On the floor, on the stairs, in my truck while I make you scream my name for anyone passing by."

My head spins. It's too much and not enough, all at once.

He shifts, rolling his hips in a way that makes stars explode behind my eyes. I gasp, my back arching, and he grins down at me, drinking in every reaction.

"See, angel?" His fingers tilt my chin, forcing my

dazed gaze to his. "You're mine now. My perfect little Omega."

I barely register the words before he thrusts harder, sending me spiraling, his name tearing from my lips as I shatter completely beneath him.

Hunter's rhythm falters, and his grip on my hips tightens as his body tenses. I feel it—the way he swells inside me, stretching me even more, locking us together.

A ragged growl tears from his throat, low and primal, his breath shuddering against my skin as he pushes deeper into me, all the way to the hilt. Heat floods me, his release filling me until the pressure is undeniable, overwhelming.

Oh, fuck.

I'm shaking hard as I clutch his shoulders, my body hypersensitive, my mind spinning. I know what's happening. He's knotting me, coming inside me.

Hunter's head tips back, his jaw clenched tight as another groan rips from his chest. His hands flex against me, gripping like he can't stand the thought of letting go.

"That's it, angel," he rasps. "Take all of me."

I whine for more, still pulsing around him, the sensation almost too much—the fullness, the pressure, the dominance.

His forehead presses against mine, his breath ragged. "It's all yours," he states, his words thick with satisfaction. "Every last drop, every inch—I was made to fit inside you like this."

A desperate, needy sound leaves me, my body still trembling as I adjust to the unrelenting stretch. My fingers trail up his back, nails dragging slightly, and he groans. His hips rock the slightest bit, sending another wave of pleasure crashing through me.

"Do you love it, angel?" His voice is a dark caress, teasing, knowing. "Love my knot keeping you exactly where I want you?"

My legs tighten around his waist.

"Yes," I whisper, my lips brushing his ear. "I love it, Hunter. I love every fucking inch of your cock."

His answering growl is pure satisfaction as his hands roam my body.

"Good," he murmurs, pressing a lingering kiss to my throat.

Hunter's breath is ragged, his chest rising and falling against mine as his body continues to work through the aftershocks. He's still pulsing inside me, still pumping slow, lazy thrusts as his knot holds us together, as if his body refuses to let me go just yet.

A deep, primal growl vibrates through his chest, sending little tremors through my already oversensitive body. The sound is possessive, wrecked. His fingers tighten on my hips like he can't get enough. Every nerve is still humming, caught between pleasure and the stretch of being completely, thoroughly fucked.

The heat is starting to ebb, my body sinking from that dizzying high into something softer, hazier. My muscles are heavy, sore in the best way, my thighs still quivering slightly from how hard I came. I feel everything—the fullness, the lingering tingles, the deep ache where he's stretched me beyond anything I thought possible.

Hunter's body shifts, and I let out a small noise as he moves, carefully rolling onto his side, bringing me with him. He gathers me against him, his arms a solid cage around me, his hand splaying over my lower back as if to hold me there, to keep me pressed against his overheated skin.

"Easy, angel," he murmurs. "I've got you."

I let out a breathless laugh, still lightheaded, still tingling. My legs shift, and he helps adjust them, moving one over his hip so I'm no longer trapped beneath him. Now we're face-to-face, our foreheads nearly touching, breaths mingling, and his cock deep inside me, locked in place.

Sweat clings to my skin, our bodies still slick from the heat we just drowned in. I sense him inside me, his knot keeping me so perfectly stretched that I don't know where he ends and I begin.

"That was amazing," I murmur, my fingers dragging lazily along his chest. "I never knew it could feel like that. Even now, I feel every inch of you stretching me. It tingles... beautifully."

Hunter lets out a low hum of approval, his hand sliding up my spine, trailing warmth in its wake.

"Hurts a little too," I admit. "Because you're so damn big."

He chuckles, and there's something tender in his gaze, something that makes my chest tighten.

"But it's how it's meant to be," he says, tilting his head to hold my gaze. "We were made for each other." His hand cups the back of my head, guiding me closer. "How we're meant to be."

For a moment, there's nothing but the sound of our breathing and the slow, steady thrum of our heartbeats. I sigh, letting my body fully relax, letting myself melt against him. My head finds its place against his thick bicep, my cheek pressing to the firm heat of his chest.

His scent surrounds me, strong and intoxicating, filling my lungs and settling deep inside me. I've never felt this before—not just the pleasure, not just the high... but this. This contentment. This sense of belonging with someone other than my immediate family.

Hunter's arms tighten around me, his lips pressing against my hair in a silent promise.

"I've got you," he whispers again. "Rest now, angel."

Somewhere in the back of my mind, a small voice murmurs that when the storm clears and the heat passes, nothing will ever be the same again.

CHAPTER NINETEEN
LILY

The bathwater envelops me like a warm embrace, steam rising in lazy tendrils around the vast marble tub. My muscles unwind as I sink in up to my neck, letting the heat soothe away the day's intensity. The bathroom is ridiculously big—and honestly, who needs a bath this size in their home? It's practically made for several people to enjoy, with its curved edges and multiple seating ledges. The spa jets pulse rhythmically, sending bubbles dancing across the surface, obscuring my body beneath.

I exhale. Today has been... a lot.

"Who even are you, Lily?" I mutter to myself, watching ripples form from my words.

The old Lily—the one who color-coded her recipe books and triple-checked her alarm—wouldn't recognize this version of herself. That Lily had plans. A five-year business strategy. A carefully cultivated collection of vintage aprons that had never seen the business end of a flour explosion. That Lily would never have found herself in this position, caught among three Alphas like some twisted fairy tale.

This Lily? This Lily, who has only ever had sex with one other guy, just experienced her first Omega heat and handled it about as gracefully as a cat on roller skates.

My cheeks burn at the memory. The laundry room. Hunter. The way my body had simply taken control, leaving my rational mind in the dust.

I'm blaming biology, I decide, emerging with a splash. It's not my fault I have broken wiring that turns me into some sort of... desperate romance-novel heroine. "Oh, Alpha, please knot me!" I mimic in a high-pitched voice, then gag dramatically. "God, I actually said that, didn't I?"

Outside, night has fallen, casting the bathroom in eerie shadows. Only the underwater lights illuminate the space, giving everything a surreal blue glow. It matches my mood—suspended between reality and something darker, more primal.

I slept most of the day away after—well, after. When I woke, I found my room stocked with enough snacks to feed a small army. I devoured most of them before making my way here, carefully avoiding any potential Alpha encounters. The mere thought of facing them makes my stomach flip in a way that has nothing to do with the eight protein bars I inhaled.

"It's perfectly normal," I tell myself firmly, reaching for the control panel to increase the jet pressure.

"Adults have… adult situations. In laundry rooms. While begging to be—" I cut myself off with a groan and slam the jet button harder than necessary.

When the jets kick in with renewed vigor, something shifts inside me. A pressure builds, familiar and urgent. I freeze, eyes wide, feeling the heat spreading through my lower abdomen.

You've got to be kidding me. I glance around the empty bathroom, half expecting to find someone controlling my biological responses with a remote. *Already? Seriously?* What am I, some kind of Omega stereotype come to life?

That side apparently doesn't understand the concept of recovery time. Or dignity. Or the fact that I have a bakery to run, bills to pay, and a life that doesn't revolve around which Alpha I'm going to beg for attention next. The sensation intensifies, a deep ache flaring through my insides like a slow-burning fire.

On instinct, I shift positions, finding a seat on the ledge where one of the stronger jets streams directly between my thighs. The relief is immediate and intense, a counterpoint to the chaos in my mind. I grip the edge of the tub, knuckles whitening, a soft moan escaping my lips before I can stop it.

Self-service. Independent. Very "girl boss" of me, really. Taking matters into my own hands. Literally.

The humor feels hollow. Is this my life now? Hiding in bathrooms, pleasuring myself to take the edge off? A shudder runs through me, equal parts revulsion and desire.

The water pulses against me in waves, and despite my inner turmoil, I lose myself in the sensation. My head falls back, wet hair clinging to my shoulders and back. Tension builds wonderfully as I chase the high that will quiet the insistent need, even if just for a little while. Everything narrows to the point of pleasure between my thighs, the outside world falling away as I climb higher, thoughts fragmenting into incoherence. The jet feels like fingers teasing me, and I'm here for it.

That's it. Just a little more…

Breathing deeper, knuckles tighter, I rock my hips, getting that direct pulse right over my clit. *Fuck yes!* Almost instantly, I crest with a gasp that echoes off the tiled walls, my body arching as waves of pleasure crash through me. The momentary bliss drowns out everything else—the confusion, the fear, the uncertainty of what I'm becoming.

I'm floating, enjoying the moment.

As the aftershocks ripple through me, I slowly open my eyes…

And lock gazes with James standing in the doorway.

I yelp and dive under the water's surface, emerging only enough to keep my head above the waterline. The bubbles from the jets provide minimal coverage, but it's better than nothing. My heart hammers against my ribs, panic and humiliation fighting for dominance.

"Oh my God! What the actual fuck?!" I sputter, my response embarrassingly high-pitched. "Don't you knock?!"

James leans against the doorframe, a slow smile spreading across his face. There's something sinful in his eyes.

"Payback, little baker. Only fair that you watched me, and now I watched you, though I seriously think I got the better deal here." His eyes haven't left mine, trapping me in their stormy depths. "You have any idea how fucking hot you are while pleasuring yourself? How the scent of you is driving me insane right now?"

I want to evaporate. Literally disappear into the steam filling this room. Instead, he strolls in and pulls the door shut behind him with a click that sounds like a prison cell locking. He's dressed casually in worn jeans that hang low on his hips and a loose T-shirt that does nothing to hide the broad expanse of his chest. His feet are bare on the tiles, making his approach eerily silent. The room suddenly feels much smaller, the air heavy with something unspoken.

"You should leave," I say, but there's no conviction in my voice. We both know it's a lie.

I stay submerged, grateful for the churning water concealing me. My face must be roughly the color of the red velvet cake batter I was perfecting last month. Even now, with my dignity in tatters, my baker's brain makes these inane comparisons.

"What do you want, James?" I manage.

He sits on the edge of the tub, letting his fingers trail through the water mere inches from where I'm huddled. "Did you know that after your first knot, you should take it easy. Let your pretty little pussy there cool off…" His tone drops to a rumble that I feel in my bones. "It will hurt less if you give it time."

"Shut up." I turn away from him, but another wave of discomfort rolls through me unexpectedly, stronger than before. I grasp the side of the tub to steady myself, a small whimper escaping before I can trap it behind my teeth. "I hate having no control. And I'm so embarrassed that I'm going to hide for eternity. I just gave myself to Hunter, begged him… God." I clench my eyes shut, memories flooding back. "I'm like a bad pornographic cliché. Next thing you know, I'll be calling him *Daddy* or something equally horrifying."

A dark chuckle escapes him. "I wouldn't complain."

"You wouldn't," I mutter.

"Oh, I know," James says casually, his fingers creating small whirlpools in the water. "Archer and I heard you both in there."

My stomach drops to somewhere around my ankles. "Shit!"

"Every. Single. Word." He enunciates each syllable, his expression unreadable. "Every moan. Every plea. Everything."

"Kill me now." I sink lower into the water, wishing it would close over my head permanently.

"I can't even be upset, though." He runs a hand through his copper hair, the movement highlighting the tension in his shoulders. "I did put a hole in the wall in my bedroom, but I'm over that now." His grin suggests otherwise—it's all teeth and barely contained aggression.

I should be annoyed—maybe even afraid—but instead, a strange mix of guilt and something far more dangerous coils inside me. Arousal. The idea that I could affect him like this, stir up that kind of raw emotion... it shouldn't excite me. But my skin tingles beneath the water, heat pooling low in my belly.

God, what's wrong with me?

"Sure you are," I mutter. "That's why you're here, intimidating a naked woman in a bathtub. Very well adjusted."

"I know you needed him," he admits with surprising sincerity, ignoring my barb. His expression softens momentarily, giving me a glimpse of vulnerability beneath the Alpha posturing. "And I'm here for you when you're ready again."

The ache pulses inside me, as if responding to his words, my treacherous body betraying me yet again.

"At this stage, I feel ready now, but I'm sensitive... you know... down there." I want to die as the words leave my mouth. Apparently, Omega biology also steals your ability to be articulate.

"What you need is an Alpha's touch," he says lowly. "Our soothing presence. Our scent. Our hands." His eyes darken. "Our mouths."

A delicious shiver runs through me at his promise. "Is that what they taught you in pastry school? Alpha wellness techniques? Between éclair piping and soufflé timing?"

He smirks at my attempt at deflection. "You're cute

when you're defensive. I never went to pastry school; I'm self-taught."

"And you're annoying when you're... breathing," I retort lamely.

"You can do better than that, little baker."

"What are you offering, exactly?" I eye him skeptically, trying to regain some control over the situation. "Because if this is some kind of pity party, I'm not interested."

"Pity?" His laugh holds no humor. "Trust me, pity is the last thing on my mind right now."

Without answering further, James stands and reaches for the button of his jeans. My eyes go wide as saucers, a protest forming on my lips that never makes it out. He's wearing boxers underneath as he slips the denim down his legs, but that's hardly reassuring when even those leave little to the imagination. He pulls his T-shirt over his head in one fluid motion, and my mouth goes embarrassingly dry.

James is a walking advertisement for whatever workout regimen they offer in prison. His shoulders are broad and defined, muscles shifting under skin that bears the marks of his history—a few scars here and there only add to the dangerous appeal. His chest tapers down to a narrow waist, with abs that look like they were carved from marble, ridged and firm. A trail of copper hair disappears beneath the waistband of his boxers, drawing my eye to the obvious—and intimidating—bulge against the fabric.

The muscles of his thighs flex as he moves,

powerful and predatory, and I can't help but notice the V-cut of his hip muscles pointing like an arrow to what lies beneath those boxers. Despite my best efforts, my imagination fills in the blanks, remembering what I'd glimpsed that day I caught him in the shower.

A small scar traces his jawline, barely visible against his stubbled skin. Another scar, this one larger, cuts across his right side—a story he hasn't shared. The burn mark on his left forearm—a badge from his first cooking job—stands out against his tanned skin. It's oddly intimate, seeing these imperfections on his otherwise perfect form.

"Like what you see?" His words break through my admiration, amusement and heat mingling in his tone.

"I've seen better," I lie, averting my eyes. "Much better."

"Liar," he says simply, legs dangling in the water and spreading slightly. "Come sit on the ledge in front of me," he says. The command is softened, but still a command.

I hesitate, uncertainty warring with curiosity. My body wants to obey instantly, while my brain wants to tell him to go to hell.

"I'm not going to bite," he adds, then smirks. "Unless you ask nicely."

"Your charm knows no bounds," I say dryly, but I wade through the water until I'm positioned in front of him, my back to his front. I'm still submerged to my shoulders while he sits above me on the edge. The position feels vulnerable, exposed, despite the water covering me. "So, what now? You want to braid my hair and talk about boys we like?"

James pushes my wet hair to one side, exposing my neck. His fingers brush my skin, and electricity zips down my back, settling inside me like a live wire. I suppress a shudder, but not well enough.

"Jumpy?" he asks.

"Like you wouldn't be if you were naked in a tub with a strange man looming over you," I retort.

"Strange?" He sounds offended. "We've known each other for too long to be that. I'd say we're practically family at this point."

"That's disturbing on multiple levels," I mutter.

His hands land on my shoulders, and I tense before realizing he's beginning to massage me. His thumbs press into the knots at the base of my neck, working in slow circles that send waves of relief through my body. It's not what I expected—it's better and somehow worse because there's an intimacy to it that seems more dangerous than straight lust.

"Oh," I breathe, surprised by how good it feels. His hands are strong but gentle. He works methodically, finding each point of tension and dissolving it with practiced movements.

"Better?" he murmurs, his breath warm against my ear.

I nod, not trusting my voice. The constant ache that's been my companion since my heat began is finally, blessedly receding under his touch, though a different kind of tension is building to replace it.

"You carry a lot of stress here," he says, working a particularly stubborn knot between my shoulder blades. "Business troubles? Or just the weight of being an independent woman in a world that wants to put you in a box?"

The insight surprises me. "Bit of both," I admit. "Plus, the existential terror of suddenly discovering I'm a true Omega and having my entire identity thrown into question. You know, the usual Tuesday stuff."

His laugh is unexpectedly warm, vibrating through both of us. "You're handling it better than most would."

"Am I?"

His hands pause their magical work, resting heavily on my shoulders. "There's nothing wrong with needing someone, Lily. Even for someone as fiercely independent as you."

Something in his tone makes me want to cry, a kindness I wasn't prepared for. I blink rapidly, grateful he can't see my face.

"So," I say when I can form words again, desperate to change the subject. "Tell me more about what you're planning on doing with your life now that you're out of prison. You never really mentioned it before."

"I had plans to start my own business, working with Archer and running the fulfillment part of the operation." His thumbs trace the line of my spine, sending shivers cascading outward. "I need something that will keep me out of trouble."

"And will it?" I ask.

I sense rather than see his smile. "Probably not, but I'm making an effort. After eighteen months in a cell, you start to appreciate the little things. Freedom. Good coffee. The ability to take a shower without twenty other guys watching."

"Must have been rough," I say, surprised by my own sincerity. "Being framed by family, no less."

His hands tighten imperceptibly. "Family's complicated."

"Tell me about it," I sigh. "My sister, Hannah, thinks I've lost my mind, focusing on the bakery instead of finishing culinary school. Dad is supportive but worried I'm working myself to death. And now this whole heat thing... it's like the universe decided my life wasn't complicated enough already."

"The universe has a sick sense of humor," James agrees. His hands move lower, working the tense muscles of my mid-back. "But sometimes, its curveballs turn out to be exactly what we needed, even if we don't recognize it at first."

"Very philosophical for a guy who probably has 'No Regrets' tattooed somewhere unmentionable," I quip.

"Nope," he murmurs with a grin.

"So, who do you live with now?" I ask, trying to keep my tone steady as his hands work magic on my tense muscles, changing the subject before I say something I'll regret.

"Alone," he says. "A street away from Archer, actually." He laughs, a warm sound that vibrates through his chest into my back. "We'd planned one day to just get a mansion for all three of us to live together. Maybe an Omega too."

I turn slightly to look at him over my shoulder, eyebrow raised.

"No, you didn't," I say teasingly. "That sounds like the setup for a very questionable reality show. *Three Alphas and an Omega*. Tuesday nights on cable."

"You don't know that," he counters, his eyes dancing with mischief. "I'm definitely thinking that now. Wouldn't that be convenient? All of us under one roof."

"Yeah, right." I roll my eyes. "Well, I'm not yours, really. And you're all three not mine. Just three guys who are helping me out... even if I'm super embarrassed about it." I pause, chewing my lip. "I don't know what I am anymore," I admit, the confession slipping out before I can stop it. "I had everything figured out, you know? And now..."

James continues massaging my shoulders, his touch somehow both soothing and electrifying. Then, suddenly, he stops. "Hold on," he says, standing up. He walks to the shower stall across the room, the muscles in his back shifting with each movement. He returns with a bottle of shampoo.

"What're you doing?"

"You'll see," he says, resuming his position behind me. He cups water in his hands and pours it over my hair, wetting it thoroughly. Then he squeezes a generous amount of shampoo into his palm and begins working it into my scalp.

I should protest. I should tell him this is weird and unnecessary and crossing about seventeen boundaries. Instead, I let my eyes flutter closed as his fingers work through my curls, massaging my scalp with firm, circular motions.

"You've done this before," I murmur, half accusation, half question.

"I've had practice," he admits. "My mother was sick for a long time before she died."

The admission is so unexpected, so intimate, that I'm momentarily speechless. I wouldn't have pegged James as a dutiful son tending to his ailing mother. It adds another layer to the enigma he presents.

"I'm sorry," I say quietly. "About your mom."

"It was a long time ago," he says, but the gentle way his fingers move tells a different story. It feels... pure somehow. Beautiful. As though he's caring for me in a way that goes beyond the primal dynamic that's been driving our interactions.

"So, this means you forgive me?" he asks quietly, his fingers never stopping their movements.

"Not sure yet," I say honestly. "You were kind of an ass."

"I was," he acknowledges.

He guides me to dip my head back, rinsing the suds from my hair. When I emerge, blinking water from my eyes, I realize he's turned off the jets. The water stills around us, suddenly crystal clear. I feel exposed in a way I hadn't before, every curve and freckle visible beneath the surface.

"I want to see you," he says softly. "You're so beautiful that I can't get enough. I don't want anything hiding you."

His words do something to me, awakening a confidence I didn't know I possessed even as alarm bells ring in the back of my mind. This is dangerous territory. James is dangerous—all hard edges, dark past, and Alpha intensity. He's not safe. None of this is.

The considerable bulge in his boxers strains against the fabric, and something switches inside me. My body responds instantly to the visual evidence of his desire, a slow heat building. I find myself preening at having caused such a reaction, even as the rational part of my brain screams "Caution!"

"You know what will happen if you stay," he says, not a question. "There's no going back from this."

"I know." And I do. This isn't just about physical relief anymore. It's about crossing a line, making a choice that can't be unmade.

I move closer to him, a smile playing at the corners of my lips as I kneel in the water before him. The position should feel submissive, but somehow, I've never felt more powerful. His eyes darken as he watches me, pupils dilating until only a thin ring of gray remains.

"You know what?" I say, resting my hands on his thighs, feeling the muscles tense. "I think I might be ready for that Alpha touch after all."

Yet, a shadow of doubt crosses my mind. What am I doing? Who am I becoming? And when this is all over, will there be anything left of the Lily I used to be?

CHAPTER TWENTY

LILY

I'm kneeling on the inner ledge of the spa, water streaming down my body and rolling over my exposed breasts as I face James. I'm shivering, scared, excited. His gaze follows every droplet with ruthless intensity, sharp and insatiable.

"Look at you," he moans, that dark voice raising goose bumps across my skin. "Fucking gorgeous."

There's something dangerous in his expression that turns me on, fire pooling between my thighs. My heat has wrapped around my mind like a warm blanket, muffling my thoughts like they did earlier in the day. The cool air against my wet skin, the heavy thud of my heartbeat, the intoxicating scent of James—it's all overwhelming.

"You just going to stare?" I challenge, finding my words despite the fog of desire clouding my thoughts. "Because I could get dressed and go if—"

"Shut up, Lily," he says, the command soft but unmistakable. "You're not going anywhere."

I should be offended. Should tell him to go to hell. Instead, a traitorous quiver runs down my spine.

"Make me," I whisper.

His eyes darken further, storm clouds gathering. "Careful what you wish for, little baker. I'm not as gentle as Hunter."

The mention of Hunter should cool my ardor and remind me of what happened earlier today. Instead, it only seems to amplify the ache inside me.

"Who said I wanted gentle?" The words escape before I can reconsider them, bold and brazen in the steamy air between us, just like when I asked Hunter to bind me.

"Oh, sweet girl." James's laugh is dark, almost cruel. "You have no idea what you're asking for."

He stands in one fluid motion, thumbs hooking into the waistband of his boxers. My breath catches as he slides them down his powerful thighs and kicks them aside, standing before me in all his damn glory. I've seen naked men before, but nothing compares to Alphas at their peak, stirring something raw and instinctive inside me.

He's magnificent—all hard planes and defined muscle—but it's the size of his offering that makes my eyes bulge, intimidation momentarily breaking through my heat-induced confidence. His cock is thick, heavy, a big vein running the long length, his hair above it cropped short, somehow making him look bigger.

"Having second thoughts?" he grunts, a knowing smirk playing on his lips.

I want to say something witty, something that puts us back on even footing, but my brain seems to have short-circuited, leaving me speechless for perhaps the first time in my life.

"I thought not," he states as he sits back on the edge of the tub. "Come closer."

It's not a request. It's a command issued with the certainty of someone who expects to be obeyed. And God help me, I want to obey. Want to surrender to whatever this is between us.

I shuffle closer, the water sloshing gently around me. "Bossy much?"

"You have no idea." His hand comes up to cup my cheek, thumb brushing across my lower lip in a gesture that's somehow both tender and possessive. "But I think you like it. I think you're tired of always being in control, always having to make the decisions, run the business, be the responsible one."

The observation hits too close to home, exposing a vulnerability I usually keep carefully hidden. I drop my gaze, uncomfortable with how easily he's read me.

"Hey." His fingers tilt my chin up, forcing me to meet his eyes again. "Don't hide from me."

"I'm not hiding," I protest, but it sounds weak even to my own ears.

"Liar," he says, but there's no heat in the accusation. "It's okay to want this, Lily. To need it."

"Is it?" I whisper, voicing the fear that's been gnawing at me since I first presented with my heat. "Because it feels like I'm losing myself. Like I'm turning into someone I don't recognize."

Something softens in his expression, a glimpse of tenderness beneath the dominant Alpha exterior. "You're not losing yourself. You're discovering a new part of yourself. There's a difference."

"What if I don't like what I discover?"

His lips quirk into a half smile. "From where I'm sitting, there's a lot to like."

The compliment, delivered with such casual certainty, warms me from the inside out. Before I can overthink it, I reach out, my fingers closing around his erection. He's hot and hard, impossibly smooth against my palm.

James hisses through his teeth, head falling back slightly. "Fuck, Lily."

"That's the general idea," I quip, feeling a surge of power at having affected him so visibly.

His eyes snap back to mine, and the inferno I see there nearly melts me on the spot. "Smart mouth. I can think of better uses for it."

The suggestion sends a jolt of electricity through me, awakening nerves I didn't know existed. I've done this before, but never with someone like James, never with an Alpha. The thought should be intimidating. Instead, it's thrilling.

"Show me," I challenge, my voice huskier than I've ever heard it.

"You sure about this, baker girl?"

"I'm sure." Through the heat haze, the confusion, the fear, and the doubt, one thing is crystal clear—I want James. Here. Now. Deep in my throat. "I want this. I want you."

Something possessive flashes in his eyes. "Say it again."

"I want you," I repeat, leaning into his touch. "I've craved you since we first started chatting on the phone. Then I see you, and you have those cheekbones."

A laugh rumbles through his chest, genuine amusement breaking through the sexual tension.

"They're very distracting." A smile tugs at my lips. "Almost as distracting as your ass in those jeans."

"So, you were checking me out," he says. "And here I thought you couldn't stand me."

"Oh, I couldn't," I assure him. "Doesn't mean I didn't notice... certain attributes."

His laugh fades into a devilish smirk. "And now?"

I shrug, aiming for nonchalance despite our current position. "Now, I'm wondering if you can back up all that Alpha posturing with actual skill."

It's a bold challenge, one that makes his eyes narrow dangerously. "You're playing with fire, little baker." James's hand slides into my damp hair, cradling the back of my head.

"Maybe I like getting burned," I counter, echoing

words I've said before but meaning them differently now. "Maybe I need it."

James studies me for a long moment, as if weighing my sincerity. Whatever he sees in my expression must satisfy him, because his grip on my hair tightens just enough to send a tremble through me.

"Open up," he commands. His gaze lowers to his cock.

I obey without thinking, letting instinct guide me. James's groan of approval vibrates through me as I press my lips over the tip of his cock. His pre-cum is salty, sweet, soft, warm, and all mine. He groans, a deep, guttural sound that reverberates through my body. I open wider and take more of him in, slowly, deliberately.

A heady rush of power washes over me, despite my technically submissive position. I might be on my knees, but I'm the one making this powerful Alpha lose control. And the heat is overwhelming, the carnal plea-sure a burning ache between my legs.

"Good girl," he praises, and the words send an unexpected thrill through me. "Take your time and slide those beautiful lips lower."

Time is the last thing on my mind. My heat has ramped up again, turning my blood to liquid fire, and I'm desperate for any form of relief. I push him farther into my mouth. God, he's so big.

James's hand guides me, not forcing but suggest-ing. His other hand cups my cheek, an oddly tender gesture given the circumstances.

"Look at me," he commands softly.

I raise my eyes to his, and the darkness I find there nearly undoes me. He's watching me with such force, such hunger, that I feel simultaneously vulnerable and powerful.

"Perfect," he murmurs. "So fucking perfect with those big eyes and that sweet mouth full of my cock."

The compliment ripples over me like warm honey, soothing some broken part of me I hadn't realized needed healing. I redouble my efforts, wanting—needing—more of those words, more of that look in his eyes.

"Goddamn," he growls, his thumb caressing my cheek. "Go deeper— Fuck!"

My pussy clenches so tight it throbs.

I smile around him, pleased with his reaction. My free hand slides beneath the water, seeking my own relief from the building pressure. James notices immediately, his eyes tracking the movement.

"That's it, touch your little cunt," he orders. "Make yourself feel good while you take care of me. Show me what you need."

I suck on him, my tongue swirling the length of the base, teasing and taunting. He throws his head back, his breathing coming in short, sharp gasps.

"Fuck," he says, his hold on the back of my head tightening. "Don't stop."

Continuing to suck and lick, my hand stroking up and down his shaft. He's getting harder and thicker, pulsing with anticipation.

"Deeper, Lily," he growls. "Take it all."

I obey, lowering my head down, taking him as far as I can. He's so big, so thick, that it stretches me, pushing to the back of my throat, and I gag. But I don't care, don't stop, even when my eyes water. The discomfort is quickly overridden by the pleasure, the sheer intensity of the sensation.

As I devour him, I find my clit, swollen and buzzing. I stroke it, matching the rhythm of my mouth on his cock. The combination is explosive, a tidal wave of sensation that threatens to overwhelm me.

A moan escapes me, and James's grip tightens in response.

I look up at him through my lashes, enjoying the way his jaw clenches with restraint.

"Keep looking at me like that. Want to see those pretty eyes while you take me deeper."

I comply, maintaining contact. His breathing grows heavier, more ragged, while I rub and pinch my clit faster, the rise in me moving like a storm. Building and building.

"Fuck," he hisses. "No one's ever made me feel like this. The way you use your tongue... right there... goddamn. And when I'm done with you here," he continues, "I'm going to fuck you, knot you, then make you come on my tongue until you're begging me to stop."

A whimper escapes me, my nipples tight, the ache in my gut sharpening.

"You like that idea, don't you?" He traces my cheekbone with his thumb. "Like thinking about me between your thighs, making you scream my name. Making you mine."

The dominant claim in his words has my pussy quivering with desire, and I shake and moan against him. His growls and the pressure of his hand against the back of my head keep me going, sucking down on him.

"Fuck, Lily," he groans, his hand tightening in my hair. "I'm close. So fucking close. You'll take all of me into you, won't you?"

I nod, not breaking my rhythm.

"Such a pretty girl. Born for this, weren't you? Born to be mine."

Mine. The word echoes in my head, resonating with something deep and primal inside me. It's too soon, too intense, too everything—but in this moment, with my body humming with arousal and my mind clouded, it feels like the truth.

James's breath catches, his body tensing. "Lily," he warns, giving me one last chance to pull away.

I don't. Instead, I maintain eye contact, wanting him to see my decision, my surrender.

His cock jerks in my mouth, hot jets of cum flooding me. I swallow it all, gulping, savoring the taste as I feel the tremors that rack his body.

"Swallow every last drop," he growls, his body stiff, then he hisses.

He's still holding my head, his fingers digging into my scalp.

I'm surprised by how natural it feels, how right, as if my body knows what to do even if my mind is catching up.

Finally, the spasms subside. He lets out a long, shuddering breath, his body collapsing against the edge of the spa. He's breathless, but a grin tugs on his lips. He releases his hold on me.

I pull away, my face flushed, and lick my lips. I look up at him, my heart still pounding.

"Well," I say, breathless. "That was... intense."

James stands, water sluicing down his body in rivulets that draw my attention. He's still aroused, I notice, with a mixture of surprise and satisfaction. Before he can step out of the spa, another wave of heat pulses through me, causing my body to shudder involuntarily. A small sound escapes my throat—something between a gasp and a purr—and James turns back to me, eyebrow raised.

"I know that look," he says. A slow, knowing smile spreads across his face. "I've got what you need, little baker." He slides back into the water and positions himself on the ledge, reaching out one hand toward me, fingers curled in invitation. "Come to me," he says.

My body responds before my mind can catch up. I move through the water toward him as if pulled by an invisible thread, my limbs no longer under my conscious control.

"I couldn't stay away if I tried," I admit.

"Now you understand," he states. "What they say

about Alphas and Omegas—it's not just biology. It's something deeper."

I nod, speechless for once. I do understand. All my life, I've prided myself on my independence, my control, and my ability to choose my own path. But with him, I've become a different person.

James guides me to straddle his lap as he sits on the ledge inside the tub, my knees on either side of his hips, his still-erect cock right there. I rub myself against him, the sensation mesmerizing.

The position also puts us face-to-face, intimate in a way that makes my heart race.

"You did beautifully," he says. "So perfect for me. So responsive." The water sloshes gently around us. "And I know you're still sour about earlier and said we shouldn't do anything," he admits. "But I'm going to be a selfish asshole and fuck you now. Forgive me... but I'm weak." Something flashes in his storm-gray stare—vulnerability, need, a glimpse beneath the confident Alpha exterior—that makes my breath catch.

"I want this more than anything," I gasp, unable to think straight.

A flush of pleasure ripples through me. His other hand dips beneath the water, finding my pussy. When his fingers press between my folds, sliding over my clit, pinching me, I nearly come undone on the spot.

"James, more," I say breathlessly, my head falling back.

"That's it," he encourages, his voice a dark caress.

"Let me hear you. Let me feel how much you want this."

His thumb circles my most sensitive spot, and I moan out loud, my hips bucking against his hand involuntarily. Just when I think I can't take any more, he grasps my hips firmly, adjusting our position.

"Look at me," he demands, and I force my heavy eyelids to open. His gaze is intense. "I want to see you when you take me. When you truly become mine."

I'm balanced over his erection when he pushes down on my hips, my pussy spreading, taking him into me.

"Oh God," I breathe, my fingers digging into his shoulders for purchase.

James groans, his grip moving my hips in a slow, deliberate rhythm. "You feel incredible," he reassures me.

"I wasn't expecting to be turned on so quickly again," I admit, trying to maintain some semblance of coherent thought as waves of pleasure wash over me.

He pushes into me deeper and deeper, water sloshing around my waist. He watches me with fierceness.

I try to say something that proves I'm still in control of myself, but all that comes out is a desperate moan as he shifts our angle slightly.

James chuckles, dark and knowing. "You try so hard to keep control," he observes, one hand sliding up my back to tangle in my damp hair. I pause on his lap, his cock deep inside me. "Let go, little baker. Let me look after you."

I stare at him, something in his words striking a chord deep inside me. "I don't know how," I confess, the admission torn from some place vulnerable and hidden.

His expression softens, then he presses a surprisingly tender kiss to my collarbone. "Trust doesn't come easy. But right now, in this moment, can you trust me to take care of you?"

I search his face for any sign of deception, any hint that this is just Alpha posturing. I remind myself that he lied to me already, yet everything about him makes my heart skip.

"For now," I whisper, the words feeling like a surrender and a victory all at once.

He grins. "I'll take it," he submits, and the words sink into me. "Now, hold on to me and let go of everything else."

I cling to his muscular arms, my forehead pressed against his, as pleasure builds to an impossible peak.

"Let me feel you come apart. Let me see what I do to you."

He thrusts into me, over and over, and I'm meeting every movement with my own, my breasts bouncing. He leans in and takes one in his mouth, and the teasing of his tongue on my nipple has me groaning for more.

The orgasm slams into me fast and sharp, sending me into a convulsion of euphoria. Shaking, I cry out, but he steals my screams when he claims my mouth.

Pleasure crashes through me with such force that tears spring to my eyes. James follows me over the edge with a growl that's more animal than human, his arms tightening around me as his body pulses within mine.

Inside me, he's thickening. Growing. Knotting... with strangers I barely know, yet somehow, they already own me.

He hisses, and his body shudders as I feel him flood me with his cum, stretching my insides as he locks himself in place.

"James," I gasp, clinging to him as my body trembles with aftershocks.

"I've got you," he murmurs, his arms strong and steady around me. "I've got you, Lily."

I collapse against his chest, utterly spent. My limbs feel liquid, and my mind is blissfully empty of anything but the sensation of being held, being filled, being... claimed.

"You were perfect," he says, his voice a low rumble against my ear. He strokes my hair, his touch gentle despite the inferno of what just passed between us. "So responsive. So beautiful when you surrender."

The truth is, there was surrender on both sides—his control just as undone as mine by whatever this is between us.

James reaches over to the control panel, turning on the jets. The water warms almost instantly, bubbling around us in a soothing caress.

"We aren't going anywhere for a while," he says, a

hint of a smile in his voice. "May as well get comfort-able since we might be here for about half an hour, maybe less."

Nodding, I settle more comfortably against him. The physical pleasure has subsided to a warm glow, leaving room for other sensations—the steady beat of his heart against my cheek, the gentle rise and fall of his chest, the lingering scent of cedar and dark choco-late with a hint of smoke that seems to emanate from his skin.

"I'll look after you now," he murmurs, his lips brushing my temple.

My head is fuzzy from my heat, the release, and the strange, powerful connection that seems to bind us together. I'm not sure if I heard him right, not sure if he meant it the way it sounded.

As I cradle against him, I wonder how things will be between us when the heat finally subsides and reality comes crashing back in.

I push those thoughts aside, grateful to feel semi-normal without the ache deep in my stomach.

For now, I let myself sink into the moment—the warmth, the closeness, the way he holds me like I'm something precious, something lasting. A girl can dream, right?

CHAPTER TWENTY-ONE
JAMES

It's barely past five in the morning, but I've been awake for the last half hour, hearing no noise from the storm as though it's gone to sleep.

Beside me, Lily sprawls across the bed, one leg draped over mine, her face half buried in the pillow. Her wild curls spill across the sheets, dark against the white cotton. I ease out from under her, careful not to wake her, and pull the covers over her exposed back.

"Fucking bed hog," I mutter with a grin, watching as she immediately annexes my vacated space.

God, she's beautiful. The kind of beautiful that made those eighteen months feel like eighteen years. I haven't touched a woman in nearly two years—six months before prison, then the entire stretch inside—and my body is still humming from last night. Fucking her finally. The way she stared at me, challenging and holding on to me as if her life depended on it. Despite her words and actions, I know deep down that she is an Omega longing to be loved, to be protected by an Alpha.

I move to the window, staring out into the darkness. Everything is so still. I can't make out much beyond our property line, just vague shapes and movements that could be animals seeking shelter or branches breaking free.

Looking back at Lily, something tightens in my chest. This is it. What I've been craving, what I dreamed about during those endless nights when the walls pressed in too close. Not just any woman—her. This mouthy little baker with her quick wit and her stubborn independence. This Omega who fits against me like she was made for me.

I could make a life with her. Build something real, something lasting. Give her everything she deserves—security, pleasure, a partner who matches her fire with his own. And if Archer and Hunter want a piece of what we have, I'm surprisingly okay with that. They're my brothers in every way that matters. We've talked about it before, in those late-night conversations that skirted the edge of being too personal—sharing an Omega, building a pack together. The idea should make me jealous, possessive, but instead, it just feels... right.

However, there's that shadow hanging over everything. The lies. Not outright falsehoods, but sins of omission. She knows about them now, though it still sits heavily on me, seeing as she hadn't admitted to fully forgiving me yet.

I pull on my boxers and slip out of the room, closing the door so as not to wake her. The house creaks and groans around me as I make my way down the stairs.

My sleep has been fucked since prison. Eighteen months of constant control, constant noise, constant vigilance—it rewires your brain, makes you jump at shadows and listen for footsteps that aren't there. Even here, in Hunter's fortress of a cabin, I can't manage more than a few hours before my body jerks me awake, heart racing, senses on high alert.

Maybe with Lily in my bed, that will change. Maybe her scent, her warmth, and her soft breathing will override the alarms that keep screaming in my head. Worth a shot, anyway.

The hallway stretches long and dark ahead of me as I head toward the kitchen, thinking about coffee and maybe some prep work for breakfast. Lily strikes me as the type who'd appreciate fresh pastries when she wakes up, and I've been itching to get my hands on Hunter's commercial-grade oven. It's been too damn long since I baked anything.

That's when I hear it—a low, guttural growl coming from the rear of the house, near the back door.

I freeze mid-step, the hairs on my neck rising. My body shifts automatically into a defensive stance, weight centered, muscles tensed.

Thor? Maybe. The malamute's protective instincts run deep, especially for an animal raised in these mountains. But something about the pitch of that growl seems off.

Fuck. Not a bear again. Last time one of those bastards got in, it tore up half the kitchen before Hunter managed to drive it back out. He reinforced all the doors and windows after that and installed steel-core frames and double-paned glass.

The growl comes again, deeper this time, followed by a hushed voice that's definitely not Hunter's or Archer's.

Fuck! Someone's in the house.

I move silently toward the sound, grabbing a heavy bronze bookend from the hall table as I pass. Not ideal, but it'll crack a skull if necessary. My mind catalogs what I know about the layout—where Hunter keeps his guns (mostly in the basement gun safe).

"Thor, better be you, buddy," I call softly, though I already know it isn't.

As I turn the corner toward the back entrance, my suspicions are confirmed. The door is closed, but melting snow tracks across the hardwood floor in boot-shaped puddles. Not paw prints. Not bear claws. Human. Big human, based on the size of those tracks.

Motherfucker. Someone broke in.

I move along the wall, breathing controlled, ears straining for any sound. From deeper in the house, Thor's growls intensify, punctuated by someone hissing at him to shut up.

If they hurt that dog, I'll rip them apart with my bare hands.

The study door stands ajar, a sliver of light—not electric, but the dancing beam of a flashlight—visible through the crack. I edge closer, pressing my back against the wall, and peer inside.

The room is mostly dark, but I can make out a tall figure bent over the desk where Hunter keeps the treasure map. The intruder's back is to me, one gloved hand aiming a flashlight at the framed document while the other traces across the glass edging like he's about to lift it up. Thor stands a few feet away, hackles raised, teeth bared, ready to lunge.

I calculate the distance, grip the bookend tighter, and prepare to strike—

Pain explodes across my back, a vicious blow that catches me completely off guard. "Fuck!" I arch away, turning just in time to take a fist to the face.

I stumble backward, dropping down to my knees, vision blurring, the bookend tumbling free from my grip. Another figure stands in the hallway, dressed all in black, face obscured by a ski mask. He's nearly my height, broad through the shoulders, stance suggesting he knows how to handle himself in a fight.

The man from the study emerges, also masked, but the moment he speaks, recognition hits me like another blow.

"What the fuck are you doing out here?" he hisses at his partner, then spots me groaning on the floor in the dark hallway.

Travis. Hunter's goddamn cousin. I'd know that voice anywhere—the same one that used to come to the cabin when we were young and start fights with Hunter, physical fistfights.

Thor launches himself at Travis with a ferocious snarl, and chaos erupts. Travis cries out as eighty pounds of infuriated malamute slam into his chest. I let out a piercing whistle—a signal that will bring Hunter and Archer running—then throw myself to my feet and turn my attention to the second intruder as he lunges at me.

We collide with bone-jarring force, hitting the floor hard enough to knock the wind from my lungs. His fist connects with my jaw, pain bursting like fireworks behind my eyes. I taste blood and feel the split in my lip, but the pain just feeds the rage building inside me.

I roll sideways, driving my knee up into his ribs, then follow with a kick that sends him sprawling. Before he can recover, I'm on my feet, snatching the bookend off the floor.

He comes at me again, leading with his shoulder like a linebacker. I pivot at the last second, bringing the heavy bronze down on his upper back as he passes. He crashes into the wall with a satisfying crunch, drywall cracking under the impact.

A yelp of pain pulls my attention back to Thor and Travis. My blood runs cold as I see Travis grabbing a decorative fireplace poker from the hall table, raising it like a spear.

"Don't you fucking touch him!" I roar, abandoning my opponent to charge at Travis.

I hit him with everything I have, driving him backward into the wall hard enough to leave a body-shaped dent in the plaster. The poker clatters to the floor as Thor scrabbles away, teeth still bared.

Before I can follow up, something slams into the back of my head—a sucker punch from the second intruder—and my knees completely give out. The room doesn't just tilt; it violently spins as I crash to the floor. Darkness floods in from the edges, nearly swallowing my vision entirely. I try to push myself up, but my arms tremble and collapse beneath me. My head thumps with such blinding pain that even keeping my eyes open feels impossible.

"We gotta get out of here. Now!" the second man shouts from somewhere above me.

"Not without what we came for," Travis snarls back. "The map's right there, under the glass."

"Are you insane? I hear someone moving around upstairs!"

I manage to roll onto my side, the floorboards swimming beneath me. Through the haze, I see Travis lurching across the room, clearly injured from our fight.

"Then help me, you idiot!" Travis grabs something heavy—looks like a bookend—and swings it down hard. The shattering glass sounds like an explosion in my skull.

"Got it!" Travis shouts, snatching up what must be the map. "Move!"

I force myself onto my hands and knees, but the room spins so brutally I nearly vomit. Each attempt to stand sends fresh waves of agony through my head.

"James!" Hunter's voice seems to come from miles away.

By the time I finally stagger to my feet, I careen into the wall, using it to hold myself upright as I stumble after the thieves. I bounce from one wall to another, barely maintaining consciousness as I follow the sounds of their retreat.

I reach the back door just as Hunter and Archer thunder down the last few stairs. They rush to the doorway where I'm leaning heavily against the frame, their arms steadying me as we watch Travis and his partner mount a sleek black snowmobile.

The strange silence hits me immediately. Outside, the world has transformed—pristine, untouched snow stretches out under a clearing sky, almost peaceful in its stillness. The snowmobile's engine shatters that peace somewhere in the yard filled with trees, its headlight cutting through the calm darkness as they tear away from the cabin.

Hunter darts out there with Archer close behind, both in boxers only, but Travis and his musclehead are already zipping away on the path they carved.

"What the fuck?!" Hunter's voice booms as they march back inside.

"James, Jesus fucking Christ." Archer rushes forward to help me. "What happened?"

I let him guide me to a chair in the kitchen, wincing

at the headache, the split lip, the bruised jaw, the possible concussion, and the definite contusions along my back and ribs.

"Your fucking cousin," I spit at Hunter, tasting blood again. "Travis. He and some other asshole broke in. After the map. Thor attacked Travis, and I took on the other one."

Hunter's face darkens with fury, a muscle jumping in his jaw. "Travis was here? In my house?" He immediately drops to a knee beside Thor at his side, checking him over with gentle hands. "Did they hurt you, boy? Did they fucking touch you?"

"He fought like hell. Nearly took a chunk out of Travis before the bastard grabbed a poker. Then I shoved the asshole into the wall to protect Thor."

Hunter's head snaps up, his expression murderous. "He tried to hit my dog? I'll fucking kill him."

I nod. "But Travis was in the study, looking at the map when I came down," I explain, accepting the ice pack Archer presses into my hand. He heads back outside real quick. "Had a partner with him—big guy, knew how to fight. They took the map and ran when they heard you coming."

Hunter rises to his feet and stalks to the front of the house again. "Fuck!" His fist slams into the wall.

"They're long gone now," Archer reports, returning to the kitchen. His breath comes in short bursts, suggesting he'd run all the way around the property. Ice crystals cling to his golden-brown hair, melting slowly in the kitchen's warmth. "But their snowmobile tracks are still perfectly visible, heading east. The fresh powder makes them easy to follow, and it looks like the storm might be over."

"I'm going after them," Hunter interrupts, a deadly calm settling over his features. His ice-blue eyes have gone flat and cold, reminding me of a predator assessing its prey. His jaw tightens. "Nobody breaks into my home. Nobody threatens my pack."

"I'm coming with you," I say immediately, pushing myself to stand despite the room's persistent sway. My head hurts, a reminder of the intruder's sucker punch. Blood trickles from my split lip, metallic and warm on my tongue. "Those bastards didn't just break in—they attacked me and Thor. They got their hands on your grandfather's map. This is personal now."

Thor woofs softly, pressing his weight against Hunter's leg. Hunter reaches down, fingers threading through his thick fur as if examining him more closely, seeming to find no injuries beneath his dense coat.

"You did good, Thor," I tell him. "Saved my ass when I needed it. Good boy." The malamute's tail wags once in acknowledgment.

A small noise from the doorway draws all our attention at once. The sound—a soft, sharp intake of breath—cuts through the tension like a knife.

Lily stands there, drowning in what looks like one of my shirts, the dark fabric hanging nearly to her knees and making her appear even smaller, more vulnerable. Her wild curls form a tangled halo around her face, catching the kitchen light in strands of dark brown and caramel. Her golden-brown eyes widen as they take in the scene—the dented wall in the hallway, the scattered furniture, the blood on my face.

"Oh my God," she gasps, one hand rising to cover her mouth. Then her gaze locks on me, traveling from the blood on my lip to the way I'm leaning against the counter for support. Her face pales so dramatically that I worry she might faint. "James! You're bleeding!"

The genuine fear in her voice breaks through the haze of pain and anger.

Before I can reassure her, she's darting across the room, all sleep-warm softness and concern. She stands in front of me, her expression of such genuine worry that something in my chest constricts painfully. She takes the ice pack from my hand, setting it aside to examine the cuts on my lip with gentle fingers.

"I need clean water and disinfectant," she says over her shoulder to Archer, who immediately moves to comply. Her fingers tremble slightly as they hover over my injuries, not quite touching, as if afraid to cause more pain. "What happened? Are you okay? Your poor face…"

"Break-in," I tell her, catching her hand and giving it a reassuring squeeze. Her skin is warm, soft—baker's hands with the strength to knead bread for hours. "Caught two guys in the house. We had a disagreement about them being here." I try for a light tone, but my voice comes out gravelly, tight with contained rage.

Her eyes widen further, fear replacing concern as she glances around as if expecting more intruders to materialize from the shadows. "Someone broke in? Here? With all of us sleeping upstairs? In the middle of nowhere during a snowstorm?"

"Travis and some other muscle," Hunter growls, his fists clenched so tightly at his sides that his knuckles have gone white. He's coiled tension from head to toe, a spring about to release with deadly force. "The fucking coward came during a storm, thinking we'd all be dead asleep. He's wanted that map since before Grandfather was cold in his grave."

"Travis?" Lily looks between us, bewildered, her brows drawing together in confusion. "The one you mentioned before? Your cousin?"

Hunter nods, jaw tight enough that I can hear his teeth grinding. "The same piece of shit who's convinced the map is his birthright, that he was cheated out of his *proper* inheritance."

Lily's hands are gentle as she cleans my face with the towel and the antiseptic cream that Archer brought, but I can feel them shaking against my skin. The antiseptic stings, but I welcome the sharp pain—it clears my head and focuses my thoughts.

"I can't believe they broke in for the map," she says, her voice higher than normal with disbelief.

"People will do anything for wealth," Archer adds from where he's leaning against the doorframe. His normally perfect hair is disheveled from sleep and the dash outside, giving him a wilder look than usual. "Money makes monsters of men. They could have killed you, James. If you hadn't heard them..."

He doesn't finish the thought. He doesn't need to. We all know what could have happened if I hadn't been awake, if Thor hadn't alerted me.

"Travis is going to be sorry real soon. And Thor helped level the playing field."

Lily's hands pause on my face, her golden eyes searching mine. "Are you really okay?" she asks softly, the question clearly meant just for me despite our audience.

"I've had worse," I tell her, which isn't exactly the reassurance she's looking for, judging by her frown. I try again. "I'll be fine. Nothing's broken, just bruised."

Her attention shifts to the malamute, who stays close to her. "Oh, Thor! Are you hurt too, baby?" She reaches down to stroke his head, and he leans into her touch with a soft whine.

"He's okay," I tell her. "He's fine."

"We need to go now," Hunter says. "The storm's cleared—perfect tracking conditions. If we move fast, we can catch them."

"I'm joining you," I state.

"Wait, 'go'?" Lily's head snaps up, her gaze darting between Hunter and me. "Go where? After them? Are you insane?"

"Are you sure that's a good idea?" Archer adds, his voice carefully neutral, but his eyes are sharp with concern. "No, better to just turn up at their place. They aren't going to get far."

One of Lily's hands rests on my chest, as if to hold me in place. "James, you're hurt. You might have a concussion. Maybe you should rest, let the authorities handle this."

Her concern is touching, but it can't penetrate the white-hot rage building inside me. The thought of Travis escaping after what he's done—after endangering everyone in this cabin—is unbearable.

"Fuck that," I growl, surprising myself with the vehemence in my voice. "They attacked me, threatened Thor, put all of us in danger—including you. I'm getting my fucking revenge." My hands curl into fists at my sides, knuckles already bruised from connecting with Travis and his buddy.

"Those bastards broke into our home while you were sleeping upstairs. What if they'd gone up there instead of down here? What if they'd found you?"

The thought sends a fresh surge of murderous rage through me. The idea of Travis anywhere near Lily makes my blood boil and turns my vision red around the edges. My protective instincts—something I didn't even realize I possessed until recently—roar to life.

"James..." Lily begins, but I can see in her eyes that she understands. She doesn't like it, but she gets it.

"We've got the snowmobile in the back shed," Hunter says, already moving toward the stairs. "We'll take it, and I'll drive. Let's get dressed and leave now!"

"You have a snowmobile?" Lily asks, clearly trying to keep up with how quickly events are unfolding. "Could have used that to get home."

"With how rough the snow was, too dangerous, gorgeous," Archer confirms.

"What about the police?" Lily asks, looking between us with increasing alarm. "Shouldn't we call them?"

Hunter and I exchange a look. "This is personal and something we're going to handle ourselves," Hunter explains.

"At least let me finish cleaning you up before you go," she insists. "If you're determined to do this macho revenge thing, you're not doing it while still bleeding."

Her words might be dismissive, but her touch is anything but—gentle, careful, her concern evident in every press of her fingers against my skin. I find myself leaning into her touch, craving more of it even as I prepare to leave her behind.

I turn to Lily when she's finished, cupping her face in my hands and pressing a hard, quick kiss to her lips. She looks startled, confused by my intensity, her golden eyes wide and questioning when I pull back.

"We won't be long," I promise, my thumbs brushing over her cheekbones. Her skin is impossibly soft under my calloused hands. "But we have to go now while the trail is fresh."

"You could die out there," she whispers. "Both of you. For a stupid map?"

"It's not about the map anymore," I tell her. "It's about making sure Travis knows he can't come after what's ours."

Something in my tone, in my expression, makes her breath catch. Her eyes search mine, looking for something—reassurance, perhaps, or maybe understanding of what I'm really saying.

"I'll go change," Hunter says, already halfway to the stairs. "Two minutes, James. Meet me by the back door."

I nod, then turn to Archer. "You protect her," I command. My hand clasps his shoulder, fingers digging in hard enough to make him wince. "You got it? If Travis comes back—"

"No one will touch a hair on her head," Archer interrupts. "Not over my dead body." His amber eyes flick to Lily, then back to me. "Besides, I'm armed, and she probably knows seventeen ways to poison someone with baking ingredients. We'll be fine."

Despite everything, Lily lets out a short laugh. "Eighteen, actually. The nutmeg trick is new." Her attempt at lightness falls flat, though, the worry still evident in the tightness around her eyes and the way she hugs herself as if cold.

I feel a reluctant smile tug at my split lip, reopening the wound. A fresh drop of blood wells, and Lily automatically reaches up to dab it away, her touch impossibly gentle.

"Lock everything after we leave," I tell Archer. "Every door, every window. And keep Thor with you—he'll hear anyone coming before you do."

Thor whines softly at my feet, clearly torn between wanting to follow me and staying to protect Lily.

"Stay," I tell him firmly. "Guard."

His ears perk up at the command, and he moves to

sit directly next to Lily, his large body pressing protectively against her leg.

She nods once, then stands on tiptoe to press a soft kiss to the uninjured corner of my mouth. "Go," she whispers against my skin. "Both of you do what you need to do. But come back to me. Keep Hunter and yourself safe."

Her words follow me as I head for the stairs, taking them two at a time despite the protest from my battered body. Each step sends a fresh wave of pain through my skull, but I push through it, fueled by rage and something else—something that has golden-brown eyes and smells like vanilla and peppermint.

In my room, I quickly dress, wincing as every movement pulls at forming bruises. As I'm lacing up my boots, Hunter appears in my doorway, dressed in black, a ski mask in hand.

"You sure you're up for this?" he asks, those eyes assessing my condition with the practiced gaze of someone who's seen his share of injuries. "No shame in sitting this one out."

"Try to stop me," I challenge, straightening to my full height despite the wave of dizziness that accompanies the movement. I lock my knees to keep from swaying, refusing to show weakness.

A slow, dangerous smile spreads across Hunter's face. "Good. Because between us, we're going to make my cousin wish he'd never been born." He tosses me the black ski mask. "Suit up. Time to show Travis what happens when you mess with us."

Up on my feet, I'm fucking ready.

"When we find him," Hunter continues, "we don't hold back."

The cold certainty in his voice mirrors the ice in my own veins. "Trust me," I reply, pulling the ski mask down over my face, "I won't."

CHAPTER TWENTY-TWO
LILY

The morning sun streams through the windows. With Hunter and James gone to retrieve the map from Travis, the cabin feels oddly quiet. Thor has fallen asleep by the back door, where Hunter left through, most likely waiting for his return, leaving Archer and me truly alone.

I lean against the wall in the entryway, glancing as Archer kneels by the back door, tools spread around him as he replaces the lock damaged during Travis's break-in. There's something undeniably attractive about watching him work—the focused concentration of his muscles, the movements of his hands, the occasional grunt.

My heat hasn't fully subsided yet. I feel it lingering with fire that flares whenever I'm near any of the Alphas. With Archer, it's particularly potent—perhaps because we've had fewer moments alone together than I've had with the others.

He tightens the final screw, tests the lock, shuts the door, and sits back on his heels with a satisfied smile. "That should do it. Not quite as secure as Hunter would make it, but it'll hold until we buy new locks."

"You look good doing that," I say before I can stop myself. "Being a handyman suits you."

He turns to me, eyebrow quirked in amusement. "You okay there, gorgeous? You're looking a little flushed."

I push away from the wall, drawn to him by something I can't quite control. "You should do that with no shirt on next time. For aesthetic purposes."

He chuckles, setting his tools down on the side table. "Aesthetic purposes, huh?" His amber eyes darken slightly as he studies me. "You're still feeling your heat, aren't you?"

"A bit," I admit, not bothering to deny what must be obvious to his Alpha senses. "It's... lingering."

With deliberate slowness that makes my heart race, Archer reaches for the hem of his T-shirt and pulls it over his head. Like Hunter's rugged bulk or James's solid strength, Archer's physique is just as big—all muscle and smooth planes.

"Better?" he whispers.

I fan myself dramatically. "Much. Though, now it's even warmer in here."

He laughs, throwing his head back. "I'm affecting the cabin's climate now? I'll add that to my list of talents."

"What else is on that list?" I ask, taking a step closer.

"Oh, lots of things," he replies with a casual shrug that makes his muscles ripple enticingly. "Reading ancient texts, identifying first editions by smell alone, making women in bakeries wet..."

"Wow, you went there," I protest automatically.

"Sure did." He closes the distance between us with a few long strides.

His hand is on my shoulder and curling up my neck, holding me there, tilting my head back with his thumb to meet his gaze.

The touch covers me in goose bumps. "Archer," I whisper, wanting everything from him but unsure how to ask for it.

"Yes, Lily?" His voice is teasing, but his eyes are serious, searching mine for permission.

"I want..." I trail off, suddenly shy, despite the urgency thrumming through me.

"What do you want?" he prompts gently. "Tell me."

"You," I say simply. "All of you."

Something ripples behind his eyes—hunger, possessiveness, desire—before he carefully controls his expression. "You have me," he states, still not touching me beyond my neck. "But I think we should be clear about what's happening here. Is this the heat talking? Or is this you wanting me?"

The question catches me off guard. It's thoughtful and considerate in a way that belies his playful exterior.

"Both," I admit. "The heat makes everything... more. But it doesn't create feelings that weren't already there." I glance up at him, holding his gaze. "I want you, Archer. Heat or no heat."

That's all the permission he needs. His mouth claims mine in a kiss that starts gently but quickly blazes into something more urgent. His hands frame my face, holding me as if I'm something precious, even as his lips demand a response I'm eager to give.

I press against him, reveling in the warmth of his bare skin beneath my palms. He tastes like the coffee he had at breakfast and something uniquely Archer— old books, bergamot, and desire.

"You're wearing far too many clothes," he murmurs against my lips. "Especially considering I've sacrificed my shirt for aesthetic purposes."

I laugh, tugging at the drawstring of his sweat-pants that he'd grabbed along with the shirt after the guys left. "I agree. Very unfair."

His hands catch mine, stilling them with gentle pressure. "Not so fast. I think I want something in exchange first."

"I'm fresh out of money," I quip, gesturing to the long T-shirt I'm wearing with nothing underneath— one of James's, borrowed after waking up in his bed.

"Oh, I can think of other forms of payment," he purrs, and my knees weaken. "Like hearing you say exactly what you want me to do to you."

Heat floods my face, but not from embarrassment. There's something incredibly arousing about his request—about being asked to voice my desires out loud.

"I want you to kiss me again," I begin, finding courage in the darkening of his eyes. "And then I want you to touch me. Everywhere."

"Specific," he teases, but his breathing has quickened. "I like it."

He steps closer, backing me against the wall. His body is a warm presence against mine, close enough to feel but not yet pinning me. His lips find my neck, a soft brush of heat against my skin, and I gasp as he trails kisses along my throat, each one searing and deliberate.

"More," I whisper, my voice shaky and breathless.

His chuckle is low and dark. "Greedy."

His teeth graze my skin, and my back arches into him, desperate for more. Sliding my hands into the waistband of his sweatpants, I curl my fingers around the fabric, tugging, but before I can get far, his hand catches my wrist.

"Not yet," he growls, and he spins me to face the wall, my palms flattening against the cool surface. His body presses against mine from behind, solid muscle pinning me in place. His breath is warm against my ear.

"You want me rough or tender, sweet?" His voice is low, gravelly, and full of wicked intent.

My pulse stutters. "Rough," I rasp. "Oh, rough for sure."

A sharp breath escapes him, and his hand fists the

back of my oversized shirt—the only thing I'm wearing. With one swift motion, he drags it up, baring my thighs, my hips, my back. His palm slides up my leg, fingers splaying wide over my skin as if he's savoring every inch.

"So fucking perfect," he mutters, his hand kneading my hip. "Bet you knew exactly what you were doing, walking around in nothing but this shirt."

"Maybe," I murmur, arching into his touch.

His fingers trail upward, teasing, tracing along the curve of my waist before gripping me tighter, dragging my hips back against him. I feel him—hot, hard, and relentless—grinding against me through the thin fabric of his sweatpants.

"Feel that?" His voice is a low snarl in my ear. "That's what you're craving."

I gasp, my head tipping back to rest against his shoulder. "Please."

He rolls his hips again, and a sharp, needy sound escapes me.

His hand slides between my thighs, his fingers spreading me wider.

"You're already soaking for me," he growls. "Tell me you need it. Say it."

"Fuck, Archer, you're going to kill me," I pant, my voice barely a whisper. "I need you."

His fingers find my pussy, pushing my lips apart, and my whole body jolts as he slides two thick fingers inside me. A cry rips from my throat, my legs threatening to buckle, but he presses closer, holding me steady with his other arm wrapped tightly around my waist.

"That's it," he murmurs, his lips brushing my ear. "Take it, sweetie." His fingers pump inside me, slow and deep, teasing me until I'm breathless, my body burning up from the inside out.

"More," I whimper, pressing my hips back against him, desperate for more friction, more pressure—more him.

His teeth catch my earlobe, his voice a dark promise. "You're not ready for more."

"I am," I say. "I can take it."

His growl vibrates along my skin, and suddenly, his hand leaves me. Before I can protest, he shoves his sweatpants down, the warmth of him pressing hard and thick against me. My breath catches, and the ache inside me sharpens to a desperate, burning need because he might just be thicker than James and Hunter. I wasn't expecting that.

"Say my name again."

"Archer," I moan. "Please."

With a low curse, he presses the tip of his cock to my entrance, and I'm already rocking my hips to accept him.

"You've been driving me crazy," he growls, his voice rough with hunger. "You think I didn't notice you watching me? Biting your lip every time I got close? Acting all innocent when you knew damn well what you were doing." His hand drags down my side, fingers skimming the curve of my waist before curling possessively around my hip. "You want this as badly as I do, don't you?"

"Yes," I gasp, pressing back against him. "Please... I need you."

"That's not good enough," he mutters, his breath hot against my ear. "I want to hear exactly how bad you need it."

"I need you to fuck me," I rasp, my voice breaking. "I need you to fill me... make me forget everything except you."

His low growl rumbles against my skin, and his fingers tighten on my hips. "Oh, sweetie, you're about to get exactly what you're begging for." He teases me with the head of his cock, sliding it just inside before pulling back. "You feel that?" His voice is dark. "That's just a taste. And you're not getting more until you beg me properly."

"I'm begging," I moan, twisting in his grip, desperate for more. "I'll do whatever you want... just give it to me."

"Whatever I want?" His voice is pure sin. "Careful what you promise, sweetie. I'm not stopping until you're a trembling mess against this wall."

Then he shoves into me hard and deep. My head drops forward against the wall, a strangled cry escaping my lips as he fills me completely, stretching me in a way that leaves me breathless. He doesn't give me time to adjust—gripping my hips, he starts to move, fast and rough, each thrust sending sparks of pleasure spiraling through me.

"That's it," he groans, voice gravelly. "Taking me so well. You're so fucking tight. You love this, don't you?" His tongue drags down my spine. "Love me fucking you like this—fast, rough... owning every inch of you."

"God, yes," I cry out, nails clawing at the wall. "I love it. Don't stop."

"Oh, I'm your god already. I'm going to ruin your pussy so you never forget my cock."

I moan, my body helpless beneath his, my nerves burning under the intensity of him. He's everywhere—his breath on my ear, his body pressed tight against my back, his hand sliding down my stomach.

"You're shaking already," he taunts, his fingers teasing my clit, pinching it. "Poor thing... you're gonna break for me, aren't you?"

I'm gasping, whimpering, my body on fire, too full of him and too lost to think. "Please," I whisper, my voice a desperate plea.

"Please, what?" His fingers press harder, rubbing slow circles that leave me trembling. "Come on, sweetie, tell me what you need."

"I need to come," I choke out. "To scream out."

"That's better," he growls. "Now come for me. Let me feel you lose it."

His fingers work me mercilessly, his cock driving deeper, each thrust winding me tighter until I can't take it anymore. My body locks up, pleasure crashing over me so fiercely I forget how to breathe. I sob his name as I shatter against him, my nails scraping uselessly at the wall as wave after wave rolls through me.

But he's not finished. He holds me through it, still thrusting, still grinding against me, dragging out every last pulse of pleasure until I'm wrung out.

"That's my girl," he rasps, voice rougher now. "But I'm not done with you yet."

He grabs my wrists, dragging them back behind me, pinning them there as he fucks me harder, faster, as though he's determined to leave me wrecked and ruined. My body is still trembling, oversensitive and aching, yet I crave more—more of him, more of this fire consuming me.

"You love this," he groans, his pace brutal now. "Getting fucked like this... knowing you're mine to break."

"Yes," I state. "Yes... yes..."

He slams into me one last time, his body going rigid as he shudders, a low, guttural growl emanating from his throat as he spills deep inside me. His grip on my wrists tightens briefly before he loosens his hold, releasing me just enough to pull me back against his chest.

I'm boneless, trembling, my breath coming in sharp gasps as he lowers us both to the floor. He pulls me close, one arm wrapping tightly around my waist as his lips press against my hair.

"I've got you," he murmurs, softer now. "You're mine."

I let my head fall against his chest, the steady thud

of his heartbeat slowing beneath my cheek. My body still hums with the aftershocks, the ache a reminder of just how hard he claimed me. I've never felt so spent, so utterly unraveled.

Yet, as I lie here, wrapped in his arms, his cock deep inside me, I know he hasn't knotted me yet.

"I told you I could take it," I murmur, my voice hoarse but teasing.

I'm still trying to catch my breath when his arm tightens around me, and suddenly, I'm lifted off the floor. My gasp barely escapes before he's carrying me across the room. His cock is still buried inside me, each step making me feel every inch of him as he moves. My back presses flush to his chest, and my thighs tremble as he lowers me to my knees beside the couch.

"Hands on the cushions," he orders darkly, his voice rougher now. "Don't move unless I tell you."

I obey, my fingers gripping the fabric tightly. His palm drifts down my spine, slow and lingering.

"I want you bent over... head down. I want you to feel me everywhere."

I barely have time to process before his hand flattens between my shoulder blades and presses me forward. My cheek hits the cushion, my body stretched out, rear in the air, legs spread, and completely at his mercy. The next thing I know, his palm strikes my ass —a sharp slap that makes me yelp, heat rushing through my body.

"You like that?" Archer growls, his fingers digging into my hips. "You like it when I mark you?" He grips me tighter and drags me back against him, his cock grinding deep. "You're still dripping down your thighs, sweetie. Such a messy little thing... I haven't even knotted you yet, and you're already wrecked."

I gasp, biting my lip, the burn of his slap blending with the pleasure surging through me. "I like it," I pant. "Please... more."

"You're such a greedy thing," he growls, slapping me again, harder this time. "That's what I love about you—always begging for more." He thrusts deeper, rougher now, his fingers sliding up my spine before curling in my hair. "I'm going to knot you so deep you'll feel me for days." He yanks my head back enough that his mouth hovers by my ear. "Tell me you want it."

I cry out at how deep he goes into me, how fast he thrusts.

"Yeah?" He grins against my skin. "Thought so."

His hand slides down to my hip, holding me still as he pounds into me. The force of it leaves me breathless, my moans muffled against the cushion. Pressure coils inside me, winding so tightly I can barely stand it.

"You're mine," Archer snarls.

"Archer..." I choke out, my body burning, my muscles straining. "I'm..."

"Come for me," he demands, his voice low and commanding. "Come for me while I knot you."

I scream, my body bursting from the inside out, pleasure ripping through me in wild pulses as my pussy grips his cock. He groans, low and guttural, his erection swelling, thickening, pushing against my inner walls. He's holding me still as his heat floods me.

"That's it," he growls, his hand smoothing down my spine in a rare moment of tenderness. "Such a good girl... all mine."

I'm still bellowing my pleasure, my legs shaking, lust tearing through me like wildfire.

He follows in moments.

We stay joined, catching our breath, hearts gradually slowing their frantic pace. For a moment, we remain like that, both of us breathless, skin slick with sweat, his chest rising and falling against my back. Then, slowly, he eases me back up to him, and his arms wrap around me.

"I've got you," he murmurs in my ear, his face buried in my neck. "You can rest now." He carries me and takes a seat on the couch, me in his lap, him buried inside me.

I let my head fall against his shoulder, my body still buzzing, my breaths slowing as his scent engulfs me. For the first time in what feels like forever, I don't feel restless. I don't feel uncertain.

I just feel... right. As if this is exactly where I'm meant to be.

The Arctic Thundercat 9000 Turbo growls beneath me, a mechanical beast straining against its own power. Its 998cc turbocharged, 4-stroke engine vibrates against my thighs as I guide it through the pristine morning snow. Behind me, James grips the handles at his sides, his body a tense presence against my back.

Each breath burns in my lungs, turning to vapor the instant it leaves my mouth. The storm has cleared, giving way to a deceptively beautiful sunrise—pink and gold light spilling across untouched white peaks, the kind of morning that feels like a lie after the break-in at my home.

I push the throttle harder, and the machine responds instantly. We sail over a drift, momentarily airborne, before landing with a muffled thump in the deep powder. The GPS mounted on the handlebars glows with our position, following the eastern property line toward the pass that leads to Travis's side of the mountain.

The tracks we follow tell their own story—two sets of snowmobile treads cutting through virgin snow. I recognize the distinctive pattern of Travis's Ski-Doo Renegade. The other set belongs to a heavier machine with a wider stance and a deeper tread—Deacon's ride, no doubt. Travis wouldn't go anywhere without his loyal attack dog.

The property line appears ahead, marked by the ancient lightning-struck pine my grandfather used as a boundary marker years ago. Half dead, half alive, the massive tree stands sentinel between two worlds—my domain and Travis's territory. My grandfather's attempt at Solomon's justice, splitting his legacy between two warring descendants, hoping the division would eventually heal our rift.

It only deepened it.

As we approach Travis's hunting lodge, I cut the engine, gliding the last hundred yards to a dense stand of blue spruces. The sudden silence after the machine's constant roar makes my ears ring. In the distance, smoke rises from the cabin's chimney—a thin gray line against the brightening sky.

"They're here," I whisper, swinging my leg over the machine and nodding toward the cabin. "Probably nursing their wounds, thinking they got away clean."

James pulls his ski mask down farther, only his storm-gray eyes visible. Blood has frozen in small dark crystals along the fabric where it covers his reopened cut.

We push through knee-deep snow toward the tree line's edge, staying low beneath the branches. The lodge emerges into full view—not the rustic hunting shack most would expect, but a substantial structure of logs and stone stretching out to a decent size. Two snowmobiles sit parked haphazardly out front, confirming that our targets are inside.

I tap James's shoulder and point toward the rear of the structure. "Back entrance," I mouth.

He nods, then pats his own chest twice before pointing ahead—offering to take the lead. We circle the clearing, staying within the shadows of the pines. Morning illuminates the cabin's windows, making them flash gold, then orange as the sun crests the eastern ridge. We reach the back door unseen, pressing ourselves against the rough-hewn logs on either side.

Through the small window, I make out movement inside—three figures roaming around the main room. Travis is easy to recognize, even from behind, his lanky frame and slouched shoulders unmistakable. Deacon towers beside him, a bull of a man with hands like sledgehammers and a mean streak to match. The third man is unfamiliar—shorter, wiry, moving with the restless energy.

James raises three fingers in question. I nod, then point to myself and hold up two fingers, then to him and hold up one.

He shakes his head and reverses the count.

I almost smile despite everything. He wants blood.

Silently testing the handle on the back door, I feel it turn with resistance. Holding up three fingers, I count down.

Three. Two. One.

I drive my shoulder into the door with all my weight behind it. Wood splinters around the frame as it flies inward, crashing against the inner wall. We surge through the opening together before the occupants can react.

The interior is dim despite the morning light, with heavy curtains drawn across most of the windows. A fire roars in the stone hearth, casting restless shadows across the rustic space. The place reeks of woodsmoke, whiskey, and sweat—with the metallic undertone of blood.

Travis stands by the fireplace, one arm in a makeshift sling, his face a mottled canvas of purple and black from his earlier encounter with James. Deacon looms beside him, a mountain of a man in a flannel shirt stretched tight across a massive chest. The third man stands slightly apart—lean, hard-faced, with flat eyes.

"What the fuck—" Travis begins, his voice cracking in surprise as he's pushing toward me.

I'm fuming at seeing my cousin. To think, he entered my home, hurt my friend, and was about to strike Thor. What if he'd found Lily? Lava burns through my chest with fury.

"You think you can break into my home and steal

from me?" I launch myself at Travis without hesitation, driving my shoulder into his gut. Despite his injured arm, he grunts from the strike but shoves away quickly, leaving me to stumble sideways. Behind me, I hear the scuffle of feet and glance back quickly to find James confronting both Deacon and the lean stranger simultaneously.

Travis recovers and swings his good arm in a wild arc toward my head. I duck under it, coming up with an uppercut that catches him square in the jaw. His head snaps back, but he doesn't go down.

"Your map belongs to me," he snarls, blood speckling his lips.

A crash from across the room draws my attention for a split second. I glimpse James rolling across a table, the lean man slashing a knife through the air where his head had been a moment before. Deacon charges in from the side, trying to pin James against the wall.

Suddenly, Travis's boot connects with my knee, sending a shock of pain up my leg. I stagger but stay upright, blocking his follow-up punch and countering with a jab to his injured arm. He howls in pain, lurching backward toward the fireplace.

"I should have ended you a long time ago," he spits, reaching for something propped against the hearth—a shotgun with a weathered wooden stock. My grandfather's Remington.

Heart in my throat, I lunge forward, grabbing the barrel just as his fingers close around the stock. We grapple for control, the weapon between us. From the corner of my eye, I spot James dropping to the floor and sweeping the lean man's legs from under him. The stranger crashes down as Deacon throws a punch that misses James and hits the wall instead, plaster cracking under the impact.

Travis twists the shotgun, trying to wrench it from my grip. My hands slip on the metal barrel, and I realize with cold clarity that I'm losing the struggle. In desperation, I drive my forehead into the bridge of his nose. There's a sickening crunch, and Travis reels backward, blood streaming down his face, but he doesn't release the weapon.

"Hunter, get down!" James shouts.

I drop instinctively as something heavy sails over my head—a wooden chair that crashes into Travis. His grip on the shotgun falters, and I tear it from his hands, spinning it around and backing away.

The lean man has recovered and now has James in a headlock, knife edging toward his throat. Deacon circles them, looking for an opening.

Fuck!

Travis charges at me again, roaring with rage. I sidestep, swinging the shotgun like a baseball bat. The stock connects with his arm with a solid thunk, and he goes down hard, sprawling across the floor, wailing.

In the same movement, I flip the shotgun, aiming it at Deacon. "Party's over, Sasquatch!" I shout.

The big man hesitates, hands halfway raised. Behind him, James rolls his eyes even while struggling.

"Sasquatch? Really?" James grunts.

"What? He's hairy and huge," I shoot back without taking my eyes off Deacon.

That split second is all James needs. He drives his elbow back into his captor's solar plexus, then twists violently in the loosened grip. The knife flashes, but James is already inside the man's guard. There's a sickening crack as James slams the man's head against the edge of a table. The knife falls from his suddenly limp fingers as he crumples to the floor.

Deacon glances from his fallen companions to the shotgun in my hands, calculation clear in his eyes. Blood still streams from his nose into his beard.

"Don't," I warn, tightening my grip on the weapon. "Just don't."

The room falls silent except for our ragged breathing and the crackling of the fire. The fight has lasted barely a few minutes, but my body throbs with every heartbeat, adrenaline making my hands shake. Travis groans and tries to get up, moaning louder in pain.

James moves to Deacon and slams a fist into the middle of his face, sending the asshole falling backward, and he cries out, clutching his bleeding face.

Travis stumbles to his feet. "You want everything, don't you, you fucking selfish asshole?" he roars, spittle flying from his lips. "It's never been enough!"

I hear the ache in his voice, even after all these damn years.

"This is all about what you think I took from you. A childhood. A family. Love."

"Shut the fuck up," Travis hisses. "You don't know what you're talking about."

I take a cautious step forward. "I was there, remember? I saw what your mother's family did to you. I begged Grandfather to take you in."

"Liar!" Travis shouts, but there's uncertainty in his eyes now. "You wanted me gone! You were glad I was sent away!"

"I was young," I state quietly. "Same as you. I had just lost my parents too. The only difference is where we ended up."

For a moment, something flickers in Travis's eyes—a flash of the frightened boy he once was before bitterness and resentment hardened him into the man he became. Then it's gone, replaced by the same cold hatred that's defined our relationship for so many years.

"Deacon, fuck, get up, you pussy," he says, looking toward his fallen ally. "Take care of my cousin. Break whatever you want."

Deacon struggles to his feet, face drenched in blood from his busted nose. His huge frame sways unsteadily.

I lift the shotgun, leveling it at Deacon's chest. "Just stay the fuck down." Glancing back at Travis, I snarl, "Next one who moves gets a hole where their lungs used to be."

Something in my voice—a darkness I rarely let

surface—makes the two men freeze. The third one hasn't moved since James put him in his place.

I turn the full intensity of my gaze on Travis. "You need to back the fuck off," I say, my voice low and dangerous. "Let go of the past. Shit happened to both of us, but holding on to it is only going to ruin your damn life."

Travis's face contorts with rage. "Easy for you to say—"

"Shut up," I cut him off. "I'm moving on, and you should too. Maybe one day we can find a way to patch up our differences, but it won't be now." I take a step closer, the shotgun never wavering. "I came for my half of the map, and you're lucky I leave you breathing with how fucking furious I am."

Silence fills the room despite the sounds of our labored breathing. Travis stares at me, hatred warring with something else in his eyes.

"You don't understand," he finally says, his voice cracking. "You got everything. Everything that should have been mine."

"Pull your head out of your ass," I snap. "You got the eastern ranch, a huge piece of land, and half a map. You're too blinded by jealousy to see how good you have it."

"It's not the same!" Travis shouts, a hint of desperation in his voice. "That land is worthless compared to what you got! The treasure is on your property—"

"There might not even be a treasure," I interrupt.

"And if there is, we split it fifty-fifty. That was Grandfather's wish."

For the first time, I see exhaustion beneath Travis's anger. He stares at me as though he didn't hear me right.

I gesture toward Deacon with the shotgun. "Bring me my half of the map. Now, you fucker!"

Deacon stares at Travis, who finally nods after a long moment. "Fine. It's in the desk drawer."

Deacon, with James close behind, retrieves the map piece. He examines it briefly, then winks to me. "This is it."

James grabs it and checks it out, then gives me a nod.

I back up toward the door, keeping the shotgun trained on Travis. "We're neighbors. We're cousins. Consider that your saving grace today. But I see you on my property again, and I will use this shotgun. Got it?"

Travis actually nods, a muscle twitching in his jaw. "Fuck, I got it. Now get the fuck out of my house."

"Gladly," I say. "James, let's go."

We back out slowly, never taking our eyes from them. Only when we're outside do we turn and move toward our snowmobile, the precious map piece secured in James's pocket.

As we climb onto the machine, James looks at me. "You think he'll stick to his word?"

I start the engine. "We'll see. I'm setting up more security systems around the property. Camera traps at every boundary line."

"And the map?" James asks.

I glance back at the cabin, where Travis now stands in the doorway, watching us with unreadable eyes.

"Let's get it somewhere safe," I say. "And then figure out what the hell my grandfather was trying to tell us."

The snowmobile roars to life, and we speed away across the snow-covered landscape, leaving Travis and his wounded pride behind us.

CHAPTER TWENTY-FOUR

LILY

I close my eyes in the hot shower, savoring the sensation of Archer's hands gliding over my skin, his touch possessive as he works shampoo through my curls.

"Is it strange that I feel human again?" I murmur, leaning back against his chest, letting the steady beat of his heart ground me.

His laughter rumbles through me, his arms wrapping around my waist. "We'll have to keep going at it for another week or two, to be sure. For research purposes, of course. I'm very scientific about these things."

"Two weeks?" I turn in his arms, water streaming between us, and smack his chest playfully. His skin is warm and slick under my palm, muscles firm beneath my fingertips. "My sister will go absolutely insane with no help at the bakery."

"Hire an employee," he suggests. His gaze darkens

as it travels down my body with deliberate slowness. "You can't avoid your heat. It's inescapable. Demanding." His voice drops on the last word.

I shiver despite the steam rising around us, heat pooling low in my belly. "My heat's almost over, I think. I feel... different. Better."

"Hmm," he hums, tilting his head as if considering a complex problem. "Still sounds like we need to be sure and not stop." His hands slide up my sides, thumbs brushing my breasts with featherlight pressure that makes me gasp.

"Do you think the guys are okay?" I ask, trying desperately to focus despite his wandering hands. "They've been gone for hours now."

Something softens in Archer's expression, though his hands don't stop their maddening exploration.

"I actually called Hunter on the radio when you first got in the shower. Phone lines are back. He said they're all good—mission accomplished, map retrieved. If something was wrong, he'd tell me straight."

"You're sure?" I press, worry still gnawing at me despite his reassurance. My mind wanders to needing to call my sister if reception is back.

"Positive," he says, pressing a soft kiss to my forehead. "Hunter doesn't sugarcoat. If they were in trouble, he'd say so." He reaches for the bodywash, squeezing a generous amount into his palm. "Now, turn around. I'm not done with you yet."

I obey, presenting my back to him. His hands work

in slow, purposeful patterns, massaging the lavender-scented soap into my shoulders, down my spine, over the curve of my hips. Each touch feels like a promise, like he's learning me by heart.

"What do you want to do when you grow up?" he asks suddenly, his breath teasing my ear.

I snort with surprised laughter. "Excuse me?"

"You know," he elaborates, fingers kneading the tension from my shoulders. "When you're all grown up. What's the dream?"

"I'm twenty-four," I remind him, leaning back into his touch. "I'm already grown."

He chuckles, the sound vibrating against my back. "I'm thirty, so I need to grow up quickly if I haven't already."

"Oh, six years older than me," I tease, turning to face him again. "Cradle snatcher."

"That would be James at thirty-two," he counters with a grin. "Or Hunter at thirty-four. I'm practically a baby compared to them."

"Wow, big age difference," I say, though truthfully, it hadn't even occurred to me until now. "Yet I don't feel any different when I'm with any of you. I'm just... smitten by everything you are."

Something flashes in his eyes—pleasure, surprise, hope. "Does age matter?" he asks, more serious now.

"Not to me," I admit, though a fleeting thought of Hannah's inevitable commentary crosses my mind. My sister will definitely have something to say about me falling for three men, all significantly older. But at this moment, with warm water streaming over us and Archer's hands tracing constellations on my skin, I can't bring myself to care.

"Well, I'm working on opening up a bookshop," he explains, returning to his original question. "Something small but special. First editions, rare finds, comfortable chairs where people can sit for hours, getting lost in stories." His hands move to my hair, gently rinsing out the shampoo. "What about you? Always going to be a baker?"

"I love baking," I say, closing my eyes as his fingers massage my scalp. "But eventually, I'd like to write a cookbook. Maybe focus on heritage recipes, the kind passed down through generations. My grandmother and mother have dozens that deserve to be preserved."

"I'd buy that cookbook," he murmurs, lips finding the sensitive spot just below my ear. "I'd buy anything you created."

His mouth travels down my neck, leaving a trail of heat in its wake. I tilt my head, giving him better access, as my hands slide up his chest to anchor in his hair. The water beats down around us, creating a cocoon of warmth and steam that feels separate from the world beyond the shower wall.

"Archer," I breathe, his name a question and a plea all at once.

He answers by capturing my mouth with his, the kiss deep and consuming. His tongue traces the seam of my lips, seeking entrance I eagerly grant. We fit together perfectly, bodies aligning as if designed for each other. His hands cup my face.

When we finally break apart, I'm breathless, dizzy with desire. "We should probably actually get clean at some point," I suggest weakly.

"Probably," he agrees but makes no move to separate from me, instead pressing hot, open-mouthed kisses along my collarbone. "Eventually."

"Seriously." I laugh, pushing against his chest. "The hot water won't last forever."

With obvious reluctance, he reaches behind me to turn off the water. "You're right. We have plenty of time for... further research."

He grabs two fluffy towels from the nearby rack, wrapping one around my shoulders before securing the other at his waist. I move to dry myself, but he stops me with a gentle hand on my wrist.

"Let me," he insists, his voice soft but brooking no argument.

I stand still as he uses the towel to pat my skin dry with meticulous care, starting with my shoulders and working his way down. There's something intimate about the gesture, about allowing someone else this level of care. It's not sexual, exactly, though my body certainly responds to his touch—it's something deeper, more significant.

I giggle helplessly as he kneels to dry my legs, his touch ticklish against the sensitive spot behind my knee. "You're being ridiculous."

"I'm being thorough," he corrects, looking up at me

with a grin that makes my heart flip. "And you're beautiful. Every inch of you deserves attention."

By the time he's finished, I'm blushing furiously, though not from embarrassment. No one has ever made me feel this way—like I'm precious, like I'm worth this kind of devotion.

Finally dry, we move to his bedroom to dress. I watch, unabashedly appreciative, as he pulls on a pair of worn jeans that hug his lean hips perfectly, followed by a blue-and-green-checked flannel shirt that makes his amber eyes appear even more golden in contrast. With his damp hair falling across his forehead and the beginnings of stubble darkening his jaw, he looks like every fantasy I never knew I had.

"I need to grab some clothes," I say reluctantly, wrapping the towel more securely around myself.

"Don't let me stop you," he replies with a wickedly slow smile, leaning against the dresser to watch me go. "The view as you leave is almost as good as the view when you stay."

"You're incorrigible," I accuse, but smile nonetheless.

I dart across the hallway to the guest room I've been using, Thor appearing from nowhere to follow at my heels. The malamute trots in behind me, settling on the rug with a contented sigh as I rummage through the borrowed clothes Hunter provided.

"What do you think, Thor?" I ask, holding up options. "The sweater or the T-shirt?"

Thor woofs softly, his blue eyes watching me with what seems like genuine interest.

"T-shirt it is," I decide, dropping the towel to pull on underwear and a simple black bra.

The jeans I choose are a bit tight—Hunter mentioned they belong to his cousin who visits occasionally—but they'll do. The T-shirt is long-sleeved with a deep V-neck that shows more cleavage than I'd usually display, and it rides up slightly to reveal a strip of skin at my waist when I move.

I catch a glimpse of myself in the mirror and pause, startled by what I see. It's not just the clothes or the still-damp curls framing my face—it's something in my eyes, a confidence I don't recognize. The woman looking back at me seems different somehow, lighter, happier than the Lily who crashed her sister's car in a snowstorm.

For the first time in longer than I can remember, I feel genuinely joyful, centered in my own skin.

"Come on, boy," I say to Thor, who rises immediately to follow me back into the hallway.

Archer emerges from his room at the same moment, his eyes darkening appreciatively as they travel over me. "You should wear other people's clothes more often," he says, voice dropping to a register that makes my stomach flip. "Preferably mine."

"Smooth," I reply, though I'm secretly pleased by his reaction. "Very smooth."

He pulls me close, hands settling on my hips. "I mean it," he murmurs, his breath warm against my ear. "You're stunning."

Before I can respond, his lips find mine in a kiss that starts gently but quickly deepens, his hands sliding under the T-shirt to caress bare skin. I melt against him, arms winding around his neck, and everything else is momentarily forgotten.

When we finally break apart, I'm struggling to remember what we were supposed to be doing. "We should... um..."

"Go downstairs," he finishes, though he makes no move to release me. "Eventually."

Thor whines softly beside us, clearly impatient with our human nonsense.

"Your chaperone has spoken," Archer says with a laugh, finally stepping back. "Come on, let's feed him and get some breakfast ourselves."

As we move toward the stairs, I notice a picture frame on the floor beneath a now-empty nail in the wall. I pick it up carefully, turning it over to examine the image behind the cracked glass.

"What's that?" Archer asks, peering over my shoulder.

"My grandmother with Hunter's grandfather." A photo I'd inspected days ago.

The photo shows her standing proudly in front of a tiny bakery. I remember Mom telling me that Grandma had worked in another bakery before she purchased the one we work in now. In the photo, beside her is Hunter's grandfather.

I've seen countless photos of my grandmother in her youth—the resemblance is unmistakable—but I still don't get why this picture of her here is in this cabin.

I turn the frame over, looking for any inscription or date, but find nothing. "How do they know each other?"

Archer takes the frame, examining it more closely.

Staring at him, an idea comes to me. "The phone lines are back up now, right?" I ask. "I should call my sister anyway, let her know I'm okay. But maybe I could also video-call my grandmother at Pine Grove Nursing Home and show her this photo."

"Oh, she's still alive? Brilliant idea," Archer comments. "I have an iPad we can use for the video call —bigger screen. Let me grab it from my room."

"Perfect. I'll go downstairs and call Hannah first."

In the living room, I settle on the couch, sinking into the soft cushions. Thor claims the spot beside me, his large head resting on my lap as if it belongs there. I scratch his head absently as I turn on my phone, noticing a number of messages suddenly popping up on my device as it catches up. Mostly from Hannah. My stomach sinks. I dial my sister's number.

She answers on the first ring, her voice tight with worry. "Lily? Oh my God, are you okay? I'm so fucking worried!"

Guilt washes over me instantly. "I'm fine, Han, I promise," I say quickly. "I'm so sorry I didn't call again after the first message. The storm knocked out the phone lines, and everything's been kind of... intense."

"Intense? What does that mean? I'll borrow Dad's car and come get you right now. I have the address from Martin."

I hesitate, suddenly faced with a reality I've been avoiding. The storm is over. The roads will be clearing. My heat has mostly subsided. There's no reason for me to stay here anymore, right?

Except for the three Alphas...

The thought of leaving—of being separated from James, Hunter, and Archer—feels like someone's reaching into my chest and squeezing my heart. But what exactly are we to each other now? We haven't actually discussed what happens next.

"Maybe... that would be great," I say, the words leaving a bitter taste in my mouth. "I need to arrange to have your car towed from where I crashed it anyway."

"Are you sure you're okay?" Hannah asks, her voice softening with concern. "The bakery wasn't that busy during the storm, and the tasting was delayed due to the weather, but I really need you back. And I want to make sure you're all right. God, Lily, you've been staying with total strangers. They treated you okay?"

"More than okay," I admit, feeling heat rise to my cheeks as memories of the past few days flash through my mind. "They've been... incredible."

"Incredible how?" Hannah asks, suspicion creeping into her tone. "You're being weird."

"I'm not," I protest, though my voice comes out higher than normal. "Just tired. It's been a long few days."

"Uh-huh," she says, clearly not believing me. "Well, I'll close the shop early. That work?"

"Perfect," I agree, ignoring the hollow feeling in my chest. "I've missed you, Han."

"Missed you too," she says, her tone softening. "You sound... different."

"I promise I'm fine. Better than fine. See you soon." She gives her farewell, and I hang up.

Archer returns with the iPad, settling beside me on the couch, with Thor on the other side. "Everything good with your sister?"

"Great," I say, forcing brightness into my voice, unsure if I'm ready to deal with telling him everything or the awkwardness that I'll need to leave, I guess.

"What's the nursing home's number?"

I give him Pine Grove's information, and he dials it on the iPad. The call connects to an audio-only line, and I explain to the receptionist that I'd like to video-chat with my grandmother, Maddie Smyth, in room 214.

"It might take a few minutes," I tell Archer as we wait. "They have to set up the iPad in her room and help her figure it out."

"No rush," he says, sliding closer until our thighs press together. His fingers dance along my side, finding the strip of exposed skin at my waist and tickling lightly.

I squirm, laughter bubbling up despite my attempt to maintain composure. "Stop that! I need to be serious when—"

The screen suddenly illuminates, showing my grandmother's face, peering curiously at the camera. Her silver hair is styled in the soft curls she's worn for as long as I can remember, barely reaching her shoulders. Her bright golden-brown eyes—the same ones I inherited—are magnified slightly by reading glasses perched on her nose. Despite being in her eighties, her skin is remarkably smooth, with fine lines at the corners of her eyes. She's wearing her favorite lavender cardigan, a strand of pearls visible at the neckline.

A nurse hovers in the background, giving her instructions.

"I can manage it myself, dear," she tells the nurse firmly before turning her attention back to the screen. "Lily! Oh, darling, I've missed you so much. I hope you and Hannah are safe after that terrible storm."

The sight of her familiar face fills me with warmth. "We're fine, Grandma. How are you doing?"

Her eyes shift from me to Archer, who hasn't moved from my side, and a slow, knowing smile spreads across her face. "Lily, please tell me you have good news and that you've found your Alpha, because that man by your side is gorgeous for you."

Heat floods my cheeks instantly. "Grandma!"

But Archer merely leans closer to the screen, his

most charming smile in place. "Mrs. Smyth, it's a pleasure to meet you. I'm Archer Sterling, and I can assure you that I absolutely adore your granddaughter."

I elbow him gently but can't help admiring the way he speaks to her—respectful but warm, genuinely engaging rather than humoring an elderly woman the way some might.

"Call me Maddie, dear," my grandmother insists, practically beaming at him. "Any man who looks at my Lily the way you just did has earned first-name privileges."

"You're too kind, Maddie," Archer replies smoothly. "Lily tells me you're the one who taught her to bake. I have to thank you—her cinnamon rolls are life-changing."

I roll my eyes at his shameless charm offensive, but my grandmother is clearly delighted.

"Flatterer," she says, eyes twinkling. "You must come visit me soon. I need to ask you some very important questions to make sure you're right for my granddaughter."

"I look forward to the interrogation," Archer replies with a wink.

I clear my throat, desperate to change the subject before they start planning wedding cakes or baby names.

"Grandma, I actually called because I found something interesting." I hold up the photograph to the camera. "Is this you... with someone from the..." I pause, turning to Archer. "What's Hunter's last name?"

"Thorne," he says without hesitation.

I turn back to the iPad, my gaze locking on my grandmother. "With someone from the Thorne family?"

My grandmother's expression transforms, softening with nostalgia. "Oh my," she breathes, leaning closer to the screen. "Where did you find that? It feels like just yesterday." She sighs deeply. "I heard Malcolm passed away recently. My heart hurt when I found out. He was such a wonderful man."

"So, how did you know him?" I ask, curiosity burning through me. "You weren't... dating, were you?"

She bursts out laughing, the sound so full and rich it makes me smile despite myself. "Oh, no, nothing like that! We were just friends... business friends. Malcolm lent me the money to finally buy a new bakery when no bank would give a loan to a *silly woman with flour in her hair,* as they put it. He let me pay him back without charging a single penny of interest." Her eyes grow distant with memory. "He was a true soul, a heart of gold. We need more people like that in our world."

Her gaze returns to us, her smile widening. "You two really do make a lovely couple. You must bring him to visit me, Lily. I need to make sure his intentions are honorable."

"I'd be delighted to prove myself worthy," Archer says before I can respond. "Though, I should warn you, I have a tendency to charm elderly ladies. It's my superpower."

"Cheeky boy." My grandmother laughs. "I like him already, Lily."

I set the photograph down on the coffee table, shaking my head at their instant rapport. "So, Malcolm Thorne was just a friend who helped you start the bakery. That's amazing, but I wonder why Hunter has this photo."

"Oh, Malcolm cared for his family so much," my grandmother continues. "He was always talking about his grandson, worrying about how he and his cousin fought constantly. He actually planted a treasure hunt for them to get along after he was gone. Isn't that beautiful?"

Archer and I freeze, exchanging a startled glance.

"Wait, what did you just say?" Archer asks, leaning toward the screen.

"About the treasure hunt?" My grandmother looks surprised at our reaction. "Yes, Malcolm mentioned it a few times in his last years when he would pay me a visit occasionally. He left each boy half a treasure map in his will, hoping they'd have to work together to find it. A rather clever plan, I thought."

"What else do you know about this treasure hunt?" I ask, my heart suddenly racing.

She chuckles, adjusting her glasses. "Well, the funny part is, there isn't actually any treasure on the map."

"There isn't?" Archer's voice rises in disbelief.

"Not on the map itself, no," she explains, a mischievous smile spreading on her mouth. "Malcolm found the gold himself years ago. After building his properties and securing the land, he hid a significant portion of the treasure in each house. He told me once he concealed it in the basement walls. If the boys ever found the *X* on the map, they'd discover a note explaining this."

Archer and I stare at each other, stunned into silence.

"Grandma," I say slowly. "Do you remember exactly where in the basement he might have hidden it?"

She shakes her head. "No, dear, he never shared those details. Just that it was somewhere in the walls, I believe." She peers at us curiously. "Why? Are you two treasure hunting now?"

"Something like that," Archer murmurs, his knee bouncing with barely contained excitement.

We chat for a few more minutes, but I can feel Archer's impatience matching my own. Finally, my grandmother glances at her watch.

"I'm afraid I have to go now, darlings. Bingo starts in ten minutes, and Ethel always tries to steal my lucky seat if I'm not there early. The woman is eighty-seven but moves like a jaguar when free pudding or prime bingo spots are involved."

"Of course, Grandma," I say, sending her a kiss through the screen. "I'll visit soon. I promise."

"Bring that handsome man with you," she insists. "And be careful treasure hunting! Malcolm always said the real treasure was family, but a few gold bars never hurt anyone."

Archer offers a charming farewell before ending the call. The moment the screen goes dark, we turn to each other with wide eyes.

"Oh my God," I breathe, my mind racing with possibilities.

Without another word, Archer and I are both on our feet from the couch and racing toward the basement door off the kitchen. Thor barks excitedly, following as we thunder down the wooden stairs into the cool, dimly lit space below.

I've been down here before—James showed me the freezers where Hunter stores game meat, and I'd joked nervously about it being the perfect place to hide bodies. The basement is utilitarian—concrete floor, exposed beams overhead, walls constructed of field-stone and mortar. Two large chest freezers hum against one wall. Shelves lined with emergency supplies occupy another wall, while tools hang in neat rows above a workbench in the corner.

"Start checking the walls," Archer instructs, already running his hands over the rough stone surface. "Look for anything unusual—loose stones, hollow sounds, weird patterns."

I move to the opposite wall, tapping and pressing methodically. "I can't believe he buried it in the house. It's pretty genius."

"It's kind of amazing they knew each other at all. What are the odds?"

We check every inch of wall space. "It's not here," I finally say, leaning back against the wall in defeat. "Maybe we misunderstood what she meant, or—" My elbow presses against what should be solid stone but instead gives slightly. I freeze, then press again, harder. Something shifts behind me.

"Archer! I think I found something!"

He rushes over as I examine the stone more closely. It looks identical to those surrounding it, but when I push, it moves inward slightly. Archer joins me, both of us pressing against the stone until we hear a faint mechanical click.

A section of wall about three feet wide swings inward, revealing a dark space beyond.

Just then, heavy footsteps sound overhead, followed by voices calling our names.

"Where the hell is everyone?" Hunter growls.

"Get your damn asses down here now!" Archer shouts back. "The treasure was in the house the whole time!"

Thunderous footfalls rush down the stairs. Hunter appears first, his tall frame filling the doorway, followed closely by James. Both men look exhausted, faces wind-burned, with small cuts and forming bruises visible on their exposed skin.

"You're back," I say, relief flooding through me so intensely it makes my knees weak. I move toward them without thinking, needing to confirm with my own hands that they're really okay.

James catches me first, strong arms wrapping around me in a tight embrace that lifts me slightly off the ground. "Told you I'd be back," he murmurs against my hair, his voice rough with fatigue but warm with something else—something that makes my heart flutter.

Hunter steps in as James releases me, his large arm wrapped around me. "Everything's fine," he assures me, pressing his lips to mine. "Got the map back, sorted Travis out."

I examine them both more closely, noting the way James favors his right side and how Hunter winces slightly when he turns too quickly. "You're hurt," I accuse, hands fluttering over them uselessly. "Both of you."

"Just bruised," James dismisses. "Nothing serious."

"What happened?" I ask, eyes scanning them both for hidden injuries.

"Later," Hunter says, his attention caught by the open stone door. "What the hell is that?" He points to the secret compartment in his wall.

Archer quickly explains our discovery—the call with my grandmother, the revelation about his grandfather's true treasure plan.

"Are you fucking kidding me?" Hunter groans, running a hand through his disheveled hair. "It was in the house the whole time? That's exactly the kind of thing Grandfather would do!"

"The old man had a twisted sense of humor," James adds.

"Well, don't just stand there," Archer urges, gesturing to the opening. "Let's see what's inside!"

Hunter produces a flashlight from a nearby shelf, and we crowd around the narrow opening as he goes in. The beam illuminates a tiny, confined space, no larger than a closet, carved directly into the foundation. Against the back wall sits an old wooden chest, its brass fittings tarnished with age.

"My God," Hunter whispers, stepping carefully into the space. "It's really here."

The chest isn't locked. Hunter kneels before it, hands shaking as he lifts the heavy lid. Golden light seems to spill out as it opens, reflecting off the flashlight beam.

Inside, stacked in neat rows, are dozens of gold bars, each about the size of a smartphone. Mixed among them are leather pouches Hunter picks up, and they clink with the unmistakable sound of coins.

"Holy shit," James breathes, crouching beside Hunter. "How much do you think is in there?"

"Millions," Archer estimates. "Gold prices today… this could be worth five, maybe ten, million."

I stare at the gleaming treasure, struggling to

process what I'm seeing. It's like something from a movie, not real life—not my life, certainly.

Hunter reaches in among the gold and pulls out a sealed envelope, yellowed with age, then he comes out into the basement. His hands tremble slightly as he breaks the seal and unfolds several pages of hand-written text.

"It's from Grandfather," he whispers, as if it's hard for him to contain his emotions. He clears his throat and begins to read.

My dear Hunter,

If you're reading this, then you and Travis have finally put aside your differences long enough to solve my little puzzle. For that alone, I am proud of you both.

I must confess something that may anger you initially: I have known the location of the "lost" Thorne treasure for over forty years. I found it one summer, hidden in a cave system on the north ridge where no one had thought to look before.

I did not keep this discovery secret out of greed or self-ishness. I used much of it to rebuild our family's legacy—the cabin where you now stand, the ranch that has provided for our family for generations, the additional land that ensures our privacy and self-sufficiency.

The remainder I have divided equally—half here in your home, half in an identical hiding place in Travis's lodge. Yes, there is a secret compartment there as well.

I know Travis is difficult to understand. His path has been harder than yours in many ways. The abuse he suffered at the hands of his mother's family haunts him still.

I tried to gain custody of him, fought through legal channels for years, but I failed him. This treasure is my small attempt to make amends for that failure.

My deepest wish is that you boys find a way to make peace. Family is the only treasure that truly matters in this life. Everything else is just metal and stone.

The gold is yours to do with as you see fit. I ask only that you consider what truly brings you happiness before you decide how to use it.

With all my love and faith in you both, Grandfather Malcolm.

Hunter lowers the letter, his ice-blue eyes suspiciously bright in the dim light. For the first time since I met him, the mountain man looks vulnerable, his usual stoic demeanor cracking to reveal the pain beneath.

Without thinking, I move to him, wrapping my arms around his broad shoulders. For a moment, he stiffens, then relaxes into the embrace, his head bowing to rest against my shoulder. James places a steadying hand on his back while Archer rests a palm on his arm. The four of us connected in a moment of shared emotion that tightens my throat.

"Travis has the same amount waiting for him at his place," Hunter says finally, his voice rough. "He just doesn't know it. I'll make him aware."

I stare at the three men surrounding me—Hunter with his intense strength, James with his protective possessiveness, and Archer with his addictive affection. Men who were strangers just days ago but now feel more essential to me than almost anyone else in my life.

I think about the bakery, about Hannah coming to pick me up today, about the reality waiting for me outside this mountain cabin. Something twists painfully in my chest at the thought of leaving.

"So what happens now?" I ask, looking from one man to the next. "With the treasure? With Travis?" *With us*, I want to say, but the words refuse to come. My chest is clenching really hard.

Hunter carefully folds his grandfather's letter. "We need to pull the treasure out first," he says, practical as always.

James and Archer move to help, the three of them working together to slide the heavy container out of its hiding place. Thor watches from the stairs, tail wagging with excitement at all the activity.

"As for Travis," Hunter continues once the chest sits in the middle of the basement floor, gleaming dully in the overhead light. "Maybe someday we can make up. Maybe. He's still the one who broke into my home and endangered everyone here."

"One step at a time," Archer suggests, resting a hand on Hunter's shoulder. "The old man was right about one thing—family matters."

"Family isn't always blood," James adds quietly, his gaze moving between all of us.

The words hang in the air, full of meaning I'm almost afraid to examine too closely. I don't know if that includes me... not sure how it can when we are just getting to know one another. Am I just a guest they helped, someone who'll leave their lives as quickly as I entered them?

My stomach turns with uncertainty, but as I watch them, I'm struck by how right it feels to be here with them. How natural.

"We should celebrate," Archer announces suddenly, breaking the somber mood. "This calls for champagne, or at the very least, some of Hunter's expensive whiskey."

"It's barely noon," I point out, though I can't help smiling at his enthusiasm.

"It's five o'clock somewhere," he counters, slinging an arm around my shoulders. "Besides, how often do you find millions in gold hidden in your basement wall?"

"He has a point," James concedes, the corner of his mouth lifting in that half smile that does ridiculous things to my insides.

Hunter nods, some of the tension easing from his shoulders. "Fine. But first, we need to secure this properly." He glances at the open wall compartment. "And figure out if there are any other secret spaces my grandfather built that we don't know about."

As the men discuss logistics, I stand slightly apart, watching them interact and how well they get along.

For a moment, I'm struck by a sense of not belonging, of being an outsider. But then James pauses at the bottom of the stairs, looking back at me with a raised eyebrow.

"You coming, baker girl?" he asks.

"Wouldn't miss it," I reply, hurrying to join them.

We head upstairs, leaving the treasure for now, I assume, and emerge into the kitchen, which is currently bathed in midday sunlight that streams through the large windows. The storm that brought me here feels like a distant memory, the world outside transformed into a brilliantly white landscape under clear blue skies.

"Table," Hunter directs.

We drink, the whiskey burning pleasantly down my throat, warming me from the inside. For a moment, we sit in companionable silence. Yet something aches deep inside me, knowing that as much as I love it here, do I really belong?

Thor pads across the room and flops down at my feet with a contented sigh, his blue eyes watching us all with canine curiosity.

"So," Archer says finally. "What's the plan now? With the treasure?"

"Whatever we want," Hunter says finally. "Fulfill all our fantasies and dreams."

Suddenly, they all turn and look at me. My cheeks flush under their combined gaze, heat spreading down my neck.

"What?" I ask, trying to sound casual despite the butterflies taking flight in my stomach.

James moves first, crossing the space between us in two long strides. His fingers brush a curl from my face, lingering against my cheek. "I think you know exactly what."

Archer appears at my other side, his hand finding the small of my back. "The question is, what do you want, Lily?"

Hunter completes the circle, standing directly in front of me, his imposing presence making me feel deliciously small.

My mouth goes dry. They're so close, surrounding me with their combined scents—cedar and chocolate, pine and woodsmoke, old books and bergamot.

"I-I..." My words tangle in my throat, my heart thumping so hard I feel the room spinning. I know what I want—them. Fuck, I want them for good so badly it hurts, yet a fear tumbles within me that our storm time was just that. Fun. Helping me. But now reality settles in.

I open my mouth to say something—to tell them I would love to give us a chance, a thousand times yes, beyond just our attraction and my heat—when a sharp knock at the front door freezes us all in place.

We pull apart slightly, exchanging confused glances.

"Who the hell is that?" Hunter growls, his protective instincts visibly flaring.

CHAPTER TWENTY-SIX
LILY

The knock at the door comes harder.

Hunter strides toward the door, his posture instantly alert. Thor trots at his heels, his ears perked forward with canine curiosity. James and Archer remain close to me, their touch lingering as if reluctant to break contact.

My heart hammers against my ribs, partly from the interrupted moment and partly from apprehension. Is it Hunter's cousin, Travis, again?

Hunter pulls the door open, revealing a slender figure bundled in a pristine white parka, dark hair escaping from beneath a matching knit hat.

"Hannah?" I gasp, recognizing my sister immediately. I rush forward as she steps into the entryway, throwing my arms around her. "You're here! Already!"

"The roads opened faster than expected," Hannah explains, returning my hug. "They had extra plows out because of all the people stranded by the storm." She pulls back, examining me with that big-sister scrutiny that hasn't changed since we were kids. "Are you okay? You look... different."

I feel my cheeks warm, knowing exactly how I look —like a woman who's been thoroughly kissed and adored.

"I'm fine," I assure her. "Better than fine, actually."

Pulling back, I take in my sister's appearance. Despite having just driven through post-blizzard mountain roads, she looks immaculate as always. Her dark chocolate-brown hair falls in perfect waves around her face, not a strand out of place. The French twist she normally wears for work has been let down, but she still looks like she just stepped out of a salon. Her makeup is flawless, her clothes—designer jeans and that ridiculously expensive cashmere sweater she splurged on last Christmas—unwrinkled. The only hint of her journey is the slight flush on her cheeks from the cold.

"I've been so worried about you," she says, her eyes traveling over my face. "Your message was so vague, and then nothing! I thought you'd been murdered by mountain men or something." Her gaze flicks over my shoulder, widening slightly as she takes in the three very large, very real mountain men standing behind me. "Oh," she breathes. "You didn't mention they were... um..."

"Alphas?" I supply, unable to contain a small smile at her reaction.

"I was going to say 'enormous,' but yes, that too,"

she murmurs. Her attention darts between the three men, her cheeks blushing slightly.

"Come in." I tug her inside, out of the cold entryway. "I'll introduce you properly."

Hannah follows me into the warmth of the cabin. She's always been the detail-oriented one between us, noticing everything, so I spot her taking in the gorgeous home.

Thor approaches her, nudging her hand with his nose. Like me, Hannah loves animals, so she bends to pat his head, her perfectly manicured nails disappearing into his thick fur.

"Well, hello there," she coos. "Aren't you handsome? Yes, you are."

I smile, watching her usual composure dissolve in the face of canine charm. Some things never change—Hannah may count her steps between tasks at the bakery and organize sprinkles by color, but put a dog in front of her, and she turns into a puddle.

"That's Thor," I tell her. "He's Hunter's, but I think he's decided I'm his new favorite person."

"Smart dog," James murmurs behind me, just loud enough for me to hear.

I make the introductions quickly, gesturing to each man in turn. "Hannah, these mountain men are Hunter, James, and Archer. Guys, this is my sister, Hannah."

She straightens, smoothing her sweater with a nervous gesture. "Thank you for taking care of my sister," she says, adopting the slightly bossy big-sister tone she uses when she's feeling protective. "I owe you so much for doing that."

"You owe us nothing," Hunter replies, closing the door firmly behind her.

Hannah glances back at the closed door, a flicker of unease crossing her face. For all her poise, my sister has always been slightly claustrophobic, a childhood fear that never fully dissipated.

"Well, we won't stay long," she states quickly. "I came to get her out of your hair. I'm sure you're ready to get back to your normal lives."

The atmosphere in the room instantly shifts, like the pressure drop before a storm. All three men go utterly still, their expressions transforming from polite welcome to something darker, more intense.

"You think you're leaving us?" Hunter asks in my direction. "Is that why your sister is here to pick you up? You don't want this? Us?"

"What's going on?" Hannah looks between us, confusion evident in the furrow between her perfectly shaped eyebrows. "What are they talking about?"

I pinch my lips, my stomach twisting madly, slightly confused. My throat tightens with emotion as I struggle to find words.

"I just thought... after helping me and stuff... then things go back to normal, you know?" I manage, my voice small and uncertain. I wrap my arms around myself, suddenly feeling vulnerable. "You have your lives and don't need someone like me and—"

"Lily, stop," James interrupts, moving closer. His

gray eyes are wide, stormy with emotion. "Don't even finish what you're saying."

Within moments, all three men surround me, creating a circle of warmth and masculine energy that makes my knees weak. Thor sits at Hannah's feet, watching the proceedings with bright, curious eyes.

"We can't allow that," Archer says, his hand finding mine. His fingers lace through mine, warm and steady. "When we, as Alphas, claim you, you are ours forever. When we help you through your heat—"

"You had your heat?" Hannah gasps. "With them? All three?" She looks them up and down again, taking in their size, their obvious strength, in a new light. "God, they're so huge."

"You have no idea," I choke out, half laughing, half on the verge of tears. The emotional whiplash of the past few minutes has left me raw and vulnerable. "It was... full-on."

"That's an understatement," Archer mutters with a grin.

"That's our fault for not telling you this earlier," Hunter explains. Then, to my utter shock, he drops to one knee before me.

James and Archer exchange a look, then follow suit until all three Alphas are kneeling at my feet. The sight is so unexpected, so overwhelming, that I'm momentarily speechless.

"We heard you like groveling," James states with a hint of that dry humor I've come to adore.

I glare at him, heat rushing to my cheeks. "But—"

"No," Hunter interrupts firmly. "We don't want to lose what you showed us, the happiness we knew we were missing." His ice-blue eyes, usually so controlled, are raw. "All three of us want you, only you."

"You crashed into our lives—literally—and somehow fixed something none of us even realized was broken," Archer adds, his usual playfulness replaced with earnest sincerity.

"You make us better," James says simply. "Together and individually."

Tears well in my eyes, spilling over despite my best efforts to contain them. It seems impossible—that these three incredible men could all want me, could be willing to upend their lives for me.

"But you barely know me," I protest weakly.

"Sometimes a week is all it takes," Hunter murmurs with a grin. "My grandfather used to say he knew my grandmother was 'the one' the moment he laid eyes on her. Took him three days to propose."

"And we've had less than a week with you," Archer points out. "So, we're practically taking it slow."

Hannah watches from a few feet away, her initial wariness gradually replaced by a slow smile spreading across her face. She's always been able to read me better than anyone, and whatever she sees in my expression seems to reassure her.

"What are you waiting for?" she whispers, loud enough for me to hear. "If you adore them, then yes, try this out. Don't you dare give up now."

"Your sister is very wise," Archer adds with a

theatrical wink toward Hannah. "I think you should listen to her. She clearly has excellent judgment, impeccable taste, and—if I might add—a remarkable resemblance to you that suggests beauty runs in the family."

"Laying it on a bit thick there, Arch," James murmurs.

"Flattery will get you everywhere," Hannah replies dryly, though I can see she's charmed despite herself. Her posture has relaxed, the protective big-sister stance softening.

"What do you want?" James asks me. "Because whatever it is, we'll make it happen. We'll move to Whispering Grove if we need to."

"I'm not sure Hannah will like having three Alphas move in with her," I point out.

Hannah makes a strangled sound that's half laugh, half cough. "There is not enough space. Literally. Our apartment above the bakery is tiny. I can hear Lily singing in the shower from every room."

"My singing isn't that bad," I protest automatically.

"It really is," she counters with sisterly frankness.

"We'll buy a house there," Archer suggests promptly. "Something with enough room for all of us."

James's eyes light up with a new idea. "We could open our own bakery, the four of us. You and me as the bakers." He turns to Hannah. "Imagine the lines of women coming to buy baked goods from Archer and Hunter in pretty aprons."

"I'd pay good money to see that," Hannah agrees, grinning.

"Hunter in an apron? Now there's a visual," Archer muses, tilting his head as if picturing it.

"Don't push your luck," Hunter growls, but there's no real heat in it.

"A book café attached," Archer adds enthusiastically. "Rare editions on display, reading nooks, literary events. I've always wanted to combine my love of books with a public space."

"And I'll handle the business side," Hunter says, his deep voice practical but warm. "Funding, management, logistics... but only if that's okay." His eyes move between Hannah and me. "We don't want to break up the bakery sisters or take business from you."

Hannah is already shaking her head. "Not at all. This is perfect, actually." She hesitates, then continues. "I've been wanting to branch out more on my own and wasn't sure how to tell you, Lily."

"You were?" I stare at her, momentarily distracted from the three men still kneeling before me. "What are you going to do?"

"I've actually been looking into starting my own event planning business," she continues. "I've already made some connections in the industry. Maybe I can order baked goods from you..." She pauses, an idea clearly forming. "If you want, I can sell you the bakery. You'd be amazing at running it yourself."

"Yes," Hunter states immediately, rising to his feet. "She'll buy it from you, and we can set up there in town but expand it. Make it something truly special." He turns to me. "If that's okay with you?"

My head spins with how rapidly everything is changing, possibilities unfolding before me that I never dared to imagine. "This is moving so fast," I say, feeling slightly overwhelmed. "Okay, one bit at a time, please. I haven't even officially agreed to stay with you yet, and we're already planning business ventures."

They laugh, the sound warm and real.

"She's right," Hunter acknowledges. "We're getting ahead of ourselves." He turns to Hannah. "Please, come in properly. We can have coffee. Join us, and we can get to know each other better."

Hannah glances at me questioningly, and when I nod, she smiles. "I'd like that a lot." She walks over to me, wrapping an arm around my shoulders and pulling me close. "You're so lucky, girl," she whispers in my ear.

The words catch me off guard, bringing fresh tears to my eyes. Hannah has always been the successful one —perfect grades, perfect appearance, everything meticulously planned and executed. To hear pride in her voice, directed at me, feels like a gift I didn't know I needed.

"Thanks," I whisper back, hugging her tightly.

"So," Archer says, clapping his hands together. "Coffee for everyone? Or something stronger, considering we're apparently planning both romantic and business mergers simultaneously?"

"Coffee is fine." Hannah laughs. "I'm driving back later."

"I'll make it," James volunteers, heading toward the kitchen. "Lily, show your sister around while I get that started."

"You're going to tell me everything," Hannah whispers to me, linking her arm through mine. Her gaze travels meaningfully to the men moving around the cabin. "Especially about James." She raises a brow.

"Later," I promise. "When I'm not in danger of being overheard and thoroughly embarrassed."

As I show Hannah around the main floor of the cabin, I'm struck by how naturally the men adjust their movements around us.

We settle in the living room, Thor moving between us, accepting pets from everyone but eventually settling at my feet with a contented sigh.

"So," Hannah says. "How exactly is this going to work? The four of you, I mean." She gestures between the men and me. "Not judging, just thinking for my sister. I have a friend who recently found three Alpha mates, and now, with Lily, I'm starting to feel left out." She laughs, and I nudge her with my shoulder.

"We're going to figure it out as we go, as it's all new to us," Hunter answers honestly. "But the important thing is that we all want the same thing—Lily's happiness."

"We're a pack," James says quietly, his eyes meeting mine across the room.

The word resonates through me, feeling right in a

way I can't fully explain. It's not just about the Alpha-Omega dynamic, though that's certainly part of it. It's about belonging, about finding people who complement and complete each other.

Hunter's hand brushes casually against my shoulder, sending a wave of tingles down my spine. Across from us, Archer winks at me over his steaming mug of coffee, that mischievous glint in his amber eyes making the butterflies in my stomach take flight.

"Is living out here always this peaceful?" Hannah asks, curled up in the armchair adjacent to the sofa. My sister has been watching the three men fuss over me all afternoon with equal parts amusement and astonishment—bringing me coffee, adjusting pillows behind my back, and making sure I'm comfortable.

"Most days," Hunter replies, his fingers absently playing with a strand of my hair, leaning on the couch behind me. "Though, it's never been quite like this before."

"The isolation must be nice," Hannah continues.

James shifts closer to my side on the couch, his hand coming to rest on my thigh with a casual possessiveness that sends warmth spreading through me. Archer moves from his chair to squeeze onto the sofa on my other side, the three of them forming a protective circle that should feel overwhelming but instead feels like sanctuary.

Is this really my life? I wonder, looking at each of them in turn. *Three Alphas want me?*

I can't stop the smile that spreads across my face,

probably making me appear ridiculous, but I don't care.

"I believe," Hunter says, "we were confirming whether Lily wants to be ours."

Three pairs of eyes turn to me, filled with hope, desire, and something deeper that makes my heart race. Even Hannah has gone quiet, her expression soft as she watches this moment unfold.

"Yes," I say simply, the word feeling like coming home. "Yes to all of it. To all of you."

The next few moments are a blur of movement and sensation—Hunter lifting me off my feet in a spinning hug, Archer pressing jubilant kisses to my face, James holding me so tightly I can feel his heart hammering against mine.

"I still can't believe this is real," I admit. "That you all want this. Want me."

"Believe it," James says firmly, his hands warm on my waist.

"We'll prove it to you every day," Archer promises, tucking a curl behind my ear.

"For as long as you'll have us," Hunter adds, his usual stoicism melted away to reveal the depth of feeling beneath.

My sister is smiling so big, and I love that she gets to be part of this, to understand that I am falling for these men so hard.

Surrounded by three men who look at me like I'm the answer to a question they've been asking their whole lives, I'm struck by the beautiful absurdity of it all. A week ago, I was just a baker with a crashed car and an approaching heat. Now, I'm... what? The center of a pack? The heart of something new and wonderful?

"What's that smile for?" James asks, his thumb brushing my lower lip.

"I'm just thinking," I reply, meeting the gaze of each man in turn before glancing at my sister, who watches with tears of happiness in her eyes. "That sometimes the worst wrong turns lead to exactly where you're supposed to be."

CHAPTER TWENTY-SEVEN
LILY

Months Later

The soft golden glow of string lights illuminates our bakery name and sign—Flour & Fable Bakery—hanging proudly above the entrance. Hunter hand-carved a brand-new wooden sign himself, and James designed the logo—a whimsical cupcake with an open book as its base.

Through the gleaming front windows, I spot the line of customers stretching down the block, a colorful queue of eager faces in the crisp October morning. Orange and black bunting frames the windows, and artfully arranged pumpkins flank the entrance. Inside, paper bats hang from the ceiling, dancing slightly in the warm air circulating from the ovens.

"Five minutes to opening," Hunter announces, checking his watch.

I smooth down my apron—black with orange trim,

our seasonal uniform—and take a deep breath that does little to calm my fluttering nerves. Three months of renovation, planning, and preparation have led to this moment—the grand reopening of Flour & Fable Bakery, just in time for Halloween. It took us longer to transition, to buy a new house, to have all my Alphas move in with me as they sold their houses. Well, except the cabin in the woods. We love that place and use it as our getaway. Besides, we had to do a world trip holiday, and then we finally started to expand the bakery.

"We're going to crush it," James assures me, sliding a tray of pumpkin-shaped cookies into the display case. His black T-shirt stretches across his broad shoulders, our orange logo emblazoned across his chest. Every time I look at him—at any of them—in our matching shirts, I feel a ridiculous flutter in my stomach.

Archer emerges from the bookstore section, adjusting the display of vintage Gothic novels he's curated especially for the season. "First editions of *Dracula* and *Frankenstein* on prominent display," he reports with a satisfied grin. "Plus, all the modern Halloween favorites. The reading nook is ready with those ridiculous pumpkin-shaped pillows you insisted on."

"They're adorable, and you know it," I counter, nudging him with my hip as I pass.

He catches me around the waist, pulling me against him for a quick kiss. "They're gauche, and I adore them because you do."

"Less kissing, more prep," Hannah calls, emerging from the kitchen with a tray of her signature caramel apple tarts. She's taken time away from the event-planning business to help with our opening day, a gesture that means more than she knows.

The bakery itself is unrecognizable from its former incarnation. Where once stood a charming but cramped space, we now have an expansive, open-concept establishment. Hunter used part of his inheritance to purchase the building next door, and we knocked down walls to create something truly special.

The front section houses the bakery counter and café tables, warm wood and soft lighting creating an inviting atmosphere. A gorgeous stone archway—Hunter and James built it themselves over two sweat-soaked weekends—leads to Archer's bookstore, where comfortable reading nooks and carefully curated shelves invite customers to linger.

"Your adoring public awaits," my father announces, emerging from the back office. With silvery hair and laugh lines that deepen when he smiles, he's embraced his role as our cashier with unexpected enthusiasm. "And may I say, the register system is remarkably intuitive for an old dinosaur like me."

"That's because Hunter spent three hours programming it to be dad-proof," I tease, earning a mock-offended look from my father.

"I'll have you know I was using computers while you were still in diapers, young lady," he retorts, but his eyes dance with humor.

One of the most surprising developments of the past few months has been how seamlessly my father has embraced my relationship. When I nervously introduced him to all three men, explaining our situation with halting words and flushed cheeks, he'd simply looked them over carefully and said, "Well, you always did have a big heart, Lily girl. Guess you needed more than one man to match it."

Now, he treats them all like the sons he never had, especially Archer, who shares his passion for obscure historical facts and terrible puns.

"Two minutes," Hunter calls, adjusting a Halloween display of skeleton-shaped cookies. His ice-blue eyes scan the space with characteristic thoroughness, looking for any imperfection that might have escaped our notice.

"We're ready," James says confidently, coming to stand beside me. "More than ready."

I lean into his solid warmth, drawing strength from his certainty. "I can't believe we pulled this off."

"I can," Hunter says, joining us. "You're a force of nature when you set your mind to something."

Archer completes our circle, his arm sliding around my waist. "Our very own hurricane in baker's clothing."

My chest tightens with emotion as I look at them— my three Alphas, dressed in matching black T-shirts and aprons, ready to help launch my dream into reality. Hunter, solid and steady, the backbone of our operation. James, passionate and precise, whose baking rivals even my own. Archer, charming and creative, whose book café has already generated buzz in literary circles across three counties.

How did I get so lucky?

"One minute," Hannah announces, adjusting a display of miniature pumpkin pies. "Places, everyone!"

I dart into the back for one final check, making sure the first batch of cinnamon rolls is ready to bring out once the initial rush begins. The kitchen gleams with new equipment.

Steel racks hold trays of Halloween-themed treats —ghost-shaped meringues, bat-winged cupcakes, pumpkin spice everything, and our signature item, Spellbinding Spirals, cinnamon rolls with orange-tinted icing and edible black spiders made of chocolate.

As I grab a tray, I hear a soft whimpering from outside the back door. Frowning, I set down the pastries and move toward the sound, unlocking the heavy door and peering outside, expecting to find the family of raccoons who have been coming often for food. I always feed them, even if the guys tell me not to encourage them. Then Hunter went and built them a little hatch in the alleyway in case they needed protection.

Cindy stands in our back alley, hugging herself tightly despite the mild October morning. Her mousy blonde hair is pulled into a tight ponytail, her normally bright almond eyes wide with what looks unmistakably like fear.

"Cindy?" I step outside, concerned. "Everything okay?"

She nervously glances over her shoulder. "I just need to come inside, please. Quickly."

I usher her in, shutting and locking the door behind us. "What's going on?"

"Just someone I've been trying to avoid. I think he's in town." She hugs herself tighter, shoulders hunched. "I swear I saw him on Main Street earlier."

"Let me call Garrett," I offer, reaching for my phone. "He might know—"

"No, please." She places a hand on my arm, stopping me. "He already does so much for me, and as my boss at the brewery, I hate to drag him into my troubles. I just need to lie low. That's all."

Something in her expression reminds me powerfully of Ruby, my best friend who runs the bar across the road, during the months she was trying to escape her asshole uncle. The same hunted look, the same false bravado covering genuine fear.

"Well, you're welcome here or to stay upstairs at my old place," I tell her firmly. "Whatever you need if you're in trouble, okay?"

Relief loosens the tight lines around her eyes. "Maybe just here for a bit, and I'll slip out soon."

"You're safe here. I promise." I guide her to a stool in the corner of the kitchen. "Stay for as long as you need."

"Thank you," she says softly. "You're always so kind."

I bring her a plate of cookies—chocolate chip, still warm from the oven—and a glass of milk. "I've got to get out there. We're about to open the shop. But make yourself comfortable, okay?"

With one last concerned glance, I grab my tray and head back to the front, nearly colliding with James as I enter the shop.

"There you are," he says, catching me by the shoulders. He presses a quick kiss on my forehead. "Hunter is about to open the doors."

"Sorry, Cindy from the brewery is in the back. She seems upset about something."

James's brow furrows with concern. "Is she okay?"

"I think so, just hiding from someone. I told her she could stay as long as she needed."

He nods, understanding without needing further explanation. "Good. Now come on, your adoring public awaits."

Just then, Hunter unlocks the front door. He stands tall and imposing in his black T-shirt, the muscles in his arms clearly defined as he welcomes the first customers with a smile warmer than most people ever get to see.

The Halloween playlist Archer curated begins playing through hidden speakers—a mixture of spooky classics and ambient music that creates the perfect festive atmosphere. The scent of cinnamon, vanilla, and pumpkin spice fills the air, mingling with the comforting smell of old books from the adjoining room.

People pour in like a river, excited voices rising to fill the space. I catch snippets of conversation—"So beautiful!" "Look at those cupcakes!" "Did you see his muscles?"—as I move behind the counter to help with the initial rush, giggling to myself.

What I also notice is the effect my Alphas have on our predominantly female customer base. Women pretend to study the menu while stealing glances at Hunter's impressive body. They linger over James's pastry recommendations, entranced by his storm-gray eyes and gentle smile. They ask Archer increasingly specific questions about obscure authors, clearly delighting in his enthusiastic responses and charming grin.

Sure, a tinge of jealousy rises in me, but I also know they are all mine.

Hannah catches my attention from across the shop and makes an exaggerated fanning motion, nodding toward a group of women openly admiring Hunter as he carries a box of books through to the other room. I stifle a laugh and shake my head.

"Looking good, sis," she says, sidling up to me during a momentary lull. "This place is going to be the talk of Whispering Grove."

"Thanks to you for helping," I reply, squeezing her hand.

By noon, we've sold out of three signature items and are running low on almost everything else. The Spellbinding Spirals were gone within the first two hours, prompting James to start a second batch that's now filling the air with its mouthwatering aroma.

During a rare quiet moment, I find myself standing behind the counter near my dad, both of us taking a breather. I take in the scene before me. Customers chat over coffee and pastries at our café tables. A young woman curls up in one of the reading nooks with a half-eaten ghost meringue on the plate beside her. My father moves to serve a group of elderly ladies, regaling them with stories from his youth, their laughter mingling with the background music.

And my men—heart be still.

I place a hand on my stomach, still flat beneath my apron but harboring the secret I've been keeping for the past two weeks. The pregnancy test tucked in my bedside drawer confirmed what my body had been telling me—our family is about to grow.

Tonight, after we close up shop and celebrate our successful opening, I'll tell them. I've already planned how—three tiny cupcakes, each with a letter: *D, A, D.* Simple but effective.

I wonder how they'll react. Hunter will probably be stoic at first, then break into that rare, brilliant smile that transforms his entire face. James might cry—he's the most openly emotional of the three. And Archer will undoubtedly make some joke about his virility before bombarding me with questions about how I'm feeling.

"Penny for your thoughts," James interrupts,

appearing beside me with a fresh tray of pumpkin scones.

I smile up at him, my heart so full it feels like it might burst. "Just thinking how lucky I am."

"That's funny," he replies, pressing a quick kiss to my temple. "I was thinking the exact same thing."

Hunter stares at us from across the room, raising an eyebrow in silent question: *Everything okay?* I nod, and he returns to helping a customer, satisfied.

A moment later, Archer slides behind the counter, snagging a cinnamon cookie from a display. "I've got a long waiting list for the book club starting next month."

"Amazing. And no eating the merchandise," I tease but can't help smiling at his enthusiasm.

"Baker's privilege," he counters, offering me a bite, which I accept despite my own rule.

The afternoon continues at a steady pace, the initial rush giving way to a constant stream of curious locals and word-of-mouth visitors. By four o'clock, we're nearly sold out of everything.

As the afternoon sun slants through our windows, casting long shadows across our nearly empty display cases, I think about everything I've been through and how things turned out.

And I wouldn't change a single step of the journey that brought me here.

CHAPTER TWENTY-EIGHT

The last customer leaves with a wave and a promise to return tomorrow, the bell above the door jingling cheerfully in their wake. I flip the sign from "Open" to "Closed" and lean against the cool glass, utterly exhausted but radiating satisfaction.

"We did it," I breathe, turning to face my three Alphas, who look just as worn out as I feel.

"We didn't just do it," Archer states, collapsing dramatically onto one of the café chairs. "We crushed it, demolished it, absolutely annihilated opening-day expectations."

Hunter, ever practical, is already counting the cash drawer. "Final tally will be impressive," he confirms. "We sold out completely. Even those experimental matcha ghost cookies James wasn't sure about."

"People will buy anything if it's shaped like a ghost in October." James shrugs, wiping down the last of the counters. His sleeves are pushed up to his elbows, revealing strong forearms dusted with flour. Even exhausted, he radiates a quiet competence that still makes my heart flutter.

My father emerges from the back office, hanging up his apron with the careful precision that defines every-thing he does. "I'd say that was a successful first day," he announces, his weathered face crinkled with pride. "You kids knocked it out of the park."

Hannah joins us from the kitchen, her perfect French twist showing not a single hair out of place despite the hectic day. "I counted the final receipts," she reports. "We made almost double what the former bakery made on its best day ever."

"That calls for a celebration," my father declares. "Dinner on me? That new Italian place downtown?"

My hand instinctively moves to my stomach before I catch myself. I can't tell them all yet—I need to tell my Alphas first, in private. The thought sends butterflies swarming in my belly, making me slightly queasy.

"Maybe tomorrow night, Dad," I suggest, forcing a smile despite my sudden nerves. "We're all pretty wiped out."

"Tomorrow it is. I'll book us in," Archer agrees. "Today has thoroughly kicked my perfectly shaped behind."

"Old Mrs. Grove certainly seemed to think so," Hannah teases, making Archer groan and the rest of us laugh.

"What happened with Mrs. Grove?" my father asks, eyebrows raised with curiosity.

"She pinched his butt. Twice," Hunter supplies with uncharacteristic glee. "Said he reminded her of her third husband."

"The horror in your eyes right now is exactly how I felt," Archer tells my father.

I burst out laughing, as does everyone else.

We finish the closing tasks together, my father and Hannah pitching in despite my insistence that they head home. Finally, we're all standing outside the bakery, locking up for the night.

"I'm so proud of you, Lily girl," my father encourages, pulling me into a tight hug. "Your mother would have been too."

The mention of my mother brings unexpected tears to my eyes. I blink them back.

"Thanks, Dad. I miss her so much," I whisper, holding him a moment longer than usual.

Hannah hugs me next, her eyes narrowing slightly as she studies my face. "You okay? You look a little pale."

"Just tired," I assure her, hoping she can't read me as well as she usually does. "Nothing a good night's sleep won't fix."

She doesn't seem entirely convinced but doesn't press the issue. "Call me tomorrow," she says instead.

After our final goodbyes, we separate—Hannah and my father to their cars, the four of us to Hunter's F-350 parked behind the building.

The drive through Whispering Grove is brief but beautiful in the late afternoon, with autumn leaves drifting onto the quiet streets and Halloween decorations glowing from nearly every porch. Despite my nerves about the revelation to come, I can't help but feel a wave of contentment wash over me. This town, these men, our life together—it's more than I ever dreamed possible.

"Earth to Lily," Archer teases, turning from the passenger seat to face me. "You're awfully quiet back there. Plotting world domination?"

"Just thinking," I reply, leaning against James, who has his arm draped around my shoulders in the back seat.

"Dangerous pastime," James teases gently, pressing a kiss to my temple.

"I heard at least three women trying to slip you their phone numbers today," I counter, grateful for the distraction. "Should I be worried?"

"Please," Archer scoffs before James can answer. "Those women don't stand a chance. Our baker boy here only has eyes for you."

"As proved by the fact that I didn't even notice anyone trying to give me their number," James adds with perfect honesty.

Hunter catches my attention in the rearview mirror, his steady gaze somehow both assessing and reassuring. He's always been the most perceptive of the three, quietly noticing what others miss. I wonder if he's already guessed my secret.

"I thought Mrs. Hawkins was going to faint when Hunter carried that bookcase into the reading nook," Archer continues, launching into a dramatic reenactment of the elderly woman's reaction. "I swear I heard her whisper, 'Mercy me,' while fanning herself with a cookie."

The banter continues all the way home. By the time we pull into the driveway of our Victorian house, located an hour out of town, I'm laughing despite my nerves, some of the tension easing from my shoulders.

Our home welcomes us with warm lights, thanks to the timers Hunter installed. Hunter unlocks the front door, James checks the mail, Archer immediately heads for the kitchen to forage for snacks, and Thor waits for us indoors, rushing toward me and curling around my legs for pats.

"I'm going to grab a shower," I announce once we're all inside, needing a few minutes alone to gather my thoughts.

"I'll order dinner," James offers. "Pizza? Thai? Too tired to cook."

"Pizza," Hunter and Archer say in unison, making me smile.

"Pizza it is," I agree, heading for the stairs. "I'll be down in fifteen."

In our master bathroom, I stand under the hot spray, letting the water wash away the day's tension. My hand drifts to my still-flat stomach.

After my shower, I pull on comfortable leggings and one of James's soft T-shirts that hangs nearly to my knees. In the walk-in closet, I retrieve the small gift bags I've been hiding behind my winter boots for the past week. Inside are three tiny pairs of baby shoes—one blue, one pink, one yellow—each containing a rolled-up sonogram picture.

Not as elegant as my cupcake plan, perhaps, but it will have to do, as I'm too tired to bake tonight. And the shoes were my initial idea anyway. My secret has been burning inside me for too long; I can't wait another day to share it.

Downstairs, I find my Alphas sprawled in the living room. The scene is so domestic, so perfectly ordinary, that for a moment, I just stand in the doorway, drinking it in.

Hunter notices me first, of course. "Feel better?"

"Much," I confirm, moving to join them. Instead of taking my usual spot on the couch, I remain standing, suddenly nervous again. "I have something for you. For all of you."

Their attention focuses on me immediately, three sets of eyes curious as I produce the three gift bags from behind my back, then hand one to each of them.

"What's the occasion?" Archer asks, reaching for it eagerly.

"Just open it," I say, my heart pounding so hard I'm sure they must hear it.

Each of them pulls out a tiny shoe box, all their expressions puzzled. They open the boxes simultaneously, revealing the miniature shoes with the sonogram photos tucked inside.

For a moment, there's complete silence as they process what they're seeing.

"Lily," Hunter says finally, his voice uncharacteristically unsteady. "Is this...?"

"I'm pregnant," I confirm, twisting my hands nervously. "Eight weeks along. With twins."

The silence stretches for three more heartbeats, then—

"TWINS!" Archer whoops, leaping to his feet with such force that Thor startles and barks. He crosses the space between us in two long strides, lifting me off my feet and spinning me in a circle. "We're having twins!"

His joy breaks the spell. James is suddenly there, tears already streaming down his face, pulling me from Archer's arms into his own.

"Twins," he whispers against my hair, his voice thick with emotion. "Two babies. Our babies."

Hunter's face transforms instantly, eyes widening as the tiny blue shoes slip from his suddenly trembling hands. He catches them mid-fall, clutching them to his chest as a smile breaks across his face— slow at first, then crescendoing into something radiant.

"We're... you're..." he stammers, voice cracking with joy. "Twins? We're having twins?"

The practical concerns still flicker across his face, but they're secondary to the pure elation radiating from him. He crosses to me in two quick strides, not walking but bounding.

"Yes," I assure him with a matching smile. "Everything looks perfect so far. Eight weeks and two days, according to the doctor."

Unlike the others' exuberant displays, Hunter's joy manifests in its own unique way—he lifts me off my feet in a gentle spin. His eyes shine suspiciously bright, a laugh bubbling up from somewhere deep as he presses his forehead to mine.

"Twins," he whispers again, voice filled with wonder and unmistakable excitement. He kisses me with such tenderness that it brings fresh tears to my eyes.

"So, I'm guessing pizza isn't the best dinner choice for you right now," James says. "I should make you something healthier. More nutritious. With vegetables."

I laugh through my tears. "Pizza is fine. I'm pregnant, not sick."

"Still," he insists, his nurturing instincts already shifting into overdrive. "You need proper nutrition. You're eating for three now."

"Three," Archer repeats, sounding dazed but delighted. "There'll be six of us in this house. Seven, counting Thor."

"A real family," Hunter says softly, and something in his tone makes my heart contract. I remember what he told me about his childhood—losing his parents young, the strained relationship with Travis, and losing his grandfather recently.

"Our family," I correct gently, taking his hand and placing it on my stomach.

He nods, a rare, full smile spreading across his face. "Our family," he agrees.

We settle on the couch as they bombard me with questions. How am I feeling? Have I had morning sickness? Do I have cravings? When is my next appointment because all three plan to attend?

I answer each one, basking in their genuine excitement and their immediate acceptance of this unexpected development. There's no hesitation, no doubt, just pure joy and anticipation.

"I know it's fast," I say finally, voicing the concern that's been nagging at me. "We've only been together for less than a year, the bakery just opened..."

"Lily," James interrupts gently, taking my face in his hands. "We've never been more excited about anything in our lives."

"Ever," Archer confirms, dropping to his knees before me to place his hands over my stomach. "These babies are a miracle. Our miracle."

"And we're going to spoil them rotten," Hunter adds, his voice unusually soft. "All three of us."

"Three dads, two babies, one very lucky mama," Archer quips, his eyes suspiciously bright despite his teasing tone. "The math works out perfectly."

They spend the rest of the evening making plans—nursery designs, baby names, childcare schedules. Archer wants a literary theme, naturally. Hunter suggests woodland creatures. James just can't stop grinning.

"We can combine both," I suggest diplomatically. "Woodland creatures reading books."

"Perfect," Archer declares. "Just like you."

As we finally eat our pizza, which arrived 10 minutes ago, Thor settles at my feet with a contented sigh while my three Alphas continue to stare at me with wide smiles. I feel a sense of completeness I never knew was possible.

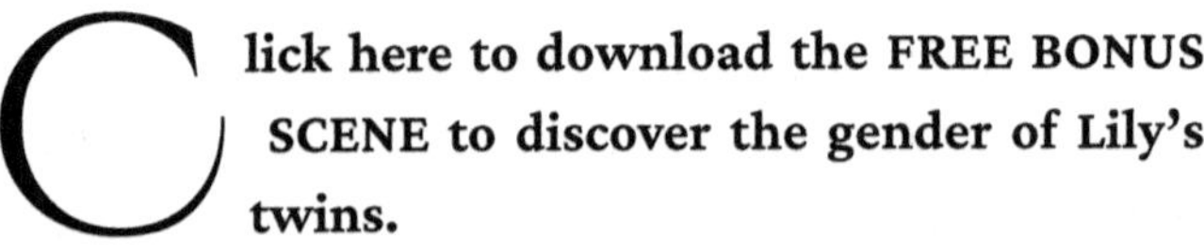

Click here to download the FREE BONUS SCENE to discover the gender of Lily's twins.

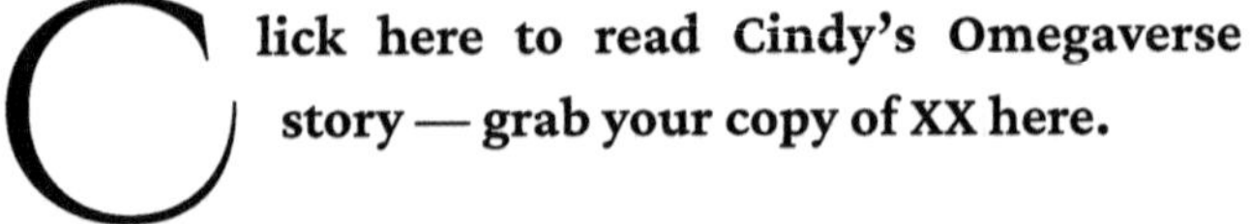

Click here to read Cindy's Omegaverse story — grab your copy of XX here.

Seven Months Later

"Breathe, Lily," Hunter instructs, his voice steady despite the white-knuckled grip he has on the steering wheel. "Just like we practiced."

I try to focus on his words, on the breathing techniques we spent months perfecting in birthing classes, but another contraction rips through me, stealing my breath and replacing it with a groan that sounds nothing like me.

"Five minutes apart," James reports from beside me in the back seat, his eyes fixed on his watch. "Lasting about forty-five seconds now."

"Can't you drive any faster?" Archer demands from the passenger seat, twisting around to look at me with barely concealed panic. "She's in pain!"

"I'm driving exactly nine point five miles over the speed limit," Hunter replies. "The optimal balance between speed and safety, according to traffic statistics."

"Screw statistics!" Archer yelps as I grab his outstretched hand during another contraction. "Those babies are coming, and they're coming now!"

"They're not coming in the car," Hunter says firmly, though he does press the accelerator a little harder. "We're almost there."

My water broke at 3:17 a.m., startling me awake from a dream about floating in a sea of cinnamon rolls. I'd shaken James awake first, as he was closest, and within minutes, all three men were in various states of controlled chaos—Hunter calmly executing our meticulously planned hospital route while simultaneously calling the doctor, James timing contractions with scientific precision, and Archer running around gathering last-minute items while alternating between excited whoops and nervous babbling.

Now, as we speed toward Whispering Grove Memorial Hospital, I'm caught between amusement at their reactions and the increasingly insistent pain in my body.

"Almost there, Lily love," James soothes, pressing a cool cloth to my forehead. Ever prepared, he somehow produced it from the hospital bag at the first sign of my discomfort. "You're doing amazingly."

"I haven't done anything yet," I pant as the contraction eases. "The main event is still to come."

"You've been growing two humans," Archer counters, still holding my hand despite what must be numbing pressure. "That's already the most badass thing any of us has ever done."

Hunter pulls into the emergency entrance with surgical precision, and before I can blink, a flurry of activity surrounds us. The hospital staff, alerted by Hunter's call, are waiting with a wheelchair. James has my bag. Archer is reciting my medical information from memory to an impressed-looking nurse. Hunter's hand never leaves the small of my back.

"Mrs. Thorne-Blackwood-Sterling?" a young nurse asks, looking slightly overwhelmed by the length of my hyphenated last name.

"Just 'Lily' is fine," I manage through gritted teeth as another contraction begins.

"And you are…?" she asks, glancing between my three hovering Alphas.

"The fathers," they reply in unison, causing the nurse's eyes to widen momentarily before she composes herself.

"All three of you?"

"All three," I confirm, unable to suppress a laugh despite the pain. "Hope that's not a problem."

"Not at all," she assures me quickly. "Just making sure I understand the situation. We'll need to prepare a slightly larger delivery room to accommodate every-one." She wheels me through the automatic doors, my Alphas close by.

"You're all going to be amazing dads," I tell them during a brief respite between contractions. "Stop looking so terrified."

"We're not worried," Archer protests unconvincingly. "We're ready."

"Speak for yourself," Hunter mutters. "I'm terrified."

This admission makes me laugh, which quickly turns into a groan as another contraction hits, stronger than the last.

The next few hours pass in a blur of pain, encouragement, and medical attention. I'm admitted, examined, and settled into a delivery room. My men never leave my side, rotating positions so that one always holds my hand, one keeps cool cloths on my forehead, and one runs interference with the medical staff, ensuring my birth plan is followed to the letter.

It all feels like a haze of agony and excitement.

I notice more than one nurse's lingering glance at them. But as James predicted months ago, they might as well be invisible. My Alphas have eyes only for me and the impending arrival of our children.

"Eight centimeters," the doctor announces after checking my progress. "Moving along faster than I expected for a first-time mother with twins."

"She's always been an overachiever," Archer quips, earning a weak smile from me before another contraction claims my attention.

The pain is unlike anything I've ever experienced—wave after wave of pressure and burning that makes me question every life choice that led to this moment. I'd opted for minimal pain intervention, wanting to be fully present for the birth, but now I'm reconsidering the wisdom of that decision.

"You can do this," James murmurs, his lips close to my ear. "You're the strongest person I know."

"We're right here," Hunter adds from my other side, his large hand engulfing mine. "Not going anywhere."

"And just think of the story we'll tell these kids," Archer chimes in, massaging my shoulders with surprising skill. "How their beautiful, badass mother brought them into the world while three grown Alpha men nearly fainted at the sight."

That earns him a strangled laugh that morphs into a cry as the most intense contraction yet seizes me.

"It's time," the doctor announces, suddenly all business. "These babies are ready to meet their parents."

Pain beyond imagination pulses through me, interrupted by moments of clarity so profound they feel almost spiritual. My focus narrows to the encouragement of my three men, their voices grounding me through the seemingly impossible task of bringing our children into the world.

"I can see the head!" James exclaims, tears flowing freely now. "Oh my God, Lily, you're doing it!"

"Push when you're ready," the doctor instructs calmly. "Nice and steady."

I bear down with everything I have, gripping Archer's and Hunter's hands, a primal sound tearing from my throat I barely recognize as my own.

"That's it, that's it," Hunter encourages, his usual stoicism completely abandoned. "You've got this, Lily. You're amazing."

With one final, monumental effort, our first child slips into the world, a cry filling the room that makes all four of us gasp in unison.

"It's a boy!" the doctor announces, placing the squirming, red-faced infant briefly on my chest before the nurses whisk him away for initial checks.

"A son," Archer breathes, looking shell-shocked and ecstatic. "We have a son."

Before I can fully process this miracle, my body reminds me that we're only halfway done. The contractions resume, somehow both less and more intense now that I know what to expect.

"Here we go again," the doctor says encouragingly. "Baby number two is eager to join the party."

The second birth happens faster, painful and rushed. With a series of pushes that drain the last of my strength, I'm huffing and screaming out. Our second child enters the world, another cry joining the first.

"A beautiful baby girl," the doctor announces, and this time, I notice a glimpse of dark hair before she is taken as well.

"One of each," James says wonderingly. "A son and a daughter."

"Perfect," Hunter agrees, his voice suspiciously rough.

Archer seems beyond words for once, his eyes fixed

on the two tiny bundles being tended to across the room.

After what seems like an eternity but is probably only minutes, the nurses bring our cleaned and swaddled babies back, placing one in my arms and, after a moment's hesitation, the other in James's waiting hands.

"Hello, little ones," I whisper, staring down at the perfect face of my son. "Welcome to the world."

Hunter and Archer crowd close, all four of us forming a tight circle around the newest members of our family. Our daughter yawns in James's arms, her tiny fist escaping the swaddle to wave in the air.

"She's going to be a fighter," Hunter predicts, gently capturing the miniature hand with one finger.

"And he looks like a thinker," Archer adds, gazing at our son's serious expression. "What are we naming these perfect creations?"

We'd spent months debating names, never quite reaching a consensus. Now, looking at their faces, I suddenly know exactly what they should be called.

"Sage and Blake," I suggest, watching for their reactions. "Herbs, not just spices—essential ingredients that make everything better, just like they will."

"Sage and Blake," James repeats, testing the names. "I love it."

"Just perfect for them," Archer approves.

"Strong names," Hunter adds. "Names they can grow into."

"Sage Olivia and Blake Malcolm," I elaborate,

adding the middle names we'd agreed on months ago —Olivia for my mother, Malcolm for Hunter's grandfather.

As we sit together in the quiet aftermath of birth, our small family expanded, I'm overwhelmed by a wave of gratitude so deep it brings fresh tears to my eyes.

"Thank you," Hunter says suddenly, his voice barely above a whisper. "For giving us this family."

"For trusting us with your heart," James adds, his finger gently stroking Sage's cheek.

"For crashing your sister's car in that snowstorm," Archer finishes with a watery smile. "Best accident ever."

I laugh through my tears, exhausted but happier than I've ever been. "Thank you for finding me. For keeping me. For loving me."

Our twins sleep peacefully. How fiercely they are already loved. I can't stop smiling.

And as Blake yawns and Sage stretches in James's careful hold, as my three Alphas exchange looks of wonder and pride, I know these tiny humans are born of love, hope, and just a touch of magic. They are the sweetest, most precious creations we've brought into the world.

Our family recipe—unconventional, unexpected, and absolutely perfect.

Click here to read Cindy's Omegaverse story - PUMPKIN SPICE, KNOTTY NIGHTS next...

ABOUT HARLEY KNIGHT

Hi, I'm Harley Knight! I'm a romance author who's absolutely obsessed with books, writing, and happily-ever-afters. I love creating stories filled with emotion, passion, and unforgettable characters that stick with you long after the last page. When I'm not writing, you'll find me lost in a good book or dreaming up my next big adventure. For me, there's nothing better than crafting love stories that remind us all why love is worth fighting for.

*Contact: **knightharleyus@gmail.com***